KINDRED
AND
WINGS

A SHIFTED WORLD NOVEL

KINDRED
AND
WINGS

PHILIPPA BALLANTINE

an imprint of **Prometheus Books**
Amherst, NY

Published 2013 by Pyr®, an imprint of Prometheus Books

Cover illustration © 2012 Cynthia Sheppard
Cover design by Grace M. Conti-Zilsberger

Inquiries should be addressed to

Pyr
59 John Glenn Drive
Amherst, New York 14228–2119
VOICE: 716–691–0133
FAX: 716–691–0137
WWW.PYRSF.COM

17 16 15 14 13   5 4 3 2 1

Library of Congress Cataloging-in-Publication Data

Ballantine, Philippa, 1971–
    Kindred and wings : a Shifted World novel / by Philippa Ballantine.
        pages cm
    ISBN 978–1–61614–779–2 (paperback)
    ISBN 978–1–61614–780–8 (ebook)
    1. Good and evil—Fiction. 2. Imaginary places—Fiction. I. Title.
PR9639.4.B39K56 2013
823'.92—dc23

2013012124

Printed in the United States of America

For my daughter,
who came into my life as vibrantly and wonderfully as a dragon taking flight.

CONTENTS

ACKNOWLEDGMENTS

As Talyn is beginning to find out, you need people around you to help you get anywhere in this world. As a writer I learned that a long time ago. So here are some people who made this book possible, and have kept me on the straight and narrow.

Lou Anders, whose knowledge and guidance helped me find my way to finally writing about dragons! His hand on the editorial tiller is something I will never take for granted.

Gabrielle Harbowy, for being my rudder in the sea of commas and red ink. Thank you for working with me all these years!

Laurie McLean, my agent who first saw potential in this tale of a woman in need of redemption. Thanks for taking a fledgling writer on, and holding her hand through the woods of publishing.

My cover artist, Cynthia Sheppard for giving form to two of my favorite creatures, and making them as wonderful as I imagined.

And I could not forget to thank all the fans, readers and listeners who have traveled along with me. You've made this writer's dreams a reality.

CHAPTER ONE

THE HUNTER MUST HUNT

I t was always about proving herself. Standing in the pale moonlight on the hilltop, her hand on an unfamiliar sword, Talyn felt the irony of that sink into her bones; she had traded in proving herself to the Caisah to proving herself to some new masters. In a world of chaos like Conhaero, it was strange to have everything stay so much the same. She pushed her dark and now damp hair out of her eyes, and kept her gaze fixed on the road.

It was a symbol of permanence on the ever-changing face of this world, where even mountains could not be relied on to be permanent from one week to the next. It was not a symbol she welcomed, since the Caisah had placed all the roads here. That tyrant who sat on the throne at Perilous and Fair was still her enemy.

The hill on which she had taken up position looked over a town, though it was now shrouded in mist, so that even the pinpricks of light from the buildings below dwindled to nothing. The chill damp of it clung to her skin, but the Third Gift of the Vaerli stopped it going any further. Her new masters, like her old one, had seen that some of the gifts taken from her people clung to her.

Still, it was not as it had been. Her lungs sang with the cold.

The mist had another effect: every sound was muffled, so even her sharp ears could make out no hoof beats on the road below.

The courier had not come this way yet—she was fairly certain of that. Talyn's jaw clenched as she checked the powder in her pistol. It was the one the Caisah had given her on entering his service, and yet she couldn't bear to part with it. Considering how much she had once loathed it, Talyn knew this was a curious reaction. She liked to think that it reminded her of what had happened to her before.

Still, if she stayed in this mist much longer the powder would be too damp to be of any use at all.

Finally, it was the faintest of shudders running up from the ground that told her that a horse was galloping up from the village below. It wouldn't take him long to crest the ridge. From there it was a straight shot down the valley, and in another two days he would reach the capital of Perilous and Fair. That couldn't be allowed to happen. If he arrived there, the item she needed would be totally out of reach, so she had to hurry.

Racing along the top of the hill, pumping her arms, Talyn caught a glimpse out of the corner of her eye: the flash of a gray horse with a caped figure clinging to its back.

Lowering her arm, she fired her pistol at the courier, but she dared not stop to aim properly. Without all of her Kindred gifts it was an awkward shot, almost backwards from the direction in which she ran, so of course it went wide. The gallop now sounded broken, as if the mount was spooked, which in this mist was understandable. Horses were fine animals, but they were not native to Conhaero, and therefore not used to the shifting of the land. It tended to make them stressed and unreliable.

"Hah!" the rider yelled at his mount, probably unsure just how many people were accosting him. If he'd been able to make out the small female figure he'd have been a little less worried, but if he'd recognized the erstwhile Caisah's Hunter he would have been terrified. Talyn had plenty of experience working with the terror she generated.

The Vaerli, though, knew she was not what she had been, and she also knew there was no way she was going to be able to catch the man if he got much further away from her. Just as that realization hit her, a prickle of heat ran up her spine and sudden energy filled her limbs. Her breath caught in her throat. This was the third time in as many months that she'd been made aware that her new masters were keeping an eye on her.

It was an unpleasant thought, but she shoved it to the back of her mind as she crouched low and leapt from the slope. Talyn had judged it perfectly. She landed behind the courier just as his horse surged forward. She did not have enough mass to unseat the man, but the mount reared as her weight came down on its hindquarters, frothing and snorting at this sudden disruption. Vaerli generally unnerved animals, especially when they jumped on them from out of nowhere.

The courier swore, struggling to both keep his seat and reach the knife at his side. Her gifted strength would usually have allowed Talyn to dispatch him quickly, but she found herself floundering to hold him off. The strength her new masters gave was a fickle thing—not nearly as reliable as the Caisah's.

The courier's elbow caught her in the diaphragm directly below her rib cage, knocking the wind out of her. When the courier kicked his heels, the horse surged forward. Talyn grabbed a second too late for the saddle, and she was jolted off the haunches of the creature.

Some small portion of her previous talents kicked in, so she landed on her feet, more frustrated than hurt as the courier galloped off once more into the mist. Pushing her hair out of her face and stuffing down her rage, she considered her options. There were not many.

A sudden nudge in the small of her back made Talyn whirl around, her hand going to her sword, but the green hairy face with the flaming eyes was not what she'd been expecting. It took a heartbeat for her to recognize it.

Talyn's lips lifted in a rare smile, and something unclenched deep down within her.

"Syris," she whispered, eyes burning with threatening tears. Her fingers immediately found the razor wire that was his hair. The tangled green strands of it drew blood, and just as she had many times before, she held out her fingers to let her mount lick the scarlet drops from her skin. The great dark eye regarded her while his neck tossed proudly, saying that their reunion was on his terms, and taking all the credit for it. Taller than any mere mortal horse, Syris contained chaos and was bound to her in ways that remained mysterious to Talyn. It was odd to find that one of the many things she'd thought lost was found again. It felt a little like hope.

The last time Talyn had seen him it had been on the edge of the Salt Plain. Yet she'd never meant to lose him; she'd reckoned on coming back to him, or perhaps ending up dead. It was always an option.

As it turned out neither of these things happened. Her new masters had come and taken her, and she'd never been able to get back to him. When she had thought of the nykur she'd imagined him returning to the chaos that was his home. It had been a form of comfort for her.

Having lost her direction, her people, and her place in the world, to find Syris here at her back was deeply moving. Her hand bunched around those dangerous strands of hair, and she did not care how deep they cut.

However, Talyn couldn't afford to savor it as she might wish. Saddle-less as he was, she still mounted him, feeling his sharp hair slice her thighs even through her pants. It was a good feeling to be on his back again. She'd had too much of no feeling at all recently. The thick, seaweed smell of the nykur was cloying and wonderfully familiar. Despite her age and her predicament, Talyn let out a whoop of excitement. Let the courier wonder what that meant.

Unlike her prey, she had no need to urge her mount forward. Just as it had always been, the great beast of chaos followed her thoughts. With the sound of his saber teeth sliding against one another, he wheeled about and followed after the courier, great muscles bunching and firing under her. It was the essence of raw power.

As the Caisah's Hunter, Talyn had undertaken many pursuits. This one was pitiful compared to those. Even if the courier's horse had been the finest in Conhaero it wouldn't have mattered. The nykur's broad cloven feet pounded like rapid drum beats even on the unnatural road. It was the symbol of permanence the Caisah had carved on the heaving face of a world never meant to be still. Certainly there was irony that a creature of pure chaos was using it.

Ahead in the mist, she could once again make out the courier's cape flapping wildly, and then the sound of the horse's heavy breathing. Syris, by comparison, raced almost silently; head down, great green ears folded against his head. Talyn knew for sure that he was enjoying the race.

It was a taste of the power that had once come so easily. By the time the courier had heard their approach and glanced around, she and the nykur were on him. This time she leapt true and stuck.

Talyn and the courier crashed together, and her momentum unhorsed them both. He landed hard, all the breath expelled in one sharp gasp, and then she was on top of him, knife drawn. He never had any chance to recover.

The moonlight fell on his face and she realized how young her prey was. It had never mattered before, and it didn't matter now. In the past, the Caisah pointed and she obeyed, dishing out death as required. This time she needed his dispatch—not his life.

"The Hunter," the young man whispered his recognition, his eyes wide and terrified. It was the expected response. He smelled of sweat and fear. Syris, rearing and stamping behind her, must have also had made quite the impression.

Talyn smiled and did not correct him. Her own particular history with the Caisah was not one she was going to share with this, his smallest of minions.

"Give me the scroll," she hissed over her teeth, hand clenching on his shirt. His fingers scrambled for the bag over his shoulder, but she was pressing him down and the knife at his throat was distracting.

Finally seeing his problem, Talyn slid to her feet and pushed him over on his stomach. Slitting open the bottom of his bag, she took out the long wrapped shape of the scroll. Even bundled up like this she could smell the musty paper that suggested it was indeed as old as she'd been told. She itched to open and read it. As ancient as she was, she could still be excited and curious, thanks mostly to the memory discipline she practiced. Nemohira meant she could pick and choose which memories she kept; it made her always acquisitive for new things.

Straightening, Talyn—once called the Hunter—looked down at the form of the shivering courier. The man had his face pressed into the ground and would not meet her eye again. As soon as he'd recognized her, the fight had seeped out of him into the hungry earth. He should be killed, as the Caisah would be eager to hear of her whereabouts, and this man would carry word of her. With the magical bonds broken, he could no longer track her, and Talyn wanted to remain elusive. This trembling man would race straight to the nearest outpost, and the Caisah would know her location by the morning. Undoubtedly there was a bounty on her head, so she had enough to worry about. She didn't need the Rutilian guard tracking her down, too.

The weight of long-bladed knife in her hand told her what really needed to be done. In her time as a Hunter she'd done worse than kill an unarmed man in the dirt. It would be stupid to change her methods now.

Her fingers tightened on the hilt in preparation for the blow, and then the world dropped away.

Finn was lying on his stomach on the edge of the stream, stripped to the waist, his bare feet muddy while he concentrated on his outstretched hands in the water. Talyn laughed at the deadly serious expression on his face. The light slanting through the trees dappled over his back and lit his hair up all gold and foxy red. The laughter dried on her lips as she realized how beautiful that moment was. The kind you'd trap in amber and keep if you could. Just beyond the curve of the river, she could hear the sound of the surf. The trout Finn hunted were nearly home.

Talyn's body still tingled with their afternoon of love, the places that had been scratched and licked remembering. It was strange to be so aware of her flesh. It made her feel normal—maybe even mortal.

The man glanced over his shoulder at her, his smile quicksilver and pure joy, before wriggling his fingers in the water some more. She was just about to say something, maybe make a joke at his expense, when Finn threw up his hands, letting out a whoop of delight. A gleaming brown trout flicked through the air, twisting and turning.

Together they raced to get hold of it, scrambling in the leaves, gasping and giggling. Talyn felt her breath choking with laughter. His fingers and hers got about the fish at the same time. Finn's hazel eyes met hers with the kind of directness that rooted her to the spot. "You'll remember this, won't you, Talyn . . . I know I will . . ."

The accusatory tone of her love's voice was the last thing she heard before the after-time let go of her. She came back to the present with a jerk. The courier was motionless on the ground, only now trying to glance out of the corner of his eye; trying to ascertain if this breath would be his last.

Talyn swayed slightly on her feet, considering with horror what had just happened. She cleared her throat. "Get up, get on your horse and ride for your life. If you're not gone by the time I get to Syris . . ." She paused, hearing his shuddering breath, and went on. "Well, you understand the rest, I am sure."

The mad scramble that followed Talyn was only barely aware of. The courier moved fast for one of the Manesto, catching his horse, mounting, and racing off in admirable time.

Talyn didn't even turn her head to watch him go; her own thoughts were too big to entertain anything else. She was nemohira; it was one of the memory disciplines that made immortality possible to bear. Talyn had deliberately discarded all memories of loving Finn. They should never have been able to come back. They should have been lost forever.

Shakily she turned and walked over to Syris. The nykur's hot breath on her neck was intensely real and helped drag her back from the edge of panic. Pressing her fingers in among his razor hair, she at least knew the present had her for the moment.

The nagging question remained: how had Finn done this? He was only a man, only a stupid Manesto talespinner, and yet he had returned memories she had chosen to throw away. It was impossible!

"By the Flames," Talyn swore, spun around and, leaning against the burning heat of Syris, looked up at the stars. Finn had to be more than he seemed, and the most infuriating part was that she had no idea why. The more she tried to stuff down thoughts of him, the more the images bubbled up. None burned more brightly than the recollection of him Naming a Kindred, making him dragon. Of all the Names he could have given that primal creature of chaos, he had given him the greatest and most dangerous one.

It had been thrilling and terrifying, and it was something she had not revealed to her new allies, the Phage. It was a weakness she was not willing to expose to anyone—especially when she wasn't sure what it meant.

Syris jogged sideways, his teeth making sounds like knives being sharpened as he curled his head about to regard her. Then he lowered that head and kicked with his back legs, as if to emphasize something she was missing.

Talyn flicked her head up, eyes suddenly darting around the trees, looking for shadows that might be holding gun or sword, or something far worse. For a long moment she thought the nykur was just riled up by the race and being reunited with her. Then the sky began to dance above them.

The former Hunter tilted her head and watched the clouds gathering above. She had seen every kind of weather in her time, and Conhaero's skies could be almost as tumultuous as the land below, but she had never seen such a strange thunderhead. It was higher in the sky than was normal, and though it was flickering with blue light, no rumbling reached her.

Syris rolled his eye and stamped, narrowly missing her foot. By the time she jigged back out of the way, the odd formation had slid and rolled away with startling speed. It was almost as if it were being pulled by some enormous hand. She watched it for a few more moments, her insides twisting almost as much as the clouds. The clouds moved off beyond the mountains, flickering with occasional light.

Tilting her head, Talyn wondered what signs she wasn't seeing. When the Harrowing had come upon her people, she had been young, not yet taught all the ways of the Vaerli. Not for the first time did she wonder what she'd missed. It mattered little now. Should she touch another of her kind, both of them would burn thanks to the curse placed on the Vaerli by the Caisah. It severely limited how much she could learn. However, there were some of her kin that she could ask.

With a great deal of weariness she mounted Syris. The smell of salt water rose from his body, an unwelcome reminder of memories she didn't want.

"Time to introduce you to my new friends, old friend," Talyn whispered into his ear. "You might not like it, but I am very glad to see you."

If he had been a horse, he would have neighed to communicate his dissatisfaction, but the nykur was a creature of the Chaos, and the strange, distant storm had fired something within him. Syris reared on his hind legs before bolting off into the mist with her clinging to his back. Talyn tried to concentrate on the momentary joy of that as best she could. It was all she had.

Finn was used to bar fights—but usually observing them instead of being involved. He ducked as another chair came flying his way and knocked one of the enthusiastic participants full in the face. He dropped with a grunt, and Finn took the chance to clamber over his prone body.

The tiny inn was shaking and seemed in danger of coming apart at the seams. Barmaids howled like harpies and laid about them with their wooden trays with real vigor. One man was thrown over the bar before another energetically leapt after him. It was truly amazing how one small question could set off a chain of event in so spectacular a manner.

Finn felt his shirt suddenly being caught in a fist and was forced to jerk his elbow back savagely. His attacker's startled curse was very satisfactory. As Finn slipped out of that situation, he found himself in a new one quickly: two larger men were bearing down on him. Unlike the majority of the brawlers, who were only interested in having a bit of rough entertainment, this pair had the air of determination in their stride. Their eyes were fixed on Finn as they shoved the mass of fighters out of the way. Formerly, he'd been able to make himself seem inconsequential, but he'd been made aware recently that the power he usually relied on in these situations was not working as it once had. Perhaps it had something to do with Naming a dragon . . .

Finn glanced over his right shoulder to where the door seemed a very long way off, then back to those approaching men. His eyes caught the glint of a knife in the hand of one of them. While he wasn't afraid of an honest knife fight, Finn was certain that they had no plans to be particularly honest.

Planting his foot on the back of a fallen patron, he leapt up onto the nearby table that was miraculously free of bodies, and from there swung up into the rafters of the inn. This was no great house, so the timber under his feet was narrow oak, and he had to stoop to avoid rupturing the straw roof. Still, this was a better way of making it to the door. Feeling somewhat confident, he grinned down at the two burly men who were contemplating just how nimble they would have to be to follow.

They were not in the scarlet of the Rutilian Guard, but every town in Conhaero was full of informants ready to earn the Caisah's coin. Finn dared the same question that had started this whole thing off, "Do you know the way to the Castle Shadryk?"

"You little dog's bollocks," the tallest and baldest of the men yelled, pointing a thick finger at Finn only barely out of reach. A over-enthusiastic brawler charged him midway through what might have proved to be an informative speech. For his trouble, the man was picked up by the collar and thrown across the nearest table.

Finn winced when the furniture collapsed underneath such a blow. The other man, shorter but somehow slightly more intelligent looking, glared at Finn. "Shadryk was where the Kiv ruled this land from, and emotions remain high about that. How about you come down and I'll give you all the history lessons you want, boy?"

Finn had always been of the opinion that when people used the word "boy" they never meant it kindly. He couldn't help the slight laugh that escaped him as he judged the distance, leapt between the beams and nearer to the door. They would be close behind but considerably slowed by the brawlers. It was almost like old times, and for a bit he could forget everything that had happened since he had last spoken in a tavern.

He made it across to the third beam easily, but his swing down toward safety was not as well timed as it could have been. Landing awkwardly, he tumbled into a knot of squawking barmaids now busy clawing each other's faces. His struggle to get out of that meant he lost almost all of his advantage. Scrambling to the door he yanked it open and dashed outside, only a heartbeat ahead of his pursuers.

And that's where an ordinary talespinner would have been in serious trouble, possibly earning a beating—most likely something worse. Finn was not anything close to ordinary any more. He'd passed that point back at the Bastion of the Vaerli.

Turning to face them, he realized that they were both armed. Still, he felt it was honorable to warn them. He raised his hands. "Look, if you just throw down those knives, you can walk away from this."

As he had been expecting, they laughed—he would in their position, too—but the other warnings he could have given would only have reduced them to paroxysms of laughter.

The air above shifted as if a great storm was moving in: heat, darkness, and a presence suddenly appearing over them. The men slowly turned their faces up, and the magnificence of Wahirangi was reflected in their shocked looks. Finn's eyes followed his attackers' gaze, and despite the fact he'd spent many weeks with the dragon already, awe washed over him once more as well.

The great golden sides of the dragon gleamed in the moonlight, and the sparkle of stars gleamed in eyes of clear opal. Larger than any of the meager buildings in the village, his wings blocked out all other light in the evening sky while his sculpted head turned on an elegant neck to observe those below. The hovering Wahirangi did not convey rage, but more poised curiosity.

The men did not seem to notice this; they had dropped to their knees, overcome with an emotion between bliss and horror. The dragon had that effect on every living being. Legend called it dragonfear. It expressed itself in either uncontrollable awe, mind-bending terror, or as in this case, a mixture of both. Finn heard horses in the public house's stables cry out, ready to bust their way free, while rats from the nearby heap scurried for safety.

Looking up, the men witnessed a curl of blue flame lick along the edge of Wahirangi's jaw and ooze out from between the rows of curved fangs. It was the stroke of a master showman and made Finn wonder if he was influencing the great dragon a little too much.

"Shadryk Castle," the great beast's voice rumbled out, at this distance enough to make bones shake. "I believe my friend asked you where it is."

One man was quite beyond answering, his jaw hanging open and a long thread of drool hanging down. The other, white and swaying slightly, was a little more lively. "North, my lord," he stammered, "In the foothills above the marsh. Not far . . . not far at all."

Wahirangi's long neck arched against the moons, and the flames flickered out. "Very well. Flee now, before hunger overcomes me."

If the CloudLord's kindness was enough to make a man weep, even a hint of his wrath had the same effect. Finn almost felt sorry for them, running as fast as they could but attempting to keep the dragon in sight even as they fled.

In the years where he'd been traveling by himself, Finn had always wondered why no one would listen to his tales of the Caisah's reign of tyranny. Now he knew that he would have gained far more attention with a dragon at his shoulder. However, that long time of solitude was now long gone; he was now more than an honorable talespinner.

The words of his long-dead mother—the one he'd never known about until only a month ago—kept him awake at night. *My beautiful hybrid son.* Hybrid, half-Manesto and half-Vaerli, was a thing that everyone had assumed an impossibility. Yet, now here Finn was—that impossible thing.

"And more, not the only one."

Wahirangi's eyes for a brief instant were wreathed in flame, and hinted at his real nature. Inside that body still burned the power and mystery of a Kindred.

"My brother," Finn said with a sigh, thinking of the boy he had found in the simple string pattern he'd woven between his fingers. He'd spoken to that boy, and never understood that they were brothers—there was a huge age difference, and Finn had never known his true parents and heritage. It had been a great deal to take in.

Though his mother had said Wahirangi would know where Ysel was, she had been wrong. His mother was dead, and only the information of a tiny sliver of herself remained in places throughout Conhaero. She was not omniscient, and many things had changed in the chaotic world since her death hundreds of years before. Such as her son's location.

Following the trail from place to place had taken time, and always there had been obstacles, setbacks, and false hope. Ysel's guardians had moved him about, apparently afraid of something. Eventually, with clues Finn had recalled from speaking to his brother, they had decided the long-abandoned fortress of Shadryk was the most likely place. Unfortunately, it also had an unwholesome and difficult reputation.

The dragon ceased beating his wings and landed in the narrow confines between buildings. His form took up the whole length of the street and caused a house across the way to creak alarmingly.

Finn quickly scrambled up the dragon's offered leg to sit behind the mighty shoulder blades on the rude saddle he'd constructed. After only one day flying with Wahirangi, he'd worked out that if he didn't want to end up a smear on the landscape he would need something to hang on to.

As he contemplated life atop a dragon, it still seemed so impossible that merely by giving a Kindred a name he had caused this to be. Every time he sat on this spot it made him feel both glorious and terrified. Glorious, because he sat on the back of a dragon—something that had only happened in legend. Terrified, because it was such a magnificent feeling of power that he might grow to love it too much.

"It is a good name, the one you gave me." The dragon's huge head turned back to look at him with something that could have been pleasure gleaming in his opal eyes. The curious linking of their minds had been growing stronger, something that Finn was vaguely concerned about. While his own dark moods had not overtaken him recently, he did wonder in the odd moment what would happen if he shared them with a dragon. "When I was Kindred I never realized how wonderful it would feel to have my own name and my own shape."

It was a kind thing for Wahirangi to say, something to soothe Finn. The dragon, for such a large creature, was surprisingly generous—not at all what Finn would have expected. It felt good to have a friend and ally in all this madness.

"We should find this Castle Shadryk, then," Finn said, though the desire to do so was draining from his body. The closer they got to their goal, the more he was worried what he would say to Ysel when they finally met in person. It was very strange to find a brother, let alone one that was mysteriously so much younger than he.

The dragon did not make comment, but shook himself like a great golden dog, and then thrust with his legs, propelling them both upwards into the sky. Finn's stomach lurched dramatically, and he closed his eyes as the sky spun in several directions at once. On each side of him, wings like sails on a great ship flexed and beat the air. For a long time, until they reached warm air on which to glide, all the talespinner heard was the rush of the wind about him.

They flew silently through the night; Wahirangi's wide wings powered them up into a sky scattered with stars and illuminated by the white of the moons. Below, the world of Conhaero passed by. Hidden by night, the only way to tell wilderness from civilization were the pin-pricks of light from houses. Yet, Finn did not like looking down. He understood this was how the Vaerli must have felt; aloof and powerful.

They did not have far to go, and soon enough the dragon began a slow circling descent. For a dragon, the miles were nothing, and Castle Shadryk was easy to find with instructions. They followed the narrow Itea River where it cut through the mountains, trapped in stillness thanks to the Caisah's spell. Conhaero's lands were meant to be in movement. The bond between man and dragon made Finn uncomfortable about that. Everything should have been moving in the eyes of the Kindred; even those with Names, like Wahirangi, felt it.

The remains of the castle were not immediately apparent to Finn, but the dragon's sharp eyes soon made them out; a huddled and broken shadow on a wooded hilltop. The woods at least were capable of movement, growing up around any structure civilization abandoned. The faintest human malkin, the will to keep things permanent, held this place together. When it faded Conhaero would swallow the remains.

As they circled lower, it was apparent that it must once have been a grand structure. Two tall towers, one now half fallen in on itself, soared above the main building which also looked rather as though a large child had kicked aside blocks of it. Alongside was the wreckage of a collection of smaller buildings, most likely stables.

"Not made for defense," Finn commented. "No moat, no walls to speak of, so it's something more like a grand hunting lodge than a real castle."

Wahirangi dropped elegantly to the ground and looked about. "So much for an attempt at permanence. Not much malkin holds this place together— amazing it has lasted so long." He might be a dragon, but he had only been Named barely a month, and as a Kindred he'd never had much experience with people. It had been nearly a thousand years since his kind had walked the earth in partnership with the Vaerli. Sometimes Finn had to remind himself of that fact.

As the talespinner walked around the forgotten garden, the smell of rotting wood and wet earth was thick enough to choke on. He did not like this place much either. It felt as if it were a stale memory, and he hated to think that this was where his brother had spent his time.

"I smell old violence here." Wahirangi's wings shuttered open and shut almost like a great eagle that had been disturbed. Like all Kindred, he also had a strange perception of time. Something that happened hundreds of years ago was as yesterday to the creatures of chaos. Finn, despite their bond, could only imagine how the slim line between now, the before, and the future appeared to the dragon.

Wahirangi shook his head and snorted, shooting tiny jets of blue flame across the courtyard.

Finn wandered over to the remains of the gate lying on the ground. It was hard to know how long it had lain there, but it was still possible to see the scars of axe blows on its surface. He sighed as he put his foot under the rotting wood and lifted a piece. It had the sign of the running river on it—a piece of ancient heraldry now fallen out of favor. "This does look like the symbol I glimpsed briefly when I first found Ysel in the pattern."

"Then this could well be where he was hidden. Make haste, Finn, this place reeks of death." Wahirangi's claws rattled on the aging cobblestones as he turned to look up at the two towers above them. Sometimes the things Wahirangi said revealed a great deal about the Kindred. Now, for example, the talespinner knew that they could in fact comprehend death, and it made them uneasy. Interesting, indeed.

His companion did not expand upon his comment, and after a while Finn decided to make his own study of the place, from the inside. The door to the inner keep was also hanging loose with axe marks even more evident. Finn managed to kick it apart enough to shoulder his way through.

Wahirangi lowered his head and peered in after him, his opal eyes gleaming like lanterns in the darkness, yet he could not follow. "Be careful." His voice was low and concerned, though blue flames flickered at the edge of his mouth.

Finn smiled at little. "I will be. I managed to take care of myself well enough before you were Named. You can go no further without bringing the whole place down. Please, wait here."

It was impossible to read the dragon's expression, but he did not push further in. Finn walked into the corridors, and the aerial impression was confirmed; the place had been abandoned for a long time. The mosaic floor underfoot glittered in the weak moonlight, while moldering curtains hung off the remains of gilded rods. The chill in here was not the only thing that sent a shiver up Finn's spine—the place did indeed reek of death and ancient wrongs. He knew that was not just his talespinner training.

As he walked down the long central corridor he could see that it had once been a picture gallery. Shattered carved frames leaned drunkenly on the walls where long-dead looters had left them. Several times Finn had to step over the sad remains of statues that had been flung to the floor. An artist himself, he didn't like to see art despoiled in such a manner, but he knew that these were the least of crimes committed here.

Just as his talespinner imagination began to work even harder, something caught his attention: a noise. Finn stopped, his heart pumping furiously. It sounded like something rough sliding over the marble, perhaps something being dragged. As blood surged in his straining ears, the noise came again. Something was moving in the shadows, making a low scraping noise that sounded very ominous, even with a dragon outside.

Finn turned and looked over his shoulder, considering for a moment calling Wahirangi; but the dragon would never fit in here and quite possibly would destroy any clues that Putorae might have left. Still, he eased his hand down to his boot-sheath and took out one of his long hunting knives. It could be just a case of a virulent rat infestation.

He went on more cautiously, trying to minimize the sound of his own footfalls. Behind doors, both intact and otherwise, he found a collection of what must have been elegant rooms. It was hard not to imagine the strains of music and laughter in the damp, crumbling salons and mirrored rooms he found, but it was one room in particular that made him stop.

Up a narrow flight of stairs, he found a smaller bedroom. On moth-eaten carpets he picked up a clutter of strange wooden lumps. Taking them to the window, Finn twisted them around in the moonlight until he was able to make out that they were in fact small toys; carved remains of little animals. His heart leapt—so it was a child's room, then.

On closer examination, Finn found curled ancient leaves of paper lying scattered all about, though he couldn't make out what might have once been drawn there. One thing among the papers caught his eye. Finn bent and picked up a curl of purple string. It was looped, so without thinking he threaded it between his fingers and pulled it taut into a perfect cats-cradle.

"Ysel," he whispered, his head shooting up as if the boy would appear over his shoulder, but it was only the moon sliding out from a cloud that had caught the corner of his eye. They were in the right place, of that he was now absolutely sure. Questions remained, though: where had they gone, and why?

A breeze whispered past his ankles, chilling and unexpected. He stood and looked around him as the tattered curtains fluttered in the moonlight and the skeletons of dead leaves skittered through the room. They were all blowing in one direction, and on instinct he followed them, the thread dangling from his fingertips.

Some way off he could hear Wahirangi's call, like a distant trumpet with no real meaning to him, as he went back down the stairs. The swirling papers danced on the wind in front of him as he walked through a set of double doors with their mullioned windows smashed to pieces, and into a room that once must have been a ballroom. It seemed to his talespinner eyes that he could almost discern the ghosts of laughing dancers whirling over the broken wooden floor, and hear the strains of music. Perhaps that was his Vaerli blood, looking back into the past. It was hard to tell.

"What is this place?" he whispered to himself as he picked his way through the shadows toward the darkness of the far wall. This palace looked as if it had been abandoned decades ago, but it was still more magnificent on the inside than he could have imagined. Surely, he would have heard of such a place before. He thought he knew all of Conhaero and her stories.

Finn shivered and tugged his thin coat tighter. The wind swirled and danced before a large marble mantelpiece, and the artistry in it made the talespinner blink. Creatures of chaos were carved in relief on each side of where the fire would have stood, but above them all, with her arms spread wide, was a woman looking out into the room. Her hair was beautifully curled, and wrapped around her face and shoulders, but it was her eyes that commanded attention.

It was Putorae, the last Seer of the Vaerli, and his mother. She had spoken to Finn when he was within the Bastion, and she had told him there were other portions of herself tucked away all over Conhaero. There had been no time for him to gather details.

The wind around him suddenly stopped, the leaves and papers frozen in their dance across the shattered floor. Finn knew what that meant. He turned his head toward the face in the marble. He was not surprised when she moved, blinked, and came alive. It was the face of a seer, beautiful but aloof. She was not the mother that he might have wished for, yet he could feel the connection tugging him.

"Son," she breathed, her voice eerily failing to echo in this large space, "you have come too late, your brother is gone."

Finn was beginning to feel a little testy. "Yes, Mother, I am aware of that." He held up the string before him. "But instead of going haring off after him, I am not moving until you answer some more questions. Tell me how I can possibly have a brother so much younger than myself, if you please."

The shade flickered, full of moonlight and mystery. Perhaps she was surprised that he was almost literally putting his foot down.

"Tell me, or I go no further," Finn said, calmly. "I will take Wahirangi and fly off to my own affairs."

For a moment he worried that this sliver of Putorae was overwhelmed by his questions; he did not know the limits of this construct. "You and your brother were born together on the very edge of my death," she spoke finally, her eyes not meeting his. "And on the very edge of the revelation to me. I knew the only way to save you was to send you to different places and times. It was important that you were separated and hidden."

Finn was not impressed. A dragon, a tangle with the most dangerous woman in Conhaero, and he was not going to settle for a seer's prevarications. His mother—or at least the trapped memory of her—floated across the ballroom floor, her feet never quite meeting the solid surface. He waited.

Her arms swept out in an abrupt gesture, and suddenly he could see the ghosts he had only imagined. Finn's eyes widened as he watched the long-dead Vaerli dance and spin around a smooth floor, in dresses seemingly made of spider-silk. The women all reminded him of Talyn. The men that he saw were lithe, handsome and smiling; in such a situation he would have been the same, himself.

Strains of music whispered in the corners, and he saw creatures among them that must have been Named Kindred: fauns, centaurs, and patterned snakes. It was a beautiful if unusual scene.

"I thought," he said through a dry throat, his eyes never leaving the scene Putorae conjured, "that the Vaerli did not make places. The chaos of the land surely makes such buildings . . ."

"There are places kept aside for us," his mother replied, and her translucent eyes also seemed lost in the vision. "Places such as V'nae Rae were made for the government of our people, but others were made for the celebration of our gifts. Here, we danced and sang."

Even the shifting shadow of it was beautiful, and Finn felt an ache lodge in his chest. It was wrapped in melancholy and loss, and those bittersweet moments were the stuff that talespinners dined on. He had never felt able to make his own stories, only ever repeating the traditional ones, but in this moment and place the urge came over him. He wanted to create their tales; these lost people who were unraveling in front of him like yesterday's dreams.

Yet, this was not the most important thing—not for the moment at least. He did not know how long he had his mother for. "I don't understand," he pressed. "How did you save Ysel here, when you have been dead for a thousand years?" Once the words were out of his mouth he wished them back again; it seemed very rude to point that out to her.

She did not seem to mind. She simply raised one hand, as if she might be able to touch his face. "The Kindred do not know time. In the deep wells of this world, they live apart from it. When you and Ysel were born, that is where they kept you. You remained suspended in that state until they brought you here, Ysel they also returned, but a fraction later. When you . . . when they feared you would not suit their task."

Her long-dead eyes were locked with his. "You know, deep down, when that time was. When you found another, different purpose."

Finn knew. He didn't have to think overly on it. He licked his lips before replying, "When I met Talyn, when I fell in love with her. That was the moment they lost faith in me?" The haunting strains of the music grew fainter now, and the lines of the dancers grew sketchier, as a child's drawing that was being erased.

"Yes," Putorae said, and though her silvery ghostly form could not breathe or sigh, it somehow conveyed a great disappointment. "They brought Ysel up from the chaos, and he grew through childhood here. No one could have guessed the connection you still shared, or how you would find each other."

Finn glanced down at the yarn in his hand, wondering at it himself. Ysel had been trying to learn the same small gifts his brother had developed. It hurt him deeply that he'd not been able to find him and help him with that.

He'd always been the talespinner, the troublemaker, and had known that he was not important. The message was all-important, not the speaker of it. It would take some getting used this new condition where he did matter, dragon aside.

"What is the point?" he asked, staring down at the floor, not wanting to see it all dissolve away before him. "Why did the Kindred protect us like this?"

The unfair spirit did not answer him; there was so little of her left here. "Go to where you were most happy, beloved son. They already know. Your brother does, too. Find me there once more . . ."

Then she was gone, now a memory too. Finn was left standing among the gray dust and the debris, his hands clenched in angry fists, his mind already darting to where she was sending him. He knew where he had been the happiest in his life. The sea. It had been with the sound of the ocean in his ears.

Finn had never wanted to go back there. Now, however, he knew he would have to.

CHAPTER TWO

BEING WITHIN THE FLAME

"**W**ell, I must say that this is a lot cooler than I imagined," Pelanor said as she turned and smiled at Byreniko. The scarlet flame that contained them described a circle of about twelve feet—a circle that gave off absolutely no heat. Byre waited in the middle of it, crouched down, hands on his thighs, content to see what would happen.

"You could at least say thank you," Pelanor growled, tossing her long dark hair over one shoulder. The Blood Witch always lingered on the edge of anger, ready to boil over into action. It was that blatant and simmering danger that made her even more attractive than Byre would admit to anyone. Letting out a long slow sigh he folded his hands together.

The last thing he should be considering at this moment was how Pelanor drew his eye. He'd just seen his father murdered by the Caisah and had entered the world of the Kindred, the place of trial for his ancestor Ellyria Dragonsoul. Primitive sexual emotions were not something that he could entertain at this point.

Ellyria—that was who he should be thinking of now, since she had been the only other of the Vaerli to enter into the realm of the Kindred as they just had. The tales of the terror and pain she had endured were not very comforting.

"I should mention that I don't like being ignored." Byre was always surprised how quickly the Witch moved—and almost as silently as the Vaerli once had. She now sat with her face only a few inches from his own. Her eyes flicked from green to blinding gold, like a cat's caught in the light.

"I can see that," he replied quietly, watching her more carefully. He'd thought that the Kindred were the creatures that he would have to watch for. His sister Talyn's gift of the Blood Witch was an added complication, but she had saved his life when the Caisah had appeared, so he owed her something. "I am not ignoring you. I am simply examining our situation."

Her eyes flickered over his face, and he realized that she was young indeed for one of her kind. Most Blood Witches were studies in composure, from what he'd heard—but his one seemed constantly on a knife-edge.

Pelanor tilted her head, and something changed behind her dark eyes. "I miss my *gewalt*," she said it simply, and the longing in her voice ran deep.

Byre glanced down, twin slivers of white fangs rested delicately against her full lower lip. The Phaerkorn relied on blood, preferably the blood of their *gewalt*—but in an emergency another would do.

A stir of eroticism roused his contrary body, which obviously did not know the difference between passion and danger. The twitch of Pelanor's smile told him it had not gone unnoticed; Phaerkorn could smell even better than a hound. Yet Byre wasn't about to say anything about that. Instead he reached up, tucked his hair back behind his ear and turned his head away from her. "Then drink from me. We will both need our strength for whatever is ahead."

She let out a little gasp which sounded hopeful and shocked. For an instant Pelanor leaned forward a fraction, but then her face clouded over and she leapt back as if she'd been burnt. Her hand was shaking as she wiped the back of it over her mouth. "You don't know what you're . . . you shouldn't . . ." She stopped suddenly, as her eyes remained fixed on Byre's exposed throat and the racing pulse there.

The confident and powerful Witch was gone, revealing a shaking and very young Phaerkorn. She was holding herself still, as if afraid that movement would break her composure.

Byre sighed and turned his gaze on her. "Think of it, Pelanor; they left us here and we haven't seen them for . . . well, however long it has been. It's impossible to tell time in their realm. What if this is the test? Sooner or later you will have to eat, and if you leave it too long you may not be able to control yourself."

She looked down at her small brown hands that were shaking. Clenching them into fists, the Witch's gaze narrowed and her lip pulled back from her fangs. "You are as ignorant as everyone else in Conhaero! It is not just a matter of you opening a vein for me. You are not my *gewalt*, so the only time when feeding is simple is when I kill someone. If not, there is . . . there is a bond formed."

Byre sat back on his heels. Everywhere in Conhaero there were pacts, geasa and bonds, but nothing between Vaerli and Phaerkorn. The Blood Witches were killers. Everyone feared them. Was it a wise move to align himself with them as his own long-lost sister had done?

His sister—the one everyone knew as Talyn the Hunter—had sent Pelanor to protect him, and Byre had to believe that it meant something.

Holding out his slightly trembling hand to the Witch, he smiled as reassuringly as possible. "There is already a bond, Pelanor. Talyn saw to that, and I trust her. I trust you."

"You trust me?" She slid across the rocky floor toward the Vaerli. Her eyes were now exclusively gold, the tip of her tongue pressed against those sharp canine teeth. She reminded him of a child being offered a boiled sweet by a stranger; all cautious anticipation but also strangely ready for flight.

Byre forced a smile onto his face. "I know you want to live through this as much as I do, Pelanor, and to get through it we will need each other."

The Blood Witch ran her tongue over her upper lip and considered for a moment.

"You," she whispered, kneeling before him, "are quite remarkable Byreniko of the Vaerli, and a much better person than your sister." The Witch's fingers rubbed lightly against the stubble of his goatee beard, tracing the line of his jaw.

Knowing she was playing with him, Byre caught her fingers in a vice-like grip. Her changeable eyes flared wide in shock; Phaerkorn were not used to anyone else having faster reflexes or being stronger than they were.

"Just go ahead and feed," Byre said with a hiss, giving her hand a sharp squeeze to emphasize his own strength. "No need to play games with me."

Her gaze narrowed for an instant, and then she moved. Byre couldn't help a small grunt of surprise as she launched herself forward. He'd been expecting her to latch onto his neck, but thinking of it, that would have killed him, most likely. One of the Caisah's torturers had tested the limits of the Vaerli healing gift, but she had not been trying to kill him. Pelanor might be young, but she knew the ways to feed. The places where it was best.

All these thoughts sped through his mind as she ripped the top two buttons off of his shirt in her haste to take up his offer. Byre steeled himself, but after what he'd suffered in the Rutilian Guards' fortress he knew he could withstand any pain.

Certainly there was a little; a sting just below his collarbone as she drew her teeth across his skin there. Then there was a drowsy enjoyment, and a thrust of pleasure down his spine as her tongue lapped delicately at the wound. Byre drew in his breath shakily as his body mixed signals of delight with the frisson of pain. The long slip of her tongue over his skin was delicious, and though he tried to keep his jaw closed a sliver of a groan escaped him. She made no move that indicated she had heard him.

Pelanor drank as delicately as a cat licking up cream, and Byre felt something unfolding within him; something more profound than just the desire of the flesh. A sound like the roar of a storm entered his head, as if from a long way off a woman was howling in rage and despair. His body felt as though it were falling away from him, spinning into nothingness with only the feeling of his blood entering Pelanor holding him awake. Then he felt the plunge of something metallic go through him, sharp, sudden and deadly.

When Byre finally did find his way back to his body it was to Pelanor's lips and sharp teeth against his, breathing into him and kissing him at the same time. He tasted the iron of his own blood, but he could also feel his own strength flowing through her. The spiral of desire and need for blood was heady, and Byre could feel himself drowning in it.

With a groan he pushed her away and struggled upright. She stayed where she was, legs folded, looking up at him, wiping the line of scarlet slowly from the corner of her mouth. For an uncomfortable moment they stared across at each other in silence as she licked the remains from her fingers.

Byre cleared his throat. "Is that what you wanted all along, Pelanor? More Vaerli blood?"

She sighed. "You offered, Byre. Your sister gave hers willingly to seal our deal, but her blood is not as powerful as yours." Pelanor got to her feet, walked to him, pressed against his chest and traced the bottom of his lip. "You are nearly Vaerli as they once were, full of power and Gifts." Leaning back she fixed him with a smug look. "Tasting you is like tasting the past, and I like it very much."

Whatever smart words Byre could have summoned died away when he became aware of a figure in the flames behind the Witch. The Kindred was part of the fire: an alien shape, tall with a great curved head, but otherwise formless as a statue before the carver set to work. Byre had only seen it because in the moving fires it was utterly still, a black shadow in so much brightness.

As far as he knew they had been alone since they arrived, but now he wondered if he'd been mistaken all that time. What had he and Pelanor revealed to them while they were trapped in the circle of fire?

Catching his suddenly alert pose, the Blood Witch turned around to see what he was looking at, and then backed away. It pleased the Vaerli to see the witch cowed so quickly; she was not so young as to not be awed by the Kindred. Pushing her behind him, Byre tried to keep his own bravery intact, but it was hard.

The Kindred were the original spirits of the land, the masters of the chaos that had been its natural state before the arrival of the other races. His own people's contract with them and the Gifts they had given in return dated back many thousands of years. Still, the Vaerli did not truly know the Kindred. Time and the elements were their home, and they had not been seen above ground since the curse had been laid on the Vaerli by the Caisah. Byre had come here to recover that ancient pact and the Seven Gifts, as his father and all his race wanted.

He was not foolish enough to imagine that it wouldn't be bought with great sacrifice. As the Kindred's towering form moved beyond the flames, within feet of the Vaerli and the Blood Witch, Byre recalled the tales of Ellyria. His long-ago ancestor's suffering at the hands of the Kindred had been what secured the Pact in the first place. He imagined that the oncoming Kindred was about to deliver the same to him.

Up close, the Kindred was not completely solid. The rocky floor could be seen through it. But it did give off a tremendous heat, almost like staring into a blast furnace. The etheric form it wore was one Byre had seen before, but he knew it could just as easily construct another from the earth all around them.

You are ready. The voice came from no body, but was rather inserted into the skulls of those it wished to communicate with. The sensation was not unpleasant, but Byre caught Pelanor out of the corner of one eye, shaking her head as if it pained her.

"Is it time for the testing?" he asked, wondering at how strong his voice managed to sound when inside he was quaking.

Your test is not to be the same as Ellyria's. The Kindred flickered and wavered, bending to winds Byre could not detect. *There can be no fresh pact-making for the Gifts.*

"But that is why I came." Byre took a step forward, thinking of all he had been through and his own father's sacrifice.

The flames around them grew suddenly furious and hot, so that his skin began to sizzle.

"Careful." Pelanor grabbed hold of his arm, her long nails dragging sharply into his skin. "You may not burn, but I think I could."

Despite being angry with her for the interruption, Byre did not want to see her go up like a candle. The Kindred's eyes now flickered with blue fire. *You came here because the after-time and the before-time brought you here.*

Pelanor's eyebrows rose in surprise. The way the Kindred lived was almost as much a mystery to Byre as any Blood Witch was. His own people, if they had known any more, had never had the chance to impart it to him. He was only aware that the Kindred did not exist in time in the same way as any other creature in Conhaero. Even the Vaerli had to abide by the hours and minutes, but the Kindred were far more than that.

When he looked up the blazing creature, almost indiscernible against the flames, Byre knew he was in grave danger. His throat was dry, but he managed to croak out, "What would you have me do?"

Cast yourself upon the tides of time. The fire arched and spun, and then flowed aside leaving a gap just big enough for two to pass through; the end was in darkness. *Live as one of the Kindred and see what you may learn.*

"And the Blood Witch?" Byre croaked.

The Kindred's eyes of flame raked over Pelanor's small form. *She is part of you, so she may travel at your side, but make sure she does not stray too far from your side. We cannot protect her.*

So there was only the darkness now for both of them—that and the uncertainty of time.

"Deeper and deeper," Pelanor murmured. "How much farther can there be to go down?" Her voice was full of both fear and desire. She certainly had the spirit of an explorer. Together they moved forward, though this time he would not hold her hand.

As they went past the barrier of flame, the sensation of heat abruptly left them for another less familiar, less identifiable feeling. Byre felt his skin shudder to a cool touch that stabbed through to the bone like thousands of long needles. The sensation passed through his whole body in waves, and by the way Pelanor shook her head he realized that she was laboring under the same peculiarity.

This discomfort was merely the appetizer. Whatever was beyond the flames was stronger than Vaerli or Phaerkorn, and they had stepped right into it. Minds were knocked sideways, and all that Pelanor and Byre were became totally irrelevant. In the tides of before-time, all that they were washed away, long forgotten.

The Rutilians were moving down the bleak valley, looking carefully around them, ready for an ambush. Equo, crouched behind the outcrop of rock in the ridge above, felt the sweat begin to bead on his forehead. The summer sun was so strong up here that he almost wanted to be down in the canyon, out of the shade—almost.

Glancing to his right, he caught Varlesh's eye. The man jerked his head up in acknowledgement and raised the square of glass upward to the sky. Sending the flash of brilliance into the clouds was his task, while Equo did the same but across the canyon.

That was all it took. Baraca's troops, concealed under canvases with a light covering of the red soil of the area on top, emerged among the crevices in the cliffs and poured down in the valley, as well. While his soldiers were well concealed, the commander was not. Spurning any camouflage, Baraca himself leapt across to a teetering outcrop with the agility of a teenager. It was impressive and a little disturbing. He was a great burly man—or had been before the power of the Void had entered him. Now he was an scion. Seeing him standing there, gesturing to his followers, Equo could understand a little of why they were all so fanatical in their devotion.

The eye kept drifting to him, but not because he was particularly handsome. Instead it was as if the air bent around him; it hung around his shoulders like a cloak. Equo was only glad that the eye patch remained in place; no one who had seen beyond it wanted to see it again. The raw magic of the Void between Worlds had taken up residence in there and changed him forever.

Baraca had once been a friend to Equo, Si and Varlesh; an old companion that was now leading the rebels against the Caisah. It was the first major uprising in mortal memory. The trio of men, however, remembered the previous one.

Perhaps that was what caused the knot of dread in Equo's stomach. The tyrant had put down more rebellions in his immortal reign over Conhaero than any of them could count. His methods had not become any more diplomatic with time. This one appeared to be beginning well for the rebels, but so too had many of the others. Equo did not have much optimism left to spare on this endeavor.

When the howls came from above them in the clouds, Equo felt his spirits lift. The Swoop dropped from the sky like vengeance personified. Hawks, eagles, buzzards and falcons, birds of beak and talon, moved together in a formation that no natural predator would have contemplated. They shot over the heads of the descending rebels and split neatly into two sections; one peeled off north while the other descended to the rear, where as yet the Rutilian guard had not noticed anything different.

Across the canyon, One-eyed Baraca was nearly down among the guard, leaping energetically from outcrop to cliff face with more athleticism than any mortal could manage. The sword in his hand gleamed, and Equo could almost feel sorry for the Caisah's troops.

The Swoop sealed the trap at both ends. The white light bloomed where the birds swooped to the earth; when it cleared, there were the scions of the Lady of Wings in all their glory, young women in shining silver armor.

Originally they had been the defenders of the Manesto, following the scion that had led their tribe through the Void to Conhaero. Then the Caisah had come, done away with the scions somehow, and taken the Swoop for his own. Now, under the leadership of Azrul, the Swoop had managed to break free of that and dedicated themselves to this new Avatar, One-eyed Baraca. Whether that had been a good decision had not yet played out, just as it remained to be seen for Equo, Varlesh and Si.

The time for thinking was not now. Equo took a place at Varlesh's side as they joined the hurried scamper down to crush the guard in their pincer movement. Si, their fey, gentler part had remained behind at the camp with the Vaerli seer Nyree.

The narrowness of the canyon certainly leveled the playing field. With the Swoop acting as a plug at each end, the number advantage the guard always had was nullified; in fact, it began to work against them. As troops at front and rear went hand to hand with the fury of the Swoop, others behind were rendered unable to move or get into action, so that when troops above them in the canyon began to fire arrows into the mass, panic began.

Baraca's pikemen began to use the extra length of their weapons to punch down into the confused mass of guards. It was terrible work that should have made Equo ill, but his brain was no longer engaged; the mob and the rush of blood had taken over.

The smell of sweat, blood and spilled guts was primal and compelling. He found himself yelling along with the rest, thrusting and stabbing whatever he could find. Standing in a rank of fellow soldiers, he and Varlesh abandoned themselves to the unit. It was a taste of the power they had experienced when they had been not three but one.

Flesh had been the domain of the Form Bards, and yet here they were cutting and destroying it. The Song they had shared had been about beauty and control, but now they were destroying with madness just like everyone else.

It was not what they had ever meant to be about—reduced to mere mortals. All of this Equo was aware of, but only dimly. He let go of self and let himself become part of something much bigger and far more dangerous.

When he surfaced again, the battle, if it could be called that, was over. Around him Baraca's troops were grinning wearily, splattered with gore, slapping each other on the back. The mixture of this with the red soil made for a truly horrific sight. Varlesh grasped Equo by the shoulder, turning him around. His eyes, too, were dark and sad.

That touch steadied Equo a little. Lifting his pike wearily, he looked down onto the field of carnage, and noted with horror that there were few survivors. Those that lay about groaning were being dispatched by troops moving among them with thin blades. The Swoop had gone—retreated once more to the sky. Only their leader Azrul remained behind.

It would be pleasant to strike vengeance and then fly away before the real horror settled in. The rest of the army did not have that luxury.

After looting the corpses for anything useful, the troops regrouped for the march back to their camp. Equo would have taken a place happily at the rear, but Varlesh maneuvered them through the tired and jubilant crowd to the front where Baraca and Azrul were.

The tall woman with her silver armor was talking animatedly with the rebel leader. Even though he couldn't at once make out the discussion, Equo observed that her tone was deferential, even while she didn't appear to be agreeing to whatever he was saying. To the Swoop any scion was the highest authority, but he recalled Nyree's horror when they had first discovered One-eyed Baraca. It was this that made him cautious about their once-friend.

Azrul finally gave up whatever argument she was having, bowed once, and retreated from the scion.

Varlesh, though, had no such compunction; he elbowed his way forward to talk to Baraca. Equo smiled grimly. He, Varlesh and Si might have been one person once, but time had changed them. For himself, he had no desire to talk to the scion.

So, while Varlesh began discussing tactics with the rebel leader, Equo's mind wandered, and he gradually let himself drop back a little into the camouflage of the crowd.

Their camp was not far off, and it didn't take them long to get back to it. It was not much to come home to—in reality a pitiful affair. The scattering of campfires was desperately small compared to the might that the Caisah could muster, but nevertheless Equo found himself jogging toward it.

The few people left behind—the wounded, the healers and the children—began trotting toward the returning soldiers with cries of delight. Only Nyree did not.

The seer stood next to the healer's tent, as beautiful as ever. She was small like all other Vaerli, with dark hair and caramel skin; hers was different, though, covered in the word magic that proclaimed she was the made seer—the *oidnafan*. The silvery script twisted over her flesh made it powerful art, and though it meant a great deal to her, every time Equo saw it his heart sank a little. It was one more thing that separated them.

The Vaerli eyes were also completely dark and full of pinpricks of light. Most called them stars. The Harrowing, the Caisah's curse on the Vaerli, had denied them most of their Gifts. The one he loved had not reclaimed the Gifts of the Kindred, but she had found her seer's powers. He was afraid of what she saw—and even more worried that it meant she could not love him as he loved her.

Seeing her, though, Equo couldn't help himself—when she smiled, he rushed in and embraced her. Her small form tucked neatly in against him. Her dark head rested against his shoulder in just the right way. Nyree hugged him back, but not for as long as he wanted.

Pushing back, she glanced around him to where Baraca was receiving the adulation of his remaining troops. Her spine stiffened and her lips twisted. Her inability to convince anyone that the arrival of a scion was the beginning of a new Conflagration was frustrating her.

"Did you see Baraca use any magic?" she asked, glancing up at Equo with those haunting eyes.

"No, I don't think so." He frowned and considered what he had seen. "He took the front line, but I didn't see anything obvious."

Her shoulders relaxed a little. "Well, that is something, I suppose . . . but we have plenty of other worries."

Equo caught Varlesh's eye, and his brother followed after as Nyree turned once more back to the center of the camp.

The heat of midday was some hours off, yet already the temperature was working against them all. The two men paused to unwrap and soak their headscarves in a tub of water kept for this purpose in the middle of the camp. The chill was a great relief—even if just for a moment—but Nyree only let the men rest for a heartbeat. She hurried them into her tent, where the shade provided only minimal comfort from the oppressive weather.

Si, the third fragment of the whole they'd once been, was seated near the trestle table, and spread out before him was a strange collection of items: the wing of a seabird, a handful of mottled blue stones, a twisted and bleached branch of wood, and a skein of tangled red wool. The ways of seers were indeed mysterious.

The splintered Si was just as bad. He toyed with the objects as if they made perfect sense to him, his brow furrowed and concentrating on arranging them just so. Nyree stood at the entrance to the tent watching him out of the corner of her eye, hands on her hips, and spoke in a low voice. "The courier from the west did not arrive."

Varlesh slumped back into the deepest shade in the tent he could find. "You mean we have no way of knowing if they are rising in rebellion, as well?"

"It is hard for me to see." Nyree tapped her fingers on the table and looked out the flap. Baraca's honor guard could be heard giving him a rousing round of cheers. "Something, or perhaps someone, is blocking my vision. I am more worried by what that could mean, than about the chance of any further people joining us."

Varlesh cleared his throat. "I am sure Baraca is worried about supplies, troops, and all those things reinforcements bring with them. This is important."

"Is it?" Now Nyree was describing a small circle in the tent, her hand pressed over her eyes, as if by narrowing her vision she could see the way ahead better.

Si leaned back in his chair, watching her but contributing nothing.

"You don't know what you are saying," Varlesh muttered while digging his clay pipe out of his pocket. "A scion has returned. If that is not a signal to rebel against the Caisah, then I do not know what could be!"

He was just saying what Equo was thinking, but Nyree rounded on him. "Have you ever considered," she said through bared teeth, "that there is more going on in this world than the Caisah?" Her eyes flickered between the three men who all seemed equally in danger from her sudden wrath.

Seeing that they were not going to answer, she pulled out the remaining roughly-made stool and sat opposite them, for a moment saying nothing. Equo was sure that some of the fine writing on her skin was actually moving, flexing, almost as if it were alive or responding to something else.

Pushing a hand through her hair, she looked down at the scattering of odd objects. When she spoke her voice was slightly unsteady. "I've been trying to understand what I see—there is so much. I can see it . . . but . . . I can't understand . . ." Nyree trailed off.

"It is not your place to do this," Si said, reaching across the table and taking her hand. "Things will make themselves clear at the right time. You are the made seer, you need the born seer to make a complete vision."

The two of them looked hard at each other, until Equo felt a little twinge of jealousy. The Vaerli shook herself as if she were a suddenly soaked cat, and leaned back. "That is as may be, but she has not been revealed in a thousand years, so we have to go on with what we have."

"And what we have is bugger all," Varlesh muttered. "You seers are always rabbiting on with never a bloody point."

The moment turned abruptly quiet again, and Equo wondered if the other man had pushed a little too far. Finally, the seer laughed, breaking the tension. "Then let me make this plain, old friend: there is one thing that Si and I agree on. One thing we have seen. If Conhaero is to survive the coming destruction, your people, the Ahouri, must rise and be as they were."

"Crone's nails!" Varlesh's pipe snapped suddenly in his grip, while Equo leapt up as if scalded. Si alone remained calm; the only sign he had even heard her was a slight tilt of his head.

Equo pushed aside the tent flap and glanced frantically left and right, but luckily no one was nearby. Turning back, he grabbed Nyree's arm, fingers digging into her flesh. "To even say that name, to even think it . . ." He stopped, shook his head, and then glared at her. "You must be insane!"

Nyree looked up at him as if he was a complete stranger, and under his palm a sudden heat bloomed. Equo felt it as if it were his own flesh burning—which in a way it was. He did not let go, though, stubborn in his absolute fear of the Ahouri being discovered. His jaw clenched tight, but after a minute Nyree smiled and laid her hand over his. She had made her point.

"It is time, Equo." Her voice was low and soft, but there was no mistaking the steel at its very core. "Your people have lain hidden for far too long, and now they must come out of the shadows. All of the races of Conhaero must stand together when the Conflagration comes. The White Void will not be ignored."

"The shadows are all we have, woman," Varlesh barked, flicking the remains of his pipe into the corner of the tent. "If we come out, if we show ourselves, then what your own people suffered will look like a picnic by comparison. Do you think we did this terrible thing to ourselves without consideration? Do you think that we went to ground lightly?"

Equo couldn't stand to see his other third and his love argue like this—even if voices had not yet become raised. He stepped between them and took Nyree's hand. "The Ahouri were peaceful people, so we would bring nothing to this war of Baraca's. It is not in our nature."

She squeezed his hand, and locked her star-filled eyes with his. "It is not for the war that they are needed, dear heart. It is for something far grander and more important. Unity. The people of Conhaero must be united. Surely you know how wrong it is to be separate?"

They stared at each other for a long time before Varlesh, pulling out a fresh new pipe from his pocket, grunted. "You two can bloody hold hands all you like, but by the maid's fair touch, you will not get the Ahouri involved merely by batting your eyelashes at him."

"You can find them, though," Nyree's pitch black eyes gleamed with little pinpricks of light that appeared to be moving. "You know where they are." It was not a question, it was a statement of fact.

"They still sing to us—in our dreams we can hear them." Si's voice low, musical, and infrequent, broke through to his brethren.

Equo felt his breath freeze in his chest. Such a sensation of peace stole over him that for a moment he couldn't even feel if Nyree's hand remained in his own. The rest of the world dimmed in the face of this hint of a remembered feeling: utter calm. It was the sensation that he could only recall in dreams; knowledge that he was whole.

Just one glance across the other parts of him—Si and Varlesh—and he knew that they had felt it too. This whisper of the past surely could not be ignored.

Varlesh cleared his throat and tugged at his beard while his eyes remained riveted upon Si. Their quietest but most potent member was the one who had the keeping of the ember of their remaining power. To any stranger, Si had the appearance of a madman—one that they took care of and managed. The complete opposite was in fact the truth. They relied on him more than any outsider could possibly guess.

Equo felt like he hadn't drawn in breath for hours. "Is it really time, Si?"

Varlesh pressed his hand down among the maps and the debris of the seer's craft, leaning forward. "We have to be sure. Once done, it cannot be undone."

Si rose and straightened, for the first time in many years looking directly at the world with a clear gaze. "I am sure it is time. We must go to them. We, the broken, must now put forth the effort to heal."

Equo sighed, feeling the fear and excitement rattle through his system. They were words they'd longed to hear from Si, yet had never imagined would actually come. Equo spoke with more calmness than he actually felt. "Then I believe we know where we must go."

Varlesh carefully laid the well-chewed pipe down on the table and cleared his throat. "Better put in a bit of practice, then—otherwise they'll laugh us out of there."

Nyree couldn't understand the grim humor in it, but despite himself Equo let out a snort of laughter. "The competition, indeed . . . with us, it is always the competition."

CHAPTER THREE

PROPOSALS AND DESPERATION

If living with a madman was a delicate balancing act, loving one was a full, breathing nightmare. As Kelanim sat to the left of the Caisah under the purple awning, she knew deep down that she had chosen this path; a path that had brought her here to the arena. That one fact kept her sane.

Ever since she'd been a little girl, determination had been her strongest suit. That and her beauty combined together had gotten her farther than her older and more intelligent sisters—all of them were now married and spitting out babies for simple merchants.

Her emerald eyes and flaming hair might have caught the overlord's eye, but she had worked hard to keep it long after his passion might otherwise have waned. The impoverished but beautiful daughter of a lowly bureaucrat, she had expected to at best tolerate the touch of the Caisah, the man she had been sent to as a gift. It had come as a great shock to her that she loved him.

She flicked her turquoise and gold fan and turned her head slightly to where the rest of the Court were sitting, each according to their standing with the Caisah. Some were within the shade of the awning, while those less favored had to endure the touch of the heat beyond.

Below, where it was even hotter, they were clearing the arena of bodies and emptying fresh bags of sand to cover up the blood. Today it would take a lot of them.

The Caisah grew bored easily even on a normal day, but since the loss of his Hunter he had grown more easily distracted. The gladiatorial games he'd once relished, he now seemed to take no pleasure in. Since his Hunter's departure he had ordered more and more of them to be played out before him, but he always appeared unimpressed. Slit throats and bruised bodies didn't amuse him as they once had. Watching him from the corner of her eye, Kelanim tried to judge if that was also true of his attentions to her.

As the mistress observed him, she noticed his hand slide under the right edge of his robe and rub his shoulder distractedly. The Caisah's body Kelanim knew as well as her own; there had never been any mark on its perfection. That was, until the day that the Hunter had left.

The Caisah had not spoken of what had happened, and she knew not to ask questions that might bring his wrath down on her. She had been there, though, hiding in the shadows, when he staggered out of the Puzzle Room. She had never seen him like that in all their time together. The image of the overlord leaning against the frame of the door, bright blood staining his linen shirt, and looking beaten was one she would treasure forever. It told her that she had not fallen in love with just a god—somewhere in there was a man. A man that she could help. Kelanim guessed she should at least thank Talyn for that.

Two days later she had been running her hands over the body of her lover and had found a raised scar the length of her smallest finger on his shoulder. Her heart had raced, but she brushed her touch past it quickly, just in case he had noticed her noticing. Love him she might, but she did not trust his hair trigger temper.

Exactly what this meant, Kelanim had no idea, and unfortunately she had no one to ask, either. The Court was a fickle place where gossip had wings and rumor could run like a hot fever. As the Caisah's favored mistress she had no friends she could trust, and no maid she dared to confide in. Anyway, it was not like any of these people knew any more about her love than she did. The Caisah was a monument in Conhaero, an immortal like the Vaerli, but with none of that sad race's imperfections. No one knew where he came from, or how he had come upon his powers.

Kelanim knew she was the expert on him, and yet she was floundering to find any explanation for the change in him in the last few months.

However, there he was, touching the rough patch on his body, and there was no anger in his expression. The far-off look in his eye said that he was not with Kelanim, and the smile on his lips whispered that Talyn still had her claws in him. He had come out with not only a scar, but with something else that never left him.

The Hunter's sword, the one she had never brought into his presence, was now always hanging from his belt. Kelanim had seen it only a few times, mostly glimpses when Talyn had returned from a bounty, but she had never entered the audience chamber with it. The mistress had often wanted to get a closer look at it, but the one time she'd dared to enter the Hunter's empty chamber she'd only found a locked silver box under the bed. The Vaerli letter magic carved on it had deterred her immediately.

Now, she was heartily sick of the sight of the sword. He carried it everywhere, and she was as likely to get a closer look at it as when it was locked away in that box.

Whatever had happened in the Puzzle Room had been violent and exciting to him. It was a combination of emotions that his chief mistress knew she could not raise in him no matter how hard she tried. Talyn—even when she was gone—remained a competitor.

The crowd roared, snapping her out of that dreadful realization. The Caisah was roused from his own contemplation by what was being dragged into the arena. He sat on the edge of his seat and leaned forward, pressing his elbows into the arms of the throne. He and the citizens of Perilous had been presented with few opportunities like this, for rebels were rarities this far west. Everyone knew that the east was prone to rising, but even they had not attempted to break away for more than twenty years. So when the crowd saw the group of half a dozen men being herded into the arena they went silent with anticipation.

The Caisah frowned, suddenly looking at the seats rather than the sand. The whispering that passed through the citizens was nothing like the harsh roars when they had so recently seen the gladiators. Now, as the guards pulled the men to the center of the arena, it was deathly silent. The clank of the chains as they were fixed to the ring echoed across an amphitheatre that was meant to magnify blood for the glory of the Caisah.

Kelanim found she was holding her breath, and the exquisite fan dropped to her lap. As a royal mistress she was especially sensitive to the winds of opinion and change, and at this minute she could feel the shift, just as the Caisah could.

His eyes narrowed and his hands clenched around the arm of the gilded throne so that it creaked and then cracked. The crowd had no sounds of appreciation for his justice, but when a cloud of darkness scattered across the sky they roared with delight. More traitors!

Trouble came from the east, as it always did, but this time it was birds. A great curtain of a flock poured from the sky, sweeping down low over the high walls of the arena. Kelanim saw mostly black birds of the fields and songbirds shoot past the Caisah's purple awning. The sounds of their wings was like a thousands doors snapping shut, but it was the cacophony of their singing, all the tones and melodies at once, that made her clap her hands to her head.

Worried, she glanced around and saw everyone else but the Caisah was doing the same. Unlike their leader, their faces were upturned, not in horror, but in delight. It was the Lady of Wings that had come—that was what each joyful smile said. The scion had once surrendered her Swoop to the Caisah, a sign most had taken to mean that he ruled with her blessing. The truth was he had taken it from the Lady—wrenched it away, really. So its loss had been a terrible blow to him.

Kelanim could not hear the words that he was now shouting to the circling birds, but they could not be kindly ones with such an expression on his face. The flock dipped and whizzed over the heads of the chained men in the center of the arena. It was hard to tell if they were pecking them to death, or merely surrounding them in a cloak of wings. Kelanim struggled to her feet, hands still protecting her ears, to watch what was happening on the sand.

The men strained against the chains, and their forms flickered. It was no trick of the light. In the dancing shadows of the birds, the men were near to becoming one with the flock. She was certainly not the only one to notice; the crowd were on their feet and cheering—but it was not for the Caisah.

The almighty crash as the throne was tossed down into the arena was just loud enough to be heard over the birdsong. Seeing her love stand tall, Kelanim staggered to her feet to lend him whatever her support meant to him. He didn't even glance her way, but the air around them flexed with his anger.

It was a sensation that she had witnessed only a few times in the presence of the Caisah. The little things he did with magic, especially in his bedchamber, seemed effortless to him, but not now. Now she was in the presence of his Avatar strength. The distortion of the air and the sudden rise in temperature signaled he was ready to use what most had never seen.

Kelanim beamed, even while her skin ached and her eardrums pounded. Digging her fingernails into her palms to distract larger pains, she looked up into the eyes of the Caisah. Immediately nothing else seemed relevant. She was looking into everything, a whirling sucking void that contained every possibility and none. The white light burning from the Caisah's eyes threatened to suck her down into nothing. What a tiny mote in the eye of existence she was. A speck of sand in the vast desert of time. Kelanim would have howled, but a voice would have been useless there. The best she could do was hold out her hands against the space ready to devour her.

Somewhere she caught a glimpse of the one she loved, a tiny recognition of her existence. He turned his eyes away from her and with one hand thrust her away.

Falling to the slate floor, the mistress found she was sobbing and gasping for breath. Her chest was tight and threatening to burst, so she clutched the tiles for a long moment until the feeling passed. She could still feel the consuming light only feet away from her, but she did not dare another look and risk its might falling on her again.

Instead, Kelanim scrambled to the edge of the balcony to observe what was now happening down on the sand. The birds were circling, but as she watched they appeared to become more organized until she could imagine there were patterns being woven with beak and wing. It was so hypnotic that for a long while she didn't notice anything else.

The men on the sand were no longer standing in ready bliss—instead they were in real pain, stretched and torn like pieces of leather between two quarreling dogs. It was impossible to hear their screams over the storm of birdsong, but their faces—revealed now and then among the chaos of fluttering wings—were twisted, while their hands reached toward the birds in supplication. As if they could be saved with just a little more faith.

Something had to give; reality could not tolerate such a battle. The Caisah bellowed, a sound so beyond what any mortal could make that many of those who were already turning to scatter from their seats were knocked down to the ground. Now the screams were not just from the birds and the men on the sand.

Kelanim felt blindly out with her hand for him, terrified and wary of looking up at the Caisah again. Her fingers grazed across his ankle, which was bare and burning. The mistress could not have said what compelled her to hold on, but she did, feeling the power vibrate through her bones. Though her mind was numb with fright, she had to see, she had to know what was going on—even if her eyes were burned from her head.

Kelanim managed to get to her knees and wrench her eyes open just a fraction at the very moment the Caisah roared again—and everything broke apart.

She hadn't even time to blink or draw breath before flame, blue and white, erupted from the stained sands of the arena engulfing the struggling men. For an instant they burned skyward like consumed candles, their arms flung back almost into the shape of wings, flames erupting from their mouths and from the tips of their fingers.

The cloud of circling birds broke away in disorder, no longer a flock, merely terrified animals as the fire rolled and spat around them. The Caisah was still screaming with a ragged throat, a word that might have been "no." It went on beyond reason while everything below was engulfed.

Not content with the condemned, the conflagration whirled about on itself and smothered the first ten rows of the stadium seating in blue-white flames. Normal citizens of Perilous and Fair were swallowed by it. Children, the elderly, or Rutilian guards—it made no different to the conflagration. They were surrounded and gone in a moment. Families scrambling to get away were swamped by the fire that the Caisah had unleashed. Old men and women not moving as fast were caught up and gone in ash. Others, trampled by their peers, screamed in agony and died even in the furthest reaches of the stadium. The flames cut a swath through lower half of the amphitheatre, licking and consuming their way up the steps like an angry tide before sliding back and disappearing. People had been running, so perhaps the carnage wasn't as great as it might have been, but Kelanim saw enough to haunt her dreams.

The mistress dragged herself upright, clutching the edge of the balcony and staring out at the remains of the day with wide eyes and a soot-stained face. The sand was gone, burned to white glass, while stone walls were blackened and twisted like the creations of some maddened sculptor. Of the people there was no sign; all that they had been was consumed and wiped away.

Spinning around, Kelanim examined the Caisah. He was blank-faced, most likely in shock. In all her time with him, Kelanim had never seen the like of it; the power had been magnificent and wild. He must have been unable to control it. Surely, all those people dying had to have been a mistake.

He shook his head, his eyes once more just eyes. His voice, when he spoke, came out hoarse and strained. "They do call this place Perilous for a reason."

His guards, having pulled themselves back into formation and regained their composure a little, laughed in a strained way. Kelanim scanned his face, certain she could see regret there. His people had died, after all. When he held out his hand to her, she took it without hesitation.

"Are you well, my lord?" Her voice was small but steady, she thought.

He cocked his head, an oddly bird-like gesture that seemed to convey momentary confusion. "I am . . . I have had my fill," he replied in a flat, expressionless tone.

The horror always took a toll on him that no one else seemed to see. However, to Kelanim the Caisah was still the most beautiful man, and if he made mistakes, then that only proved he was human.

With the Rutilians close about them, they left the arena as quickly as possible.

He was silent all the way back to the Citadel, watching out the window of their carriage as people rushed away from the stadium. It was a scene of carnage as burned and terrified people streamed into the streets in an effort to get home. The Rutilian Guard kept them from slowing down their leader, pushing people out of the way of the carriage.

Kelanim ventured only one comment the whole ride: "Perhaps we should distribute some alms to the houses of healing?"

The response she got told her that the Caisah was deeply hurt by what had happened. "Traitors, every one of them," he said with a snarl, and that was the end of that.

When they reached the safety of the Citadel he said nothing, but strode away, leaving her to make her way to the harem as best she could.

Every return to the shady confines of the ladies' quarters was in itself a defeat—one that never went unobserved. Nanthrian, the statuesque ebony beauty, was leaning against the cooling stonewall and making no effort to disguise her smile of victory.

She was younger than Kelanim, and her maneuverings within the harem of mistresses were getting more blatant. Unfortunately, the Caisah had called for her twice the previous week alone.

Tonight, though, the elder mistress knew he would not be pleasant company. It could, in reality, be deadly to be around him. Deadly. That was a thought. Kelanim stopped next to Nanthrian and glanced up, as she let her fan droop to her side.

The younger woman's deep brown cleavage was pushed up high by a deep scarlet robe, and this was not the type of robe the mistresses customarily wore in their chambers. Nanthrian must be ready to stage her feminine coup, willing to take a chance to lure the Caisah's eye. Kelanim was not unaware of that sort of tactic—she had used it herself in the early days when she'd first come to Perilous.

"You are looking particularly prepared tonight," she said.

The younger woman's brown eyes flicked over the other's disheveled hair and torn dress. "And you, madam, are looking less than you should. The Caisah should always be surrounded by beauty . . . not soot." Her sneer was not her most becoming feature.

Kelanim straightened and took a step forward. "I shall be ready for my lord quickly, for he will call."

Nanthrian laughed, stretching her long elegant neck and tracing the curve of her own bosom with one finger. "Not as quickly enough, old woman."

Before Kelanim could open her mouth, the raven beauty had gathered up her skirts and strode off toward the door to the Caisah's chamber.

As soon as that scarlet clad back was turned, her elder smiled to herself behind her fan. Let the young fool rush to him. The only thing he would want this night would be flesh to punish and a throat to hear screams come through. He might even kill the hapless girl, who was so very sure of the power of her beauty. If not, Nanthrian would be bruised and unattractive for a while. Kelanim could do with respite from the competition.

After her maids had loosened her robes, she dismissed them and finished undressing alone. Splashing rose water on her face, she loosened her auburn hair and flung off her corset. It was only then that she noticed the slip of paper tucked under the copper bowl.

Years in the oppressive atmosphere of the hall of mistresses had taught her the folly of opening such a flagrant note—the chance of deception and falling into one plot or another was too great. However, there was something about this particular note that made it different. Like the one she had received after the ball, this one was sealed by a single silver letter of Vaerli script.

Kelanim knew what they looked like, she had studied all she could find on the subject, even though she had never learned what each of them meant. The swooping sigil was the same, and sigils were often used to lock items.

When she laid her finger on it, it opened underneath her touch. Her maids were certainly not responsible for this.

Inside, it was not written in Vaerli. She could read the one word clearly: *Stables.*

It appeared this day was not yet done with surprises.

Talyn let Syris have his head. She did not guide him in any particular direction and had no desire to. It felt good to let the chaos have its way with her for a time. She had not the Phage's way of using the White Void, and she was glad of that.

The nykur carried her faster and faster until the world blurred into that halfway place where the landscape dropped away. Beyond the pull of reality, they could run as far and as quickly as they cared to.

The razor wire of Syris' hair swirled around her face, cutting her cheeks and forehead. The pain was tiny—but better than the confusion that boiled inside her head. Finally, when it all had reached a level she could no longer endure, she called out to Syris until her voice was raw.

The nykur's powerful legs ceased pounding the earth with such terrible vengeance, and instead slowed enough for him to take instruction from Talyn's heels. Regretfully, she turned him deeper into the Chaoslands were primeval powers ruled and her new allies awaited.

The Phage were strangely solitary creatures. While they claimed to be the purest of the Vaerli, they were at odds with what Talyn remembered of her people before the Harrowing: they had been the most sociable of creatures. Her childhood memories, which she had picked out to be cherished and retained, were all raucous gatherings and laughter. Perhaps that was what niggled away at her—the worry that she had not chosen well in that mad moment after losing the Caisah. An even darker thought had begun to grow in the time since then: perhaps she had been manipulated in that darkness by the Phage themselves.

Luckily, before she was totally overrun by her thoughts, they reached water. Three days before, the lake had been much bigger, but this was the Chaoslands and nothing remained still or certain for long. The land, even as

Talyn rode, was shifting upwards, thrusting into a mountain, and the lake draining away into a river. Soon there would be another environment. The Phage seemed to flourish in such wild places.

Talyn pulled the nykur to a halt. He stamped and clashed his long fangs together in protest, but obeyed. When she slid down from Syris he danced an angry circle around her. It would have been death for any other, but for her it was mere display. He finally came to a halt before her, not even breathing heavily after such exertion. "You won't leave, will you, old friend?" Talyn asked, wrapping her hands around his muzzle and kissing the tip of the nykur's nose. It was the only gentle part on his body—as soft and velvety as a horse's.

The beast settled and hung his head, for all the world appearing resigned to remaining, and let out a long, very equine sigh. Everything around Talyn was wrong but this.

"I see you have found your beast." The Phage emerged from the water as silent as a Kindred. The water had enveloped her, but she was not wet—another in a long line of curious things about her. Talyn wondered if it was because everything natural was repelled by them. Certainly, her own skin prickled and her stomach rolled when they were near.

Yet, she had not come alone as she had last time. At her side, with her small hand in the adult's, was a child. Talyn was a poor judge of such things, but she thought that the girl looked to be about ten years old—if she had been mortal. Knowing the Phage even as little as she did, Talyn suspected she was not. The child had a heart-shaped face, soulless black eyes, and most horrifying of all, a tiny row of shifting, shadowy nubs sprouting from her collarbone. Talyn counted four trapped Kindred already in service to the girl. But that was not what caused her hands to clench into fists.

Dark lines ran down the girl's shoulder, from underneath her eerily wet shift dress. The *pae atuae* were written on the skin of the seers of her people, to help them see the path for the Vaerli. The Phage were a breakaway group of Talyn's people, but they had never had seers of their own. Things had changed, apparently.

She averted her eyes for a moment, steeling herself to look at both of them. Behind her, she saw Syris recoil, stamping his cloven feet and shaking his head. She was pleased that he stood his ground. She did not want to be alone with her new master and the frightening child who had her gaze locked unflinchingly on Talyn.

Finally, the once-Hunter gathered enough resolve to meet those eyes. The Phage waited at the water's edge, with her hand now on the child's shoulder, rubbing back and forward in a dire parody of maternal pride. While the child displayed the nubs of her forming Kindred, the older Phage was keeping her prisoners hidden. Talyn was thankful for that small mercy. For the moment the only hint of their presence was a slightly raised scar running around her neck just above her collarbone. The first time that Talyn had seen the snarling, snapping many-headed creature, her blood had almost frozen in her veins. Now she knew that only when using magic did the Phage need that nightmarish circle. Such knowledge gave her little comfort.

This Phage was the one she interacted with most often—though she had seen others. It had taken the longest time for this one to even deign to give Talyn her name. Naturally it was not her true name, but at least it gave the Vaerli something to use when addressing her. She did not introduce the child at her side, but her smile was parental enough to induce plenty of chills.

The Phage inspired fear in all who saw them—even without the circle of trapped heads—but there was one thing that kept Talyn from fleeing them: the sensation of connectedness.

As always the sensation of empathy fluttered on the edge of her senses— like a timid bird hovering near food. It was certainly not how she remembered it being before the Harrowing, but it helped her believe there was hope to be found in their presence.

Still she remained cautious—much as Syris was. The Phage might have offered her power, but they had yet to deliver on their promises. The tasks she'd been set might well be testing her capabilities and her integrity—or they could be a way to get her to dance to their tune without explanation.

Sliding the scroll tube out from under her belt, Talyn it held it out as casually as possible toward the adult Phage. "I have got you what you sent me for, Circe."

The child, standing in the water, smiled at Talyn, and suddenly that dangling hope of connection did not matter one little bit. The once-Hunter wanted to turn about, throw herself on Syris, and ride until she passed out. She could not help but let her eyes linger on the dark lines peeking out from under the girls dress. Though she feared what the words might be, Talyn still wished she could get a better glimpse of the dark parody of Vaerli power.

Only the seers ever wore the *pae atuae*. It was a way to connect with the true power of this land, the Vaerli. Her mind whirled with exactly what that could mean, and she feared very much that it meant the Phage were trying to make their own seer. That thought alone was enough to fill her veins with ice and make Talyn wonder, even more strongly than before, what she had done allying herself to the Phage at all.

She had been hollowed out by the Caisah's epic deception, the one in which he had sent her hunting and killing all over Conhaero for decades, for nothing. Her broken kin had known exactly the moment to strike.

As she looked down at the scroll she held out to Circe, she also began to mull over what was in the scroll.

The other woman's eyes narrowed and she flinched away, not a great deal but enough for Talyn to take note of it. "You must keep hold of it, because your next task is to destroy it."

That comment made her spine tingle. The empathic link was indeed weak but she could sense Circe was masking whatever her true feelings were. That also was something no Vaerli would have even attempted. The joy of the link was the sheer honesty of it. The coil of unease unraveled even further in the pit of Talyn's stomach. At her back she heard Syris stamp his hoof in an echo of that distress.

Feeling her anger and consequently her frustration grow she tossed the scroll of parchment down at the edge of the water. "Do it yourself. Find yourself a fire and be done with it."

Only now the child reacted, when she pulled back her teeth and hissed at Talyn like a feral cat. Circe slid her arm around the girl and pulled her behind her.

"You should have that taken care of," Talyn said, managing to keep her voice flat and calm, even though her skin was almost ready to crawl right off her.

Circe let out a little laugh. "Little Veleda is just feeling a little fragile, not quite ready for the world." Talyn could have sworn she felt more words hovering just on the tip of Circe's tongue: *But soon. Very soon . . .*

As Circe patted the girl's slick hair, she crooned something to her that Talyn could not understand. It did not sound pleasant or soothing to her ears, though. When she was done, she turned back to Talyn. "What you should be concerning yourself with," she said with an eerie tilt of her head, "is that scroll and its destruction."

Talyn's hands curled into fists at her side. She had heard that tone of voice many times, standing before the Caisah. It meant she had much experience keeping quiet in the face of it.

Circe patted Veleda on the head as she went on. "It will not be easy. What is made with power cannot merely be burned or shredded." She smiled slyly. "Surely you have not forgotten the ways of the *pae atuae* so quickly?"

Word magic was the most ancient of Vaerli magics. Its use stretched back beyond the time that her people had been summoned to Conhaero. The myths had it that *pae atuae* had been one of the ways they had survived the great white of the Void.

"It was never going to be my magic." She found herself skirting the issue, even as she watched with some trepidation, the little girl emerge from behind her elder. Veleda had such a look of adult cunning on her face that Talyn feared what the *pae atuae* carved on her body, but hidden by her dress, might actually say. She would bet that they were twisted versions of what the real seers should have worn.

"Even so," Circe snapped as shadows began to twist like smoke around her shoulders, "you must know that the great words once set down are not easy to destroy. It must be in a certain time and place and by the right person. You— as a descendant of Ellyria—are the right person."

"And the place and time?" Talyn asked, certain she would not like the answer.

The bunching of shapes at the Phage's shoulder was resolving itself into the shapes of the Kindred, and the nubs around Veleda began to rise and sink like terrifying pustules. Syris was suddenly at Talyn's back, pressing his tall shape against her and filling her nose with the scent of greenery, like fresh seaweed. The beast had no words, but he was well able to make her feel a little better knowing he was there.

Which was a fine thing, since now the tormented heads of the Kindred were breaking free of Circe's flesh as well and beginning their odd, horrific and yet mesmerizing dance.

"The time and place will be of your choosing," the Phage said finally, "because only dragon fire can destroy what Ellyria Dragonsoul made."

A dragon, and there was only one of those that Talyn knew. It was not the dragon that worried her, as much as it was the one who had Named him.

Finnbarr the Fox, who was so much more than a simple talespinner. Talyn swallowed and looked away.

"Wahirangi CloudLord will not do as I ask," she whispered. "He was not Named by me, and dragons are not something I know how to deal with . . ."

"But you know how to deal with the one that Named him." The Phage's pale face looked even worse when it was plastered with a smile.

Veleda made Talyn start when she spoke. Her voice was high and clear, and made every hair stand up on the once-Hunter's skin. "The Fox is hunting for his brother, and we happen to know where he is going. She who told him is weakened greatly. The dragon and the means of the scroll's destruction will come to you."

Talyn met her new master's eyes and felt bile rise in the back of her throat. She opened her mouth and tried to find words. She wanted to rage—and not just at the Phage. She'd traded the mercurial Caisah in for the chill determination of these twisted versions of her own people. Now they would force her into contact with the one man she feared to see again.

For an instant she considered pulling out the pistol the Caisah had given her and shooting them both then and there. However, she had seen things in the months since her change of masters that made her realize that would be pointless. Much like the tyrant, the Phage were harder to kill than that.

It would be better to play along and see where all this was going.

Finally, she croaked out the words she did not want to let out. "Where shall I go?"

The blank eyes locked with hers, while the heads of the imprisoned Kindred moaned in eerie accompaniment. "You shall go to the sea. Where he was most happy."

The words ran her through as sharply as any sword would have. "No," she whispered, shaking her head and backing up a step. "Not back to the sea." It was where she'd met Finn, fallen in love with him, and lost herself. Thanks to his breaking of her control, she remembered each of those precious dangerous moments as if they had happened yesterday.

The snarling, snapping circle of Kindred heads were suddenly silent, all watching her. It was so eerie that she suddenly wished for them to go back to their pain. The Phage watched her from cool, dark eyes. "Is the Hunter so very afraid of one little fox?"

"I am the Hunter no longer," she replied, half-shouting so that she showed none of her vulnerabilities, "and Finn means nothing to me."

At her back, Syris pawed the ground, snorting through his nose and showing how little he cared for Circe and her small minion.

Yet it was Veleda who spoke again. "Then ride your beast to the sea, and manipulate the talespinner into destroying the scroll. He has a weakness for you that will prove useful."

Then, as if dismissing her, the pair of Phage turned about to slide back into the water. Talyn spoke. She was curious, after all, and had no one else to ask: "I saw something in the sky just after I retrieved the scroll . . ."

The twin rings of Kindred flicked back, their tormented eyes burning into hers, while Circe and Veleda did not. It was an eerie effect that set Talyn's teeth on edge. "The sky?" the child whispered under her breath.

The former Hunter watched with trepidation as the mass of heads stilled. She was used to them twisting and turning as if they were burning. This was different; they barely moved while their eyes scanned her face. Their regard was a hefty weight to bear.

"Yes," she said, her heart suddenly beating hard in her chest. "A strange cloud moving with brightness, that looked like lightning, but there was no thunder and no bolt to the ground. Syris acted very strangely."

"There are many strange things in Conhaero," came the reply, hissing from the mouth of the younger-seeming Phage, though she did not turn. "Even the mighty Vaerli have not seen all of them."

Then, dismissing Talyn as if she were a frightened child, both of them strode back into the water, sliding under it and disappearing with not even a ripple. Even the Caisah had not dismissed Talyn that casually.

The Vaerli was not so much of a fool; she understood that the Phage was keeping something from her. When she had tied her fate to theirs, Talyn had thought she was going to learn some of the secrets she had missed out on due to the Harrowing. Instead, she was only now beginning to comprehend the true depth of her mistake—but what other paths were open to her? It was this or seek out a fellow Vaerli who wanted to end in flames. She was not yet at that point, so Talyn turned to Syris. "To the sea, then. We will await Finn and his dragon there."

When she climbed onto the back of the beast, and his razor sharp hair cut her hands, she barely felt it. Already her mind was on the shore, wandering, wondering where she had gone wrong, and if there could possibly be a path back for her.

CHAPTER FOUR

CALL OF KIN

"**W**e must be careful how we proceed." The fact that a dragon was saying this made Finn more than a little nervous.

He settled back in his place on Wahirangi's shoulders, readjusted the straps of his saddle, and tried to think of what his companion meant by that. What could cause a dragon to be so concerned? Certainly nothing that flew in the sky could bother such as he was.

"Is there something you are not telling me?" he asked finally, though asking such a thing of a dragon felt a little dangerous too. He knew all sorts of stories about the secrets a dragon might be prone to hold onto.

Wahirangi swiveled his golden head about and regarded his passenger with those probing opal eyes. Finally, he dipped his head and admitted, "While you were inside I searched the grounds. The smell of the Named is all over this place."

Finn took a deep breath as his insides clenched. Wahirangi was one of the Named, but the other Kindred who had also received names were an unknown quantity. Ysel was in great danger if they were involved. All this time he had been communicating with his brother, and never known he was kin or that he was in such danger. "What can that mean?"

"You and your brother are the sons of the last Seer of the Vaerli," Wahirangi said, his voice full of sadness. "You are both something that should not exist. The Named could find a use for such a thing." A flicker of blue fire danced around the dragon's jaws. "You have seen them before, when they attacked us in the desert?"

Finn swallowed hard, remembering the panic in the gathering, and what the creatures had done to mere mortals. "Yes," he ventured, "but I didn't get a close look. There was smoke, and it was night so I . . ."

"You saw what they can do, though," Wahirangi pressed, while a long sigh rippled through his body.

"But aren't you one of the Named now?" Finn asked, leaning forward in his saddle. "Doesn't that mean you can communicate with them? Tell them what to do?"

The dragon flexed his wings, though he did not lift off from the ground. Finn had not known Wahirangi for long—and indeed the dragon had not known himself for long in this form either—but silence so heavy seemed something alien to his great presence.

"Yes," he finally replied, "you Named me, and it was wonderful thing to be given a name, but for some Kindred the process is not nearly as wonderful. You see, the Named receive many things from their maker, including portions of their personality and . . ." the creature paused, raising his head to look up at the swirling stars, ". . . well you might call it their soul."

He shook himself suddenly and so hard that Finn was glad he had his legs locked in the saddle and his hands wrapped around the pommel. Wahirangi's tail lashed back and forward, and flickers of blue flame ran along his jaw. All signs, Finn had learned, of the dragon's inner turmoil.

A low rumble formed in his chest. "The Named you met, Finnbarr the Fox, were not whole creatures. They were released from their prison after many cycles, and their original Namers are lost to them. Then there are the new Named that are being created . . ."

"New?" Finn whispered, his hands clenching white around the saddle horn. "Who is making new Named?" Even as the question popped out of his mouth he thought of the vision he'd shared with Talyn; the terrifying woman out on the Salt, the one with the Kindred trapped in the fabric of her body. The writhing shapes of the Kindred attached around her shoulders had haunted his nightmares.

As if he could feel what Finn was recalling and could not bear it, Wahirangi let out a trumpeting cry and thrust himself up into the air. For a long few moments the rush of the wind about him, and the feeling of his stomach dropping away from him was all Finn could concentrate on.

When they reached the level of the clouds, and his face was damp and cool, he found his mind could work again.

"Where are we going?" he shouted over the rush of air and the relentless thrum of the dragon wings on each side of him. He had not told the dragon where he had been the happiest, so this seemed like a mad venture.

Wahirangi made no reply, merely extended his neck out straight before him.

The dragon had his head arrowed toward something—that much was clear—so Finn was forced to sit back in the saddle and be a mere passenger. He trusted the dragon as he had trusted the Kindred it had once been. That Kindred that had saved him and his friends in Perilous, it was also the one that had protected him in the Chaos wastes, and most definitely been the one he had finally given a Name to.

In fact, he trusted the dragon more than he did himself. After all, all the years of his traveling had really been about one thing. Now, given some distance from it, he was able to acknowledge that. He had been pursuing Talyn, hoping above all hope that he could make her remember their love. Wahirangi and the ghost of his long dead mother had helped him understand that his dreams were in vain. The Hunter had chosen to forget their moments together—a conscious decision that he could not pretend had not happened.

Now he had to find his brother and understand their strange connection. That did not mean he didn't think about Talyn in idle moments such as these. As he peered down on the land laid out like a dark map before him, he wondered where she was and what she had done since their parting. Had she returned to her ways as the Hunter, or perhaps found a new path? Unlike his days as a wandering talespinner, he had not spent much time of late in public houses or on the road. His usual method of gathering information was rendered impossible when in the company of a dragon. It was hard to get reliable information out of slack-jawed or terrified people.

"Do you see them?" Wahirangi's bellow jerked him out of his reverie, and he sat up in the saddle with a jerk.

With the light of the moons glimmering on the tops of clouds, there was plenty of light to observe their surroundings. They were beautiful, magical, and they were sharing them with two distant figures. Two figures that appeared not to want to get too close. With a dragon beneath him, Finn could appreciate why exactly that was.

He narrowed his gaze. Finn did not have much experience judging distance or size in the air—it was difficult without any landmarks to compare things to. The shapes were flying parallel to them, skirting the edges of clouds to their right and to their left. They did not come closer, but Wahirangi's eyes were much sharper than Finn's mere human ones could ever hope to be.

"Griffins," the dragon said, his head turning from side to side, while he glided on. "Some of Ellyria's old flock perhaps."

The mention of that name made Finn's already dry throat tighten even more. Ellyria Dragonsoul was the most famous of the Vaerli. "I thought she only Named a dragon . . ." he croaked out.

"You apparently did not hear all the tales of the Vaerli." It was impressive that Wahirangi could discern his words over the sound of the air rushing past them.

"Why are they following us?" Finn asked, pressing himself harder against the saddle, just in case they were forced to make any sudden moves.

"A dragon has not been Named for nearly a thousand years—that tends to draw attention." Finn could not be mistaken, there was heat now rising off Wahirangi, as if something deep within him had been kindled. They had not had many reasons to fight, but flickers of flame had threatened now and then. It felt now as though Wahirangi was brewing something.

The dragon gave Finn no warning. He suddenly twisted his wings, and banked right in a split second. Finn managed not to cry out in surprise, but he was very glad that he was already locked in place on the dragon's back.

Streams of blue-white fire were running from Wahirangi's jaws, but his bellow was even more terrifying. The giant chest expanded beneath Finn's thighs, while the wedge-shaped terrifying head opened wide, and the cry the dragon let out could have knocked down a platoon of Rutilian guards—and most definitely would have sent them scurrying for cover.

If it were directed at him, Finn was certain he would have turned tail and run for it. He made a mental note that it was now confirmed; dragons did not like to be challenged in the sky. Another thing was also made obvious; griffins did not want to tangle with dragons. Moonlight reflected off Wahirangi's golden scales as he turned in pursuit of the impostors. His muscles bunched and flexed beneath Finn, powering his broad wings.

It was a strange sensation for Finn to experience; trapped between the ice-cold air and the building heat of the dragon. He didn't even try to restrain the dragon with words—that would have been fruitless and possibly painful. He simply held on as the dragon turned this way and that in his chase. It reminded his rider of a falcon with his eyes locked on his prey, all focus and determination. The talespinner realized he would have as much chance of stopping the falcon as the dragon.

The turns became sharper and more stomach churning as Wahirangi closed in. That was when the griffin began a series of steep dives and climbs in an effort to shake him off. However, Wahirangi was relentless, and seemed not to tire.

His powerful wings snapped hard and fast in the climbs, and when they plummeted into the breath-stealing dives his streamlined form resembled a shot arrow. Finn could not be sure that he wasn't screaming.

He was no rider. He was a passenger on the world's most insane ride. Even Talyn's nykur could not have offered more dangerous travel than this. Several times mountains loomed on each side of them, and he was sure they were going to smash into them. His mind conjured up images of himself being crushed like a bug while the dragon continued his heedless pursuit. Would Wahirangi even notice the destruction of the human until the end of it?

The griffin was closer now, its white-tipped wings standing out brightly in the moonlight.

Finn might have no experience in flying combat, but he was sure he could make out the signs of fatigue in the beast. The dragon could not make tight turns like the griffin, but as long as he stayed close, Wahirangi would wear him down. Nothing about the dragon showed the least sign of exertion. Every muscle that played beneath Finn was working as hard and as flawlessly as it had when he began.

Finally, the griffin must have realized this as well. They were reaching a mountain pass, and the griffin dropped desperately toward the narrow ravine and dark trees, seeking a chance at sanctuary there.

Wahirangi was not deterred. His neck snapped back, his jaw opened, and the blue-white flame erupted from his mouth. He sprayed the air and nearest trees with an explosion of light and heat that made Finn fear for his skin. The griffin let out a squawk like a terrified pigeon. Its tail feathers had nearly been caught in the flame, and it tacked right and left to keep out of the direct line.

It was strange how the dragon had missed his target, but Finn was not about to question it. Wahirangi roared again, and his wings beat harder. The dragon must have been able to sense victory—even Finn could see it approaching. He was imagining that the beast would let forth a stream of fire to engulf the creature that had enraged him so. Strangely, that was not what he did.

Instead, when Wahirangi's flame came, it tore the night apart to the right of the griffin. Finn bent low over the dragon's neck and couldn't help but let a grin grow on his lips. It felt good to be the hunter rather than the prey for a change. Again, Wahirangi let off another burst of blue flame, this time to the left, and the griffin tacked away.

Now Finn understood; the dragon was driving the smaller creature before them, but for some reason he didn't want to incinerate the creature.

Finn opened his mouth, and tried to yell above the screaming wind, "What are you doing?" Apparently, their connection did not make the dragon compliant to all of the talespinner's wishes, because Wahirangi's head flattened out straighter before him, and he flew on even faster.

Finn had no recourse but to clench his increasingly cold hands on the saddle and wonder if he was going to end up a mere splatter on the ground below. Riding a dragon had sounded like a great deal of fun, but it was not without its perils.

Finally, they had the griffin cornered in a narrow valley. Now its advantage of tighter turns meant little. Wahirangi was able to use his own greater speed to loom over the smaller beast. His long legs flashed out, and the only way the griffin managed to avoid being caught in them was to plunge down.

With a sharp cry, the dragon followed, driving the griffin to the ground. Still he did not use his fire. When they landed only twenty feet from the griffin, Finn saw at once that the creature was terrified.

It took him a moment to remember what it had been like to see Wahirangi for the first time. Dragon fear was no magic—it was a genuine terror to be confronted by a creature such as he was. He could only imagine how that would be magnified if the beast had been chasing you through the sky.

The griffin itself was a wonder. Long blue-black feathers that gleamed in the moonlight, a long curved golden beak, and eyes that flashed with fire. It half opened its wings, but there was the suggestion of a tremble in its manner.

"Wahirangi CloudLord." Its voice was deep like a bell, but not nearly as impressive as the dragon's. "In the name of kinship that exists between all Named, let me pass." It did not exactly cower, but the effects of the nearness of the dragon were wearing on it. It did not seem as though it even noticed the human perched behind the shoulder blades of the dragon that blocked the way.

The dragon made a sound like steam being ejected from an angry machine. "You were following me, bird, and no kinship exists between us. Nothing can, while you call poison master."

Finn's mind darted back to the creature he had seen on the Salt, the one his mother saved him from. Everything about him had recoiled from that warped and twisted being which had trapped so many Kindred to do its bidding. Was this what the dragon meant?

The griffin tipped its head, suddenly looking cunning. "When the Vaerli were scourged, we Named were locked away. As Kindred, time means nothing, but given form and shape we felt its weight." Its avian eye fixed on the dragon. "That was when they came to us, found us, and freed us. You cannot judge, you never felt."

Wahirangi spread his wings, the moonlight gleamed off every golden scale, illuminating the ravine. "You gave in to them. You, Drynis Alorn, and all the rest. They who would bring this world down around us. And now you would steal her child. This I cannot allow."

The griffin stepped around in a little tight circle, placing its feet carefully. "You are dragon, but we are many, and the Vaerli have no strength to lend you."

This standoff was more powerful than any story Finn could have told, but his skin ran cold with the knowledge that they were talking of his brother, and this was important. He was so concentrated on the tension between the dragon and the downed griffin that nothing else seemed important.

It was lucky that a dragon always has sharper senses than a mere human. Finn was nearly shaken from the saddle as Wahirangi leapt into the sky. His head jerked back and all the breath was stolen from his body. He was lucky that he didn't bite off his own tongue. For a few moments, he struggled to understand what was happening.

Then he heard the screams. The griffin was not alone; he was part of a flight. As Finn turned and looked around him, it felt as though the sky was full of wings. Suddenly a lone dragon did not seem as great a thing.

Equo, Varlesh, and Si. It had always been the three of them . . . well, as far as their separate memories would go.

They walked away from the encampment together, and when Nyree asked to come with them, Equo quietly but firmly told her no. Beyond the encampment, the Chaoslands had them, so there was a little peace. Unlike the Vaerli—at least as they had been—they could not feel the Kindred or the land, but they did not pass over it unnoticed.

Si's eyes flickered over the trees, and his whisper was not of the comforting kind. "We are being watched."

"We were once their friends," Varlesh said, his voice going into a growl. "The Ahouri, the Form Bards, it didn't matter what we were called, we always aided them. Now what are they doing?"

The scion of the Ahouri, Woman of Faces, had been the first to reach Conhaero, drawn through the White Void to the call of the Vaerli. When she had led them down onto the Steps of Sacrifice and into the world, it had been a marvelous thing. Later, when the Caisah had destroyed the Vaerli, the Ahouri, as their greatest allies had been his next target. His magic had been attuned to find them when they sang, and the Ahouri had never been able to go long without singing—at least in those original forms.

"Do you remember the last song?" Equo asked of his brothers.

They turned their eyes away from him, but it was Varlesh that spoke out loud their shared anguish. "How could anyone forget it? It was . . . painful and beautiful."

Equo could recall the agony as it had passed through their bones, the magic tearing them down to nothing. Only the Song had saved them. Unconsciously he rubbed his arms, feeling again the moment when they turned their song on themselves, tearing themselves apart before the Caisah's power could destroy them completely.

"The weakness of his magic was its specifics," he murmured. The Ahouri, by breaking themselves apart, had given the magic no focused target, and it had dissipated. It was only later that the three of them, now brothers instead of one being, discovered that they had not been the only Ahouri to think of the solution. Their numbers had been decimated, but some had survived with the Caisah none the wiser.

How they would respond to a call to arms was another matter altogether. It had been nearly a thousand years since they had walked as one rather than as trios.

"This is a good enough spot," Varlesh said, turning about and facing his brother. "Nice and quiet, distant . . ."

"Yes," Si confirmed, running his eye over the well-vegetated hollow. "It is already a natural bowl. It will suit our purposes."

The three of them formed a rough circle, linking hands, closing their eyes. As always the sound was created by Varlesh, passed to Equo who formed it into words, and then it went on to Si who let it loose in the world. It was the music of this world, the place that the Ahouri had found after so long searching. Pilgrims from another world where they were persecuted and feared, they had found this world of chaos. It was in its essence a song of great love.

The song told of their joy of finding Conhaero, and the thanks they had for the Vaerli for leading them to it. Then the song of rejoicing became a song of something else. A plea. A reminder of that special closeness Vaerli and Ahouri shared. How they had stood together, and paid the price for it under the Caisah's cruelty.

The song was not directed to the Vaerli, who no longer had the ability to hear it. Si, Varlesh, and Equo were singing to quite another audience altogether, one that they knew very well was listening out in the damp forest. The Kindred.

These creatures of chaos, the first creatures, had remained untouched by the Caisah. They endured when all else was so altered. Varlesh's notes grew deeper, the words Equo formed more melancholy, and the song that exploded from Si's lips now resonated through the rock to the Kindred directly.

Always Watching. Always present. Give to us what we need.
Bring back what was lost, form again to battle at your side.

The Ahouri sang on even when it appeared no one was listening, and the air began to grow warm around them. A circle of flame sprang up outside the tiny circle formed by the three of them. It was close enough that Equo felt as though they might be engulfed by it, and for a moment it appeared that was what the Kindred meant to do. However, the Form Bards went on without slowing or giving up. Their plea rolled on, even though the flame licked perilously close to their toes. They knew enough about flesh, not to care about it.

Then the flame that flickered so close began to move out and away from them—but at no normal rate. It went faster and faster, out in an ever increasing circle of red heat. It consumed the trees near them, burning them to a cinder.

It was no regular fire, lit by a mortal hand. This was the fire that burned deep within Conhaero, the flames of the Kindred. The fires of chaos. Within only a few moments the three of them remained, still singing, in a cleared circle of burnt earth with the taste of charcoal in their mouths. Nothing stood within eyesight but blackened rock and cinder.

The Ahouri sang on; eyes half-shut, the music consuming them.

The time has come. The Ahouri will arise to stand beside you again.

Bring us close, land of sanctuary, help us become what was.

Dark shadows flickered at the edge of Equo's vision now. He strained his eyes to each side, but all he could discern were shifting patterns of smoke and ash. He was not sure he wanted to see the Kindred—not all of them. He could feel their presence and that was enough.

Beneath his feet, he heard the land shift. Conhaero was always shifting . . . but not at this accelerated rate.

All three of them kept singing—they dared not stop now. It was all they had. A tremor ran through the portion of ground they described with their circle. A fissure snapped and cracked around that circle. The sound of it was disconcerting, but Equo felt his brothers' hands reach out, one on each side, and grip onto his. They kept singing.

The rock circle that remained firm under their feet, began to descend. As they looked up, mouths still full of song, they saw that they were dropping away into the earth. The precarious rock beneath their feet was rapidly becoming part of a bowl in the earth, perhaps more like the pit of a volcano. It was a terrifying thought, but the brothers did not miss a beat in their song.

Equo closed his eyes for a moment, as their rapid descent caused his stomach to lurch painfully, and his ears popped. It was hard to sing under such circumstances, but the song had always described the Ahouri. It would not fail them now.

After a terrifying few moments, their descent slowed and then, thankfully, stopped. The earth around them shifted, even as their song died away on Si's lips. The dark shadows moving through the earth never formed into recognizable shapes, but they had eyes that alternately glittered like stones or burned with fire.

Ahouri, you call us. One loomed closer, forming a body out of the nearby rock, so it might glare at them with flaming eyes.

You summon us with reminders of ancient, long lost debts. A second emerged from the soil below.

"But you came," Varlesh growled. "For you those debts are like yesterday, as they are for us. Time is nothing to the Kindred or the Ahouri. We all remember."

"We need your help," Equo went on, feeling the heat in the depression grow stronger, as sweat beaded and ran down the back of his neck. "We need you to help us gather the rest of our kind."

The shadows slowed their circulation, and now the earth seemed alive with eyes; none of them looked happy or welcoming.

The chaos is stirring, Ahouri. Rising up. Conhaero serves a great purpose and that purpose has been denied for too long. We have much to do.

"As do we," Si said. His voice, so rarely heard, echoed around the earth bowl. "All the races have their part to play in the future. The Ahouri most of all."

To speak to one of the Kindred—especially in that way—was a dangerous thing to do, but Equo liked that their third was speaking at all. It did flash through his mind that the Kindred could easily collapse the hollow of earth and bury anyone they viewed as an annoyance.

Perhaps you are right. Long have we contemplated the place of the other races in Conhaero's story. Though we did not call them here, regardless they remain.

A shape formed in the rocks above them, a looming shadow that flickered and burned, standing three times as tall as they. Kindred might not be mortal or human, but they still understood the worth of a little drama.

Send word, then. Send the Ahouri your song to see if they will come. Gather at the place we will prepare for you. Then we shall see if the broken can truly mend themselves.

The earth shifted again, but this time it was not beneath the three men. Around them the walls of the formed amphitheatre cracked and groaned as thousands upon thousands of fissures opened. They were vertical, long, and deep.

Equo knew what was happening. He had seen it before. Many times the Vaerli and the Kindred had allowed the Ahouri magic to pass through their domain.

The Conhaero is listening, and now it is your time to sing, Ahouri.

The Kindred seemed ready to act as their audience.

The brothers looked at each other. It had to be the greatest song that they had ever created. It had to bring together the broken parts of the Form Bards and make them listen. It was a daunting task that should have made all of them terrified to even attempt it.

Equo could feel it from his brothers as easily as he could feel it in himself. This was what they were meant to do. All of their trials and tribulations in this world had brought them to this point. This was the reason for this moment, and it was perfect.

Varlesh created the power, the air that brought it forth. Equo formed it in his throat with muscle and flesh made for solely for this purpose. Then it was Si who let it out. His lips and tongue gave it final form, and let it loose into the world.

It was a calling to flesh, magnified by the powers of the earth. It would break the heart of the lost. It would remind them of times past. Equo hoped it would make them weep—and perhaps dream of better days that might lie ahead.

As the Ahouri call went out from the broken men, it would be heard everywhere on Conhaero. Anywhere a Form Bard stood, they would hear it in their bones.

The call went out, and it only remained to be seen how many of them would answer it.

CHAPTER FIVE

THE HEART OF THE DRAGONSOUL

The darkness suddenly gave way to light, and Pelanor and Byre staggered out onto the rough ground like children who had just learned to walk. Like children that had been beaten, that was.

The Vaerli wrapped his hands around his head, for a moment letting his own sensations come back to him as best they could. When he finally felt capable, he lifted his eyes to his companion. The Blood Witch was on her knees with her hands pressed to her face, and long shudders were running through her body as if she were freezing cold. It gave him some measure of satisfaction that the powerful Phaerkorn was worse off than he.

Looking about through his dissipating confusion, Byre at first could not believe what he was seeing. To his left the rocky ground dropped away down to a wide plain, a place he somehow assumed would have been a river. Up to his right was a place he could immediately identify, even though it did not look as he remembered.

Peripherally, he heard Pelanor walk to his side. Her voice was shaky and raw when it finally left her body. "Is that . . . No, I recognize it—that is Perilous and Fair." Her fine face was folded into a deep frown.

"No," Byre whispered, "you are mistaken. It is V'nae Rae." The hill that rose before them was heavily wooded but also heaving with activity. The walls of the city were just as he remembered at the pinnacle of the hill, but further down they were still under construction. The running of the many waterfalls throughout the city made the air full of a kind of delightful music. The Phoenix Gates carved in lapis lazuli were up, but the surrounding walls of white stone were only half done, and their marvelous mosaics not yet in place.

All of this was wonderful and beautiful, but not as shocking as what Byre saw. All over the city, even from this distance, he could see Vaerli; his own people walking, talking and working on building the city as if it were an everyday thing. Laughter mingled with the sound of the waterfalls.

Byre's throat went dry while tears welled in his eyes. He had not seen so many of his own kind since he was a small child. That was not all; he could feel them. In his own time, the empathic feeling had been dulled by the Harrowing, reduced to only a vague awareness. Now Byre was flooded with connections, much as he had been in the Caisah's torture chamber.

He choked and gasped, struggling to hold the feeling of his own self together under so much information. Thousands of emotions, both complex and very basic, flooded him.

Also, the Vaerli were aware of him. Their examination of him, this new thing in their consciousness, felt like thousands of hands on his skin. Up on the hill some of them stopped and turned to look toward the two newcomers. He could feel their eyes on him as if they were handshakes or even joyful slaps on his back. It was overwhelming.

"Byre? Byre!" Pelanor wrapped her small hands around his shoulders and gave him a little hard shake.

Slowly Byre's Vaerli instincts kicked in, the fog cleared and he smiled. He knew his grin made him look drunk.

If this was the test, then it was one he thoroughly approved of. "Come on," he said, grabbing her hand, and tugging her after him. He didn't need to touch any of these Vaerli; he already had a far more intimate meeting with them. However, there was one person he really wanted to see.

He and the Blood Witch walked up the hill, bare of the Caisah's Road. All the way, Byre found that he was only just managing to control himself from breaking into a run. It was a homecoming as he had never imagined having.

Pelanor did not seem quite as enthralled. Her sharp eyes darted over the Vaerli, hard at work. "So we're somehow travelled backwards, and these are really your people. If so, what are they to make of me?"

Byre stopped and with real surprise realized the Blood Witch was nervous. Even though he hadn't known Pelanor for long, and had never been that good at judging people, he understood this was not her normal manner. She was young—something he barely remembered being—and despite her great strength, she was uncertain. This world that the Kindred had flung them into was one in which no Phaerkorn, or any other latecomer, had yet to arrive in.

"You're with me," he murmured and touched her smooth dark cheek. Despite Byre's awareness of his kin around him, it did not get past him how smooth and delicious that skin was. Beneath it, he could feel his own blood pulsing in her. It felt like an age ago that she had drunk from him, and the memory made him start with a little shock. For if he was aware of his own blood coursing in her, then so too would his people be. What would be their reaction to that?

The corner of her mouth twitched. "My protector now . . . is that how it is? How gallant." Yet she did not flick away his touch on her cheek. Instead, she clasped her hand in his, and together they walked hand in hand up the slope to the nearly complete city.

Vaerli were walking down to meet them, and Byre nearly choked on his own emotions.

They were a short race, but in this time, with no one else to compare to, it didn't matter too much. Byre ate up the details of their forms and faces as they came close enough for him to make out. Even while part of him clenched with the vague fear that the burning death of the Harrowing had not been left behind.

The women came forward first, expressions open and curious, pushing back their long dark hair from their faces to regard these new arrivals. Byre swallowed a laugh of delight; there were stars in those great black eyes, and no trace of the deep despair he had always known to reside there. The image of his broken sister yearning for death in his arms was burned into his memory, though that had not occurred here . . . not in this time.

This, then, was the Vaerli as they were meant to be: confident, powerful, and utterly at home in their world. Now he could feel their minds lightly reaching out to his, questioning but not invading.

Pelanor tugged on his arm twice, drawing his attention to the rear. There, standing among the crowd of Vaerli, were five Kindred. They wore bodies of rock and earth rather than the more terrifying fire form, but Byre knew they were no safer. From where they stood it appeared that the Kindred had actually been helping the Vaerli construct this portion of the white stone wall. None of the Kindred made a move toward Byre and Pelanor.

Only the Vaerli did. A bearded man with strands of gray in his long hair greeted them. "Welcome to V'nae Rae, young one." His brow furrowed when his gaze alighted on Pelanor, but he said nothing nor made a move to confront her. "I am Yafet. I sense you have come far to join us."

It was not a question; what need was there for questions when all that Byre was lay open to every Vaerli. He felt almost tongue tied, unable to decide what was an appropriate greeting.

He was saved from embarrassment by a sudden darkness that fell over them all. Everyone looked up, but Pelanor alone was the one that swore. "By the Goddess' Twelfth Mouth!"

The sunlight gleamed off a long silver belly and outspread wings while a carved, intelligent head turned downwards. It was a dragon and Byre knew her name, a name that every Vaerli infant knew: Morleth the First. Stories whispered in the night were not enough to prepare for the sheer grandeur of her. Larger than the complete section of wall and blocking out the sky, she still did not instill fear in him. Instead there was an absurd joy in laying eyes on the dragon.

Barely disturbing the rock, Morleth landed as lightly as a cat, and turned her huge frilled head to examine Byre. "You are damaged, little brother."

Her eyes, bright blue eyes with flecks of gold in them, narrowed, and he felt as though she were looking into his head, though there was no sensation. Folding her wings tightly against her body, Morleth wrapped her tail over her front paws.

"But you are expected." Her voice was sharp like crystal in his ears, but hearing it made tight tears form in the corners of his eyes.

He was hearing and seeing and feeling the legendary dragon. The Kindred's idea of testing had not been this in his imagining, and part of Byre wondered when he was going to be snatched away from it all.

His other problem was that he had absolutely no idea how to address a dragon properly. He paused for a moment, feeling all the eyes of his people on him, and then awkwardly sketched what he hoped was an elegant bow for her. At his side Pelanor followed suit, and he was surprised and pleased. The Phaerkorn were not known to be overly fond of abasing themselves before others. He imagined that dragons made as much of an impression on Blood Witches as they did on all the other races.

The Vaerli around them laughed gently. Morleth's rumble of amusement was strong enough to run up through the earth into their bones. "Little brother, there is no need for ceremony. We are all children of the chaos here. One and the same."

Byre did not understand what that meant, but found he was blushing as if caught in some foolishness by a relative.

"Ellyria is waiting for you," Morleth boomed, extending her gleaming silver arm. "Come fly with me."

"Sacred blood," Pelanor hissed, and actually took a step backwards behind him.

Byre turned on her and grinned mischievously. "You can always fly yourself if you want to, no need for a dragon to take you."

The Witch's gaze flicked between him and the shining dragon as she appeared to consider her options. Then a slow smile spread across her face, wicked and fearless. "A dragon flight is something even a Phaerkorn cannot turn down."

Then, just like that, they were climbing up the silver leg of Morleth the First. When Byre's hand came down on the dragon's skin, it was warm and surprisingly smooth, like polished leather.

In all the stories of Ellyria's dragon, it had never been mentioned how kindly her great curved eyes were. Byre had been raised on tales about how Morleth had been terrible and perilous, yet as he pulled Pelanor, almost giggling, up behind him, he couldn't see the danger in her.

The dragon was magnificent and shining like polished steel. Just looking on her was enough to bring a smile to anyone's face, he thought. Then all rational thought was jerked out of his head as she sprang upwards into the sky.

Byre laughed while Pelanor squeezed him tight, her abrupt gasp of surprise a heavy breath in his ear. Morleth's wings snapped wide, thrusting them through the air higher and higher. A few wide, deep beats of her wings and they were among the clouds—higher than birds. V'nae Rae was spread out below them, like some child's drawing of the city. Byre, despite his slight fear of heights, was mesmerized by what lay before them. Pelanor's hands tightened on his waist, and she pushed her narrow face in against his shoulder.

Such magnificence couldn't last forever. Eventually, they spiraled down, circling the ragged mountains that were even at that moment being smoothed by Vaerli and Kindred so that the city would have a place to remain static.

The citadel was much as Byre remembered—but fresher, whiter and sharper than it had been, or would be with the Caisah in residence. The *pae atuae* would show up best under moonlight, but even under an afternoon sun they glinted from time to time. It lifted his heart to see everything as it had always been meant to be—and not how things had devolved under the tyrant.

He did not want to think of that man or that time—not right now.

"The Waterfall Gates of Iilthor," Byre said turning and pointing to the fluted and carved niche where the two gushing rivers splashed to each side of the silver bound doors. Everything was familiar and somehow so very different.

Morleth trumpeted a laugh, one that they could feel deeply in their flesh and bone. "What a wonderful name! I think we shall call it that. You Vaerli have a real ability to name things—it is so delightful!"

Byre felt a shudder of strangeness run through his spine, as the vagaries of time began to make themselves apparent. The Kindred who lived without the tides of time became stranger and stranger to him.

It was a much-needed reminder that they were alone in this place, and it would have its own dangers and rules that they best discern quickly. Byre kept his mouth closed on the subject of any more names, lest he create too much of a disturbance in time.

Instead, he turned his attention to the place they were moving toward. He observed a sweeping balcony at the highest point of the Citadel that poked out of the red cliffs like a admonishing finger. It looked fragile and filigreed, but incredibly the vast bulk of Morleth landed easily upon it. Not even a creak sounded beneath them.

Byre stroked the dragon's smooth, strong hide, uncertain if he wanted to get down. What would be the chances of him ever being able to get back up again? It was the kind of experience he did not expect to repeat.

The dragon's head swiveled about and she regarded her passengers. "You came a great distance to find my lady, Byreniko-of-the-future, so I think you should talk to her while you may."

His mouth dropped open, ready to ask a thousand questions, but then the flicker in Morleth's eye reminded him: she had once been a Kindred. A Name had not changed everything, necessarily. She was still of this earth and knew more than he ever could.

Taking the hint, Byre slipped down and held out a hand to Pelanor. She looked down at him, head cocked. Her voice, when it came, was almost admonishing. "I am very far from my *gewalt* here, Byre of the Vaerli. I hope you know what you are doing . . ."

He didn't reply, because to reply would have meant having to lie. He did not want to do that to her. Instead, he mutely kept that hand extended to her. Eventually she gave in, took it, and stalked after him as he went inside the Citadel.

It was a beautiful, moving thing, this palace. The walls shifted and danced with mosaics of the Vaerli and the Named. Centaurs capered around the corner of the hallway that opened out onto the terrace, and seemed to dare them to follow as they moved ahead of the newcomers. The tiny stones that made up the decoration flared different colors in an amazingly complex pattern. Byre had no idea how it was done, but suspected it was leading them somewhere.

Pelanor's hand clenched in his. Her eyes widened at the fine silk curtains fluttering in the wind, and the cut crystal above them that lit the way, but with no discernible light source.

Finally, by virtue of following their flat, impossible guide stones, they found her.

It was madness how she was simply there. Ellyria Dragonsoul, the first of the Vaerli, the one who had made the Pact with the Kindred. She was the one individual who had always been upheld as the greatest of their kind, and thus she was an ideal more than a real person, woven in myth and surrounded by holiness. Byre stopped suddenly, as if he'd been struck from above.

Hearing them enter the bare chamber, Ellyria turned to regard them. No aura of anything particular surrounded the woman standing in the white stone chamber. She was not haloed by light, or burning with righteousness, but it was also impossible to pretend she was normal.

She looked young, with a heart-shaped face and sharp cheekbones, but her eyes reflected a great age. Her shiny black hair was folded into a thick plait that lay straight against her spine. Mother of the Vaerli she might be, but Ellyria Dragonsoul was also completely naked. However, it did not shock or titillate. Instead, it seemed the most natural way to find her. Her nudity made the words carved on her body clearly visible, like blue snakes spiraling around her limbs, encircling her breasts and twisting across the flat plane of her belly. It was hard not to follow the curving lettering, to try and discern what it might mean, but Byre managed to pull his eyes away when he realized something: Ellyria was his great-grandmother; kin and blood.

At his side Pelanor was unusually silent, and he wondered how Ellyria looked through the Blood Witch's sharp senses. One thing he could be sure of was: she was somehow catching a whiff of power from the leader of the Vaerli. He was unsure how much the Phaerkorn knew of Vaerli mythos, but she did the right thing: dropped her eyes to avoid staring, and waited hopefully to see what he did.

Byre bent to one knee and inclined his head also to the floor. It was a gesture he had never seen a Vaerli make, but in the face of the mother of his people it was entirely appropriate. He waited, breathing hard, until he saw her bare feet appear in his vision. Then he felt a slight touch on the crown of his head.

"You have made a long journey." Her voice came out strangely hesitant, and softer than he might have imagined. "I see how sad and hurt you are. I am very sorry for it."

Byre glanced up. Her eyes were like the other Vaerli's, full of stars, but there was no focus within them. Getting to his feet, he watched her wander away from them in a dissolute manner. She flicked her gaze over one shoulder and smiled. "Come into the Puzzle Room."

Both Byre and Pelanor jumped when Morleth's crested head appeared at the window Ellyria had just been standing before. The dragon was large enough to twine herself around the Citadel and peer in any window she might fancy.

"She is as you find her." Morleth rested her smooth, gleaming head close to the window and watched the Vaerli disappear deeper into the Citadel with one blue slitted eye. "Her struggle with my Kin did not leave her scarred on the outside, but the inside is another matter. It is difficult to be both born and made seer."

"Both?" Byre stiffened. This was something he had never heard before. "Ellyria is a seer?"

The dragon let out a great sigh, her talons shifting on the white stone. "Such vision is a great burden," was all she would say, before she pulled her head back from the window and disappeared from sight.

"What is this born and made business?" Pelanor asked, tucking her dark hair behind one ear in a sharp gesture. Phaerkorn were haughty folk indeed—even in such strangeness.

"There are always two seers among the Vaerli," Byre replied as evenly as possible, even though he wanted to dash after Ellyria. "One is born into the role and one is made into a seer when she reaches maturity. They work together. The born has the gift of interpretation while the made has only the strength to see. I never knew . . . no one ever told me that Ellyria was both."

"She is expecting you to follow," Morleth said, appearing again, thus proving her hearing was sharp, "but be careful." The dragon tilted her head as she peered in, and Byre was reminded of a child peering into their toy house. The effect was disconcerting.

Byre did not direct Pelanor to follow him, but he could feel that she did. The Vaerli blood in her made her a shadowy echo in his new perception. Trying to ignore her, he concentrated on observing more of the interior of the Citadel. He had never seen the inside in his own time, so could not judge what the Caisah might have done to it. The deeper they went, the fewer mosaics there were. Instead, the *pae atuae* was everywhere. It danced through and over the mosaics that were opposite each window. Light flooded every nook and cranny so that no shadow dared to linger.

Byre would have loved to stop and examine the word magic—for he had never had the chance to learn it—but down the end of the corridor he could sense Ellyria. She was the center and the beginning. If ever he had a chance to find out answers to those questions, it was down there.

He'd heard of the Puzzle Room, the place where his sister had earned pieces of the answer the Caisah dangled before her. The idea that it had been made by his own people was a new one.

Cautiously, aware of Morleth's warning, Byre pushed open the door. Ellyria was standing, hands on hips in the middle of the room that was flooded with a curious golden light. Spread out on the floor was not the Caisah's puzzle, but something infinitely more complex.

Mosaics depicting fire were fanned out on the floor before her. From this center radiated other interconnected pieces. There were several colors that joined together before separating and interconnecting with others. The whole effect was of ribbons wiggling their way out in a bewildering pattern that made Byre's head hurt.

Ellyria Dragonsoul was staring at it though with the kind of fixed attention that reminded him of only one person: his sister, the one the world knew as Talyn. He hesitated to speak and break her concentration.

Pelanor, coming up behind him, was not nearly as diplomatic. "Well, that is quite a mess."

The mother of the Vaerli looked up, her eyes for a second completely alien, but a sharp smile danced across her lips. "Indeed it is. A mess."

Her concentration trailed off as she seemed to suddenly become engrossed with her own arm. The *pae atuae* flexed and swiveled on her skin, an effect that made Byre nervous. His father had been a master of the word magic, and so his son knew the power they could contain. The marks of the made seer were an unknown quantity. Though his mind buzzed with unasked questions, he couldn't find it in himself to query the mother of his nation.

Naturally, Pelanor had none of those qualms. She strolled over to stand within a hairsbreadth of Ellyria's back and looked down at the pattern spread out like an octopus before them on the floor. After a second with her head cocked, she pointed to the dark gray ribbon. "But that is the twelve-mouthed goddess."

Byre, despite his reverence, darted over the pattern to stare down at what she had recognized. The tiny wooden pieces that were locked together in this strand were indeed marked by the symbol of the Phaerkorn's goddess.

"How can that be?" Pelanor asked him in a demanding tone. "My people are not even here yet."

"The buried avatar." Ellyria nodded. "The female energy we require."

Byre turned about slowly, looking with great care at the puzzle of interlocking pieces twining away from them. With careful inspection he was able to make out sigils and signs of the Lady of Wings, the Rutilian Guard—and even the Caisah himself, the spread winged eagle.

"And here you are." Ellyria dropped to her haunches and touched a narrower band of red. The sigil of his name was immediately apparent. "And here is the little Witch." Pelanor's section of the puzzle was also red.

"Mother," Byre whispered, "how can you know so much? This has all yet to happen." He turned around in confusion, suddenly understanding what the puzzle behind him meant. "It has happened."

Ellyria gripped his hand hard. "They gave it to me, all I asked for." Her eyes were frighteningly clear and piercing. "The Pact was made—but there is always a price." She pointed down to the floor. "They broke away and everything was ruined."

The ribbon she pointed to was as wide as that representing the Caisah, but he did not understand the sigil. He pronounced the unfamiliar word. "Phage . . . the Phage?"

"The Pact breakers," Ellyria whispered. "I have not been able to see the way to stop them. I have tried. I've laid the pieces again and again but it just won't fit."

He followed the slithering length of the pieces that were so obviously distressing the Mother of the Vaerli. Up ahead its broad swath cut through the more fragile lines of his and his sister's. "What does that mean? Where do we meet these breakers?"

Whatever clarity she had briefly held onto slipped away like summer mist. Ellyria the Mother, the most revered of the Vaerli, fell into muttering to herself and scrambling on the ground.

Pelanor walked over the puzzle, entranced, then leapt lightly over pieces so as not to disturb them. Byre stayed very still, concerned that if he moved in the slightest he would lose his senses.

Clearing his throat, he tried to refocus and get past the rush of actually being in the presence of Ellyria Dragonsoul.

"Look here!" Pelanor's sharp eyes seemed to making better sense of the puzzle than his. "Is this the Harrowing?"

The conjunction of pieces made this spot appear like a tangle of wool. Some he expected, like the Caisah, but to see the dark skein of the Phage was unusual. He'd been there that day at the Bastion, he recalled none that would have been described as Pact breakers. As much as Byre wanted to ask Ellyria about that, he sensed this could well unbalance her. He had another question, the one that he'd battled to have answered.

"Grandmother," he said softly, "can you end the Harrowing and give back the Gifts to our people?"

Her eyes never left the *pae atuae* on her right forearm as her left index finger traced them. "The Gifts are not lost. The Harrowing is from your time, and it is you who must fix it." The words were not said in a cruel manner, but Byre felt them hit him as if they had been. Ellyria Dragonsoul looked up at him suddenly, examining him as minutely as she had the *pae atuae*. "You were there, you know what happened and how to fix it."

Now, both women were looking at him. A confused smile spread on Byre's mouth. They had to be playing some kind of cruel joke. "I was . . . I was a child when that happened. I was there on the Salt Plain, but I was definitely not in the meeting when the Caisah came and—"

"But you were there." The seer stepped closer to him. This near, it was impossible to ignore her nakedness, and not to let his eyes trace the *pae atuae* over her body. She was a work of art. When she tapped him in the middle of his chest with her index finger, he felt his heart slow, and his eyes grow heavy. He'd been wrong; she was not a work of art, she was more like a drug.

Growing up in the wilds, away from his people, he had not been idle. Peon was the inhaled smoke of choice, and two local farm boys—ones not afraid of the fact he was Vaerli—had introduced him to it. The spectacular but empty visions he had shared with them, he had mostly done for the far more heady taste of acceptance. Ellyria was like that.

When she touched him, colors exploded at the back of his eyes, and nothing seemed to matter except the movement of her lips. Each of the words from her mouth were intensely important.

"You were there," she said in a low tone which he knew was only for him. "The lines of connection and time run from you back to there." The seer pointed behind him, and Byre blinked. It felt as though she had pulled back a curtain for him. The world was so much more than his eyes could possibly tell him. Trailing from his body were threads, such as might be found in a magnificent carpet. They ran from him—from everyone in the room—backwards.

"Do you see?" Ellyria asked, her voice the tone of a teacher showing something new and special to a student. Byre nodded as he concentrated.

It was no longer just a thread. It was everything. As he stared at his past, he could see the moment he had decided to trust the dragon, the place where he had been tempted to give up while in the custody of the Kindred, and further back, the choice he had made to follow his father.

The moment that he saw that, Ellyria stepped away from him. The once simple trail spun like a tangled skein of wool and became impossible to read.

Byre gasped and bent over, clutching himself. His mind felt suddenly scrambled, much as it had years before when tasting peon for the first time.

With focus and concentration he managed not to throw up before his childhood hero. What she had shown him was magnificent and also terrifying. So many junctures and possibilities that it bent the mind to hold them all— let alone understand them.

When Byre straightened up he looked at Ellyria with new respect. He also suspected that the *pae atuae* were holding her together, like something bright contained in a jar. Without them she might fly apart altogether. She smiled slightly. "I see you understand." The seer turned to the back wall. "He's ready to go."

The Kindred were there, waiting. Maybe they had been there all along. The flaming eyes and the indefinite forms still chilled him, but he knew that to go ahead he had to trust in them. He jumped when Pelanor's hand slipped into his.

The Blood Witch squeezed his fingertips and smiled. Women everywhere were mesmerizing him, because for a moment he could not take his eyes off the points of her teeth on her lip.

"I've always wanted to see the Salt," Pelanor said, and then laughed. "But you are going to have quite some explaining to do about me. I guess I will just have to stay close."

CHAPTER SIX

A DARK HORSE

Day was giving way to night by the time Kelanim found a good time to sneak out of the harem. If she had been fresh to it she would never have managed it. Delios the chief eunuch was an old friend that she had cultivated for years, and he knew her devotion to the Caisah.

He also knew that sometimes the pressure of the harem grew too much. So when she appeared at the gate shrouded in a brown cloak, her face hidden behind a battered old mask, he did not make any comment. Instead, he simply held the door open.

It was not as if she could go beyond the palace walls. In fact, her usual operation was to walk the walls, drink the night's cool air, and maybe pray a little. The gods might have forgotten her, but she had not totally forgotten them.

Tonight was not for the gods. It was for her mysterious benefactor. Keeping to the shadows, Kelanim worked her way toward the stables. The stablemaster and his boys slept above their charges, but the night was helping her. The wind howling around the corners of palace and whipping up leaves into eerie hisses in the road would mask her footsteps.

Reaching the stables, the mistress slipped inside and eased the door shut. The smell of straw, horses and leather washed over her, and despite the rawness of the odor Kelanim appreciated it. It was honest—more honest that the smells of the harem. Sandalwood, jasmine and rosewater dominated her life, and hid the reality. Here at least was truth.

The trouble was, she didn't know who she was meeting. For the last few months she'd been receiving cryptic messages in the most unlikely places, and always they had seemed to make life easier. Talyn was gone because of them, but Kelanim still didn't know who her benefactor was.

Something moved in the stables, a horse shifting from foot to foot in its sleep, but she jumped.

"Mistress, you are right to feel fear." The voice that came from the stall, made her heart leap into her throat, and she grabbed for the wall. It was not the stablemaster or any of his boys—she knew that immediately. The voice was deep and resonant, the kind a person could feel all the way though their bones. "You are in the presence of the Named."

Kelanim stood frozen to the spot, and the whole world seemed to lose its importance. The Named. She had read voraciously all she could find on the Vaerli and the Kindred. She knew that the Named were the creatures created by Vaerli, and they were rare and powerful creatures.

Though her heart was racing, Kelanim took a few hesitant steps closer to the voice.

"A brave creature then," her visitor went on, "but then, you must be to fool the Caisah so completely." Whoever was speaking was within the middle stall in the line, and when the mistress reached the railing she saw why. A centaur. She blinked hard and her hands tightened around the wood of the rail until her palms hurt. The centaur remained there, as huge and irrefutable as could be imagined. His back half was a jet-black carthorse, while the human shaped portion was an equally massively muscled man, and that was merely the outside. Being Named, he would have other resources.

Kelanim ignored his goading remark. She flicked a look over her shoulder to make sure they were really alone. "How could you get into the palace like . . ." she gestured helplessly to encompass all the centaur, "as you are?"

"I am not alone," the centaur said, glowering at her. "I am part of the vanguard, the things to come. Others of the Named can come and go through the palace with perfect ease. This place was never made to hinder Kindred, Named or un-Named."

The idea of imagined creatures like the centaur roaming through the corridors of the palace was very uncomfortable. Her mind darted through all the possibilities of what that could mean; the horrors and delights of childhood stories unleashed in her world. However, she did not move from her spot, though every ounce of her wanted to rush back to the harem, bar the door, and hide beneath the silk covers of her bed.

The deep mahogany of the centaur's laughter rolled over her. "Such a little woman, but full of great bravery . . . and all wasted on the Caisah."

"I love him," she said with more strength than she actually felt.

Strangely, he did not scoff at her protestations of love, but simply folded his arms in front of him and stared down implacably at her. She had never felt so small—even when the man she loved had struck her.

"Your Caisah has learned one of the terrible things about immortality," the centaur said, each word falling on her like a hard stone. "That love is a myth to comfort those with small lives. Love cannot endure a never ending existence."

Kelanim's mouth went dry, and her hands clenched at her sides. She wanted to protest that he did not know the Caisah, but something in those dark centaur eyes made her hold her tongue.

"It is not your fault." Now the beast sounded almost comforting. "You cannot compete with the weight of history."

The mistress thought of his restless sleep, and his quickness to anger.

"You would deny him the delight of love once more?" The centaur stamped one hoof, and it was so loud in the quiet of the stables that Kelanim jumped.

He was making a persuasive argument, and perhaps she'd been a fool not to see what the centaur pointed out so easily.

"Imagine how your moth-like your existence must seem to the Caisah," the centaur said, his voice sliding around her senses like balm, "and think on how many moths have passed through his life."

Tears filled her eyes, and she suddenly realized how many of the harem women would have paid good money to see this: Kelanim, the hard-nosed, icy first mistress, brought low.

The centaur and the horses observed this crumbling of her reserve, but Kelanim no longer cared. When her tears overflowed and ran down her cheeks, she let them, and tilted her head up defiantly. "I will still love him, even if he cannot return it. I will endure until there is nothing left for me."

The centaur stepped forward, out of the stall, to stand only two feet away from her. This close the smell of him was impossible to avoid; an odd combination of horse sweat and powerful man. It was not unpleasant. "Why should you endure, when there is a way for him to love . . ."

She was no fool. The centaur had just told her the solution, and though her heart leapt with the possibility, she had not got so far in the harem by being reckless. "I will not harm him," she replied, and even dared a half-step forward, "and I would be doing that by taking his immortality from him."

The centaur was silent for a moment, his great dark eyes drifting around the barn, taking in trappings of man and beast. "You think immortality is such a gift?" His hand suddenly clamped down on her shoulder, and Kelanim felt the heat of it go right through her while the weight of it nearly brought her to her knees. "I was once a Kindred, little human. I lived on the tides of chaos, and time was nothing to me. When I was Named all that changed, and I was fixed in place. For a long time it was a wonderful thing to me, to experience time, but all things wax stale for me now. Beauty, love, tragedy and even friendship mean nothing to me living this way. Can you imagine that?"

Looking up into his eyes was like looking up into the face of a statue, implacable and terrifying. Kelanim bit her lip in order not to cry out. He was doing a fine job of making her feel inconsequential. "Then why did you summon me here?" she snapped, feeling as if something inside her might break.

The snort that came out of him would have made someone of weaker constitution flee in terror, and when his massive hooves stamped on the cobblestones in front of her, Kelanim did feel the urge to cry out. Only some inner core of character kept her shaking, but upright. The centaur leaned down, so that his breath was on her face. In anyone else that would have been an almost erotic gesture; with him it was the most terrifying experience. "We have helped you get rid of the Hunter." One of his huge hands closed around her throat. "And we shall help you free the Caisah so that he may truly love you. Isn't that what you want?"

Kelanim could breathe, but she was well aware his fingers could tighten at any moment. He had been the one to send the note that encouraged her to manipulate the Caisah into sending Talyn after the talespinner. That had worked wonderfully. Carefully, she nodded, and then gasped out, "Yes . . ."

The centaur considered her, twisting her head from side to side as if she were some exotic bug he had captured. Then, finally, he released her. "You are doing the right thing for the man you love," he added, his voice rumbling through her bones in this close proximity. "Think of it, does he sleep well?" The centaur's eyes bored into hers.

Kelanim found herself breathing hard and fast, but her mind followed him along the path. The Caisah did not sleep well; he often woke screaming in the night, or muttered terrible things in his sleep.

"Immortality was not meant to be his." The centaur's hand was not pressed on the top of her head. The heat from a moment before that had terrified her, now seemed a comfort. "You know this."

She licked her lips, and dared to reply, "You are right. He has said so before, in fact."

"Then you must take it from him, relieve his burden." He stepped back into the shadows again. "It can be done, and then he will be as other men, able to live and love as they do."

For a split second Kelanim was terrified; the idea that she could have a hand in taking away her love's protection hit her hard. However, she remembered the pain in his voice, and how much she wanted to feel his love in return. "Then tell me how to do it," she whispered. "I would have him live a whole life, not a half one for all eternity."

The centaur bowed his head. "It will not be an easy thing, and there are many dangers for you, too. Immortality, when given to a mortal, can crack their sanity."

"I know that," Kelanim replied, her hands clenching into fists. "Every day I am with him is a danger, so do not think to turn me aside with that."

"Very well." The centaur reached back into the saddlebags he carried on his withers. He handed the mistress a small bag. "Place this piece of paper under his pillow while he sleeps. It must be near his head."

She opened the bag, just to be sure that it was nothing poisonous, but it did indeed appear to be a piece of faded vellum inscribed with the *pae atuae*. Kelanim swallowed hard, her throat suddenly seemed as tight as it had when the centaur had his hands on her. "It . . . it won't hurt him will it?"

"Has anything written by Vaerli ever had a chance of hurting the Caisah?"

It was a good point. "So then," she continued, folding the paper carefully and putting it back in its pouch, "this will restore his mortality by morning?"

The centaur's laugher filled the stable, making the nearby horses snort and shy away. Kelanim worried that the stableboys might come back to investigate. "As if the gifts of the Void can be so easily taken away from a scion," the centaur said. "No, this is only the first part."

"Then tell me the rest?" the mistress demanded.

Another laugh, this time lower. "All in good time, little slattern. First, you must prove yourself to us, then we shall see how to proceed."

He turned, adroitly considering his great bulk, but then paused at the outside stall door. His shape was outlined by the moons' light, revealing his thick locks of hair running from his head, over his shoulder, down his back, and transforming into a mane along the way. It was bizarre and beautiful.

The wind from outside blew his scent once more over her, and now a shudder went through her. The centaur was primal and terrifying—something the Caisah fired in her as well. "I will find you again," the centaur rumbled. "Do as we ask, and all will be well."

Before he could get away, Kelanim—perhaps inured to danger by her time with the Caisah—blurted out, "What is your name?"

When he turned and glared at her, that feeling in the pit of her stomach became almost painful, and she added, "I need to have something to call you." For a moment she wondered if she had gone too far with what was essentially one of the most dangerous creatures in Conhaero. Would she end up with her throat crushed and tossed beneath the horses?

Finally, the centaur turned back once more, and spoke, "You can call me Pholos. It is not my true name, but it will do for you."

Then he sprang away from her and out into the night, disappearing before she could take another breath. All Kelanim, mistress of the Caisah, could do was tuck the pouch he had given her into her belt, and turn back for the palace.

If she was prone to prayer, now might have been the time for it.

Riding toward the sea was not the thing Talyn wanted to do. She had not been to the sea since her time with Finn, and even though she had purged that memory, somehow, some little part of her still abhorred the ocean. Now, the Phage were sending her there, and she felt as broken as she had when she'd been the Caisah's Hunter.

Bending low over Syris' back as he raced east, she tried not to think of what she was doing. Tried and failed. She had given up everything to be the Hunter, and had comforted herself in the night that she was at least working toward getting the Gifts of her people back. Lifting the curse that had been placed upon them had seemed like a goal that was worth her own sacrifice.

Since that had been revealed as a cruel trick by the Caisah to keep her close and amuse himself, she had fallen into despair. The Phage had seemed the only option.

She brushed her eyes with the back of her hand. The speed at which they were traveling was playing tricks with her vision. In her mind's eye she could see the puzzle pieces laid out before her, and the revelation that when formed together, they had made the image of Putorae, the Last Seer. The Caisah was impossibly cruel. He had told her the answer to the lifting of the curse was in the puzzle, but one long-dead seer was not the answer. He was a liar.

Everything was a lie. As Talyn watched the world fly past in a gray blur around her, she was surprised by one thing: she had not killed herself. Some damned annoying little spark of self-preservation still burned on. Even when things were hopeless, she couldn't bring herself to take her own life—not when so many Vaerli had never had the chance.

Syris' muscles bunching and clenching beneath her served to remind her that forward momentum was possible. Yet she was not as she had been. Time on the back of the nykur was not easy on muscle and bone—even for a Vaerli. Leaning forward, Talyn whispered into the long curved green ear, "Rest, my darling."

Syris slowed from his ground-eating gallop to a quick trot, and the world resolved back into its normal state.

They were on a wide plain, where the Road of the Caisah was beautifully absent. It was unmitigated Chaosland—just as it had been before the coming of so many people. Talyn leaned back in the saddle and stretched her aching back. The smell of grass and fresh air buoyed her spirits slightly, reminding her that the world was not all bad.

Conhaero, the land of chaos and change, the refuge of the people through the White Void. It must have looked awe inspiring and delightful after the madness of the swirling between worlds.

Bouncing on her saddlebags, the scroll caught her eye, and for the first time curiosity began to chew at her. The Caisah had sent for this scroll, presumably from some hidden store of his. Immortal beings tended to collect a lot of objects and items; Talyn knew that her own people often hoarded such things.

Once the libraries and storage vaults beneath V'nae Rae had been bulging with scrolls of history and lore. Many had contained *pae atuae* since only so much word magic could be inscribed on walls and other surfaces.

As Syris brought himself to a halt, stamping and tossing his head, a dreadful thought came to Talyn. The man who had inherited the city, who had renamed it Perilous and Fair, had been free to plunder those teachings. He had been able to read every one of their stories. Some were written in ancient Vaerli, impossible for even her kin to decipher now, but others would have told him much about her people.

Now she glanced down at the scroll in a totally different way. What would the Caisah want so urgently? What could he have hidden?

The patterned tube that contained that information was only a hand's breadth away. She slipped down from the nykur, but stood still for a long moment. The Phage had said only dragon fire could destroy the scroll? Who else apart from that fool Finn had ever had a dragon?

Her fingers traced the canister, feeling the raised pattern and the tight seal of wax that provided proof that it had not been tampered with or opened. Her mind raced. Dare she open it now?

With a ragged sigh, Talyn turned away. The Phage were not to be taken lightly. The thing she had to remember was that they were the enemy of the Caisah—that was the only fact that mattered.

So instead, she tempered her curiosity with practicality. The scroll had to be destroyed, and anything that kept a little more power away from her former master had to be a good thing. Talyn set herself to getting a little rest. Night was drawing in fast, and she did not like the purple clouds gathering. It would probably be rain.

Syris' dark eyes followed her as she set up a circle of stones, lit a fire, and made herself as comfortable as she could be in this lonely place. It was not the first camp that she'd been forced to make for herself.

She sat on her blanket, looked up at the menacing clouds, and chewed on a bit of dried meat. Lonely had become the normal for the Vaerli, but it had not always been. Talyn thought back to the Gatherings of old. It was an odd recollection to be having, and she had not had much reason to think of them lately.

When she had taken Finn there, she had been haunted by memories of those days, but since then she'd been working to block their memory. She had not stricken them from her memory, which she could have done as nemohira. Talyn swallowed the tack, and tilted her head back to watch the plain swallow the glowing red ball that was the sun.

No, if she had consigned those memories to dust then she would have lost the last precious glimpses of her mother and her brother. Instead she hoarded those memories like an animal hiding food for the winter.

It was the curious half-light moment, when the rays of the sun turned the clouds to violet, and there was a feeling of oppressive humidity in the air. Syris would not settle. Talyn looked over at the great green beast and watched him curiously. It was not like her mount to be upset over a little weather. The nykur was the nearest thing to a Kindred, attached to the chaos in ways that not even Talyn could understand completely. When he began to paw the earth and roll his black deep eyes at the sky, she listened to what he was trying to tell her.

Slowly getting to her feet, she looked up at the clouds with a more searching glance. They began to flicker with white light, as if someone was lighting and dimming a lantern in the heights of the sky, but there was no sound of thunder to accompany it.

Syris pawed the ground, ripping up great chunks of the earth. The shadow of his arched neck blocked out a portion of the sky. Conhaero was home. Even without the gifts, Talyn knew it as she knew her own body. She did not know this particular weather that did not obey any of the rules of the land.

Walking forward, she laid her hand on the nykur and waited to see what would come. The sharp smell in her nostrils overwhelmed even the mossy odor of Syris. Above, the lightning became more than flashes. Now it was blinding claws of white darting from cloud to cloud. The movement was unnerving, and her right hand drifted unconsciously to the handle of her sword—though what that could do to a storm she did not know. This was no chaos storm, she'd seen plenty of those in her time. They rolled in—or perhaps more accurately, out of—the earth itself. They blinded the senses and could easily unhinge a Vaerli mind. This was as if the sky itself was lowering.

The lightning increased its tempo, making Talyn feel uncomfortable deep down in the pit of her stomach. Syris was on the edge of something, circling around her as if he could sense danger somewhere, but could not make out where it was. When the rumble came, it was deeper than thunder somehow, as if it were roaring from somewhere further away. The flash of lightning illuminated the ground, and Talyn narrowed her eyes.

The shapes scattered on the plain before her had not been there a moment before. Her jaw tightened. The Kindred, maybe a hundred of them, stood motionlessly staring up at the sky, too. Their dark shapes looked like they had been pulled from the earth. They might have been primal statues, but she knew they could move when they wanted to.

"What is happening?" she whispered to herself, though even Syris could not have heard her over the menacing rumble of the thunder. The Kindred had never shown themselves after the Harrowing. The one that had saved

Finn had been the only one she'd ever seen. Yet now here they were in great numbers . . . for some reason.

The clouds were rolling, twisting as if in pain, and then they finally disgorged something. Or many somethings. She had heard enough stories at her parents' knees. The White Void through which all peoples of this land—even her own, back in the darkness of history—had come. It was legendary for its terrors. Any that ventured into it, if they were lucky enough to emerge, were forever changed. It was what had destroyed gods and created the Scions.

Talyn could scarcely believe that she had not fallen into one of Finn's ancient stories. She clutched onto Syris. He too was awed by what was happening above them. The clouds were shredding, coming apart like the funnel of a tornado reaching down to the earth below. This was no mere wind. The shapes bearing down on them were tearing, burning with light that made her eyes hurt even to look on it.

Blood was trickling down her arm from where her fingers had been cut on the nykur's sharp hair, but it was a nothing compared to what she was seeing. All of her fears and concerns paled in comparison to this. The Song of the Pact rushed back to her—the words taught to every Vaerli child at her mother's knee.

"Beware the Void they called with frightening sound,
Cursed you will be if it comes and you sing.
Hold fast your word, and flame may be held at bay."

Suddenly her throat was dry, and she thought of what she had been meant to be; a maker of song magic. Now her mind was a barren place, and no music formed in it. Once, their magic had even used the White Void to travel, but they had only dared it for tiny moments. If it opened fully then they had no chance at all.

The White Void was opening, as the Kindred had warned. The end of Conhaero. The roaring sound above was now so close it felt as if it might break her bones. Talyn looked up and saw her own personal doom coming. The crushing light of the White Void, as one of those tornados pushed down on her from above. She didn't move. Whatever it was, she would take it. Maybe it would be better than the Phage, the Caisah, and even Finn had done with her.

The nykur stood with her; sharing whatever fate was coming. The cold of the Void was nearly upon her when something scarlet moved between her and the oncoming end. A circle of bright red splashed up and away from her, as if someone were casting water from a bucket before them.

An ear-popping rush of sound enveloped Talyn, and she felt every hair standing on end. The Void was gone—so were the Kindred. The plain was empty, except for herself, Syris, and another woman standing only a few feet away from them. She was small, dark skinned, and holding the soft flesh of her forearm up to her mouth.

What she was most definitely *not* was Vaerli, but she had moved as fast as they could. She could only be one thing.

"Thank you Blood Witch," Talyn said, and with shock realized her voice was trembling. The White Void had taken a toll on her that was not confined to merely physical strain. She cleared her throat and removed her hand from Syris. Now the pain and blood were making themselves felt.

The Blood Witch's eyes darted to the stream of scarlet, but she lowered her own arm from her mouth. "You could have given it some of your own, then."

Talyn looked up at the sky, but even the clouds had gone. She glanced down at her savior. "I am—"

"I know who you are, Talyn, once the Hunter for the Caisah . . . now something far worse." The Blood Witch looked at her with a slight frown on her forehead, but Talyn was not entirely happy about being judged.

"As compared to how you allowed one of your own to take me as their prey." She had not forgotten Pelanor.

"Sharp words from one who just saved you." The other woman tilted her head and smiled. "My name in Anduin."

The other tribes of Conhaero gave away their names so easily, but maybe they meant less to them. Talyn glanced at Syris, who usually did not care for the smell of Blood Witches, but the nykur was strangely quiet, only watching Anduin out of the corner of one gleaming eye.

"So tell me, Anduin," Talyn said softly and with great calmness, "how did you manage to see the White Void all by yourself?"

The woman's tiny frame did not seem mighty enough to contain enough power for all that. "Blood," she replied simply. "Everything may be bought with sacrifice." She turned and gestured back across the plain. "As you can see."

Talyn took a step forward, looking where the witch pointed. The Kindred were gone. For every one of the rips in the White Void, there had been one waiting. They were now gone. A chill ran through her body as she realized what that meant.

The Witch was at her shoulder. "They have bought your people time, Talyn. Time to decide."

The once-Hunter turned on Anduin, her brows drawn together and her hands clenched. How dare this creature speak to her of the Vaerli and the Kindred. What could she possibly know?

"The Pact is broken, my people scattered or burned to ashes—so what exactly do you suggest they do?" The Pact was part of the Vaerli. It was who they were and where their pride came from. It made them special in a way that no other race in Conhaero could claim.

The Witch must have been nearly as young as she looked, because she backed away in the face of Talyn's growing rage. "That I do not know. They will not speak of it."

The Kindred were speaking to other races, but not to the Vaerli? A fire lit in Talyn at the concept. After all that her people had suffered, this was one more humiliation that could barely be stood.

She grabbed Syris' mane, wrapping her fingers deep in the sharp hair, and pulled herself upwards and onto his back. The plain ahead of them was quiet and empty again.

Looking down, she met the eyes of the Blood Witch. They were ancient where they should not have been. "My race has already been dead for a thousand years," she said simply. "I tried to save them, and I failed. Now, if the end of the world is coming, then so be it. We have nothing to live for!"

She glared out at the empty landscape. She knew they had to be there watching, and listening; that, after all, was all they were good for. "As for our former allies, they did nothing to stop the Harrowing because they are cowards and liars. Perhaps now they begin to understand a little about fear and despair."

As she kicked Syris and urged him into a gallop, there were tears in her eyes. Why was she bothering to breathe? Perhaps dragon fire was a worthy way to end it all. At least she would get to see the ocean one last time.

CHAPTER SEVEN

PLACES UNEXPECTED

The Kindred wrapped around them, pulling Pelanor and Byre down into the earth once more. Pelanor was reminded of her own journey into the maw of the twelve-mouthed goddess.

Her stomach rumbled at the thought; it was the memory of her *gewalt* that did it. They had shared blood and become locked together, and yet she didn't even know his fate. Her fellow Blood Witches had him, and would not let him go until she returned with the blood of the Vaerli hunter Talyn to satisfy them.

A quick glance out of her dark eye toward the Vaerli who stood at her side reminded her how she had failed at that task. Her *gewalt* could be suffering for it.

She had not killed his sister, but rather had taken up the pact with her instead. She had allowed ambition to cloud her judgment. The Blood Witch had never imagined that it would lead her here—into the strange timeless world of the Kindred.

Another stab of hunger pierced her through, and was followed by a wave of light-headiness that made her sway on her feet. Byre was beside her, his strong arms wrapped around her waist, and she did not fall.

"Pelanor, you're not well." He might be the closest thing to a full-blooded Vaerli, but he was still a man—with all the foibles of that sex; like stating the bloody obvious. They shared a look.

He was beautiful, Pelanor realized as trembles began in the tips of her fingers. It was not the blood hunger that made her notice that, but it certainly helped. Byreniko of the Vaerli smelled delicious, like warm bread left out on the windowsill to cool. She'd experienced the delight of such fragrance before she had pledged herself to the goddess. It made her mouth water and a shudder of desire wash over her. Craven and debauched images flashed through her head; naked, writhing flesh, where he was inside her, and she was drinking.

The hunger was making her crazy; she was pledged to her *gewalt* and he alone. Yet when this Vaerli held her she could barely remember her *gewalt's* name.

The flame and earth around them were moving them, but Pelanor was sure of one thing, she was not going to be able to last without blood—not for much longer. She would need to drink from Byreniko again soon.

A flicker of understanding passed over Byre's face, his eyes taking in the signs of the hunger that were writ on her. "You must drink," he said, and by the goddess those words sounded so erotic, she nearly moaned. If she kept drinking from him he might as well become her *gewalt.*

Just as she was going to have to make up her mind how to respond, the Kindred let them loose. The white of the blinding midday sun caught both of them by surprise. From the cool of Perilous and Fair to this made Pelanor stagger a little.

She pulled herself reluctantly away from Byre; she would not have her weakness be so apparent in all this openness. As they looked around them, it was obvious that again the Kindred had transported them to this place and time and then left them.

The Blood Witch did not think much of their hospitality. It was not the most welcoming of places. A flat, wind-blasted plain, with nothing but salt lying ahead of them. The odd stubborn stunted bush punctuated it, but that was all. The smell of this arid place burned her nostrils, while the sun gleaming off all the whiteness was almost blinding.

Luckily, she was not without her own resources: her extra eyelid slid over her delicate eyes, reducing the sunlight to a more acceptable level. It was a handy ability for her kind, which might not burn to death in the sun, but did not enjoy its touch.

Beside her, Byre was not moving. His breath was fast and shallow. He was as rigid as a board, with his gaze fixed on the horizon. He must know where they were.

If she touched him, Pelanor knew she might not be able to control herself, so instead she said his name, a whisper to hopefully bring him back from whatever strange place his mind had plummeted to. After she had spoken it three times, Byre jerked his eyes away.

"The Salt Plain." He turned to her, and his eyes were so wide. "The gathering place of the Vaerli. The Bastion."

She looked out on the expanse and could not control her words. "Not exactly the setting I would have chosen, but I suppose it suits your kind well enough."

His smile was faint as if he were trying to be amused, but then he frowned. "Pelanor, there is one thing—this place is meant only for Vaerli. You will not survive setting foot on it."

When she looked down at the salt it appeared innocent enough, but she was not going to dismiss his concerns. The option of staying behind was not one she would contemplate—after all, the Kindred had a nasty habit of whipping him away at a moment's notice. She most certainly did not want to become marooned in the ugly past.

A rumble of her stomach reminded her. When Pelanor looked up at him, it felt as though the pain was spreading to her bones. "I . . ." she began, but ground to a halt. What was there to say? The strength of her people was also their real weakness. Her *gewalt* was so far away now it was impossible to feel him.

"You need to drink," Byre said, stepping nearer to her. His burnished brown skin looked like salvation, and this close she could almost feel his pulse in her head.

Pelanor swallowed hard, not sure if she wanted to reveal how close to the edge she was—or how she was terrified that she might drink him dry, should she step over.

Silently, she shook her head, backing away a step. It was all she could manage.

Relentlessly, Byre moved forward, closer than she had moved away. Now his warm, throbbing blood was only an inch away from her skin. His voice seemed to come from very far away. "Take my blood, Pelanor. Drink, and the Salt will accept you as Vaerli, at least for a while."

It made perfect sense, but she was terrified. When Talyn had given her blood willingly it had been heady and powerful—but it had also come with a price. The Blood Witch held herself ramrod straight, and kept her mouth tightly shut. She did not need another *gewalt*.

"I give it freely," Byre said, and touched her. He raised her fingers to his neck, placing them right where the pulse raced. Though she closed her eyes, she could not pull away.

"I trust you," he whispered, and every part of her body reacted.

"I don't trust myself," she muttered, keeping her eyes closed firm. "I could drink you down to nothing and then where would I be? Trapped in the past, lost forever to my *gewalt*. I would die."

"Then take what you need, and leave the rest." Byre wrapped his arm around her waist, but no longer in a concerned way. He pulled her tight against him, and Pelanor discovered that she was not the only one fighting her desires.

Her nature could only be denied for so long, and she was not a Kindred to feel nothing. Pelanor wanted the Vaerli badly, in every way possible for human or immortal. She wanted his flesh in her and under her tongue.

When Byre tilted his head down and kissed her, she tasted his desire as well. She had kissed her *gewalt*, and when she'd been mortal, plenty of men too—but this was Vaerli . . . a Vaerli on the edge of recovering his gifts.

It was as if hot flame plunged into her. Every nerve and sinew was directed toward one aim: having as much of him as she could. Even the power of the goddess was not this.

Behind her eyes Pelanor saw and felt the power of Conhaero; the roiling mass of chaos, time and power. Byre was a conduit to all that, and she wanted to bathe in it. His hands on her were only taking what she wanted him to have. Clothes were ripped and torn apart as they ended up on the hard packed earth.

Pelanor's teeth found his neck, and she opened her throat and drank.

The Vaerli's cry as she did so thrilled her darkest desires. His blood burned through her, even as he entered her, making a perfect circle of lust and completion. All the discomforts of the hard ground were washed away in sensation. He was all Vaerli and she all the goddess made.

Pelanor drank him down, as his body drove into her.

Orgasm was not the word for what it was. It was pain, loss, anger, and beauty all rolled into one.

When Pelanor came back to consciousness, it was to find Byre's body lying across hers. On her lips was the taste of his blood, still rich and good but cooling. She realized that in the moment, she'd had no thought of control, and was suddenly terrified.

"Byre?" She touched his shoulder with genuine trepidation. He felt cool, but then just as her fear choked her, he murmured something and levered himself from her.

His eyes widened as he looked down at her, and Pelanor knew she looked a sight. Her fangs, lips and chest were covered with his blood—and she was as naked as the goddess had made her.

"I'm all right," he assured her, his hand touching the line of her face. "But I . . ." He broke off, and licked his own lips. "I wasn't expecting . . ."

"That?" she offered. Usually when sharing her body with someone not of her kind, she left quickly. Pleasure was a passing thing for a Blood Witch, but a strange sensation was washing over her.

He looked almost embarrassed, but helped her up. Both of them struggled to pull their clothing back together, but did not meet each other's eyes. Finally, there was nothing for it. She had to know.

"Is it always like that for your people?" Pelanor demanded.

Byre blushed, and pushed his hair out of his eyes. "I . . . I really don't know. I was so young when the Scourging happened that I never got to touch another of my kind."

She'd been an idiot. "Yes, I suppose burning and dying when you touch another Vaerli would make that difficult. How about with mortals?" Pelanor had to know. It wasn't about stroking his ego. Something had happened, something more than sex.

When Byre shook his head, she felt an odd little surge of happiness. "No, never." Then he took her hand gently in his own and squeezed lightly. "You have to understand that Vaerli seldom lie with other races—especially before the Harrowing." Then, perhaps to ease her mind, he kissed her again.

It was there, underneath the passion: a hint of fire.

Pelanor knew that her blood lust was sated; she felt light and powerful once more. She still would have gladly pulled him down onto the hard earth again—would do so in this instant. It was not just his blood.

When she had passed through the last mouth of the goddess she had felt more sure of herself than she ever had before. She had known her place in the scheme of things. She had become part of something much larger and better than she was. Now, standing on the edge of the white Salt Plain, all of that was blown away. For if she was a Blood Witch, then why had lying down with a Vaerli pleased her so deeply?

Love was something reserved for the *gewalt*. It was he, and he alone that should make her complete—not some Vaerli.

When she kissed him back something was shifting within her. Could there be a reason she was here with him, feeling these things? Her kind did not believe in fate or predestination. They believed in blood and kin. Yet Byreniko loomed large in her vision now, and Pelanor didn't quite know what to do with that. It was terrifying and exhilarating.

She tried to keep her voice light when she replied, "Perhaps there is a reason for that."

A slight smile lifted Byre's mouth, but he put his hand over hers and squeezed. "I don't know what it means, Pelanor. Your kind and mine—we never had much contact. Perhaps it is the blood."

She closed her eyes and felt it pulse in her. Every time she drank from a person not her *gewalt* she'd been disappointed . . . until she drank from Talyn. That had been heady, but drinking from her brother was different again.

"Perhaps," she said, buttoning the last of her shirt, and dusting off her skirt. It was hard to believe it, but these were the same clothes she'd worn went she left the coven, the same clothes she had fought his sister in.

As she looked out over the white plain, she thought of what had brought her here, and wondered with a little trepidation what lay ahead. "What is out there?" she asked him, turning and looking over her shoulder at him.

Byre sighed, and taking her hand, kissed the palm of it. "Let me show you."

He led her out on the surface of the lake, the place where the white salt cracked under her heel and the Vaerli territory began. It was a strange, barren place, but it was not that which chilled her.

"It feels like I am on ice," she whispered to him. "Like I might slip and fall."

The Vaerli tightened his grip on her, and she felt a little more sure of herself. "I won't let you," he replied softly, and together they walked out a little further. Suddenly the blood in her veins that had made her feel so powerful, did not feel so much so.

As they walked, Byre talked to her; at first merely comments on the color of the sky, or the bleakness of the place. After they had gone far enough into the Salt that the edge was no longer visible, he began to open up to her.

"This is the last place I remember seeing my mother." His voice was carefully neutral, but she could tell that those words cost him. "She was injured in the Scourging, badly. She, my sister and I were separated from my father."

The Harrowing of the Vaerli was a part of legend. In her coven there were Blood Witches who had been alive then; ancient, gnarled old women who claimed to have been terrified to drink the blood of the cursed Vaerli—even as they had watched them flee.

His words made Pelanor start. She managed not to blurt out what she was thinking, but she knew it had to have been running through Byre's head from the moment Ellyria had the command to come back here. He might see them again. Not only his recently dead father, but also his long lost mother and sister.

She couldn't imagine how that would be. Pelanor cleared her throat. The salt was shifting under their feet again, but in a very different manner. Every step they took felt like the ground was spinning beneath them. The distance they walked in one stride was impossibly long. The earth couldn't move that fast, even in Conhaero . . . could it?

Glancing up at Byre, she knew not to ask him. Too many things were plaguing his thoughts, and she suspected the nature of this place was meant to unsettle. Still she couldn't just leave him to remain silent.

"Do you remember what happened at the Harrowing?" she ventured, leaning in close against him. "None speak of it—certainly not the Caisah, from what I have heard . . ."

Byre's eyebrows drew together until he resembled nothing so much as a stern mask. "What do people think happened?"

She shrugged. "Some say he called down lightning. Others say it was like a great whirling cloud of pestilence."

"It was none of those things." His eyes closed briefly, as if summoning the memory from deep down and far away. "I was a child, so I was not at the meeting. I don't know what happened, but I saw the aftermath."

"What was that like, then?"

His words made her wince just a little. "You will see, Pelanor. It is coming soon enough, and you will be witness to it."

The white was endless and mind-numbing. Pelanor felt like it was inside her head, wiping out everything that was in there. She could not imagine how it might be without a Vaerli at her side and his blood in her veins.

"It seems easy to walk," she commented, more to try and get him to talk than anything.

"That is because we are Vaerli," he murmured. "The Salt has its protectors. It is more a living thing than a place, but just be grateful that you do not see it."

He never let go of her hand, and despite being a Blood Witch and her own private universe, Pelanor was grateful.

Then a thought struck her. "But what of the Caisah then? How did he get across the Salt Plain?"

"You mean, how will he get across the Plain?" She glanced up at Byre, and saw a flicker of pain cross his face. This was a bitter homecoming for him. "I do not know, but I suspect we will see it all."

They walked on, their feet seeming to skim across the dire salt, and yet it felt as though they were not getting anywhere at all. Time had little meaning here, but it seemed to drag on Pelanor.

Then, just as she felt as though she was reaching the end of her sanity, something gray appeared on the horizon. She blinked rapidly, wondering if her eyes had finally decided to give up on her. However, as they moved closer and closer to it, the shape resolved itself into a long line of caravans, wagons and horses.

She squinted. Or *were* they horses?

It was quite the gathering. She had thought the gathering she'd witnessed in the sand with Finn the Fox was impressive. This made that look like a tiny family get together.

"So many," she said, her eyes flickering over the transport, the fires, and the emerging hubbub of the crowd. "So many Vaerli . . . I never imagined there were so many of you."

"Once we were numerous . . . at least, my father told me that. It was said the Vaerli rode the land in a multitude."

It was a strange thing to think of them that way. In her time and place they were so scattered and so few. Pelanor began to have more of an appreciation of what they had suffered. It also brought her some measure of relief: they would not stand out so much in this crowd.

"This is a sacred place, Pelanor." Byre pulled them to a stop, and looked down at her with a sad and serious expression. "And we cannot change what will happen here today—not even if we yearn to."

She knew immediately that he was talking to himself most of all and not to her. The things that lay ahead would be a dreadful temptation: a chance to see his father, mother and sister again, as well as soak in the community that he had lost at such a young age.

The blood they shared warmed Pelanor, and she blamed it for the empathy she was feeling for the Vaerli. She rubbed his back a little. "Then let's go on. We have much to learn and not long to learn it."

The scream that issued from the mouth of the dragon was enough to shatter eardrums and rend sanity. The Named fighting against each other was an abhorrent thing, and Finn had never heard of it happening—not in any of the stories.

As the griffins circled lower, he felt smaller and smaller. Wahirangi remained on the ground, trumpeting his anger to his fellows and flexing his wings. He seemed unwilling to take the fight to the griffins even though they were making their intentions plain. Finn's gaze darted around, as he felt at any moment they would be overwhelmed and destroyed.

Finally, the dragon could no longer safely remain where he was. Wahirangi leapt into the sky, thrusting his way through the press of griffins; angry squawks and feathers flew around them. Finn crouched low over the dragon's back as his wings swung hard and deep, but he did not use his fire, not once to clear the way. Beaks and claws raked along the great length of the dragon, but he did not turn and retaliate. Finn yelled in rage and frustration, as the dragon angled himself almost straight up, the griffins in close pursuit.

"Fight back," the human clinging to his back screamed. "Burn them out of the sky."

Any illusion that Finn had that he was in charge was swept away as they went higher and higher, but no flame appeared.

The screams of the griffins followed them, but the higher Wahirangi climbed the fewer of them there were. Finn realized that though the griffins were nimbler at the turns than the dragon, they could not match his stamina and strength in the air. As he climbed higher and higher, the griffins dropped away one by one.

But Finn could not really enjoy the success, because by this time he was gasping for air and having increasing difficultly hanging on to the saddle. His vision was blurring and the little air in his lungs felt like knives.

"Wahi . . . Wahirangi . . ." he choked out.

The golden head turned, regarding him for a moment as a human might stare at a bug, but then the dragon folded his wings and dropped lower. Relief flooded through Finn as he was finally able to see clearly, and even think a little. As he craned his head, left and right, and did a sweep of the air below him, he realized that they had swooped down far from where the griffins could follow. He could see them as distant curves on the horizon, but they would not be able to catch up from that distance.

He threw himself down across the dragon's back, wrapping his arms around the scaled neck, and took in a few more luxurious breaths. When Finn finally levered himself up, he asked one question. "Why did you not burn them? Wahirangi, you could have destroyed them all in an instant."

A deep note thrummed through the dragon, something that might have been vague displeasure. He did not look at Finn when he finally spoke. "Think on it for a moment, human . . . who are the griffins and what am I under this skin?"

He felt like an idiot. "You are Kindred, both Named I guess—but they are no longer your kin—and they would have killed you if they had the chance."

"So that makes it right for me to kill them?" the dragon asked, his voice liquid and sad. "They are Kindred, and we do not kill our own. They have been blinded by the power of others, but that does not mean they can't be saved. I have hope that it may happen one day . . . though being in this form makes it hard to see how that might happen."

"You might be able to get them back from the Phage?" Finn demanded, wondering if the beast was about to show him some more magic. He was ready for it.

"No," Wahirangi replied, as he stilled his wings and began to glide for a spell. "Not I. That is beyond my power, but they can indeed be saved."

"But not by you? So then, by someone else?" the talespinner pressed. "Who would that be?"

The dragon was silent for a long time, content to soar the skies with the clouds. "You," he finally replied. "You are the son of Putorae, the Last Seer, and you have her powers deep within you."

Finn opened his mouth a couple of times, seeking words. It was one of the few times that he could not find any to do the job. Finally, he sat back on the dragon's back and thought about that.

He could not imagine what Wahirangi was talking about, but then again ever since leaving Perilous and Fair he had been trying to catch up with himself. He'd Named himself a Kindred after all, and still didn't know how exactly that had been done.

He'd said no words that he could recall. So if the dragon was expecting him to battle the Phage for the Named then he should at least give him some idea how.

"I know you saw her," the dragon said, obviously deciding he'd had enough chance to digest the information. "You saw Putorae. I can smell her on you."

The idea that his long-dead mother had a smell was the least disconcerting thing about the day. "You know her," he croaked out.

The dragon's wings beat for a moment, and Finn was pressed in the saddle as the dragon sought warmer currents of air. Flocks of birds passed beneath them, squawking in protest. Wahirangi snapped at them, and Finn could feel the dragon's irritation in his own belly, like restless flame. The great beast could not survive on such meager fare—he preferred to hunt larger prey by himself— but these questions were bringing up a storm of emotions in Wahirangi.

When they reached the height where the landscape was reduced to blue and purple shadows, and clouds flickered between them and it, the dragon spoke again. "I knew her in the time before the Harrowing. She was a bright star that drew my kind to her like moths. She was . . . the word you would use might use would be . . . entrancing."

Such language used about one's mother might have been unnerving, but Finn had no memories of her himself. He found he was eager to learn more, but most of all one question he had not dared ask the fragments of her he had run into.

"How did she die?" He swallowed, cleared his throat. "Was it in the Harrowing? I thought that she died in the Harrowing . . ."

"You should be doing what you need to do to find your brother." The dragon's voice was suddenly hard, where before it had been full of compassion.

He did not need to weave the yarn to know. Putorae had already told him. Of all the stories he had learned in his time as a talespinner, none was as important as this one Wahirangi had to give him.

Leaning forward, Finn pressed his hands against the smooth, warm, neck of the dragon. This was a creature of the Chaos, but he had Named it. He knew from the stories that Ellyria Dragonsoul had loved her dragon, but it had also obeyed her. "I am the one who Named you, Wahirangi. I need you to tell me what happened."

The dragon flew on, but his golden head flexed on his long neck, peering back at Finn. The talespinner didn't need reminding how insignificant he was, and how precarious his position was, perched on Wahirangi's back. He'd just been told how damned important he was by a seer, and that had gone to his head a little.

"Tell me," he repeated.

"It was after the Harrowing," the dragon rumbled. "People say she died in it, but that is not true. She survived both it and your birth, but she did not survive your father."

"My . . . our father killed her?" Finn felt as though he'd been doused in ice water. It was chilly riding dragons, but this was the kind of cold that he felt he would never shake. First a mother, and then a father. Too many thoughts were suddenly trying to cram their way out of his throat. He'd been an orphan, raised by the talespinners, and often wondered about his family. Eventually the stories, legends and myths they taught him had filled all those cracks and empty spaces. He had not thought of his father for a long time, so to hear him mentioned caused all sorts of tumult.

A peculiar shudder went through the dragon, and he swung his head about, looking above and below them.

Finn realized then that a dragon could disassemble just like a mortal, and Wahirangi knew more than he was letting on. It was like when Finn had sat at the feet of his master of myth, and asked for the whole story. Except that the talespinners liked to leave a dangling plot to draw a listener back for more. The dragon did not want him to ask any more questions, but there was one that hung between them.

"Who is our father?" Finn whispered to himself first, barely disturbing the chilly air with it. Then, as anger began to rise in his chest a little more, he sat taller in the saddle and asked it in a more demanding tone. "Wahirangi, who is our father?"

The dragon beat his wings harder, beginning a rapid climb into the cloudless sky. Finn did not know how things went with the Named. Could they lie to their creator? Could their creator demand knowledge from them? He liked the dragon, and he had much to be thankful to it for, but he had to know.

"I think I deserve . . ." he gasped out, finding his head curiously spinning the higher they got. It was harder and harder to think straight, but the dragon showed no signs of breaking off his climb.

"You already know," Wahirangi replied, seemingly not bothered by the altitude, or the bone freezing cold. "Think on it. Who would your mother go to such great lengths to hide you from? Who has the power to make a creature such as you? Only a scion."

Now Finn's head felt as though it were stuffed with wool, but he knew that there were no scions left in Conhaero. He would have said as much, but he had so little energy left in him to do anything.

Wahirangi must have felt he had made his point; he folded his wings, and they dropped like a hawk through the air. For a short but terrifying moment, all that Finn could think about was hanging onto the saddle, and not ending up a smear on the ground.

When they finally leveled off, for a while Finn just breathed, feeling the wind over his skin as a blessed relief, and the sunlight on his face. Yet, he would not be distracted completely.

"No scions remain in Conhaero," he stammered out, hating how unsteady his voice was.

"One never left," Wahirangi said, and that was all he needed to say.

Finn leaned back in the saddle. He thought about the Caisah, and the one time he had seen him. It had not been a good view of him, since he'd been wearing a mask and manhandling Talyn. Could it really be that he and Ysel were the sons of the Caisah—the man that everyone knew was immortal and impotent?

Clearing his throat, Finn had to admit to himself that it was quite the turnaround to his past. Only a few months before, he had been considering himself below anyone's notice, and had to trek to Perilous and Fair in an attempt to be taken seriously. Now, his mother was the last Seer of the Vaerli, and his father the destroyer of that race.

He was just about to compose another question, when the dragon let out an almighty bellow that rattled through his being and split the air in front of them. It was loud enough to make Finn clap his hands instinctively over his ears, lest they be destroyed. It was a very good thing that he was tied into the saddle otherwise he would have fallen to his death. He had never heard Wahirangi make such a sound.

His head was ringing and his body shaking, but he leaned forward to demand why the dragon had done such a thing. His voice died in his throat because his eyes finally saw what Wahirangi had seen first: a sinuous shape on the horizon, with great wings and a head shaped like an arrow blade.

It had appeared out of the clouds, and was descending sharply and quickly toward them. Finn licked his lips. "Is that . . . that can't be another dragon?"

"You are not the only one with the power of Naming," Wahirangi hissed, as his head oriented toward the ominous shadow. "There are others . . ."

"Who would that be, then?" he asked softly, resting his hand on the long knife sheathed at his side—though he knew it for a ridiculous gesture. "Is this who you mean has corrupted the other Named?"

The dragon was silent a moment, pumping his wide wings to climb higher. An eagle, Finn remembered, always struck from above. Wahirangi had no desire to be the prey. "Indeed. The Phage," the dragon growled. "A sect of the Vaerli long hidden, but always looking for a way to trap and use Kindred."

"Never heard of them," he replied. "I've studied all the myths and legends of all the races of Conhaero—even the Vaerli. How can they . . ."

"No one speaks of them." Wahirangi's voice usually was clear, like a bell, but now there was a guttural, angry tone to it. "They Name Kindred for their own purposes, and feed off their power."

"How can they do that?"

Something rumbled deep within the dragon's chest, a threatening storm ready to break free. He banked left, catching an updraft that lifted them above the clouds, and for a moment they could not see the other serpentine shape. Wahirangi's head swiveled around, so he could obviously pierce the clouds with his superior vision. It did not make Finn feel any more secure.

"They found a way to manipulate the Pact," the dragon finally replied. "They turned our Gifts to the Vaerli around on us. Twisted them to make us prisoners. Unnamed Kindred are all in peril when the Phage are near. Named with strong Namers, we are another story."

The last part ended with growl that ran through Finn's legs and into his chest. Wahirangi was gathering himself for something. The talespinner had always heard stories of the implacability of the Kindred, but now he was beginning to understand how all that changed when they were Named. The shape of dragon came with a set of parameters that he had a feeling he was about to discover the meaning of.

Carefully he checked the tie around his legs that held him into the saddle, and wrapped his fingers tight around the pommel that rose between his legs. Then, leaning forward, he tried to keep his heart from leaping out of his own chest.

All around were damp clouds and gray light that let him see only a few feet in front of him. Wahirangi, his neck stretched out before him, could see more, and that was all the talespinner could rely on. Still, it would have been nice at this point to have at least some of those Vaerli gifts that he was apparently entitled to. All he had were his knives and a growing dread.

He dare not say anything to Wahirangi, because it was obvious that the dragon was intent on something, and besides that the talespinner did not want to break the thick silence that was all around.

When Wahirangi wrapped his wings around his body and dropped through the air, Finn managed not to scream. The air raced past his face, and everything grew numb. The talespinner was thrown backwards as Wahirangi collided with something. For a moment Finn worried it was the ground, but then a coil of granite gray skin lashed against his dragon's shoulder, and he realized that they had found the interloper.

Finally, Wahirangi had managed to find the high air and had taken advantage of it; plunging down with his taloned feet, he had latched onto the menacing creature, and was now engaged in striking at it with his saber long teeth. The beast's wings were tangled, and both riders and dragons were falling. Finn could hardly breathe or think as the air whistled around him. The snarls and screams of the dragons would have driven anyone mad, and Finn was trying his best not to be crushed as they wrestled back and forth.

Wahirangi had not taken the opportunity to ask his rider if he should attack, so his rage had to be at boiling point. Finn could only hope that the dragon's sense of survival was as strong as his towering anger.

The talespinner managed to work loose his knife on his left boot, and twisting around plunged it again and again into the gray flesh of the dragon. He had no idea if it was doing any good or not, but at least it was something.

As he did so, he caught a glimpse of the other dragon's rider, and what he saw chilled him to the bone. Eyes that looked as though they were full of pitch glared at him over the rough gray of her dragon's hide. She was a child, but like no child Finn had ever seen, and though they were falling to their death, this vision before him terrified him more. A suggestion of something else lurked around her shoulders, as if shadows clung to her, writhing.

Finn lost sight of her as the beasts plummeted to the ground, twisting and trying to get the upper hand. Wahirangi's talons eventually tore loose from their grip of the rough hide of his foe. Both dragons spread their wings and managed to catch air before catching the ground.

Finn was jerked free in the commotion, and lost his knife as the dire dragon pulled away and began to furiously try to gain height. Wahirangi quickly moved to do the same. The strong thrusts from his wings snapped Finn back in his saddle, and he had to struggle to regain his seat. He would have asked what the plan was, but he was afraid he might bite off his own tongue in the process. Also, there seemed little point in trying to argue with an angry dragon.

Instead Finn crouched low, readjusting his fingers on the pommel again. The gray dragon with his back spines appeared out of the cloud to their right, and his head turned in their direction like a snake ready to strike.

The figure on his back shouted something, though what it could have been was lost in the rush of air. The dragon's head snapped back. The meaning of that action suddenly flashed across his brain, but Wahirangi apparently knew it better than he did.

Flames rushed toward them, curls of red and gold meant to incinerate and destroy them, but at the last moment Wahirangi banked sharply to the left, turning his belly to the onslaught. The legendary toughness of the dragon skin turned away the edges of the flames, but Finn felt the reflected heat wash over him.

As he climbed, Wahirangi snarled his defiance to his enemy, and then dipped sharply, banking down toward him, with his own flames jetting from his mouth. How much dragon fire the beast beneath him had, Finn was unsure of; the legends differed on the answer to that. Certainly Wahirangi did not seem to have any shortage, as he shot toward their enemy. Was it Finn's imagination or did the creature actually look worried.

He dropped away from them, folding his wings tight and angling directly below, toward the sea, swooping low over the waves.

Finn leaned forward, prepared for the pursuit. Wahirangi, however, circled for a moment rather than following. In those seconds their adversary disappeared into the clouds and the distance.

"We aren't going after her, Wahirangi?" the talespinner asked. He could feel his blood pumping hard in his veins and was ready for more action. He had already lost one knife but was ready to lose another.

The dragon swiveled his golden head about and regarded Finn with his opalescent eyes. "I too would love to give chase, but there is something that tells me this attack has another reason."

Finn leaned back in the saddle and rubbed at the spot on his arm where the fire had come the closest. "They mean to distract us from finding Ysel?"

"Possibly," the dragon said, turning himself about to once more follow the coast. "Her Named creature is very young to engage in battle with me. We grow in strength fast, but by the taste of her blood she has been Named only recently. Perhaps for this one purpose."

"Do you think they are close to finding Ysel?"

"They sought both of you through time," the dragon reminded him. "So there is no reason to think they would give up now."

"Then that unholy child will just have to wait. We shall meet her and her dragon again," Finn said with confidence.

"She is not yet come to her powers," Wahirangi growled in warning. "And the strength of her dragon will only grow as she does. We were lucky this time. Once she has harnessed more Kindred they will both be a greater danger."

Finn shivered at that idea. "Then we must find Ysel, and before they do."

"Indeed," the dragon agreed. "And let us hope we fly faster and better than they do."

CHAPTER EIGHT

A FAMILY GATHERING

"**I** do not know what you expect to achieve by this," Baraca said, adjusting the patch over his eye. "The fight for the world is here with us."

Nyree, her skin softly glowing with the silver lettering of the *pae atuae*, stood at his shoulder, looking at Equo, and it was her eyes that he could not meet.

"I understand that the Caisah has done terrible things," Equo said, "and he deserves to be punished, but the time has come for my people to return and take up the song once more."

"You mean to fight with us?" Baraca asked, his voice full of disbelief. "You people were never much for the fighting before."

"And neither are we now," Varlesh broke in. He had taken a seat in the tent of the rebellion's leader, but he did not look much impressed. "We were the friends and allies of the Vaerli. It was to them that we owe our allegiance."

"The Conflagration is coming," Equo broke in, looking to forestall any arguments. Baraca and Varlesh had never been best friends when the rebellion's leader had been human. Now that a scion had somehow filled him, it didn't seem to have made any difference. "All of us must stand up, or the world will be consumed by fire once more. Nyree, you have the gifts of the seer—you must understand why we have to leave."

Her eyes, dark and full of stars, raked over him. He missed what they had been. When her eyes had been as his were, there had been some chance that perhaps she would fall in love with him, as he had her. Now, he knew she was lost to him.

"The Conflagration is coming, as you say, Equo," she said, her gaze no longer locked on him, "but it is imperative that we destroy the Caisah before it arrives. You can help that happen."

Equo exchanged a look with his brothers; his other selves quite literally. Si, the deepest part of their triumvirate, did not look moved by her pleas. "The Ahouri will be there at the end," was all he would say.

It did not look like it pleased the seer.

"Go then," Baraca barked, "leave us for your kin if you must, but I think it is a fool's errand. The Caisah is the greatest threat to this land."

They departed from the tent as if they were dogs being chased from a town. Equo, for one, would not go with his tail tucked between his legs.

"I am sorry." Varlesh's hand came down gently on Equo's shoulder. "Nyree meant a lot to you, I know."

"She means a lot to all of us, if you think about it," he replied, trying to keep the mood light. "I just wish I believed her visions."

As they walked to the outer edges of camp, Si kept nodding, his face an unreadable mask. Deep within him, Equo felt a curious lightness. It felt as though every step he took away from Nyree and Baraca was the right one.

Si glanced at him and smiled, as if his other half was only now beginning to reach a conclusion that he had done so long ago. Equo could have kicked himself. Had he been blinded by love and an ancient belief in the infallibility of the Vaerli for all this time?

He grabbed his brothers by the arms and pulled them behind a tent, beyond the reach of prying eyes. "Nyree," he paused, gathered his thoughts. "Nyree . . . do you think it is possible that she did not get her talents back from the Vaerli?"

Varlesh's brow furrowed. "Where else would she get them from?"

"Think on it," Equo went on. "Nyree has been the made seer of her people since the Harrowing, but she has never got her gifts back until now. Do you not find that strange?"

Si glanced up at the sky, and didn't seem to notice that his other two brothers were paused, waiting on him. "The Kindred have not returned the gifts."

That was for certain. If they had, then things would have been very different in Conhaero.

The three of them stood closer; they all knew that there was one group of Vaerli that could be responsible. "The Phage," Varlesh growled, his voice so low it barely disturbed the hairs of his beard.

The three of them considered. The faction of the Vaerli, the ones who had advocated Naming all the Kindred they could, of using them to overcome the Caisah. It was not a name that they had uttered in hundreds of years.

Equo frowned. "It would make sense though. Think of all the signs: the

Kindred on the move again, the Scions appearing. If this Conflagration is happening, then the Phage will be able to use their trapped Kindred. They could have broken loose."

The Phage had been imprisoned below the sacred Salt Plain—some said by the Caisah himself. In the days after the Harrowing, legend and myth were fairly mixed up. If the Conflagration was coming, the normal rules could be bent, if not broken.

"If that is the case, then the Ahouri must stand against them," Varlesh said, and a song seemed on the edge of his tongue. "But Brothers, should we go tonight? Nyree knows of it. Perhaps we can put it off—"

"It must be tonight," Si interrupted him, his voice stern and his dark eyes flashing in the torchlight. "Tonight or not at all."

Equo and Varlesh shared a tense look. "Very well then," Equo said, "but can we leave Nyree here, with Baraca? We know her, we know that she wouldn't be part of the Phage knowingly. Whatever and however she got her powers back, I know she is innocent. Perhaps we should take her with us?"

"Do you think we can take her away?" came the chilling reply from Varlesh. "We are not what we once were, brother. If we plan to stand against a scion and the made seer, we must go much further into the healing process."

"And so must all the others," Si added. "We must all be united, or we will fail." They stood together under the wheeling stars and considered.

"Then sing," Varlesh slapped them each on the back. "Let us sing into forms that can carry us from here—and let them be mighty forms, too. Echoes of the greatest of this world."

They had already announced their presence to everyone who had ears to hear—there was no use pretending otherwise. It was time for the Ahouri to show what they could do.

The song was of flesh and bone. It was of joy and freedom. None of the three of them cared that the whole camp could hear them. The Form Bards' song wiped away everything for the three of them. They became lost in its depths, losing all awareness of their bodies.

The Ahouri called all of life and creation and chaos, part of the One Song. Everyone was a note or a rhythm in it.

The song wrapped around them, taking what they were and making it into something else. Equo felt himself ripped apart and the sensation was deeply satisfying. They had not turned the Song on themselves for a long time, terrified that it would draw the attention of the Caisah.

Equo, Varlesh and Si remained separate beings. That song could not be sung by one voice, and could not be undone by one, either. Instead, they arose from the music as three creatures, but different.

Behind them they heard the cry of the warriors, shock or outrage it was hard to tell. Three dragons, tiny replicas of the Named Kindred only as large as a human, leapt into the sky. Varlesh wore the pale green, Equo the scarlet red, and Si was the velvety black of deepest night. They would not rival the dragon of Ellyria Dragonsoul, but they claimed the air as easily as she had. Below, Conhaero was laid out like a detailed map, one where the line of the Road cut through like a knife.

The three dragonets screamed and spun around each other in delight. The air, Equo thought to himself. They had forgotten the joy of the air. This was the domain of the Swoop and all the other birds of the Lady of Wings.

It was freedom.

They passed over the forming hills and mountains, hearing the call of their kin ahead of them like a beacon flaming on the horizon. They could no more ignore it than they could the breath in their own bodies. Still, they took the chance to experience the measure of the land, too.

As Ahouri, they could feel the people below, flesh crying out to theirs. So much pain in the world, and some of it was completely unnecessary.

Equo's sadness was mirrored in his brothers' hearts too. Once the Ahouri had been healers, beloved and cherished. Now they were fearful and fewer than ever.

The lure of place, of permanence in people's hearts was strong, and the Form Bards spoke to change and impermanence. The other tribes who had come later to Conhaero were not as in tune with it as even the Ahouri had become; they feared that change.

The three tiny dragons flew on, knowing that anything they offered to help ease suffering would be viewed with fear and disgust. Equo for one could not understand it, but it was not their goal tonight to right all wrongs, merely to find those that they had lost.

A lake had formed on the spot of the Ahouri's last meeting. It had been all manner of things before: a desert, a tall spire of a mountain, even a spouting volcano. Today it was a lonely island in the middle of a vast lake that ebbed and flowed with tides. Long amphibians that would travel with the water, existed beneath the surface—the Form Bards could feel them—but they were the only creatures in this lonely portion of Conhaero.

Certainly there was nothing to mark this spot as sacred to them, but then, that was what made it sacred. The dragonets flew to the island, and found they were the last to arrive. Not that it was a vast gathering.

Twenty or so Ahouri waited on the island, in over sixty forms. All of them were triumvirate beings, so their numbers looked greater than they actually were. They stood on the green slope of the island and looked at each other. Many wore the shape of humans, but there were a number of bird forms, and even another group of dragonets.

All of them looked concerned and wary. Varlesh began the song of change, and the throats of their forms changed to human. As wonderful as it was to wear other shapes, the human form was best for communication in groups.

The odd sensation of nerves washed over Equo. These were his people, but he had not seen any other of his kind since just after the Harrowing of the Vaerli. Their own particular destructive event had happened shortly after, but was far less known to most folk. The Ahouri had been a small group even back then.

"This cannot be all," he whispered to Varlesh, who was standing next to him eyeing the rest of their kin with something close to anger on his face. For a Form Bard he was not prone to diplomacy.

"It is all." An Ahouri who wore the shape of a tall dark-haired woman, stepped forward. Her others remained in the shadows. "After all these years, these are all of us who remain. Many, of course, are crippled and cannot take shape."

Equo bowed his head. He did not like to think of it, but it was true; if one member of the trio was killed, then the others could go on. These cripples, however, would never again know the joy of the change. They were Ahouri in name only. Given the choice, most of these Form Bards chose total death.

Time had not been kind to his people.

"Then, there are those that will not come," a man with more gray in his beard than Varlesh said, sitting on a rock and looking Equo up and down. "But even they would not double this company."

Varlesh folded his arms over his chest. "Once when one of us called, all of the Ahouri would answer!"

"Those times have passed," another near the back of the group shouted, and his voice was full of anger. "Since the Caisah fell on us, it has been each for ourselves, surviving as best we can."

At that, Equo's heart did sink. They were right. The Form Bards were nothing like they once had been. Any call to arms was going to run straight into their own desire to survive.

"Think of something else they want more," Si whispered into his ear. When he pulled back his eyes remained locked with Equo's.

The other felt the tug of loss at that. Once they had stood tall, stronger and better than they were now. They had been whole and it had been magnificent. They'd stood for something, been useful, and friend to the Vaerli. Most of all, they had a purpose.

Now looking out over the shattered remains of his people, Equo began to see it. What they wanted.

He stepped forward and held up his hand. "You are right, we have been surviving as best we can, but the time has come to point out that survival isn't everything."

A murmur passed through the audience. The trios drew together fractionally, perhaps worried that one of the Ahouri had succumbed to final madness. It would not be the first time for that either. An insane Form Bard could cause untold devastation.

He looked over them and felt genuine pity. They had sung the song of separation as a way to avoid the Caisah, and had never thought of the consequences. They had lost far more than just their unity, they had lost the will to be who they were always supposed to be.

As Equo began walking among them, he looked into their eyes, and what he saw told him the real truth. "We are already dead," he said, touching a hand or a shoulder as he went among them. "We are the broken pieces of the Ahouri, remembering what it was to be whole and real." He touched his throat. "When my brothers and I were forced to sing one of the songs to save innocent lives, I was terrified."

"We all were," Varlesh continued, finally understanding what was happening. "But it felt right." He pointed to the tall woman and the older man.

"And you know what we mean, because you felt it again tonight, when you took the form that brought you here."

Many of them hung their heads or looked away. Equo felt his anger finally begin to kindle. The Ahouri had suffered so much, but he had never thought they would lose their strength. Even when the Harrowing had come upon their allies, and the Form Bards had been so few in number, they had still stood with the Vaerli. Now they were saying that they would not risk it. He knew there were few of them, but if they surrendered now, then there was no point in going on.

Despite the rightness of what they felt, they were going to turn away—he could see that. Coming here tonight was as far as their bravery would take them.

Equo was just sinking back into despair and frustration when Si rose to his feet. He was their soul, their conscience and their compass. Equo expected there to be nothing that he could say that would move the remainder of the Ahouri to action.

"When we came through the White Void," Si began, his low voice surprisingly resonant around the hill, "we were forged like steel. We wandered through the terrors for longer than any other race that came to Conhaero."

These were by far the most eloquent words Equo had even heard his brother utter, and they sang with deep truth. He shared a shocked look with Varlesh, who only shrugged in disbelief before crossing his arms, sitting on a nearby log, and watching.

For Si was not done. "We were few, but we were powerful. All the forms of life we encountered in the Void we learned, and there were many. We understood there was always more to learn, so we avoided arrogance, which is the danger of all powerful people." Now their brother turned and pointed up. "So, we did make one mistake. We forgot about the White Void."

Every eye on the hill followed where he pointed, and every one of the Ahouri gasped in horror. Lights were pouring across the heavens, like a child's paint box spilled on a wide canvas. Rising to his feet, his body tight with wonder and horror, Equo now understood why his brother had insisted on tonight.

It was beautiful, eerie and terrifying. All of those who had passed through the White Void knew it well. They had tasted its power, and seen its coming before. When One-eyed Baraca had lifted his eye-patch and a portion of the

Void looked back, Equo had been delighted. A scion returned, but he had not wondered overly on how that had happened.

The scions were creatures of the White Void; leaders hammered and forged by the space between worlds. Magnificent, yes, but also storm crows. It was the uncomfortable truth about why they had been gone for so long.

Now as the Ahouri craned their necks upward and looked on the trickle of light running across the ceiling of the world, they had plenty of cause to recall those things.

Si's voice, so seldom heard, seemed a perfect portent for the end of things. "We must learn to be strong again, because the Void is coming, and no song we make can change that."

The Salt was pushing them forward and Byre knew he could not resist it for long. The gathering that was emerging from the haze of the Salt Plain vision was just as he recalled. Those memories he had of his family he had kept extra safe.

He wondered if what was ahead would enhance or perhaps destroy his childish recollections. Pelanor, his new lover and blood partner, was at his side, and he could feel her now in his bones. Vaerli sharing blood with one of her kind was something he had never heard of—let alone lying down with one.

What would his mother have thought? A shudder ran through him at the idea, but it was done now. There could well be stranger things in the future for them both.

The first sound to reach them was the singing; the Vaerli had made magic with their art and music was a very popular choice. Pelanor tilted her head, and one of her rare smiles flickered over her lips.

"That is so beautiful," she murmured, "but I don't understand the words."

He was ashamed to admit he did not either. The ancient language of the Vaerli, the one learned in the White Void, he had not yet learned before the Harrowing. He did not want to risk a sad discussion, so he waved his hand and dissembled. "It is about the joy of the gathering . . . they don't even suspect a thing."

Shortly, he was able to make out figures moving about among the tents and wagons, their dark skin standing out amongst the glare. Some were standing on the outskirts of the gathering, looking at him and Pelanor with hands providing shade above their eyes.

So many Vaerli, and all of them together, was an almost physical shock. His pulse raced, and he thought of the burnings he had witnessed when his kin tried to touch each other, but here they were, before all of that, kissing, rubbing each other's backs, clasping hands. A hundred little gestures that they couldn't know would soon be stolen from them.

He let go of Pelanor's hand. "If you were my mate, then we would not be holding hands," he said to her before she could get offended. "A Vaerli woman stands on her own with no man required."

His eyes flickered over her. She was dark enough to pass as one of his people, but she would stand scrutiny. She had no Gifts . . . how to explain that?

Then it came to him. "Hold your hands around your belly, Pelanor. Act as though you are pregnant."

She blinked at him. "You don't think that you have . . ."

"A pregnant Vaerli appears as a blankness to others—since she cannot use the Gifts without harming her child." He could feel that he was reddening slightly, especially after what had passed between them, but it was the only thing that would protect her.

When she bit her lip, Pelanor looked so much younger than she was, but she nodded, wrapping one hand protectively around her stomach. The Blood Witch was admirably brave to follow him like this. He doubted his sister had all these things in mind when she sent Pelanor to protect him, but she was becoming much more than that.

Byre tried not to think about her supple flesh wrapped around him, and the explosion of his senses that occurred when they shared blood as well.

Three women stood on the outskirts of the gathering, and he struggled to remember what the welcoming trio were called in his language. He cursed—not for the first time—that he had been so young when the Scourging had happened. So much of his education had been lost.

"Maybe I can pick up a bit of it here," Byre muttered to himself. The *aethai*. The memory darted up from his dim consciousness just as they came up on the women.

The overlay of memory and reality was hard to pick apart. These were not just any *aethai*—these were the exact same women who had greeted his family when they came to the gathering. They would already be there. He was already here.

How the Kindred managed to live in this curious flux world where past, present and future meant nothing was a total mystery. The aethai began to sing: a young woman with the glow of the very young on her, a second with the smile of a mother, and the third a silvered-haired matron.

It was hot on the Salt, and they wore little in order to make up for that—a loop of leather around their waists, and not much else. Byre had forgotten about this custom.

However, he had not forgotten about the other one. He sang back, just a few notes of thanks. They did not need much in the way of identification, since the Salt protected this place, but they smiled none the less, stepping away and trailing in their wake.

Byre had to keep his jaw tight, least he exclaim every few steps. Pelanor kept pace with him, her head turned resolutely forward, though he knew that she had to be longing to peer about.

The tents and wagons smelled of cooking and spices, and his mouth watered at the recollection of his kin's food. He heard, mixed in with the laughter of children and the low murmur of folks inside the tents, sounds of animals, but not any animals that the Manesto would know of.

They passed a nykur, standing patiently at the rear of a tent, its long green hair blowing in the warm wind, and he thought of his sister. Yet this could not be her beast, it was someone else's. He almost ducked when a griffin screamed above, and couldn't help sneaking a look. The black shape was startling against the bright blue sky. Pelanor flinched slightly, since she must have heard many terrifying stories of the Named.

Luckily, no one was taking particular notice of them, and Byre led them confidently forward, though he had no real idea where they were going. Ellyria had only told them to discover the truth about the Caisah. She had given them no instructions on how to act, or what to do in the meantime.

Byre had thought that he was leading them in a directionless manner, but as soon as he saw the tent directly in front of them, he realized that he had been very wrong. Some strange beacon had drawn him here.

He stopped and could not help but stare. He didn't care in that moment if he drew attention, or what anyone thought about him. Pelanor was somewhere at his side, but the rest didn't matter. It was his family's tent, and he couldn't decide if he should turn and run, or turn and run inside.

The Blood Witch at his side made a strange hissing noise, as if she was trying to get his attention, but he ignored that, trapped in indecision.

"It's theirs, isn't it," she said, and then her fingers wrapped around his arm. She was trying hard to tug discreetly at him, but he was a rooted tree.

"Come on," she whispered. "We have to find the meeting." He could feel his blood racing in her veins. It was an odd, but decidedly erotic sensation.

Finally, Byre let her pull him away from the tent with its flapping red banner, and back toward what they had come for.

Pelanor was trying desperately to keep his attention on her. She squeezed his hand. "So, tell me what you know of the Caisah's coming. I know you were only a child, but . . ."

Byre closed his eyes and thought back. He had been small, yes, but he had also been a child of the Vaerli. His memory was perfect back then, like a crystal pond before the Gifts came. As he sorted through those recollections, he felt the disconnect of reality and the past. The sounds and smells he was experiencing now were exactly the same ones he had experienced then. It made the line between memory and now blurry.

He saw his mother's face as she had turned to leave the tent. Her words echoed back from then. *The meeting has started. You have made me late, Retira.* Then she had bent to kiss his father on the brow, a genuine smile of love and respect on her lips.

With a lurch of his stomach, Byre understood his mother. She had loved them. He had always been so wrapped up in the memories of her leaving them that he had been unable to see past to those other, just as important moments.

"Mother left," he muttered under his breath to Pelanor. "She headed . . ." he opened his eyes and oriented himself within the scope of the camp once more. "In that direction."

Pelanor followed his finger, and they both saw the huge green tent that stood a little apart from the rest. It had been set up near the wide entrance to the underground part of the Salt Plain. The Blood Witch rolled her eyes, and he understood. They had both been so consumed by the chaos and heartbreak of the gathering.

They stood there for a moment, hands pressed together, and must have looked like a bonded couple. "You two lovebirds, out of the way!"

And there he stood: Drynis Alorn, the centaur. Pelanor blinked up at him, and Byre felt her whole body go stiff. She had faced Alorn in another, similar gathering place. She had told him it all, in those days trapped by flame.

He was certainly an impressive Named; thick, muscular horse-like legs, attached to an equally massive human torso. He'd been Named many years before Byre had been born, and as a child he had actually been terrified of Drynis Alorn. As a little boy he'd run screaming for his father even just hearing the crash of his hooves on the ground.

Since then, Byre had seen many, many things. He stood his ground while the centaur stamped and scowled at him. They did not want to be noticed, and an argument with a centaur was bound to draw attention to them. Byre wrapped his arms around Pelanor and pulled her into the shadow of a nearby tent. The centaur let out a angry snort, and passed them. The musky scent of him was overpowering.

Pelanor stared just as angrily after him. "I see in the past he was just as charming as when I will first meet him." She looked up at him. "One thing has always puzzled me about your people; why did they Name Kindred at all?"

It was something he had wondered in his odd time. "I don't know. Once again, I was too young to be taught such mysteries." He knew there was a deep vein of bitterness in his voice, but he didn't care. "Perhaps only because they could. Perhaps to amuse themselves they decided to play with the legends of others. Maybe it was even to cow the various tribes that they invited to Conhaero."

"I hope they didn't Name any for the Blood Witch legends." Pelanor wrapped her arms herself before jerking her chin in the direction of the large green tent. "So if that is where the confrontation happened . . . I mean . . . will happen, then where did the Caisah come from?"

It was good she herself had changed the subject, because it would do her no good to find out that the Vaerli had not spared raiding the Blood Witch mythology as well. Instead, Byre scanned the white expanse that lay beyond the gathering. "I have heard tell that he came from the Salt—but that is impossible; the Salt kills any who are not blessed by the Kindred. Vaerli."

The Blood Witch at his side was silent a moment, but she had her head raised to the wind like a dog tracking prey. "Vaerli all around me," her voice was in a soft tone, almost loving. "But to the west something else . . . something mortal."

"Mortal?" Byre followed her gaze, but even his eyes could detect nothing. "Out there? Impossible!"

"We must go," she said, taking his hand once more.

"How far?" he asked.

"Impossible to tell," she replied. The idea that they might miss learning about the Caisah, maybe even stopping him, was not acceptable to Byre. He turned and strode away, leaving Pelanor to follow in his wake like a child.

His jaw was set as he approached the nykur. The dark, clear eyes regarded him from under the razor sharp green hair. It was no Named Kindred, but it was a creature of this world. It had chosen to obey his kind, and now it would have to obey him.

"I have need of you," was all Byre said, holding out his hand and thrusting all fear away.

The unnamed nykur regarded him from its great height, threatening impalement by tossing its horned head a few times. Up this close it smelled of salt and danger.

"I need to find him," Byre finally pleaded, hoping that some of his sister's abilities still lingered in him. "They told me I need to see. Ellyria did."

The nykur opened its mouth, so that all of its saber-like teeth were visible. Pelanor, who had caught up with him, caught at Byre's elbow, but she was clever enough not to say anything.

They both stood there, easily within striking distance of the beast. When it finally tossed its head and lowered one foreleg in a bow, Byre felt as though he were hallucinating.

"Isn't this stealing?" Pelanor asked, before hastily adding, "Not that I care if it is . . ."

"The Vaerli have no real concept of personal possessions," Byre replied, as he slid his hand under the nykur's nose. "Besides, there is no owning a beast like this. He is no Named Kindred that owes anyone anything. It is his choice to come and go."

When he turned and looked at her, he knew a mad grin was on his lips. "And he has chosen to go with us . . . at least for a bit."

None of the Vaerli around them took any notice as the nykur folded his forelegs and allowed them to mount on his back. The thought flashed across Byre's mind that this was how his sister must have felt the first time she climbed onto Syris.

Pelanor leapt up easily behind him. "What a wondrous beast," she whispered. "Look, even his hair reminds me of home." She held up her fingers so that Byre could see the stripes of blood on them.

When she licked them off with her tongue, the nykur was not the only one to stir. "Waste not, want not," she said with a slight smile.

When the nykur rose, there was no choice but to hold onto the hair. Unlike Syris, this beast had no saddle on him, so they were both grateful of their leather pants and skirts. Unfortunately, their hands would not have such an easy time of it.

It was a small pain compared to the greater ones he had endured. Byre wrapped his palms around two great clumps of the nykur's hair. "Hold onto me," he said to Pelanor, which she did gratefully.

No one wanted the Witch to require more blood quickly. So it was Vaerli blood that flowed onto the nykur, which seemed only right.

The beast trotted from camp, with them clinging to its backs and feeling like children who were doing something very naughty.

"That way," Pelanor said, pointing over Byre's shoulder. "I smell the blood of something not Vaerli."

It should have been impossible, but on this day of great horror, it was almost a relief to hear her say that something was different. Something was coming.

Once beyond the camp, the nykur began to run. The flex of muscle and power under him was a heady thing. Byre now began to understand why his sister was so wrapped up in the beast. The green, cutting hair flew in the wind of the nykur's passing. It kissed Byre's skin, leaving tiny cuts where it touched, but it was a small price to pay.

Riding a horse was nothing compared to this. It felt as though if Byre asked, the nykur could carry him to the end of the world itself. It was a temptation.

Pelanor would not let him just fly away. Her senses were keen, and all too quickly she was pointing again. "There!"

Now he saw it, too. The disappearing shapes of Kindred, sliding beneath the Salt Plain, back into their own world. They neither stopped to speak to the two of them approaching on the nykur, nor gave any indication that they were aware of their arrival.

However, they had left something behind.

"Impossible," Byre whispered, even as the nykur slowed first to a trot, then to a walk.

How had the Caisah gotten to the gathering of the Vaerli, had always been the question. The answer could not be that the Kindred had brought him! That would be a betrayal of the pact between the Kindred and his people. Why would they have done such a thing?

The nykur stopped feet from where the crumpled body of a man lay face down on the salt. The curly dark hair was immediately familiar to Byre; he would have known it anywhere. The costume that he wore was strange; it appeared almost to be a kilt, but armored. An unusual looking helmet had come off his head and lay a few feet away.

Byre sprang down and picked it up. It looked like iron, but the curious thing was a line of tall feathers that ran down the middle. It made Byre think of a rooster vying for attention.

With his foot, he rolled the man over. It was indeed the Caisah—but dressed most strangely, and in a position that no Vaerli from Byre's time would have recognized.

The timeless face was as relaxed and vulnerable as a baby's, yet he knew it had committed terrible atrocities. It had ordered the death of Byre's own father. What he would do with this information now was the question. A hard ball of vengeance began to gather in the pit of his belly, and the only thing Byre knew would soothe it was blood.

CHAPTER NINE

HOPE AND NIGHTMARES

Three nights the royal mistress waited, all nerves and lack of sleep. The Caisah did not call for her and the darkness was not her friend. Kelanim sat on the wide edge of the window and looked out over the sleeping city. Perilous and Fair was always at its best when under the gentle ministrations of night; the strange silvery writing and the undulating drawings that were carved on every wall and roof gleamed with moonlight. Only the Vaerli—and perhaps Kelanim's love—knew what they meant.

They also made her think of the strange writing on the old looking piece of vellum that the centaur had her slip beneath the Caisah's pillows. She twined one lock of her long, thick red hair about her finger and tried to hold back the rush of fear that suddenly filled her belly. The beast had said it would allow him to become human and mortal again. She herself had heard him wail and complain about how he hated his immortality, how it was driving him mad . . . so she could not have done a bad thing.

The cool night breeze slipped in through the window and scampered over her skin. The delicious tug of it over her breasts pulled a little gasp from her throat. It, in turn, made her think of him. Wriggling slightly, Kelanim pulled up the hem of her night robe. It was very plain, and nothing like she would wear for him. It was made for comfort, not for seduction.

She was just about to retire to her narrow bed, when movement caught her eye. White in the dark sky, a flicker of the thin moon on a shape fluttering down toward the conical outline of the Chapel of Wings.

Wings. Kelanim sat up straight, suddenly more awake than she had been for hours. The chapel of the Swoop had been sealed up when they had proved disloyal. Their loss had sent the Caisah into a rage only matched by the one he had when the Hunter had been lost to him.

Surely the Swoop would not come back now. That would be suicide for certain.

Another possibility hit her. The Named. Many of them could fly. Gathering her robes around herself, Kelanim slipped from the windowsill and to her door.

Easing it open a fraction, she was glad that she always kept the hinges so well oiled. Out in the corridor, all was quiet. The faint smell of rosewater lingered, so that meant the servants had been past recently. Every night the harem was sprinkled with the cloying water, thought to bring peace and beauty. To Kelanim it only smelled of desperation.

Her perfume was of lilacs and cinnamon, a concoction that the Caisah had expressed an affinity for. Thinking of him still made the mistress' heart beat a little faster. If one of the Named had come to Perilous, then she would be the one that they wanted to speak to. She paused only long enough to take her dark cloak off the hook behind the door and slip it on. It was not much protection from the dangers of the Court, but it at least hid her instantly recognizable hair and provided some chance of remaining in the shadows.

The old chapel was part of the inner court, so she did not have to worry about going beyond the walls. Several times, though, she had to slip into alcoves and side corridors as eunuchs and female servants moved silently around the palace. Kelanim had never thought much on the army of lesser folk that kept Perilous running, but now it felt as though all of them were determined to keep her from reaching her goal.

Patience had, at least until recently, been her greatest personal virtue. She felt none of it now. The possibility that the centaur had dangled in front of her like a gleaming jewel had made her ache for completion.

Stealing through the corridors of Perilous like a thief, she began to fantasize about a time in the future where she might be able to stalk them as queen. Once the Caisah was a mortal, he would have no need of the other women. He would be able to think on things that normal men could, like love and raising a family.

That glowing idea made her insides ache. A child for the Caisah, one born from her womb, would be the most spectacular thing.

It made the whole mad scheme worth it.

As Kelanim got closer to the chapel she felt the cold steal past her robe and thin slippers and into her bones. Her breath was now visible in front of her and she dared not touch the stone wall of the building. The seneschal had locked the great ironbound door of the chapel tight, and she didn't have access to the key.

As the mistress stepped closer, she saw with a little thrill that the door was ajar, with a thin slice of light breaking through into the corridor.

She crept forward, certain at any moment one of the Rutilian Guard would appear and haul her off to the dungeons. She felt as though she was in danger, but curiously she was excited by it. As when she stood next to the Caisah, she felt truly alive.

A sound was coming from inside the temple. The sound of wings.

Emboldened by the thought that no one should be inside, Kelanim crept through the doorway. The chapel had an entranceway where penitents could take off their shoes, and wash their hands and feet in the small pool that stood just to the right of the next door. The water was long dried up, and the mistress did not feel the need for any ablutions.

The Lady of Wings was not her scion, and she was not even sure she believed in the scions. With as much fear as she felt, standing there in the half-dark listening to the faint sound of wings, she felt no real reverence. The scions had led the various tribes and races through the White Void to this place, but they had never been present in her life. None of them had stood up for her when her own father had sold her into virtual slavery to the Caisah. Where had any of them been when she had wailed and cried out to them? She'd wept alone in her room, wracked with fear and horror at what her own parents had done. No scion had magically appeared to whisk her away to freedom.

They were not gods, and they were not saviors, so there was no value in them.

However, there was no denying that in this moment she did feel some primitive reaction to something in the other room.

Kelanim, mistress to the Caisah, had never shied away from danger. She would not do so now.

Slowly, carefully, she went forward into the chapel. It was shaped like the dome of a dovecote, an odd realization that brought a smile to her lips. The perches lined the ceiling and walls, which soared upward in a cone-shape. Strangely, it did not smell.

One thing that the acolytes of the Lady of Wings had apparently been most studious about was hygiene. Even after all these months, it should have reeked of bird business, but instead it smelled of cedar and the memory of incense—almost like the Caisah's bookshelves.

The sound of wings broke her contemplation. Turning her head upward,

Kelanim saw that one of the boards that the Caisah had ordered hammered over the lofty entrances of the chapel had come loose.

The bird that had discovered the opening was sitting on a perch not far away, looking down at her with golden eyes. It was a snowy white owl, a creature of awe and beauty. Despite her disinterest in the Lady of Wings, Kelanim was not unmoved by the creature. It had to be one of the Swoop.

It tilted its head and watched her as if she were a mouse in the barn. Perhaps to one of the Swoop, she was.

It opened its wings and dropped toward her, transforming in mid-air.

A young woman, around whom light seemed to hover, was dressed in silver armor, with a winged helmet on her head and a long sword strapped to her hip. Kelanim did not move as the girl landed on her feet. She tilted her head, much as she had in bird form, and regarded the mistress.

"I know you," she said in stern voice. "You are one of the Caisah's whores. What are you doing in my Lady's sanctuary?"

The insult was a slap in the face to Kelanim. She was fairly sure she had never been called any such thing—even by the Hunter. "This is no longer your lady's anything!" she shot back. "You and all of your Swoop are traitors to the rightful ruler of this land, and I shall tell him as much."

She was about to turn and leave when the press of ice cold steel against her neck gave her pause. The mistress looked along its length and swallowed hard. The look in the other woman's eyes was particularly deadly.

"I am here for the tyrant's blood," she said, her voice as cold as her blade. "You will show me to his rooms, and maybe I will let you live."

For a moment panic washed over Kelanim. She wanted to live just as any mortal did, but she did not want to show one lone assassin where her lover slept, either. The mistress pushed away fear and contemplated her options.

"What has he ever done but make you a whore?" The woman's eyes, still gold, gleamed in the little moonlight that managed to reach into the chapel. "I can change all that in a moment."

Her tone was so imperious that for a long moment Kelanim was not sure how to react. She was outraged that one of the Swoop would return, but also wanted to keep her neck intact.

Then something moved in the shadows of the chapel, and it was a sound that sent a thrill of fear down Kelanim's back. The whisper of dead leaves blowing over stones. Many leaves. Only one thing that could make that sound in here.

The girl of the Swoop must have understood, too. Her eyes darted past Kelanim and into the shadows. Maybe her owl eyes gave her greater abilities to see into the dark, but it did her little good.

Kelanim had barely blinked before it was all over. The intruder turned and disappeared into her snowy owl shape, and then the creature in the shadow struck.

The thick serpent's head caught the owl even as her wings spread. The teeth and jaws closed on the bundle of white feathers, and the bird had only a moment to let out a shriek of pain before it was lost among the coils of the creature.

Kelanim stood very, very still while the snake emerged out of the darkness. One of its heads was busy swallowing the owl, while the other five examined her with flat, dark eyes. The nagi.

She'd understood instantly and instinctually. Her grandmother had told her about the nagi, with all its venom and its cunning. It was impossible that such a thing could really exist, but here it was, plucked from legend much as the centaur had been.

A Named Kindred. That some Vaerli in the past had given a Kindred such a dire name was something she could not comprehend. The Nagi was a Manesto legend, present in the tales of all tribes. It was the beast of vengeance from the shadows, and used to terrify small children into behaving.

Even now Kelanim's skin crawled as the fan of heads rose above her. The smell invaded her nostrils, stealing away her breath. The nagi reeked of old leaves left to rot away, and the hot tang of blood.

In the moonlight the snake shifted from side to side, and Kelanim's eyes flickered to follow it. She did not move, standing as motionless as the statue of the Lady of Wings in the center of the chapel.

"He said you would not flee . . . I did not believe him." The snake's voice rattled and wheezed its way out of six fanged mouths.

The mistress swallowed hard on the bile burning at the back of her throat. "So he sent you."

The snake reared back, the chorus of hisses pounding against Kelanim's ears until she almost screamed with the horror of it.

"Pholos is a fool," the nagi's coils began to emerge from the darkness, and the mistress could only think about how each of those lengths could wrap about her twenty times and be done with her life. The snake's head lowered closer to her, and the smell of the beast grew thicker. "And so are you."

Kelanim coughed and choked against the waves of it. This near, she could see the curved fangs in each mouth were as thick as her arm and as long. Twelve sets of fangs all gleamed with poison, the likes of which could not be matched for deadliness in all of Conhaero.

"Then why . . ." she cleared her throat, "then why did you just save me, if I am such a fool?"

The slitted eyes of the nagi gleamed in the moonlight. "You have a purpose in this dance, as we all do."

She recalled now the meaning of the many heads of the beast: they could see in all directions, including into the past and the future. Suddenly all fear dropped away from Kelanim. Instead of terror, she now looked into the nagi's eyes with something verging on hunger. The snake could see the future, so perhaps it could see if her goal was achievable. Was the nagi, even now, able to see her at the side of the Caisah, perhaps with a child on her hip?

"I saved you," the snake went on, its head weaving and dancing to a music that only it could hear, "because you are helping us and we are helping you, but if you do not go right now and wake the Caisah, it will all be for nothing."

The strained hisses of the heads were making it hard for her to think.

"Is . . . is the Caisah in danger?" she gasped, her hand going to her throat.

"You have made him vulnerable by opening his spirit to the guardians of this world."

A slight groan escaped Kelanim, but she was not so much of an idiot that she would spring away without knowing the kind of danger her love faced. "Who . . . who is coming for him?"

In answer, one of the heads of the nagi nudged a few white owl feathers that lay on the floor where they had fallen. The Swoop!

Without further thought, Kelanim turned to run to his rooms, but the long neck of the nagi flashed out, and the iridescent loops of its body blocked the way. The mistress looked wildly about, contemplating clambering over them for a mad instant.

"First, I have a gift to give. Make haste." The fan of heads hissed in terrifying unison. The tip of the nagi's tail flicked out, and a forgotten goblet with the carved image of the Lady of Wings on it, rattled out of the shadows. "Pick it up."

It seemed it was the only way to escape the nagi, so the mistress did as she was bid.

She stood holding the goblet, mind filled with fear for the Caisah, when the fan of snakeheads enveloped her. It was a moment from her childhood nightmares. The smell of the snake was now all there was, and the slick skin of the beast was pressed all around her. She even felt the lick of multiple forked tongues on her face. An unvoiced scream echoed through her body as she stood ramrod straight, the goblet clasped against her stomach.

One of the heads dipped down and pressed its long fang against the curve of the vessel. Kelanim heard the liquid squirt into the bowl, and suddenly all her fear was washed away. The smell of the venom was sharp, and vaguely saline—not at all how she imagined it would be.

The nagi retreated, and she was left breathing heavily, looking up at it. When she finally glanced down at the goblet, she saw it was now full to the brim with white, slick venom.

"Will this save him?" she whispered.

"Not tonight." The nagi seemed to be retreating from her, descending once more into darkness and imagination. "You must save him tonight. Leave the cup here, and if he lives you must slip this into his food. Every time he eats, there must be a part of me in him. Three times is the number. Have him drink three times and he will be yours."

By the time the last words were out of the snake's mouth, it had disappeared completely, taking the smell, the sound and its terrifying presence with it. All it had left behind was the full measure of its venom.

Kelanim carefully placed the goblet on the floor—no one would find it here. If it mattered at all she would come back and find it. If it did not, perhaps she would drink the whole thing herself. Then spinning about, she ran from the chapel, her slippers flying off her feet as she tore through the palace to the back chambers of the harem.

It was not her night to be with the Caisah; he had called another to his bed tonight. No guards were in the passageway, since it was assumed none of the mistresses would be foolish enough to enter this way. Her feet made slapping noises that echoed in the stairwell; that and her ragged breathing were the only sounds . . . at least until she reached the upper levels.

The door to the bedchamber was already open, and Kelanim ran in. Perhaps it had been part of her own delusion that she had never imagined the Caisah taking another woman to his bed—not since she had given him vulnerabilities. Even though all the others of his harem had surrounded her, Kelanim had been skillful at putting that fact from her mind.

So it was quite a shock to see real evidence of it laid, literally, out before her.

In the blue tinge moonlight, the paled-skinned beauty Uinia was writhing atop the Caisah as seductively and as fluidly as the nagi had moved. The love of Kelanim's life had his hands on Uinia's full breasts, and his head tilted back admiring the show.

Whatever she needed to do, had to be done . . . and soon. The nagi had sent her here so she would see that. The snake had told her to leave the goblet, just in case she spilt any of its precious liquid.

The threat to a dragon was not from without. Finn knew that he flew one of the most dangerous and feared creatures of Conhaero. The threat to Wahirangi was Finn himself, and what he might need the dragon to do.

They had flown for days in near silence.

His brother was down there somewhere. Ysel. He was with the Talespinners of Elraban Island. If it had not been so serious he might have thought it were a joke. He had trained there in his youth, and enjoyed every moment of the rigorous training. It had turned him from an idealistic boy into a trained idealistic boy.

As Wahirangi turned his head toward the east and the sea, Finn could not understand why he was feeling unease in the pit of his stomach.

Wahirangi had protected him from every danger, but Finn was still unsure of him. The knot in his stomach just would not abate.

The dragon was his to command, wasn't he? Yet, he had not obeyed him in all things.

They flew over mountains twisting themselves into lakes, and valleys summoning the strength to rise to mountains. It was a view of Conhaero that he had never contemplated before. The vast glory of the place, with none of the complications.

"You are silent," Wahirangi rumbled, twisting his golden head to look over his shoulder. "You are not concerned about what your mother said, are you?"

Finn had the terrible thought that the dragon could read his thoughts, or perhaps sense his doubts.

"She said I would find Ysel back at the beginning and that I must protect him," he muttered, his hands clenching around the saddle. He almost couldn't remember how it felt to walk on his legs anymore.

"Doubt is the way of the seer," the dragon rumbled, turning his curved head back toward the horizon. "Their powers are seeing the paths ahead, but none of them can claim to see the way of all things. Every person in this place contributes to the future. That is a lot to hold in one's head."

Wahirangi was right, too. "I suppose," Finn ventured, looking down from the dragon's back to the world racing by under them, "that you are right. After all, if they were really that good, then the coming of the Caisah would not have been quite a shock."

"Unless it had to happen," Wahirangi returned. He paused for a while, as he climbed higher. The sound of his wings beating against the wind was the only sound for some time. "Tell me, talespinner, to master a tale, do you always have to know what is coming? Or is part of the joy that it unfurls to you? Which would you rather have?"

Finn considered for a time, remembering how wonderful his training as a boy had been. The magic of the ending of a story—yes, it was a beautiful thing. However, now that he knew all the traditional stories, he still found them charming. "I think I would prefer to know the ending."

Something like a chuckle ran through the belly of the beast beneath him. "Typical mortal answer. That is the joy of your stories. You find satisfaction in the ending because you know it, and it is safe. Unfortunately, life—even for a Kindred—can never be known. In that chaos is great beauty, and I hope one day you will see it, my friend."

They flew on some more, the land sliding beneath them like a complicated painting. Finn was glad he had picked up some dried fruits and tack-bread before they had left the cabin in the woods. He nibbled as they travelled, and then even managed to doze.

His dreams were all of bejeweled dragons, and falling and flying. He lurched awake several times, terrified of losing his footing in the makeshift saddle and plummeting to his death.

When they finally reached the sea, Wahirangi trumpeted the announcement. He jerked out of his light slumber to see the sun sinking into the sea behind a layer of gleaming pink clouds. It had been so long since he'd seen the ocean that the effect was most visceral. He thought of her, and their time by the ocean in the tiny, cramped, dark, blissful hut.

Perhaps that was why he had unconsciously wandered always away from the sea. The smell of salt, and the bite of sand under his tongue made him think of her far too much. He cleared his throat and leaned forward over Wahirangi's shoulder. "There," he said, needlessly pointing out the home of the talespinners to the sharp-eyed dragon.

A series of tall islands ran from the white bluffs of the eastern coastline down into the sea. It was as if some giant might have once used them as a staircase as he tiptoed down to the waves. None of them were big enough to sustain a village, but they were close to one another. The talespinners had brought some of their wealth back to this place and woven for themselves a spider web town that seemed to have sprung from some children's tale. It progressed across the islands, a string of bridges and narrow buildings. Every one of these constructions Finn knew better than the back of his own hand.

He had run across many of those bridges, marveling at the crashing ocean beneath, fearless as only the young can be.

He stood up in his stirrups and looked at them in wonder.

"I used to ask the masters of Elraban how this place stood when everywhere on the coast was always in constant change. They said the Kindred had blessed it, and they loved the stories too. Is that true?"

Wahirangi let out a long breath that almost became musical. "The Vaerli told us tales once, sang us music, gave us Names. It was one thing that we missed when the Pact was broken. We do indeed halt the movement of the earth here for the talespinners, so they might have a refuge. The Caisah does not like tales, as you may remember."

Finn knew he should feel delighted to come back to the only home he had ever known, but it felt a little too much like defeat. Running back to the masters when his stories had not done their work. When he had instead taken up a past he never knew about, and abandoned his dreams.

As they circled lower toward the village, he was surprised that none came out to witness the arrival of a dragon; it was an unprecedented thing, and one that should have been recorded for all of Conhaero to share. As they got within a hundred feet of landing, he saw that there were indeed some people out to greet Wahirangi.

Three figures stood outside the main entrance, and he recognized two of them immediately. One was Koth, the master of the Talespinners of Elraban Island, and he looked as disreputable as ever. The other was the smaller figure of his brother. He had seen Ysel enough times through the pattern to know his face.

Wahirangi closed his wings and dropped the last few feet to land as silently as a cat on the wind-blown grass of the cliff. For a moment none of them spoke.

Finn worked his legs loose of the saddle, feeling the cramp of far too long in it, and hoped he wouldn't make a fool of himself as he slid down from the dragon's back. He was lucky; his legs might have felt like wet wool, but they did manage to stay under him.

Ysel was looking at him as soberly as an adult; a reminder that life in the chaos with the Kindred, and then on the run from the Phage, had not allowed him to be a child. Koth, who looked even older and more ramshackle than when Finn had last seen him, smiled hesitantly, but his gaze slipped sideways to the woman Finn did not know.

A pain shot through Finn's stomach. For a moment he thought it was Talyn standing before him. Then he made out the slight silvering in her hair, and the softer curves of a different woman. Yet, she was Vaerli. The brown skin and dark eyes told him that much. She wore a sword at her side, and the way she had placed Ysel behind and to her left made it immediately clear that she was one of the protectors that Finn had heard about from the boy. What he found odd was the strands of white in her hair, and the group of lines collecting around her eyes. He scrambled to understand for a second, and then his reading on Vaerli caught up with him.

She had gone to the mountain. Few Vaerli took that option, choosing instead to keep their connection to their kin even while they wandered, were chased, or committed suicide. It must have meant a lot to this particular Vaerli to protect Ysel.

Old Koth, after seeing no one move, and casting a wary eye toward Wahirangi, bustled forward. He embraced Finn in a warm, if pungent clasp. Koth did not approve generally of washing, hence why he enjoyed being guardian of the door. Though what he could have done against an invasion was anyone's guess.

"My boy," Koth slapped him on the back for good measure, "we've been waiting for you." His eyes darted back and forth, as he kept his back to the woman and the child. "If you want to jump back on this remarkable beast, no one would blame you." His gaze sharpened, as if he could tell Finn's tale and its ending.

It was a kindly meant sentiment, but since seeing his mother, riding a dragon, and battling the Phage, Finn had no intention of turning aside. He was no longer the simple, if radical, talespinner that he had been when he left this place.

He stepped around Koth and walked toward his brother. The Vaerli did not place her hand on her sword hilt, but her stance straightened and her eyes never left Finn. He guessed this was how his brother had survived all this time.

If Ysel had been a normal child, Finn might have hugged him, or thrown his arms around him, but he was not. He looked down into the face that was a younger version of his own. This was the boy they had sent to the world when they thought that he had failed.

It was he that had encouraged Finn to continue his rabble-rousing ways, but also to be careful. The boy was far more sober than he had a right to be, but he was what he was.

"You knew everything," Finn finally said, and he hoped none of his anger stained his voice. It was not a question, but his brother took it as such.

"Yes," he replied, his eyes never leaving Finn's. "They realized that sending you to the world without knowledge had been a mistake. They told me every-thing. I am not sure if that was the best course, either." Those words from a boy that only looked to be ten, chilled the talespinner's bones. Ysel jerked his head toward the woman. "This is my protector, Fida. Fida, this is my brother Finnbarr, called the Fox by some."

Fida relaxed a fraction and allowed her eyes to take in the magnificence of Wahirangi. "I doubt that is what they will call you now."

"Humor from a Vaerli?" Finn retorted, trying to lighten the mood. "We have come to the end of the world!"

It was perhaps the most ill-chosen thing he had ever uttered. A first impression was the most important weapon a talespinner had—or so he had been taught—and he felt he had just made a very bad one.

Wahirangi, in a display of subtlety Finn had not been aware he possessed, folded one front paw and performed a faint bow toward Fida. "Thank you for your service." His voice was low and humble.

A flicker of surprise darted over the Vaerli's features, and her eyes gleamed slightly. "I serve the Kindred, as many others have served without question, CloudLord. I hope in days to come your people will remember not all of us agreed with our leaders."

Caught in the middle of this historic conversation, Koth's eyes were fit to burst from his head, and his jaw was working as if he had a thousand questions but couldn't decide which one to let out.

Finn touched his shoulder lightly. "Master Koth, I need you to keep watch on the door. My mother said to expect a visitor. Do not be frightened by what she rides up on."

His old teacher went pale. "You warn me of this when you arrived on a *dragon*?"

It was such comments that had kept Finn amused as a boy, and it was nice to feel their touch again.

Wahirangi lowered his head until it hovered only a few feet from the master of the Talespinners, and Finn could feel a tickle of the dragon's amusement leak across to him. When Wahirangi spoke, his hot breath nearly knocked the ancient man over. "I would speak with the once-Vaerli alone. I would question her on a number of things."

Finn did wonder what those might be, but he also wanted some time alone with his brother, whom he had been separated from through all time and space for far too long. He had family now, and it was something he had always wanted, yet never had before.

As Fida tucked her hands behind her back and walked up the cliff-face with Wahirangi a little, she did glance back once, but the presence of a dragon was comfort to most people who were on good terms with him. Finn, careful not to touch his brother, walked the opposite direction.

Ysel kept up with him, but also remained silent until they reached a comfortable stone only yards from the front door. It still had a splendid view of the ceaseless sea. "You know," Finn began, "I used to sit here when I was a boy about your age, and wonder about my family."

"You have all the answers now," Ysel said, hitching himself up on the rock in exactly the way Finn once had. "Father. Mother. Brother."

Finn rubbed his hand on the rock, and looked askance at Ysel. "Not quite all. I don't have the why. Why did Putorae lie down with the Caisah? Scions are supposed to be barren, and Vaerli are not supposed to be able to produce children, so why did she think . . ."

His brother let out a small laugh. "She saw us, Finn. By looking into the future and seeing it was possible, she made it possible."

Anything to do with seers, Finn was beginning to realize, was mind-bending. "If she could see all that . . . then she knew he would kill her, too."

Ysel folded his hands on his knee. "Yes, but she must have thought it was worth it. That is what it means to be a seer, after all: to be able to do what needs to be done. Our mother was the first seer in a long time that actually did it, though."

Finn thought of what Putorae had said to him, about the Vaerli and their fear. It seemed perfectly understandable to him; the White Void was a place most fled from. It had left even the Caisah a tattered mess. No one who went into it ever came out the same. Now without the Vaerli presence in it, it would tear worlds apart.

He cleared his throat. "Can we stop it, Ysel?"

The boy leaned on his knees, staring out to sea, and looked suddenly very young. "I cannot stop it. The Vaerli cannot stop it. Even the Kindred or your dragon cannot stop it for long." He turned and looked at Finn, examining him with a critical eye. "However, you can draw everything together." He folded his legs under him. "Do you have the thread you used to find me?"

It was a strange request after so many strange days, but Finn nonetheless fished out the piece of tatty string that he had kept in his pocket all this time. It did not look like much to hang the future of all worlds upon. He held it out to his brother, his face folded with a confused frown.

Ysel shook his head, and did not take it from him. "It is your gift, brother, not mine. I haven't been in this world long enough to develop one. While Fida looked after me, I did try." He shrugged, and then a tiny smile flickered on the edges of his mouth. "I guess, though everyone thought you had failed, you just took longer to develop those skills."

Finn had to remind himself that this was no ordinary child, but like himself, a son of a seer and a scion. He wasn't offended by the assumption he was a failure; it was, after all what he had thought of himself for most of his life.

Amazing how that small voice had been quelled by the arrival of a dragon. He held up the simple loop of yarn and looked at his brother through it. It had been how he found Ysel in the first place. "What exactly do you want me to do?" he asked.

His brother shrugged. "Look forward, find what must be done."

CHAPTER TEN

A MEETING OF WINGS

Talyn rode Syris until her muscles burned and her vision blurred with tears. It had to have been days that she stayed in the saddle. The nykur would run forever, chasing himself deeper and deeper into Conhaero. The world of chaos and madness that was their inheritance sped into nothing around them.

She knew where they were, could feel it in her bones. They were drawing toward the sea and its relentless pull. The power of the land was giving way to it. When Talyn finally called a stop to the race, she was the one left gasping, draped over Syris' shoulders. Every muscle burned, and she felt as though movement and emotion had wrung her out.

The White Void was coming. That was an inescapable fact. Even though she had run from it, it was still there. The roar of the ocean might be loud, but it would not drive away fact. The nykur stood motionless as Talyn slid from his back. Though she landed on her feet, they quickly gave way, and the woman feared by so many in Conhaero ended up crumpling to the ground.

She lay there for a long time, with the sky her only view and the sea the only sound. A large part of Talyn just wanted to stay there, to give up, and let her bones go back to the earth. Did she have the will not to move? Sooner or later even a Vaerli would die without food and water. Her father was gone, she knew that. Byre was a stranger to her, a dream of a little boy she had once known. Finn was . . .

Talyn sat up so abruptly on her elbows that her head spun. Suddenly she realized she had spent a long time trying not to think about Finn. Her own tarnished memories of him, and the feelings they caused in her, had blinded her to the wonder of what had happened.

He had Named a Kindred. He had created a dragon. What, by the flame, could that mean?

Syris leaned down and brushed his nose against her hair. Such a gesture was a rare thing from the beast of chaos. Blindly she reached up and laid her palm on his muzzle. His breath ran hotter than any mere horse, but he was not out of breath in the least. The hint of the nykur's teeth against her skin reminded her how lucky she was to have him as companion. Better than a human or even a Vaerli. Syris would never give up on her. So what right did she have to do that same thing?

Shaking slightly, Talyn got to her feet. "Finn," she whispered to herself, "what could Finn be, to do all that I saw?"

Only one answer could be possible; Vaerli. Yet, he could not be, because the only flames that had come between them had been of passion. So . . . Vaerli, but not Vaerli. At least, he had Vaerli powers, but the Harrowing had not fallen on him. Perhaps then only half-Vaerli.

Talyn leaned against Syris and rolled that thought around in her head. Could Finn be the product of some Vaerli and one of the Manesto? Certainly there had never been such a thing, but perhaps someone had found a way. She stuffed down her disbelief. This was a man she had seen with a Named Kindred, after all, and this was the only explanation that she could think of. The Kindred would not have given the gifts to others, not without trials completed by someone like Ellyria.

Her legs seemed to have finally regained some of their strength. Pushing away from Syris, she walked carefully to the edge of the cliff, and looked down. It was a long way to the ocean, smashing itself on the rocks below. This line of cliffs was another of the fixed points in Conhaero, but this one had not been made for the Vaerli. The Kindred had their reasons for it, no doubt, but the Folded Edge was still something of a mystery.

It was here she had met Finnbarr the Fox, and dallied with him awhile. The Phage had said he would go where he had been the happiest. This surely had to be the place, then, for it was here that they had spent the happiest of times.

The memories he had forced back onto her told her that. Back then, there had been a fishing village in the high caves of the Folded Edge. When she squinted her eyes shut she could make them out even now. The Caisah had ferreted the fisher folk out of there shortly after the trysts between them. She had caused that to happen.

Another guilt to lay on her already hefty burden.

She was so enmeshed in these uncomfortable memories that her usually sharp senses were not tuned toward anything but melancholy. It was only

Syris' sharp nudge in her back that alerted her to a bitter wind coming in from the mountains, and what it brought with it.

The Vaerli whirled around and looked up. The forest at her back was being bent by the gales racing down from the peaks. A few broken tree limbs and disturbed leaves were not all that came with the change in the weather.

It was the Swoop. For a moment a smile lit Talyn's lips. The feathered servants of the Lady of Wings were numbered among the few of her friends. She considered Azrul, their leader and her closest confidante, whom she had not seen since Talyn left V'nae Rae. When Talyn first laid eyes on the flock of predatory birds sweeping down from the mountains on the edge of the wind, her heart actually lifted.

Then she remembered. She was no longer one of their friends. They belonged to the Caisah, and she to the Phage. On the wings of that realization, Talyn leapt onto the back of the nykur, bent low over his shoulders, and let him have his head.

The beast pounded along the razor's edge of the cliffs, unable to blur into chaos and lose the Swoop unless he turned deeper into the land. Talyn kept a firm grip on his body with her thighs, and would not let him turn. She would not be chased off her mission—even by Azrul and her feathered compatriots.

The smell of the nykur filled her nostrils and his hair cut her face, buried as it was directly in the path of his mane. The birds soon caught up with them, and now she could hear their shrieks, high and piercing, coming at her.

Talyn hunkered down lower, her face almost crushed against the nykur's massive flexing shoulder, but the eagles and hawks continued to dive at her. She dared not take the bait and sit up. Flailing at them with her sword would only unlikely unseat her, and then they could reach her eyes.

The cliffs were dangerous places for the nykur to run. Twice the edge gave way under his feet, and only with a surge of his hind legs did he get free of it. The path down to the sea and the caves seemed to be a long way off, while the fluttering of the wings and the screaming seemed to get louder.

Syris surged up and lashed out with his front feet, his mouth gaping and full of saber-like teeth. None of the Swoop seemed ready to fly directly at the dangerous end of the nykur. Instead they surrounded Syris and Talyn, flapping, calling, and diving at them.

The once-Hunter sat up straight and looked fiercely up at her once-friends. She did not draw her blade on them, though exactly why that was, she didn't immediately know. The circling cloud of predators did not attack.

When the Whitefoam eagle dropped out of the flock and transformed herself into her human form, Talyn was not surprised. Instead, she was almost grateful. Azrul still wore the shining armor of the Swoop, and she still filled it well. If there was one person in all of Conhaero that Talyn knew deserved her respect, it was the woman with the kind brown eyes standing before her. But Talyn did not take the kindness in those eyes for granted. She had seen Azrul in battle, and she was a formidable opponent.

Was this how death would finally find her, Talyn wondered as she slipped down from Syris' back. Her hand didn't stray toward her sword or her pistol. If the end was going to come, then perhaps it would be best from Azrul. Maybe it could even help Talyn's friend.

The leader of the Swoop looked down at Talyn from her greater height, and there was none of the usual smile on her lips. "You shouldn't have run," was all she said.

The Vaerli shrugged. "I thought you and your kin liked a little bit of a chase." She could not meet Azrul's eyes, so instead she looked out over the ocean. "I suppose he has asked for my head . . ."

"The shackles have been broken," her friend replied, and then her smile broke through. "The Swoop no longer answers to the Caisah. We no longer do his bidding."

Talyn blinked, hardly able to believe what she was hearing. The Swoop had been his for almost as long as the Harrowing had been on her own people. Talyn let out a whoop of delight and threw herself at Azrul.

The sudden embrace must have caught the leader of the Swoop a little off guard—and truthfully it had done the same to Talyn—but soon Azrul was hugging her back.

"Something good . . . finally," the Vaerli said, finding herself laughing. "You have broken your shackles, and so have I."

They hugged, and pounded each other on the back for a long time. When they finally let go of each other, the rest of the Swoop had dropped to the ground and taken up their human forms. Each of the armored women viewed them with steely glances. The Vaerli understood their looks. She was not exactly beloved by all of the Swoop—after all as far as they knew, she was chained to the Caisah and his hound. Even when she told them the truth, she doubted it would change much.

Azrul swung Talyn around by her arm. "See here, sisters, another has found a way to free herself of the evil of the Caisah. Truly One-eyed Baraca has made this miracle."

Talyn's smile froze on her face. "Did you say One—"

"Yes," Azrul said, grinning at her as if they were both children. "A true scion has found his way back to Conhaero. The Swoop has sworn allegiance to him."

"A scion?" Talyn pushed her dark hair out of her eyes. "Are you sure?" She knew her friend had a need to believe.

A flicker of a frown passed over Azrul's face. "I know a scion when I meet one, Talyn. The mark of the White Void is unmistakable—but tell me, how did you get free of the Caisah."

Suddenly the Vaerli was ashamed of what she had become. "I had help," she said lightly. "It turned out to be easier to accomplish than I thought." The image of the circling, trapped Kindred heads flashed in her mind, and she knew she had to change the subject quickly.

"So, what are you and the Swoop doing out here on the edge of nowhere?" she asked, hoping her voice betrayed nothing more than interest. Azrul might be kind, but she was also prone to sharp observations.

"We are heading toward the talespinners of Elraban Island," the Swoop leader replied, though there was a suggestion of a frown on her face.

The talespinners! Talyn felt another memory open like an unwelcome flower within her. Finn had trained there for many years. They had met shortly after he had finished that same training. She swallowed and contemplated an uncomfortable possibility: perhaps this was not the place where Finn had been happiest.

The Phage had many cruel ways, and not all of them were physical attacks. In many ways, they were worse than the Caisah had been. When he had held her leash, her greatest pain had been the embarrassment of her predicament. The shattered remnants of her people had deliberately used her memories and her love for Finn against her.

"Talyn?" Azrul's smile faded from her lips.

It was too much to share. Talyn wanted there to be just one person in the whole of Conhaero that thought well of her. If her friend knew that she had merely traded her slavery to the Caisah for another—perhaps worse—master, then at best she might think Talyn a fool, at worst she would be a monster.

So the Vaerli did something she was ill used to doing; she lied.

"Sorry, I was just thinking of my brother; he always did love a good tale." Her eyes drifted to her saddlebags and the tall scroll of paper that was visible from it. She had stolen it from the Caisah, that was true, but probably One-eyed Baraca would also have been interested in it. Smoothly, Talyn slid herself between Syris and Azrul. "What is your business at Elraban Island? Not many people visit the talespinners."

Azrul shrugged. "Baraca has been having dreams. Dreams of the . . ." She stopped, struggling with something. "He's been having dreams of the White Void. Some of the dreams are not even when he is asleep."

"A scion having wakening dreams of the Void?" Talyn nodded calmly, as if every nerve in her body was not thrumming with fear. "And you go to consult the talespinners? All of you?"

"The Caisah has not attacked Elraban," Azrul said, "but he could. They hold much knowledge in their memory that has been lost to the ages . . . even from the Vaerli." She crooked an eye at Talyn. "Since our paths appear to be in the same direction, Talyn, would you care to have an escort there?"

Her friend could not imagine what awaited them there, but Talyn would not deny it would be good to share some time with Azrul. "I can think of no finer escort than the Swoop."

Syris, perhaps to show his usefulness to this collection of women, bent his knee so that Talyn could mount up easily. When he surged to his feet the tables were turned; the Vaerli towered over Azrul. A smile cracked on her face, and it was no lie. "Remember how we used to race?"

The leader of the Swoop was already gathering herself to spring into the air. "We are the masters of the sky, old friend. I think you are over estimating how fast that creature can carry you."

Talyn thought of the dragon that Finn had conjured, and barked out a laugh. "You think you are the masters of the sky. Let us see if that is true."

She did not need to urge Syris at all. He leapt through the air, bounding away like a hound released after a rabbit. Talyn decided she was going to enjoy this brief moment. The cliff was high and terrifying, but it was nothing compared with what was to come.

As the three unlikely companions walked down the salt-carved steps and into the Bastion, Byre nursed the need for vengeance for a moment, rolling about in his head the memory of his father crumpling to the floor and the tales of what his sister had done at the Caisah's command. The knife at his belt felt like it was calling to him.

At his side Pelanor drew in her breath, and he understood her shock. He himself felt numbed by this turn of events. Yet, her reaction reminded him of another thing: he was not the only person who had scores with the Caisah. Was it right of him to take the chance, when there were even more citizens of Conhaero who could not?

Swallowing back his initial reaction, Byre crouched down next to the new arrival. A strange smell lingered around the man, like a breath of winter in the baking heat of the Salt. Even as he examined the man, it was burning off and disappearing. Byre wondered what it could mean.

As it dissipated, they were at last left with the man himself. Byre carefully examined the clothing he wore; this was an opportunity to understand the Caisah in a new way.

He wore armor and a long red cloak. The series of iron plates over his front, back and down each arm were articulated and would have slowed even the stoutest blow. They were, like the helmet, totally alien. Byre, in his time of wandering, had seen many, many things—but none like this. Carefully he ran his fingertips over the armor. The warmth of the Salt was beating down on the metal, but he could still discern the freezing cold that it had been exposed to.

The White Void was supposed to be more frigid than anywhere in Conhaero, and it was the only way to travel between places. It made a kind of sense. The Caisah was not Vaerli—he could not have made it through the Salt's defences otherwise. However, that meant that the Kindred had helped him, opening the way to the heart of Vaerli society. It could hardly be believed, but the Kindred, who were in a sacred pact with the Vaerli in this moment of time, had delivered their greatest enemy into the heart of their kingdom from the White Void itself.

Byre glanced over his shoulder, but he didn't need to ask Pelanor if she recognized any of the Caisah's dress, because her expression was just as baffled as the one he felt he was wearing.

His many dire thoughts were interrupted when at Byre's feet, the Caisah moaned, his eyelids fluttering madly.

"Why don't we just kill him now?" Pelanor whispered, her fangs now visible and lying against her full bottom lip. Perhaps she was thinking of drinking from the most powerful being in Conhaero. What would happen if she did? It was an interesting question.

For a moment, Byre's hand rested on the handle of the long knife at his hip. The greatest enemy of his people was lying completely vulnerable before him. Only one thing stopped his hand from striking: Ellyria Dragonsoul had told him he had to watch. He could only observe. He was merely here to learn the nature of the Caisah, to see the Harrowing with the eyes of a grown man and not a frightened child. The temptation to do more was pressing down on him like a physical weight. He found he was having difficulty breathing.

Finally, Byre let out a long, tortured breath. He could barely believe what he was about to say. "No, Pelanor, we can not do that. This is the past, it has already happened. If we disrupt its progress then unintentional consequences could—"

"You are living this," she said, snatching his hand up and pressing it against her chest. He could feel his blood within her, racing hard and fast. "You have a chance to slay the originator of the Harrowing, and you will not do it?" She was looking at him with something verging on disgust.

He could see in her eyes that she couldn't understand what he was thinking.

Maybe he couldn't either, but he was trying his best to see the larger picture.

"If I spill his life here and now," Byre said, locking his fingers around hers, "then the ripple of such a mighty change could tear the future apart. We are here as observers only."

She glared at him, her fangs evident, and along the grip he had on her he could feel her trembling with desire to use them. Yet for all her excitement, this was not Pelanor's Harrowing. It belonged to the Vaerli.

"Do you understand me?" Byre said, keeping his voice hard and grim. He twisted her arm a little, knowing that her strength was far greater than his. She could have broken his grip at any moment.

Pelanor looked very young to him, standing there ready to defend a people she didn't know from a threat she didn't understand. It reminded him of his own distant youth. Quick action was the privilege of the young; the time to repent it that of the old. Byre kept his gaze steely before her. He could not afford her to run free on her instincts.

"Yes," Pelanor finally returned, yanking her hand free of his with a flick of her wrist. "I want you to remember this moment, and remember I counseled death for the tyrant. I think you shall regret it later."

It was only when the Caisah shifted on the ground before them that they realized he had been listening to them. Some time in the middle of their argument he had awakened, and had lain very still while they discussed his life and death. It seemed very unlike the Caisah Byre had encountered previously, or the one that was whispered about in hushed tones throughout Conhaero.

When Byre turned his attention once more back to their soon-to-be ruler, he realized that something else was different; looking at him was no longer a simple thing.

Byre blinked twice, and took a step to each side, just to make sure that it was not some weird trick of the blinding light of the Salt. It was not.

The air was bent somehow around the Caisah, as if every beam of light needed to touch him. Among all the whiteness of the Salt Plain, he was its brightest feature.

Byre wanted to ask him about this curious phenomena, but when their gazes locked all questions were suddenly answered. Behind the Caisah's eyes the memory of the White Void lingered. It had touched him, and made him its own in a deep way that reached beyond what he was. A sound tore at Byre's ears, though he was not sure if it was audible. Its screams demanded bone, flesh, and mind bend to its will. Now the white of the Salt paled to nothing as the real white seemed to wash over them both. Dimly, the Vaerli realized that he and Pelanor had crashed to their knees before this call. They were dazzled and undone by it.

Then the Caisah blinked; just once, long and hard. Then he shook his head, and the White Void was no longer with them. His eyes were now merely a clear, unremarkable blue—perhaps clouded with uncertainty, but nothing that far from mortal.

While he looked across at Vaerli and Blood Witch on their knees before him, Byre struggled with yet another fact. Only the scions that had seen and beaten the White Void kept it beneath their eyes. The distance between worlds was not travelled idly, and without the guidance of a scion none of the tribes that now inhabited Conhaero would have made it to safety.

He had never heard of the Caisah being a scion. His people revered scions, and when they had retreated from the world there had been much despair. The Caisah had only ever caused despair with his presence.

"Where . . . where am I?" the new arrival asked, and he sounded nothing like the man that Byre had faced over the body of his dead father. Uncertainly was written in every inch of his body, while his face resembled nothing more than a child who had lost their favorite toy.

It felt strange indeed to know that he was giving information to destroyer of the Vaerli, but Byre knew he would have to tread delicately.

"This is Conhaero," he said as calmly as he could manage. At his back he could feel Pelanor's lust still beating—perhaps now more than ever. The blood of a scion had to be a tempting target.

"Conhaero?" the Caisah repeated, raising a hand to his head as if he expected to find blood there. "Yes, Conhaero, of course. Conhaero."

So many questions raced through Byre's mind that he simply couldn't choose one. So many scholars had debated where the Caisah had come from, and how he had appeared on the sacred Salt of the Vaerli. Now that the Vaerli had managed to remind himself that he was an observer only, he realized that he should at least try to learn more about the tyrant of Conhaero.

"Did . . ." he paused to clear his throat. These next few moments could mean everything to his quest to return the Gifts of the Vaerli. "Did you come far?"

The man, who looked so young despite what he was, looked at him strangely, but did not answer his question.

Instead, he shifted slightly. "I have a message to deliver," was all he said, then he levered himself upright, and brushed the salt from his strange costume. When he finally got to his feet he was a little unsteady, but Byre did not move to help him. He was afraid if he touched the tyrant, he might be tempted to throttle or stab him.

Also, he didn't know what to say to that. If he assisted the Caisah, he was helping the man who had murdered and enslaved his own sister, but he couldn't just walk away, either. While he thought quickly about what answer to give, Pelanor raised her hand slightly to get his attention. While the Caisah turned slowly around, taking in the expanse of the Salt, she pointed out what she had found to Byre.

It was a staff, as tall as a man, made of some strange deep colored wood, and surmounted with a great golden eagle with spread wings. Byre had no time to tell her to leave it, because like all Blood Witches, she moved fast. Pelanor pried it upright and turned it this way and that, examining it in the bright noon sun.

The Caisah—who had apparently regained his strength quickly—moved as swiftly as a pouncing cat, grabbing hold of the staff and thrusting the Blood Witch aside as if she were a mere mortal. A normal woman would have fallen off her feet, but Pelanor darted backward, and glared at the man with rage that might turn to blood if the Caisah wasn't careful.

"No woman can touch the eagle," the newcomer said, his shoulders straightening, as if suddenly realizing he did possess pride.

Byre thought of the Swoop, the worshipers of the Lady of Wings. Their symbol was a bird, too, and in his time the Swoop was used by the Caisah to enforce his will. This could well be the answer to how that particular outrage had happened.

He ran his eye over the man once more, taking in the sword sheath at his side. A warrior then, wherever he had come from—but he looked so young. A scion, a friend of the Kindred. None of these things had he been aware of.

Yet, what person had ever known the Caisah? Not even the women he shared a bed with. However, all that lay ahead of him. For now, he was very new to Conhaero. He swept his cloak around him, and unnervingly turned his face toward the gathering.

"I must give my warning," he said, as if they were his underlings. "I gave my solemn oath to deliver it." With that, he set off walking toward the Vaerli meeting place, in a strange military step that Byre had only ever seen on the Rutilian Guard before. Another puzzle piece dropped into place.

A solider that had come through the White Void. If this was purely an intellectual exercise he might have been delighted, but for Byre this was far more than that. This was the end of his people.

The Caisah was walking toward history, and all Byre could do was watch him, mesmerized.

Pelanor tugged on his arm, her smaller size completely irrelevant to the pull she could exert; his blood in her veins gave her plenty of strength. "We must follow him," she hissed impatiently.

He did not want to. He had no desire to watch the wounding of his mother, the Harrowing of his people, and the flaming deaths of his kin. Yet, Ellyria Dragonsoul had endured far worse for the Vaerli.

Byre hastened his own footsteps so that they trailed the Caisah only by a little. Byre shivered at the thought that to an outside viewer it might look as if they were acting as an honor guard to him.

They approached the gathering again, and this time there was no guard to come out to them. Instead the Vaerli themselves came out. Perhaps they had felt the disturbance through the Kindred. Byre pulled up the hood on his cloak reflexively, and shot a glance across at Pelanor. She took the hint and jerked hers up, too. It would bring shame and danger on her people if a Blood Witch was recognized traveling with the Caisah. Byre certainly did not want his face associated with the Caisah, especially with what was to come.

The ranks of the Vaerli came out from their tents and wagons to watch with dark eyes as the man the Kindred had brought approached. He leaned only slightly on the staff with the eagle surmounting it, but his bearing was erect. He walked toward them, with Byre and Pelanor trailing unhappily in his wake. Luckily, he did not acknowledge them at all.

When he stopped only feet from the first of the Vaerli, they did too. Silent sentinels to what they knew was coming.

Immediately Byre was grateful that he had put up his hood, for his father Retira stepped out from the crowd. He was as he had been when Byre was a child, though he had not observed how much his father had changed when he had rescued him from the Caisah's prison. Retira had a thick mop of jet-black hair, and his beard had only a few strands of silver to mark it. His eyes, as all of the Vaerli's, contained endless points of light. Stars that the Vaerli had put there to mark the Pact.

"You are not Vaerli," Retira spoke directly to the Caisah, and Byre was grateful for that, too. He did not know how he would have reacted to his father acknowledging him. "I do not know how you have bested the sacred Salt, but you must turn back."

Several of the Vaerli wore dark looks, and many hands were on the hilts of swords. They were ready to defend what was there, and a ridiculous hope sprang in Byre's chest. What if the Caisah was killed before the Harrowing could be released? It would not be his fault if that happened. Maybe time could re-write itself?

"I am here to see Putorae," the Caisah said. The seer's name sat oddly on his lips, as if he did not quite know how to pronounce the syllables, and the emphasis was not exactly right. His words were also stilted, and Byre suddenly understood that these words were not simply chosen. This man had practiced these words many times before.

He had been schooled.

The duplicity of the Kindred grew deeper in his mind, and he almost reached for his own long knife then and there.

When he spared a glanced across at Pelanor, he caught the tiniest shake of her head in his direction. It was enough of a reminder that his weapon stayed in its sheath.

While he continued to wrestle with that awkwardness, a ripple of whispers ran through the Vaerli assembly, and he knew what they were thinking. His father's demands were a bluff. Any who crossed the Salt could only be a Vaerli, and there were no rules to contain a Vaerli at the gathering. As for the seer, she belonged to the people, and any of the people could call on her as they wished.

The Caisah's head turned as he examined all those before him, and then in one swift movement he bent and laid his sword out on the Salt for them.

Byre wondered how defenseless he actually was, but it was a gesture that all peoples could understand. As his eyes scanned the crowd for his mother, or even his sister, he could feel his heart hammering harder and harder in his chest. He did not want to see this.

In many respects Ellyria might have had the easier testing. It was a red-hot knife beneath his skin to see so many faces that he vaguely recognized, and yet to know that he would never see them again. He was trapped between awe, horror and trying to soak up as much of this as he possibly could.

"All may speak to the seer," the Caisah said, and though his voice was soft, it carried.

The word magic, the *pae atuae*, could not be disobeyed. From what Byre knew of his own people they were sticklers for pacts, oaths and honor. Slowly, the press of Vaerli parted, and the way was clear to enter.

Byre kept his head down, only daring the occasional glance up as he followed the Caisah deeper into the sacred heart of Vaerli life. He kept his jaw clenched, lest he blurt out a warning. As they followed behind the Caisah,

Pelanor drew closer to him, and her fingertips trailed against the edge of his cloak. Byre would not allow himself the comfort of her touch. It was the least of things he could do to share his people's suffering to come. Very soon they would be alone, and he would share that with them.

As he glanced out from under his hood, he caught glimpses of the Vaerli watching this odd, small procession pass them. He tried to hang on to the little details: the weapons they carried, their confused expressions, and even the musky smell of too many bodies out too long in the baking heat of the Salt. Every one of these details was something of the experience he had been too small to hold on to.

He noted that his father did not follow the Caisah down the cut steps and into the council chambers beneath the Salt. As they walked past him, Byre held his breath and clenched his hands, least he lose control and grab hold of the man who had already died for him. What he could not control was one last look as they descended the stairs.

It was just a split second where their gazes locked together, but Byre could have sworn that his father gave a slight start. As a child, Retira had always told his son how much he resembled his mother. Since Retira had never mentioned this moment to Byre, he must have cast aside any strangeness about the hooded stranger as merely some kind of hallucination in a truly evil day.

They were soon past the press of Vaerli, and headed into the chamber of the council. Though Byre had always dreamed of seeing such a holy, sacred place, this was not how he had imagined it would go.

CHAPTER ELEVEN

THE FLAME RETURNS

The Ahouri watched the sky change above them. Unlike the other times when they had been in charge of change, they did not seem to care much for it. Equo was watching his kin's reaction to this terrifying show of lights more than the lights themselves.

"It is the White Void, isn't it?" Varlesh asked, unconsciously edging nearer to his brothers.

"Yes," Si replied. "It has finally returned. The Conflagration."

"It's beautiful," Varlesh said, his gruff voice stained with a rare kind of awe.

Equo tilted his head back and watched the play of colors across the sky. He imagined how different it would have looked to the Vaerli while they were the only race to live in Conhaero. Perhaps they would have remembered the Pact they had made with the Kindred, and quailed.

A pact made in the dim reaches of time, one they had surely consigned to the back of their minds and simply dismissed as part of legend, was now coming to haunt them.

So they had run from it, tried to find a way to escape their fate. They had sacrificed their own children on the Steps, and instead of going into the Void, they had called others, like the Ahouri, to them. By adding their blood and strength, they had managed to fend off their obligations.

Now, looking up at the streaming white and blue across the whole sky, he knew it for what it was; a summons to the Vaerli. One last chance for the first people of this land to honor the Pact.

If they did not, the balance of chaos and order would be undone. It was more than Equo's imagination could manage, all the worlds in the Between that would suffer.

Suddenly the fate of his own people did not seem as important as it had only moments before.

As the Ahouri watched, the lights in the sky gathered themselves, turned and twisted about each other, until the sky was alive with hundreds of burning, spiraling tornadoes which were now reaching to the earth below like many angry fingers.

The Ahouri answered as best they could. Leaping into the sky, they claimed the forms they had used to reach this meeting place, and would have fled. Si, however, called to them, and the voice of the conscience would not be ignored.

"Fly, but the Void will have you, and that will be the end of the Ahouri."

Tiny dragons, birds, massive insects with whirling wings, all paused. The White Void was streaking down to earth everywhere. Some would escape, but the trios would be destroyed. By gathering together, they had allowed one devastation to hold the future of their whole race.

Equo knew this was his doing, but was not sorry for it. What sort of life had his people led since the Caisah had hunted them? He laughed as the wind tugged at his jacket. Maybe it was the most fitting way for the Ahouri to finally end. The White Void was merely putting them out of their misery.

He grabbed for Varlesh as the rock around them shifted. It seemed even the world was not stable enough to hold them, and they would be crushed between sky and land. As Equo tumbled from his feet, he caught the image of Si still somehow standing upright, silhouetted against the approaching White Void.

They were all falling—at least, those who were not flying. Equo could have reached for the form, but it seemed such a waste of energy. Let the Void have them. They had teetered on its edge for long enough.

When that thought flashed across his mind, he was suddenly rising. Hands that were impossibly large were holding him. Now it didn't seem an easy thing to go.

He swiveled around and looked into the flaming eyes of a Kindred. This one was not as the one that had latched onto Finn. This was larger and far more threatening. Around him other Kindred were also aiding the remaining Ahouri.

Kindred who had not been seen for a very long time.

Will you join with us, Form Bards? Will you join your blood to this world?

Equo frowned at the question. "Conhaero is our home, it was our refuge. Take whatever is needed."

The pain that went through his body was like he had been speared by something. When he was left gasping in its wake, he stared down at his body, expecting to be bleeding everywhere—dying, even. Yet nothing was missing.

When he looked up, he saw trails of Ahouri blood spiraling up to meet the blinding White Void. The roar of it was so deafening that nothing else could be made out over it. Even the screams and howls of his people. It might have been a song, or it might have been merely a primal outrage at the thing they feared most.

Equo remained silent. The White Void had too many of their songs already; he would not give it another one.

He watched impassively as the maw descended toward them, not flinching. His only thoughts were of Nyree and how he should have said so many things to her. Then, just as suddenly as it had disturbed the night, the tornado whirled back up, and away. The sound of its passing was like a beast abruptly silenced.

The quiet after it was also as painful. The Ahouri gave up their winged shapes and dropped to the ground in human form. If they had been unconvinced by Equo's admonishments, then the appearance of the White Void and the Kindred had changed all that.

One by one, they bent in bows to the masters of Conhaero who stood in an impassive circle around them, watching with them with eyes that flamed. They were shapeless masses, but they did not menace the Ahouri as Equo might have thought they would. Together they had stopped the incursion of the White Void. What could they not do?

As if it could read his thoughts, one of the Kindred turned to him. *We have not turned the White Void aside, Master Ahouri. Merely beaten it back for a spell with your blood.*

"Then what did you take our damn blood for?" Varlesh blustered, though his eyes were wide with recently departed alarm.

The Kindred were silent.

"Something has changed," Si ventured, edging closer to one of their number and peering at them. "Why have you come now?"

It was impossible for the face of a creature made of rock to convey any real emotion, but the voice projected into their heads sounded almost contrite.

We gave up on all surface dwellers. We had made a pact with the Vaerli, and they broke it. You might call what we felt despair, and we stayed long in the ground. One of our number, though, thought that change was possible. He dared to hope, and rose to find *answers. He found more than that; he was Named by one you call friend.*

It could only be one person.

"Finn Named a Kindred?" Equo felt as though there was no end to the strangeness of the day.

Not just Named. Named him dragon.

"A dragon," Varlesh whispered, his eyes darting over the clear skies as if he were imagining him there right now. Even the Ahouri had not dared that shape. It carried weight and significance beyond just its form.

As have others. The Kindred shifted through the earth drawing nearer—it could not be out of fear. *You have already seen her in the skies. She is nearly ready* *to come out of hiding.*

Equo thought of what Azrul had glimpsed in the skies above their camp and shivered. "What do you want of the Ahouri?" he asked, knowing in his heart of hearts that the answer would cost his people dearly. "We are not slayers of dragons."

No, but you are part of the Pact now. Just as we have made pacts with the *Phaerkorn, the Choana, many of the Manesto tribes. They all know what is at stake,* *and we are all bound together by blood. Now we come to you.*

The Ahouri all looked at each other. Though the Form Bards had long been allies of the Vaerli, they had never had much discourse with the Kindred. That the enigmatic masters of Conhaero should now be seeking to make pacts with all the newcomers was a definite change.

Equo swallowed, thinking for a moment how one choice to call for a gathering was now making his trio leaders in a people that had never had much call for them. When he looked around at how few there were, he could also see how none of them were stepping forward to complain. They were indeed a people on the edge of non-existence.

"What do you need from us?" Varlesh spoke for them, tilting his head up and looking as confident as he could manage. It was a bluff, but one that Equo was sure he didn't have left in himself.

You have something sacred and necessary to this world's survival. You know and *love her. You must bring her to the Belly of the World, where she will be tested along* *with all the other Vaerli. It is their last chance.*

Equo felt as though he had been punched in the gut. "The Vaerli?" he blurted out. "You mean to kill them all, then. The curse will set them all on fire. They will die if they gather as we have tonight!"

All must come, or all must die. That is their calling. You must only bring the made seer to us. Without her there will be no chance of survival. The seers must stand together or the White Void will consume this world.

One of the Kindred shifted away from his peers, and his burning face turned back the way Equo, Si and Varlesh had come.

Already, the Phage mean to make her theirs. Fly if you want to save her.

Equo had the song already forming, but it was Si who turned back for a moment. "And the Ahouri?"

We have a task for them. The Kindred replied. *They will be our heralds, and sing the songs that are needed. Have no fear for them. Fly, or lose your seer forever!*

They let the notes of change surround them, becoming the dragonets once more, and turned their heads back they way they had come. Equo was at the head of their little formation, his mind already focused on Nyree, the Kindred almost forgotten.

Without any further instruction from his brother, Finn sat down at the base of the rock, propped his hands up on his knees, and held the loop of yarn before him. It seemed like such an everyday thing to lay so much on.

When he glanced up, Ysel was watching him with absolute clarity in his eyes. He had not moved from his spot of the rock, and looked like he could have waited there forever. Such patience in one that seemed so young did not seem right.

"Too much thinking," Finn whispered to himself under his breath. "Time for some doing."

He had not worked the pattern in the thread since before his Naming of Wahirangi. A lot had happened since then, and he recalled that even before then, the pattern had fought back against him.

"You're different now," Ysel said, giving his brother a hesitant smile. "You know what and who you are."

The clamor of thoughts would hardly let him go, but he thought back to his talespinner training. Koth had taught all the youngsters the art of preparing for a performance.

Finn rolled his head round a few times with his eyes closed, letting his mind quiet as best he could. He concentrated on his breathing as if it were the most important thing in the world. That empty space was usually where he found his strength to speak before an audience, but it was also the place where he had found the pattern to reach Ysel.

Now in that space, he recalled the first time he had woven the pattern. He'd been sitting beside a meager fire, on a long night when he had been chased from another town. The stars had been his only companions, and his belly had been aching with hunger. One of his old coats had become frayed, and he'd played idly with the thread before pulling it loose. Finn recalled the feeling of utter hopeless that had washed over him as he had played with the piece of yarn. He could never say at what point he had tied it into a loop and begun to mindlessly repeat the child's game.

Holding on to those memories, Finn began to wind the thread into the familiar patterns. He did not think of what his brother wanted from him, not even what a certain dragon had seen in him. Instead Finn thought of a face cupped in his hand. He thought of dark eyes, and lips that had been made for kissing and smiling, yet had seen not much of either of those things. He recalled how happy he had been, and how nothing else had seemed to matter in those brief days. Despite the fact he had told her that she was nothing to him, and denied her to his mother, she was still in there.

The string tightened, and Finn looked down in shock to realize that he had made an intricate pattern that almost felt in danger of cutting his fingers off. It seemed like a ridiculous thing to be worried about, but for a second he panicked just a fraction. If this was his power it was not much of a one, to make a trap out of a children's game.

"Here," Ysel said, sliding down off the rock, and taking a position up opposite his brother. "Let me help."

He inserted his fingers into the pattern, and pulled the design back and forward a few times. For a moment it felt like the yarn itself was going to break, but in between the tugging between the brothers, and some low cursing from Finn, the yarn sprung apart.

Finn and Ysel exchanged a look. The shape was a cat's eye, held between their fingers.

"I thought you said it was my power," Finn said, examining the pattern they had made at as much distance as he could manage without pulling it apart.

"I thought . . ." the boy stammered, and suddenly the talespinner felt sorry for him. He'd been held for a long time in the belly of chaos, and then been hidden away for so long—yet he remained in essence a child.

"I'm joking." Finn tilted his head. "I think perhaps the magic works best for us together. Alone I always had trouble with it. It looks like the cat's eye formation, all right."

"Then look through it," Ysel said, though his voice held no real conviction.

Carefully with their hands working in unison, Finn was able to raise the thread to act like a pane of glass. At first he was looking into blackness, darker than night or loss of hope, but then it cleared through gray, white, and finally flaring red. It burned so hot that Finn almost jerked his head away.

When the burning cleared enough, he was looking out over a plain, smooth and dimly lit by a red moon. It was the moon of Conhaero, but masked by clouds that boiled with dangerous colors. A tall mountain rising dark against the skyline punctuated the plain. It was spewing out thick clouds, and the rattle of rocks sounded all around.

Finn saw another shape in the clouds, a dragon with wings spread, sailing the skies above the withering mountain, but it did not have the golden sides and curved head of Wahirangi. Its longer, more serpentine shape had a crest of long, sharp spines down its back. He squinted, concentrating harder. A small shape clung to its back, on a saddle. It was far too small to be an adult, and a streamer of dark hair flew out from behind it.

Below the dragon, on the edge of the lava and fire, stood four figures facing the interior of the volcano. None of them moved, despite the danger and the dragon apparently circling lower toward them. Their hands were linked, and Finn could feel something from them. Unity. Determination. It was like a lodestone pulling him in.

His gaze darted upwards again, and he realized that the dragon was now terribly close to the figures. Now all he felt was terror for them. He had to warn them somehow.

The dragon and rider turned their heads toward him, and those eyes flared brighter even than the red light all around them. They were staring out at him, and this dragon, like Wahirangi, could see right into him. There was no escaping it.

The yarn caught fire around Finn's vision, and he found himself throwing it to the ground with a curse. Ysel had also jerked himself backward, and eyed the smoldering piece of thread. For a moment he looked like a normal child caught at something he was not supposed to meddle with.

When he cleared his throat, his voice came out slightly squeaky. "We can get more yarn; it's not the thread that is important."

Finn climbed to his feet. He felt washed out and very, very old. "But what we saw is. That place . . ." his voice ran out.

"The Belly of the World, some have called it," Wahirangi said. Neither of the brothers had noticed his approach, which for such a large beast was disturbing.

"I have never heard of it," Finn said, somewhat warily. He'd studied his whole life the cultures and legends of the people of Conhaero. "Where is it?"

The dragon's head turned toward the sea. "Out there." The life of a sailor was not a long or profitable one. The constant changing of the land made the sea even more unpredictable. Finn knew fishermen aplenty, but none that had ever sailed out of sight of the land. Ever-changing currents and terrifying monsters of the deep kept them close to home.

"In the ocean?" Ysel asked what Finn was thinking.

"No," Fida replied. "The Belly is the place for the Kindred only. Not even shared with the Vaerli when the Pact was still whole. It is the place where chaos itself is birthed into the world. The place where it should journey out into the void to balance the forces of stagnation."

"I saw a dragon there," Finn interrupted her. "A dragon that was not you, Wahirangi."

The beast's opalescent eyes fixed on him, and he had nowhere to look but into them. "You Named me, Finnbarr the Fox, and it was a mighty deed, but there are those who have might of their own."

"The Phage," Fida said, crossing her arms. "I understand that you felt one trying to take Talyn from you on the scared Salt."

"They can make dragons?" Finn exclaimed. "Then what chance is there?"

"Only one other can do as you have," the dragon said soothingly. "But it is one you will have to face if the destruction of this world is to be avoided."

Ysel, who had been silent up until now, took hold of his brother's arm, tugging him around. "You saw the four shapes on the edge of the volcano. Of those four shapes, all of them were seers of the Vaerli."

Now Finn began to wonder if his brother was out of his mind. Surely the strain of living his life just out of sync with the rest of the world had done something to him.

"There are only ever two seers at a time in the Vaerli," he said slowly, so that Ysel would not be insulted. "The born and the made."

"Indeed, there were only meant to be two until the Vaerli were ready to travel the White Void," Ysel said, with a shake of his head. "But the coming of another two was needed, to act as anchors to hold the Vaerli in this place, while the first two went into the Void. There were always meant to be four." His blue eyes held Finn's. "You know who the new seers are, don't you?"

Son of a seer. Namer of a dragon. Finn had been forced to come to terms with many things since the disaster on the sacred Salt, and now he knew why. Why his mother had sacrificed herself, and why she had protected both of her sons as best she could. All the little coincidences—the voices of doubt in his head, the trick with the thread, and even his ability to break open Talyn's memory—now made sense.

He swallowed hard, looking around at the four sets of eyes watching him ever so closely. Did they imagine he was about to crack under the stress of it all?

He walked to the edge of the cliff, to where the sun was beginning its slow descent into the ocean. "We are the seers, Ysel, you and I, but I have no idea what to do."

"You stand up for your mother's people," Fida said, and when he turned to face her, Finn was surprised to see she how sad she looked. He was used to the implacability of the Vaerli, but not to seeing genuine emotion. It made him think of Talyn, and the smile on her face when she had remembered to love him. With that love he felt he could accomplish anything. That was why he had begun his campaign against the Caisah in the first place.

He tried to hold on to that memory. "I can do that," he replied, though his voice sounded weak to his own ears.

"You won't be alone," his brother assured him.

"But what about the other two seers?"

Wahirangi closed his eyes for a moment. "Nyree is the made seer. She studied with your mother and would have been made."

"And the born seer?" Finn pressed.

The dragon's head retracted, now towering over the mortals with the dying light running over his golden skin.

"Born but not yet revealed," Fida whispered. "The real problem is the Phage. They have—"

Ysel held up his hand, and the woman snapped her mouth shut. "Before any of that," Ysel said softly, "there is also someone you need to meet in the village. Someone who watched you for a long time. From the moment you came here as a child like me."

CHAPTER TWELVE

HOMECOMING FOR ALL

T he talespinners of Elraban Island had certainly a sense of theatre in how they lived. As Talyn crouched low over Syris bunching shoulders, she caught glimpses of their homes through his flying mane.

The cliffs turned into a promontory that thrust out into the pounding ocean, before becoming a series of broken islands stuttering their way into the waves, smaller and shorter as they went.

The talespinners buildings were strung between them; some perched on solid ground, others suspended precariously over nothing but air. A series of flimsy looking rope and hemp ladders provided access to these little islands. The major one—which was not that major—was styled Elraban. Talespinners did have a way of inflating every little detail.

The Vaerli flicked her gaze upwards for an instant to check on the progress of the Swoop. They seemed to be enjoying the chase as much as she was. The great Whitefoam eagle spun above her; Azrul was content perhaps to have the high thermals while the smaller birds of the Swoop dived around Talyn.

It was a blessed carefree moment that was about to be utterly spoiled— because now there was no mistaking the other visitor that the talespinners had. Wahirangi CloudLord, Finn had named him, and he was just as magnificent as the last time Talyn had laid eyes on him.

He was perched on one of the outer islands, his claws clenched on the crumbling rock, his wings wrapped around him, as he stood as tall and commanding as a sentinel. He had his back turned to the magnificence of the sea, and his huge opal eyes fixed on all the comings and goings of the talespinners. Without saying a word, he gave the deep and real impression that he was the guardian here—and the inhabitants of Elraban Island had never been safer.

Above Talyn, the Swoop finally saw him and scattered from their games about her. The dragon's head turned to regard the lowly creatures. They might as well have been pigeons in his eyes, the Vaerli supposed.

It was, Talyn though idly as the Swoop broke apart in squawks and keens, going to be difficult to get him to destroy the scroll she carried when he was isolated over there like that. All those problems lay ahead.

Syris pressed his head forward, and the drumbeat of his gallop increased in tempo, as if he too were feeling the sting of being smaller than Wahirangi. The nykur soon brought Talyn right to the gate of the talespinners' refuge. From this angle, she was higher than the dragon, but his head was still in view, and she knew full well she had his attention. Those opalescent eyes carried a great weight with them when they were fixed on her.

One quick glance above told her that the Swoop was confused and not willing to land. It was understandable; up until only moments before Azrul had probably been confident that she was working for the most powerful being in Conhaero. It would take some readjustment.

Talyn swung down from Syris and looked about her. Talespinners might be daring with their architecture, but they were not much on defenses. The entrance to the whole complex of homes was one simple, woven doorway, leading out onto the rope bridges.

"Welcome, once-was Hunter," a voice croaked only a few feet away from Talyn.

She leapt back, and had pulled out her pistol and aimed it in the direction of the greeting before she'd had time to think. It was not often that someone caught her unprepared, but as the features to one side of the entrance moved, she was able to discern that it was not part of the rock, but an actual man.

His clothing was perfect camouflage, blending in with the gray and brown rocks. He even wore a hat, which when tipped down obscured his face and resembled more of the cliff. As she got a closer look at him, he did not appear to be much of a guard for the entrance.

She was not a good judge of the age of the Manesto people, but she hazarded that this man was well past the age where moving was expected of him. He had the craggy features and deep wrinkles of one who had seen too much of the sun and weather. Yet his eyes, when they met hers, were gleaming with intelligence.

He had startled Talyn so thoroughly that she found herself wondering what powers he might possess. "How do you know that about me?" she demanded.

He grinned, exposing a generous band of broken and missing teeth. "By the clouds in the sky, the scampering of the ants, and the call of the fish in the sea." He laughed uproariously, slapping his knee as if he had made a fine joke. "No, I tell a lie, I know because he told me. Your lover, Finn the Fox."

It was embarrassing to feel herself flush at this impertinence, but Talyn did. She had fallen for that one. Still, she was not going to deny it—that would only make it worse. Instead she frowned at the man. "How does one gain entry to the city? Is payment due?"

She must have seriously affronted the man, because he rose off his perch and staggered a few steps toward her. "You dare," he roared, before breaking into a round of heavy coughing. "You dare to speak of money, when legend itself is being born." He waved his hand in the general direction of Wahirangi, who had not shifted his gaze one inch from Talyn.

The gatekeeper cast his eyes upwards and regained his smile. "But you have brought the scion's Swoop with you, so I shall forgive you! What a joy to see them again!" His face creased into such a beatific smile that Talyn forgot for a moment all that was around her—the White Void, the cruel Phage, and even the dragon watching her mistrustfully over the cliffs.

"May I come in then, Master?" she asked hesitantly, wondering if her presence would break something. Though she had little respect for many of the newcomers to Conhaero, the Talespinners of Elraban reminded her very much of the storytellers of her own time. That was, she suspected, why it had been so easy for Finn to entrance her. It was ironic indeed that now she was pursuing him to ask for a favor.

The old man tilted his head, and held out his hand to her. "I am Koth, First Teller of Elraban, and all are welcome here." He gave out a short laugh. "Indeed, were the Caisah himself to pay us another visit, we would still welcome him in."

It was some kind of miracle that such people survived in Conhaero, but Talyn did not say as much to his face. What was more, he knew who she was. She did not have time to ask him what he meant by "another visit" before the air was suddenly alive with feathers and transforming women.

The Swoop dropped elegantly from the clouds on predators' swift wings. Soon there were a dozen armored women facing the First Teller. He looked as pleased as if jewels had just rained down on him. Being a talespinner tethered to the island instead of out exploring the delights of the world did seem a little lonely.

"The Swoop of One-eyed Baraca!" Koth exclaimed, clasping his hands together.

Azrul made a bow to the First Teller, but did not enter immediately, and Talyn knew why. "A dragon?" was all the leader of the Swoop managed to croak out.

"Legends come to life makes for interesting times," Koth observed in what had to be the grandest understatement Talyn had heard for a good long time. "We have had many visitors of late, but Wahirangi CloudLord is certainly the grandest."

Talyn understood her friend's reaction, the dragon—even when seen from a distance—did take away a person's breath. Up close he was even more scintillating.

"Well," Azrul said, her smile bright, but her eyes wide as she tried to regain her composure, "we will be grateful that he seems polite enough."

It was not easy, but Talyn managed to conceal her grin. She knew it was not just the dragon. It had been a long time since the Swoop was welcomed in such a manner. They had been tainted by the Caisah much as Talyn had been.

Azrul cleared her throat. "We have come to speak to your dream sages, and share what our master has been experiencing of late."

The cheery grin on Koth's face faded. "Yes, we know of what you speak. Enter and take the first left into the sages' chambers. I think they have been waiting for you."

"Thank you, First Teller," Azrul said, her politeness was rather off-putting since Talyn knew her for her more brash nature. Something had softened the edges of her friend.

She drew the Vaerli off to one side as Koth settled back in his spot, blending in with the rock face.

"I will preform my charge as I must, but I want to speak to you afterward." She folded her hand over Talyn's shoulder and gave it a squeeze. "I see something new and sad in your eyes . . ."

"It has always been there," the Vaerli replied, "but I appreciate your care, Azrul. I too have my task."

"Yes, we all have our duties that pull us apart," Azrul said, and her voice was stained with genuine sadness. "Still, we will roost here until the talespinners have studied the dreams of the scion. It will be good to rest for a while.

It was apparent that today was not the day that they would get to share apple tea. Talyn thought of the last moments they had passed together, when they had really been able to talk in the sanctuary of the Lady of Wings. She did not share her doubts with Azrul, that they would never be able to have that again. Instead, she nodded and turned back to her mount.

She overheard the leader of the Swoop instructing her soldiers to wait for her here. The talespinners were bound to be leery of such a show of military force. Some remained in human form to perch on the rocks and take what rest they could, while a few others returned to the sky to keep an eye on the area. Talyn thought them brave souls, considering the dragon.

For herself, the Vaerli went to the nykur, who she could have sworn was irritated by the presence of the dragon. He was used to being the center of attention.

Ignoring his reactions, Talyn clenched her hand in his hair.

"Wait for me," she whispered to him, "it could be a trap."

The nykur tossed his green head and stomped one huge foot as if to remind her that he was his own creature. He had found her after all this time, and he was not likely to leave her behind now.

Talyn had a sudden thought, and turned back to Syris. "Oh and leave the old man's fingers on his hands, please."

The creature of chaos rolled his dark eye. She was not sure if that was a reassurance or not. Then she followed Azrul onto the rope bridge, which did not encourage much confidence when it creaked so alarmingly. Talespinners were not known for their abilities with their hands, and she wondered idly if the whole thing would end up tipping them into the rushing waves below.

Azrul found her junction easily enough, but seemed a little reluctant to go down it. She held on to the rope by her head and turned around to look at Talyn. "I don't suppose you can tell me why you are here, can you?"

The Vaerli twisted her lips. "No, I am afraid not. Don't worry, I will find you later." She hated lying to her friend, but she would not tolerate pity from her. Every sorry thing that had happened since they parted she would keep to herself.

The leader of the Swoop gave a sharp nod and headed off in the direction she had been told to go. It was hard for Talyn to tell, but she got the impression Azrul was hurt. So be it. The Vaerli would rather have her friend angry with her, than feeling other softer emotions.

Unlike Azrul, Talyn had been given no instructions to find Finn. It was largely typical of their meetings. As she picked her way along the rats' nest of swaying tubular rope bridges and tiny rooms with the occasional talespinner teaching a class, she caught brief glimpses of the dragon through the gaps in the walls.

The sun was beginning to set, and the light was striking every smooth, gleaming surface of him. The beast had undoubtedly picked the spot for this very reason. They might be mighty, but Talyn had heard the stories—dragons could be excessively proud creatures. There was certainly much to be proud of.

It did not go unnoticed by Talyn that Wahirangi's head turned to follow her as she scrambled about the rabbit warren that was Elraban Island. After a while it started to annoy her instead of frighten her. She knew a little about the Naming of Kindred, and she knew more than a little about Finn the Fox. What Talyn was fairly sure of, was that he still had no real concept of what he had done. Perhaps she would explain it to him, just in case things started to take a turn. She might not have the chance when the Phage called her to heel again.

She was thinking about that, rolling the idea about in her head, when she heard his voice. Talyn stopped abruptly, swaying slightly on the rope bridge, with her head cocked to one side. At first she thought he was telling a story—maybe educating a few trainee talespinners, but then the rhythm of the speaking told her that it was a conversation, not a myth being retold.

Finn's voice was one she could have picked out from amongst a thousand—well, at least since he had brought back all the memories of him she'd elected to lose. That was the kind of man he was. Irritating. Frustrating. Unforgettable.

She glanced to her right and caught Wahirangi flex his wings once, and then shutter them around himself. Perhaps some kind of dragon amusement, Talyn wondered as his tail wrapped tightly around the rock on which he perched. It was sometimes easy to forget that he was Kindred on the inside, but in this moment she could almost feel the creature of chaos watching her, peeling back the layers of her soul, even from this distance.

So she simply strode away from his regard, and toward where she could hear Finn talking. It was not much better walking that way, since her stomach was clenched like it had been punched, and she had a strangely dry mouth.

She and the talespinner had not parted on the best of terms, considering she had him as her prisoner and he had managed to escape.

She could not guess how he would respond to her turning up, asking for a favor from his dragon—but she knew she was going to quickly find out. Her boot heel caught in one of the loose boards of the rickety walkway and she slipped up to her knee. Being so engrossed in worry cost her the usual gracefulness of the Vaerli. As she was swearing and trying to untangle herself, she heard him speak words she could easily make out—mainly because he was standing only feet from her.

"I trust you haven't hurt yourself?"

Talyn jerked her head away from her predicament and toward the man standing in the doorway to the plaited room. His golden blond hair was scruffy as ever, but his eyes had changed. The hardness she saw in them was not the only change in the talespinner; there was a pride in his eyes now.

He stood braced in the doorway, legs slightly parted, hands above his head, holding onto the ropes. She should have expected he would be so nimble in this place. After all, this was where he had trained in his craft. For all intents and purposes this was his home.

She dropped her eyes away, and struggled and jerked her leg free of ropes. "I am all right, though I think there should be some more attention paid to the repairs in this place. It's practically a death trap."

"And you would know all about those," he replied, not moving from his place. At his back she caught a glimpse of more figures, the ones he had been conversing with.

Talyn might have hoped for a private audience with Finn, but she was obviously not going to get one. For a moment she felt suspended over more than the ocean. Should she go forward and embrace him, or would he take that as an insult? She had never much cared for others' impressions of her—at least, not for decades—so she was at a total loss how to proceed.

The boy who wriggled his way under Finn's arm to stand on the rope bridge between them at least broke the awkwardness of the moment a little. He had the same light hair as Finn, and with a sharp indrawn breath, Talyn's first thought escaped her. "Finn, you have a son?"

He had never said anything to her about such a thing before. The wriggling, burning sensation in her stomach . . . could it be jealousy?

The talespinner's eyebrows drew together, and he shot a look over his shoulder. It was indeed a woman behind him, but Talyn could not make out her features. The urge to turn about and stride away was almost overwhelming, but the Vaerli held her place.

"Ysel is not my son," Finn finally replied, but his tone said he would offer no more on the matter. Instead he asked her bluntly, "Why are you here, Talyn?"

She had not considered how to answer that question. The Phage had told her to manipulate the talespinner, but she did not have much experience with such things. Though she knew she should not launch into asking him to burn the damn scroll, she had not considered what she would say was her reason for tracking him down.

A lie would be easiest, but if she were found out, it would destroy any hope she had of his help. So a half-truth then, something that would not show on her face. "I heard you were here, and I didn't like how it ended."

"You tried to take him to the Caisah," said the boy who looked about twelve mortal years old. His green eyes were far too knowing for her liking—much like the Phage child's.

If Talyn had little experience with lying, then she had even less with children. The only ones she had contact with were the spoiled brats of the Caisah's court, or the weeping ones she tore off their parents' bodies. She licked her lips. "Yes, I admit I did that, but I am no longer in thrall to the Caisah. I broke with him when I discovered that the puzzle—which he said held the answer on how to set my people free—was a lie. The only image it showed was Putorae's, she who was the last seer of the Vaerli."

"And how do you think that was a lie?" The woman who had until this moment lurked in the background stepped around Finn. Talyn took a step back, nearly falling into the gap she had only just extracted herself from.

"You are Vaerli!" She thought it ironic that she was about to die right in front of Finn. Maybe that would calm his rage.

Yet there was no flare of heat in her muscles, no dire ache in her bones, and she knew immediately what this woman had done. "You went to the mountain . . . like my father?" Talyn could still not quite believe that anyone would do such a thing.

The Vaerli, who had the faintest streaks of silver in her long dark hair, nodded. Her eyes were an eerie brown. "Some must always sacrifice themselves for the future." She dropped her hand onto the head of the boy beside her. "I am Fida. I was your father's brother's wife, but you probably don't remember me."

Talyn shook her head slowly. "Many of those memories I chose to abandon."

"No doubt," Fida said, but her voice showed no real hatred, which was a definite surprise.

Talyn did not like the silence that followed, all four of them swinging slightly on the rope bridge, trapped in the uncomfortable moment. "So why did you go?" Talyn asked, merely because it was the first thing that came into her head, and not because she was wondering. Indeed, she could feel Finn's eyes on her like burning marks.

Fida glanced down at the boy called Ysel. "You will find out, niece." With that she guided the boy past Talyn, leaving the once-Hunter and the Fox standing together.

"Are you here for my head?" Finn finally spoke. "Because this would not be the place to take it." He gestured to the foaming water below.

"No," she replied, reminding herself to keep to the facts as best she could. "I parted company with the Caisah. I really have. I heard you were here, and I had to come."

The man's eyes raked over her, and she recalled that as a talespinner he could probably discern much about people from their expressions and gestures. It came in handy when a public house turned ugly.

"Why?" he asked mildly.

She cleared her throat and considered. When she'd been the Hunter, she had been used to taking men to bed for mere pleasure. It had been something to sate her own physical needs, but she had never kept the memories. She had thought perhaps that was why she had discarded memories of Finn—but when he returned them to her, she recalled it had not been the case. She'd cast away the memories of their time together because to her, loving a Manesto, or indeed loving anyone, was a waste of time and devotion. Her one aim had always been to save her people.

"I . . ." Talyn stammered, "I . . . I don't—"

"I have someone you must meet," he interrupted her, holding out his hand. "I think she might help you clear your head a little."

It was a moment of trust; a test that she had to pass. Somehow, with everything she had been through, this felt like a turning point. Reaching out, Talyn took his hand, and knew everything was about to change.

CHAPTER THIRTEEN

IN THE HEART
OF THE VAERLI

Byre and Pelanor had obviously been taken as some kind of honor guard for the stranger, and had also been allowed to pass. They reached the spot where the Pact of the Oath was carved in the salt. Here the Caisah paused, looking it over. If he was a stranger, Byre suddenly realized that he would not understand it.

Perhaps if he understood the words, he would understand the Vaerli. Byre stepped up closer to the new arrival. "It says—"

"—I know what it says," the Caisah replied sharply. "It is the pact between these people and the gods of this world."

Gods? Byre was for a moment confused. He had to mean the Kindred, but they were not gods. All the gods had been stripped from all the peoples that passed through the White Void.

"Gods hate oath breakers," the Caisah muttered, before striding on deeper into the carved salt corridor.

Pelanor caught at Byre's hand as he made to follow. "Don't we know enough?" she whispered to him. "Shouldn't we go now?"

She didn't understand the nature of this punishment. Byre looked down at her, and for the first time felt the real difference between them. She might have his blood flowing in her veins, but she could never truly comprehend in any meaningful way what was happening. Besides, curiosity had already exchanged places with fear within Byre. The Caisah's talk of gods and oath breakers had done that.

He looked at her with real pity in his eyes, feeling the superiority of the Vaerli race for the first time. "We need to see the whole thing to understand."

Then he walked away from her, quickly, before he lost sight of the Caisah. He hoped she would follow, because he would need a witness to all this.

Ahead the corridor began to widen to a chamber, and it also grew dimmer.

The light from above was being lost in the depths. Torches were now spaced out along the walls, and his Vaerli hearing could make out voices ahead. They were angry voices, and one of them he recognized enough to make his heart race.

Mother.

The Caisah had stopped in the shadows so abruptly that Byre almost ran into him. Only the gleam of the eagle on his staff gave any hint he was there. The soon-to-be tyrant's head was cocked to one side, like a child listening intently to parents having an argument. Byre stood at his side and listened, too.

At first he couldn't make out the words that were being exchanged like barbs, but gradually he could discern some. He recognized "Phage," which he had heard before. The only time had been a mention from his father when he was little. Retira had called them a "dangerous sect." Then he heard "Kindred" and "Pact" being bandied around.

Finally the words seemed to die down.

"Yes, that is good," the Caisah whispered. "Now is the time."

As he strode forward, Pelanor tugged on the back of Byre's hood. "Are we just going to let him go in there?"

He knew what she meant. What was coming was nothing less than the Harrowing itself. Byre licked his lips, feeling how dry his mouth was. The witch was asking how prepared he was to watch the destruction of his people, but what choice did he have?

"It's already happened," he whispered back to her, his eyes never leaving the retreating back of the Caisah. "As Ellyria said, the future cannot be rewritten, and we are only observers."

"I will abide by your decision," she replied, and slid her hand down from his back to rest inside his. Ahead, all sound was abruptly cut off, so Byre led her after the Caisah at a brisk run. He might not want to see what happened next, but he also did not want to miss it.

Their sudden arrival was barely noticed as they trotted into the council chamber. The Vaerli who were its members had risen from their seats around the carved wooden table, and were staring fixedly at the Caisah.

Byre could understand their sudden silence; they were going through the very same range of emotions that he had experienced. While they did, Byre allowed his eyes to trail around the gathering. There were seven of them. The same as the number of Gifts that they had been given by the Kindred.

He did not know any of those present, except one. His mother was among them. He'd known that she would be there. He'd been in this place before, and seen what happened—what would happen—to her after.

The rational part of Byre's brain could quite easily understand his reaction to her being there, but it was not easy to stop his eyes filling with sudden hot, bright, tears. She had not been an easy mother, he could still remember that, but he had loved her; both he and his sister had. To see her now, standing in the council chamber, outrage and bafflement on her beautiful face, hit him in the center of his chest.

Suddenly the words he had only just spoken to Pelanor seemed empty. It took every ounce of his strength to stop himself from running over to her, and getting her, whatever way he could, out of this room.

She looked very like Talyn would look one day. They called her Kourae the Light, and he could understand why now. She represented the singers on the council, but her hand was on the hilt of her sword, which was half out of its sheath.

Naturally, it was his mother who recovered first. When she spoke, her voice was bright and melodic despite the situation. "Who are you to intrude in this sacred space?"

"Not so sacred," the Caisah spoke while he leaned heavily on his staff. "No Pact means no sacred places for the Vaerli—at least not in this land."

Two of the male Vaerli, one who had a thick silver beard, walked around the table to stand at Kourae's side. "You were asked your name," the ancient old man spoke. "And you are not one of us."

The old man, Byre surmised, was in a position of power. The leaders of the various arts chose one of their number every ten years to speak for all. He had no idea which art this man represented—it didn't matter much . . . he was to be the last.

"No," the Caisah said, "I am not one of you." He paused to cough. It was a hard, wracking sound that did not speak well of the man's health. The White Void obviously put a strain on him that would linger a while. Byre would never have imagined that this was how the destroyer of the Vaerli would come into their midst.

"I am, however, sent by those you have wronged."

The council members looked at each other, and he knew that look—it was the look of shared guilt and fear.

He almost blurted out a question, like he was watching a story unfold, until he realized that they were real people, and his very real mother.

The Caisah straightened. "You know of whom I speak. The Kindred sent me, since you have stopped conversing with them. I am their burning beacon on the hilltop."

Kourae seemed to recover the quickest. Her hand did not leave the hilt of her sword. This was not at all how Byre imagined the Harrowing had begun. "The Kindred did not send you," she said, though her voice did not sound all that steady.

Pelanor shifted closer to Byre, and her pointed fangs were in evidence. Something about this excited her. For himself, Byre felt posed on the edge of a great void.

The Caisah, for all his apparent weakness, did not look worried about facing so many Vaerli in their den. Instead he straightened, and that whisper of the White Void grew closer again. The chamber was chill like death.

"It is coming," Byre whispered under his breath, so that only Pelanor could hear it. It was hardly needed. The presence of a storm was building.

When the Caisah spoke, it was as if a thousand other voices spoke through him. "The Pact was broken. You did not heed our call to the Void. Instead you summoned more people to this world to help give you strength in blood and flesh."

He stepped nearer, and Byre saw that the Vaerli flinched away. "You were afraid to fulfil your promise, the promise of Ellyria Dragonsoul. You claim superiority over all the land, and yet you are too terrified to go where I came from."

Byre expected them to deny it. He looked to his mother, hoping to see it written all over her face, but there was nothing there—nothing but deep guilt.

The Caisah was right. The person that they had despised for a thousand years, was right. What was more, he had come to this place at the bidding of the Kindred. The scene around him blurred, but not because the Kindred were taking him back.

"Byre," Pelanor said, pressing her mouth close to his ear. "Don't leave me, Byre."

Before he could answer with anything at all, another of the councilwomen stood up. She could only be Putorae, the seer. She was covered in the *pae atuae*, and her eyes were hard. "The Pact was only to warn us about the White Void. Ellyria Dragonsoul did not promise us to it."

"Why were the Gifts given, then?" the Caisah went on calmly. "Did you think that they were laid on you as a reward. They are weapons, so that you may survive the White Void."

"This is ridiculous!" Another woman walked toward the Caisah. "You come here, into our heart of hearts, and tell us that the Kindred are disappointed with us? We are the Vaerli! The people of the land! You are an intruder here on the Salt and here in Conhaero!"

"Mylise!" the leader said, laying a hand on her colleague's shoulder. "Think of how he came here . . . we should hear what he has to say."

The dark woman's eyes flashed as she shook of his grasp. "No! This is the sort of insult our so-called allies have been making for years. We sacrificed children to hold back the White Void while they did nothing to save us."

"You did wrong," the Caisah said, turning on her like a viper. "The White Void was meant to open, and you were meant to go forward into it, taking change and chaos with you. Instead you chose to use blood to call others here; wanderers that the Kindred did not intend to let dwell here. Already they are changing this world."

Kourae swallowed, her gaze darting between her colleagues but holding none of them for long. "What do you want us to do about this now?"

"The Void remains, and you still travel it in small amounts. You have a chance right now to mend the Pact. Step back into the Void." The Caisah's words fell like a death sentence on the Vaerli.

Byre shifted, and felt the regard of all the council members flick to him. Luckily his hood was down, but he knew that they would be able to feel that he was Vaerli. He did not like that they would think him a traitor to his own kind. It was foolish, but he had been so long separated from them that he had nothing else to lose but their opinion.

The woman named Mylise threw up her hands and let out a hard, painful sounding laugh. "Why not just ask us to fall on our swords now? It is suicide to enter without a scion. Some of us are still alive who remember the perils of the Void, and the friends and family lost to it."

Byre suddenly understood—that was why they feared it even more. The Vaerli gift of long life had made them more fragile than they had been when they came to Conhaero. They wanted to keep living, and the White Void was a place which would take that from many of them.

"Then the Gifts will be taken back," the Caisah said simply. "The Pact will be irrevocably broken and the Kindred will . . ."

Exactly what the Kindred would do was forever lost; the woman leapt at him. It happened so fast in the before-time, that Byre lost track of her movements. Before he could think about his reasoning, he found himself stepping forward to help the Caisah.

It was the strangest thing that had happened so far, in this strangest of days. The Vaerli woman was quick, but so was he. The Caisah made no real move to protect himself, but Byre was too busy pushing aside Mylise to have much time to wonder.

He got his arm between her and the soon-to-be tyrant and twisted, sending her sliding across the room. Pelanor appeared at his side, and hissed like a wild cat at the surrounding Vaerli. Her fangs gleamed white in the half darkness, so Byre knew there was no chance anyone could mistake her for other than what she was.

However, that was also true for him. His hood had fallen back in the struggle with Mylise, and he could feel all his kin's eyes on his tell-tale features; there was no fooling any of them now. He was Vaerli.

His mother's eyes most of all he could not meet, but he could not keep his gaze from them. It was a moment before he realized that he was swaying on his feet.

"Byre!" Pelanor screamed at his side, and it was only that sound that made him aware that the ground itself was moving. The Salt was cracking and shifting as if pounded by a giant hand. Byre heard the Caisah laugh, and it sounded as mad as the movement of the sacred all around him.

"He is doing this," Mylise's voice somehow reached over the movement all around them. "The infidel has bought destruction—and them!"

Byre, clutching hold of the taut figure of Pelanor, whipped around and saw where she was pointing. The Kindred had come.

A dozen faceless, dark shapes were all around the council chamber. They had appeared while the Vaerli were in disarray, but they did not make any moves toward them. The Caisah stood in the middle of the circle they described, his face calm and with swirling light about his head.

"Heed the Pact!" he called, and it should have been the trumpet call for the Vaerli to do as he and the Kindred bid.

Byre, standing in the middle of the tumult, suddenly understood his people. The veil of his childhood, the one constructed out of myth and pride, was ripped aside. The Vaerli had grown too powerful, and they no longer could listen to the truth.

Byre would have sunk to his knees if Pelanor had not held him up. "It was their own fault," he muttered, as his whole body shook to the rhythms of Conhaero. "All this time I thought we were the victims, and he the villain."

His watering eyes could no longer look anywhere else but at the Caisah. He was the herald that the Kindred had sent as a last resort.

Above them he could hear the screams of the Vaerli, and he knew that some of those screams were his, some of them were Talyn's. He was reliving the terror, the flying dust. He could almost feel his father's arms around him.

"I was just a child," he sobbed, barely feeling the witch's hands wrap around him. "I didn't know . . . I didn't understand . . ."

"No time for pity," Pelanor responded, shaking him hard enough to snap his head back. "This is what you came here to find out. Look!"

Getting his feet under him, Byre whirled around and saw what was happening. The Vaerli were fighting the Kindred. He saw Kourae, her blade now released from its sheath, strike at the impassive creatures, her face set in a mask of terrible rage. One of the councilmen went down screaming as an impassive Kindred fell on him like a slab of granite. Mylise, however, was doing something else; she was becoming something else.

She was a dancer—that much was obvious. For a moment he was entranced, despite all the madness about them. The movement of her arms and legs were elegant and smooth, describing patterns in the air. He knew what she was doing; he was seeing for the first time the Naming of a Kindred.

The object of her attentions did not seem to be enjoying it, though. The Kindred were so impassive, and alien to the Vaerli—usually. This one was writhing in pain, filling the chamber with wailing that might crack skulls and shatter eardrums.

A trickle of blood ran from Pelanor's nose, and she clapped her hands to her face, falling to her knees. The Vaerli turned to watch the dancer, but none of them moved to stop her.

Byre lurched forward, not knowing what was happening, but certain that he needed to make it stop. Kourae stepped between them, her bare blade acting as a barrier. Her dark eyes locked with his, and despite everything he stopped.

The Kindred let out one final cry and seemed to crumple into the shadow of Mylise. She danced on, but now there was an extra shadow hanging from her shadows like a cape. Whatever Name she had given the Kindred gave no joy to his compatriots.

Flames burst into life on the remaining guardians, while the Caisah howled. His voice cracked, and his eyes were not his own. "What was once a Gift, will now be a curse. You are so very proud, Vaerli. Content in your own company—now that, too, will be poison."

Byre felt the blow deep inside him. It was a building flame, like the one the Kindred commanded. He felt it begin to eat at him, gnawing its way toward the surface.

The council members were stricken too—all but one. Kourae, clutching her stomach with one hand, staggered toward the Caisah. Her first stab was wild, and her target fell back, clutching at his arm. Blood poured out from under his strange armor, but he faced her bravely. He appeared to have little care for himself, since he didn't draw his own sword or even move the staff to intercept.

Kourae pulled back, though her face was still twisted in a mask of pain as the Harrowing began to take its effect. Byre didn't know why he moved forward, himself. He only knew that the herald of the Kindred had to be protected.

Instinct, built up over his many years of running and hiding, welled up inside him, and took over. His blade intersected with hers, sliding into a riposte that skilfully turned her strike, and made one of its own.

When Byre looked down at his sword buried in his mother's belly, he wondered why he had not heeded Ellyria's commandment. Those final moments when as a child he had seen her blood leaking onto the Salt came back to haunt him.

He had killed her. Not the Caisah. Not even the mad Vaerli dancer Mylise. It had been his blade that had been her end. Again instinct, but a of quite different kind, made him yank back on his weapon.

A wound to the gut in this chaos.

"I'm sorry," he screamed, rushing forward to envelop his mother, as if his very presence could heal her. The world was shaking itself loose from its moorings around him, while the Harrowing began to squeeze its teeth down on the

Vaerli, and he didn't care. He was not going to let go of her. He was not going to forget this feeling of his mother's blood on his hands.

Until he was holding nothing, and there was no world. He was once more in the realm of the Kindred, his arms no more filled by Kourae. Her blood was still on his hands, both literally and figuratively. He stared down at them, unable to breathe, clenching and unclenching them.

"Not possible . . . not possible," he whispered to himself, hating even the sound of his own voice. With a guttural scream he pulled out his knife, and would have plunged it into his own belly if Pelanor had not stopped him.

She was a tiny scrap of a person, but she had his blood in her, and he could not overcome their combined strength. She did not say a word, simply cast aside the knife and wrapped her whole body around him.

He howled and screamed, and all the time he thought about her—his sister. The world though the Hunter the worst of the Vaerli . . . they didn't know her brother was far, far worse.

A storm of tears overcame Byre. He wished they would wash him away.

Finn led Talyn off the bridge through a few more swaying rooms as the wind blew in off the cliffs.

"So this is where you grew up?" Talyn found herself wanting to make some kind of small talk. The silence and the oppressive gaze of a dragon were a little much even for her.

"Yes," he said, shooting a look over his shoulder. "Is that so hard to imagine?"

The Vaerli looked around, taking in the roar of the ocean below, the beautiful vistas that could be glimpsed through the woven ropes, and the constant risk of the islands eroding into the sea. "No, I think this is exactly where I imagined you would have grown up."

"You told me that last time," he said, his voice a little stiff, even as he picked his way across yet another rope bridge.

She thought hard on the matter, and discovered that he was right—but last time she had been laughing and they had been naked. The intent had been entirely different.

"Here," he said, holding the ropes taut so she could walk past him onto the relative safety of an island. The Vaerli squeezed around him, smelling the musk of his skin and the salt of the sea on him. She recalled that smell too, and it hit her in her most primal parts. Despite being an immortal creature and nemohira, he could still affect her that way. She hoped he couldn't sense it.

They passed over some slightly sturdier bridges to a room that was actually built on solid ground. This was truly part of Elraban Island, she thought as she stepped out onto the permance of one of the tall islands that made up the talespinner's isolated home. This particular island was barely large enough to accommodate twenty people, but it had a patch of green grass, and was open to the sky. It would have been a wonderful spot to see the stars at night, were it not for the small depression in the middle filled with water. She would not have called it a puddle, but it was definitely less than a lake.

With her recent experience with the Phage, she was leery of water. It seemed a deceptive element. She turned to Finn, confused.

His eyes, which now seemed almost the deep blue of that bowl of water, had the look of distance in them. If she had not known better, she might have thought he was looking into the before-time. "I was trained here, on this island." He gestured to the pool. "We all sat around this little piece of water, and talked of the myths and legends gone before." A smile darted across his face. "Ellyria Dragonsoul was my favorite, but I never guessed a Vaerli was so close."

Before Talyn could demand what exactly he meant, the waters shimmered and the last Seer of the Vaerli rose from it. Putorae, in all her shimmering immortal glory, carved with the *pae atuae,* stood in the middle of the water, smiling like some benevolent scion.

Talyn only just prevented herself from leaping back in shock. She had seen the spectre of the seer on the Steps of Sacrifice, a trick made from placing a bit of herself into the before and future times. An impressive ability, but she would never have imagined that Putorae would do such a thing in the middle of the village of talespinners.

The Steps Talyn could understand, since they were an important site for the Vaerli, but this place made no sense. Unless . . .

She spun around and regarded Finnbarr the Fox with a new eye. Golden hair and blue eyes were unusual, but her own father had them. He was taller than she would have expected, but something about him now looked familiar.

"Not possible," she whispered. "You cannot be Vaerli! The curse is not on you, and . . ." she flapped her arm in the general direction of Wahirangi.

"He is not all Vaerli," Putorae replied. "His father was and is the scion you call the Caisah."

Suddenly Talyn needed somewhere to sit down, but she found herself pacing, hand pressed to her head. "Not possible. The Vaerli and others cannot breed . . . and the Caisah . . . he cannot . . . I . . ."

Her voice and her brain finally ran out of coherent words, so she simply stopped and looked at them. Really looked. Standing side by side for the first time, their resemblance was clear.

She swallowed hard. "I need to hear the whole story."

The spectre's eyes narrowed on Talyn. "I see I judged you harshly, Talyn once-Hunter; there is still something of your old self in there."

At that assessment, Talyn only just managed to hold back a harsh laugh. This creature was not nearly as wise as she was making herself out to be.

Finn's lips jerked a little at the corners, but he led her over to one of the rocks that he had probably sat on to study in his youth, and began to tell her a tale. The seer had not died in the Harrowing. Instead she had found the Caisah and recognized him for what he was.

At many points while Finn told her the story, it sounded just like that—a story. Yet the shimmering form of the Last Seer stood at his side, corroborating every word. How the Caisah had been sent by the Kindred to bring the Vaerli back into line, but how everything had gone horribly wrong. Putorae had sought to bring her people two more seers to hold Conhaero while another two went into the White Void as the Pact had promised.

"Seers?" Talyn said, feeling like her own world was tilting. "You and your brother are seers?"

"As are you," Putorae added, her dark eyes full of stars fixed on the former-Hunter's face. "The born seer to Nyree's made."

"Nyree?" She felt as though she was being pummeled from side to side. "I know Nyree, she was your acolyte . . . but me . . . the born seer?"

"Why do you think the Caisah saved you?" Finn pressed his hands over hers. "He may be broken and mad, but he could sense a little of what you were."

"Even my own father didn't, though," Talyn retorted bitterly. "He rejected me when I saw him last. Even my brother . . ." She stopped to a halt, and looked up accusingly at Putorae. "Why did you not tell me when I saw you at the Steps?"

The Last Seer reached out to touch Talyn's cheek. "I am only fragments now. This one is the greatest portion of me, sent to watch over my son, so that piece you met was merely a thin shard. Besides . . . would you have believed me back then?"

Talyn took a deep breath, and thought of herself then. Angry, tied to the Caisah. She had not seen a dragon Named then, and had not witnessed the horror of the Phage.

"The Phage!" She gasped, fumbling for the scroll they had given her. When she ripped it open, it was blank. Nothing more than an aged piece of vellum. Again she had been tricked. "When will I stop being such an idiot," she howled, throwing the scroll as far away as she could. "That damn puzzle was a picture of you . . . the Caisah had his joke, and now the Phage have too."

"It was a Phage we saw on the Salt," Finn said, his voice filled with concern. "They are part of the Vaerli too, aren't they?"

"They took me in," Talyn muttered, feeling shame creeping over her. "Like the Caisah, they fooled me."

"Think about it," Finn said, wrapping his arm around her while she shook with rage. "The Caisah didn't lie to you. In a way, he was right. Mother knows how to get the curse lifted. He did not put you wrong. We are seers, and we will find a way."

"Now you need only find Nyree," Putorae added. "My sons, you, and she, shall set things right. The curse can be lifted, and all can still be well."

"All seers . . ." Talyn whispered, and leaned into Finn's embrace. They sat there for a moment, while the sun continued to slide beneath the line of the horizon. The gleaming sunlight bathed the tiny island in red light.

"And like all seers, you will need training." Putorae turned and pointed out to sea. "The Belly of the World waits, but not for long. You will have to learn as much as you can in the next few days."

"Days?" Talyn blinked. She thought of Nyree and the way she had followed Putorae around like a dog for years upon years. "Surely that isn't enough time to—"

"That is all we have," Finn's mother replied, sounding peevish for a dead person. "The White Void is close."

"How much can you teach us in that short amount of time?" Talyn asked. "Surely not enough to save the world . . ." She stopped herself. There was no time for doubt. They had the amount of time they had.

Instead, she shot a sharp smile at Finn. "It seems strange that a people so unconcerned with time should have to worry about it so much at this juncture."

His hand came down over hers and gave it a slight squeeze. "We shall manage." He folded his legs under himself as he sat at the edge of the pool. "Just like old times."

Talyn followed suit, though her memories were of times at her mother's knee; her mother who had never known her daughter was the born seer. She looked across at her new instructor, one she could see through.

"I hope not," was all she said, more to herself than Putorae and Finn. She was ready for something different. A new path would be a very fine thing.

CHAPTER FOURTEEN

TO LOVE AND LOSE

The dragonets flew hard and fast back the way they had come. Even with the improved sight of this new form, Equo could hardly see in front of him. He had witnessed too many atrocities in his long life; it was far too easy to imagine them perpetuated on Nyree. He could hardly think straight.

His worst fears were confirmed when they saw light on the horizon long before they reached the campsite. Equo felt as though the heart in his chest was going to burst, as he flapped his wings as hard and fast as he could.

The Swoop was not there to protect the camp. He had remembered that fact as soon as the Kindred had spoken. Baraca had sent them on some kind of mission—he'd not said why or to where.

While the rest of the Ahouri went to be the heralds for the Kindred, Equo and his brothers were racing late to save what they had left behind. The question burned in him whether they would be too late.

Creatures were in the sky above the camp, creatures that resolved into nightmares the closer the trio got. Griffins and other fell beings with wings were pouring destruction down on the camp of the scion. The lights, they could now see, were from the burning tents, but also from another. Baraca was a scion, and he was not without his own powers.

He stood outlined on a hilltop, his feet braced against the earth, while from his mouth poured light. The Named screamed and fell back, seemingly unwilling to dare approach the light.

Equo in the red dragonet form darted forward, away from his more cautious brothers. Hope was swelling in him. No power in Conhaero could match a scion that had passed through the White Void. All would be well.

The remains of Baraca's army had gathered around him, fighting a rearguard action as creatures of hoof and fang beset them on all sides.

Equo screamed as he dived from the sky, raking his claws over the back of a creature with a lion's body but the heads of a lion, a goat and a snake. A

197

chimera, he thought as he banked up once more, ready for another pass. The Named had grown greatly in number, though who had freed them was more the question. Surely, not the Caisah—even he would not be that mad.

Si and Varlesh, the green and black dragonets, swooped low over the gathering, pouring flame down on the Named, reminding him of the power of this form. They were no dragons, but they came close.

Twisting to the right, Si narrowly missed the snapping jaws of a feathered serpent that was following close on his tail. Equo spun around and went to his brother's aide, sending the serpent fleeing as fire licked over those magnificent feathers.

The song of the dragonets cut high and sweet over the gathering, causing many of the seething mass of Named to stare up at them. The strings of the Naming were tightly woven—far more so than those of normal creatures—but given time Equo knew that they would be able to pick them apart.

The trio spun and turned about each other, singing vengeance and the rebellion of flesh. Below them, the Named began to writhe. Baraca was no fool, he took advantage of the confusion that the arrival of the Ahouri had caused. The white light cut swathes through the Named, and where it touched they burned as if the magnified beam of the sun was upon them.

The tide of the battle was turning. One-eyed Baraca's troops were lifting their heads, hopeful that they might not die this day. Some even called for a rally to take the fight to the enemy.

The trio of dragonets climbed high, preparing for another blistering attack on the crowds below. Equo could make out Nyree, standing in the middle of a knot of soldiers close to Baraca. She had a sword in one hand and a pistol in the other. She was easy to spot because of the gleam of her *pae atuae* and the light of the scion. Too easy.

A scream sounded above the dragonets, among the rolling clouds that had boiled in from the mountains, and Equo knew which shape made that sound.

The dragon struck from above, but the wave of fear preceded it. The soldiers fell back, some literally, as the dragon, darker than the storms it had emerged from, fell on them. Even Baraca the scion felt it.

Equo and his brothers were insulated by their very nature from it, but they were too far away to get between the dragon and its prey. The great reptilian shape crashed into the mass of soldiers right where Nyree had been standing.

A desperate cry ripped from Equo's throat. It was no song, just a sound of anguish. The soldiers in the impact area were knocked flying, or crushed beneath the weight of the beast. She roared and snarled, snatching up half a dozen nearby fighters and crushing them between gargantuan jaws. As the trio of dragonets struggled to reach the spot, One-eyed Baraca stood before the granite gray maw of the beast.

A small figure was now distinguishable atop the dragon. She had a blade upraised, and for some unknown reason Equo was more terrified of her than the dragon she rode. Baraca's eyes blazed, and the light which had terrified the other Named seemed to deflect from the dragon. She threw back her craggy head, and when her mouth opened flame poured from it, enveloping the scion in a circle of red light that overwhelmed him.

The light of the Void died with him. The trio of dragonets finally reached the devastation, but it was too late for the scion. Varlesh began the song, as a thrum; a song of transformation that would shatter bone and bring it into line, but the dragon sprung up from the earth, buffeting the smaller shapes the three of them wore.

The song was disrupted as Varlesh and Equo were brought crashing to the ground.

As the Named dragon leapt into the air, Equo saw the tiny, limp form of Nyree hanging from one of its claws. It was impossible to tell if she was dead or alive. The dragon fear claimed those below, like a tide of misery. Clouds swirled around the creature and lightning danced behind her.

Then she laughed, the kind of sound that made ears bleed. Many of Baraca's troops that had managed to stay on their feet until then, howled and fell to their knees when she began to speak. "You wonder, insects, why there are no more scions in Conhaero. Now you see the power of the Phage, and how we take what we want. We are the true power in this world."

With that, the dragon disappeared back into the clouds with a few flaps of her wide wings, faster and more powerful than any form the Ahouri could manage in this moment.

Equo let go of the shape as he watched Nyree disappear with the dragon. Such an ugly creature for such a magnificent name. Despair washed over him.

"She's dead . . ." he whispered to himself, scarcely able to feel his own body anymore. His mind kept repeating again and again, the moments they had shared, his dreams . . .

"Not dead," Si said, putting his hand on his brother's shoulder. "She is the seer. Remember what the Kindred told us. They have taken her because they need her."

"And what, by the Crone, will they do with her?" Varlesh wiped a line of blood from his mouth. "Did you see the dire little child riding his back?" He shook his head. "I did not like the look of her!"

"The Belly of the World," Equo muttered, trying to clear his head of distracting thoughts. If they lost their way now, Nyree would die as Baraca had. "Where is that exactly?"

"Over the water," Si replied. "The place where chaos is born. Not a good place. Even the Vaerli always avoided it."

"And yet," Equo said firmly, "that is where we will be going. The Ahouri will be going even if the Vaerli do not come."

Varlesh looked around them, at the broken remains of One-eyed Baraca's army; the dead and dying with their hollow eyes and the wounds that were deeper than mere flesh. Even the most optimistic of their trio could see what the others saw.

"If the end is truly coming," he said under his breath. "The center of the world is a good a place as any to meet it."

Kelanim had not forgotten that moment. Seeing one of her rivals riding the Caisah that night of the Swoop's invasion had made the point that the nagi had wanted made. Very well, in fact.

Yet she had not made a fuss. Instead, the mistress had simply turned and slipped out the door with neither the Caisah nor his lover noticing that she had come. She had shed no tears as she shuffled back to the chapel, took up the cup, and went back to her room in the harem, clutching the nagi's gift to her. Even when she'd shut the door, she had let none of the venom fall.

Instead, she determined that this shame would be the last. The nagi had given her more than a goblet, he had given her a way out of this humiliation.

For the next few days, Kelanim turned all of her considerable talents of attraction and wile toward the Caisah. It was a bold move, since in the past her full-on attempts to get his attention had sprung back in her face.

As she sat at his side dealing with Court matters, she noticed an imperceptible change—the faintest edge of fatigue seemed to hang around his shoulders. It was not anything that anyone but she would have noticed.

The nagi and the centaur had been right: she had her chance. She used those days to work at the edge of that vulnerability. She wore all the colors the Caisah loved on her; dark green, or vibrant purples. She laughed at all the appropriate times, smiled at him askance, and flirted as only she could. Yet, she did not flaunt herself overly.

The younger members of the harem always made that mistake. The ones that lasted were the ones who quickly realized that he liked to be the pursuer, not the prey. They dressed appropriately, if they were sensible—attractive, but not showing quite everything.

Kelanim bent all that knowledge she had gained in her years in the harem toward catching his eye. It would not be the first time that his interest in her had waned. His affections were like the tide, and she would draw him back in again.

Nearly a week after her embarrassment, Kelanim succeeded. The Caisah called for her to dance for him late that evening, and immediately she felt the thrill of victory. He spent that night in her chamber, watching her, talking with her, laying her in the bed, and most importantly of all, drinking with her.

When the Caisah first lay his lips on the cup of the nagi, Kelanim had been sure that he would take one taste, spot the deception, and fling it—and most likely her, too—out the window to smash on the stones many floors below. Instead, he had laughed, poured the wine on her body and licked it off.

It had taken every ounce of her self control to laugh along with him, and pretend that it was all pleasure and hedonism for her.

Whatever it was, that first drink helped her cause. The next day, the Caisah had eyes for no one but Kelanim. He came to her chamber again, drank deeply from the cup, and did not even need her to wind her charms around him with dance. Instead he took her on the rug by the fire.

None of this made the mistress feel better in any way. Three times, that was what the nagi had said, and so it would have to be three times.

The Caisah was sitting in his throne. General Despian of the Rutilian Guard was on bended knee before him, his scarlet jacket dulled in the shadows of the room. The news he had just delivered was the kind that should have driven the Caisah into a frothing rage, and Despian knew it. He was a grizzled old man, who had worn out his life in service to Conhaero and its ruler. Yet he was visibly trembling as he knelt.

Kelanim, lazily waving her peacock fan in front of her face and watching the scene, would have predicted this would end in a bloody fashion on any other day. She had seen a few such occasions before, and been forced to move fast to keep the hem of her dress from ruin.

However, as her eyes drifted furtively toward the Caisah, she suspected that today would not be that sort of day.

"You Majesty," the general spoke, after kneeling on a bent knee for many minutes. His gout must have been acting up for him to dare to question when he knew his life depended on it. "Majesty, did you hear that the rebel Baraca has taken Peuluis? The garrison has been overrun, and the populace is tearing down the wall."

"Yes," the Caisah replied, waving his hand. "That town has always been troublesome."

Despian cleared his throat. "And the Swoop was part of the group that helped take the town. Without their assistance, it might never have fallen."

Kelanim liked the man's forward behavior. He had never cared for the Swoop, and must have in private taken great delight in that piece of news. If he thought he was going to lose his head anyway, he might as well press the point.

The Caisah was not even looking in his direction. Instead his gaze turned to Kelanim, and a flash of a smile darted over his lips.

"Majesty?" the general ventured again. "What would you have us do?"

Kelanim felt her stomach clench. If the Caisah fell apart right in front of his people, it could be the end of his Empire. The people believed in his immortality and his almost omniscient view.

A small voice whispered in the back of her head: wasn't this what she wanted? For him to be mortal, and hers?

The Caisah was smiling at her, his eyes seeming to pierce right through her. It was as if he were looking at her for the very first time. Kelanim felt her own eyes prickle with tears, and she clutched onto her fan with tight white fingers.

"It is time," the tyrant spoke, so softly that all of the Court had to lean forward to catch his words, "for my part to come to an end."

He held out his hand to Kelanim, and she rose quickly to stand beside him and take it. She felt as though her heart would burst with pride.

The Caisah inclined his head, as though he were telling a tale to a group of children—which, from his way of thinking, they were. "I was not born in this world, but in another place just as cruel, though it was not the heart of chaos."

Kelanim could feel the Court hanging on every word that came out of her love's mouth. All of them, from solider to scholar, and from courtesan to milk maid, had always wondered and pondered on the beginning of the Caisah. Never in all the time before this moment, had he spoken of it—not even to give the slightest hint.

He walked down off the dais and she went with him, beaming with pride. Finally, they stood before the tall staff that hung on the wall. She could not remember a time it had not been there. Only now, looking up at the golden eagle with spread wings that stood atop it, did the mistress wonder what part it played in the Caisah's story.

His eyes were fixed on it now, like a drowning man might look at a piece of flotsam. "This was the mark of my honor. It was everything I had dreamed of. This was carried before the infantry that I commanded, and where we went the heathens trembled in fear. Until that day . . . the day that the mists descended, and we went into the White Void."

Kelanim gasped as his hand tightened on hers, but he took no heed of her, lost in the memory. The mistress glanced around at the Court in horror, because she knew it was not what they wanted to hear. The councilors at the back were whispering amongst themselves, and the general, who had finally levered himself up off his knee, had retreated back toward his aides. The Caisah could not afford to lose the trust of both the politicians and the army.

"Darling," Kelanim whispered under her breath, "you are not well. Let's go back to my chamber and we can . . ."

The Caisah completely ignored her, though he kept his hand tight on hers, while the other stroked the smooth wood of the staff. His voice now was more for himself than for anyone else. "They promised so much—honor, glory and power. They said I would lead the world in victory, and bring an end to cowardice. All I had to do was promise to be theirs. Be the scion that they needed."

Scion. The word flashed around the room like lightning. Now there were more than whispers, there were actually people stepping back from the Caisah. One or two were even taking the chance and slipping away. Their leader did not even appear to notice, his eyes ever fixed on the golden eagle as if it could tell him something.

Rebellion in the east, and now the Caisah was losing his grip on power. He'd ranted and railed before—Kelanim had seen plenty of that. However, this time was different. This time he seemed not to care about power at all.

Kelanim was only his mistress; she knew full well that the Court had less than zero respect for her. They would not listen to her if she spoke. Actually, if she did, her love would only look weaker. So she stood there, for the first time in her life utterly at a loss at what to do.

The Swoop did her a favor then. Windows shattered high above, raining shards of glass down on the glittering Court. Now their whispers turned to screams of horror. For a moment Kelanim smiled as the great birds of prey—a hundred at least—poured through the broken windows. Feathers and shrieks filled the air. All of the hangers-on, the beautiful advancement-seekers and the leeches, started running for their lives.

As the women of the Swoop reached the ground and slipped from bird to armored soldier form, some of the Rutilian Guards finally remembered their jobs. As they stepped between the Swoop and the Caisah, Kelanim noticed that General Despian was not one of them. In fact, she noted how he slipped back from action altogether and out the door.

The Caisah had not moved. Not even the appearance of flying women could pull his gaze away from the strange memento on the wall. The sound of sword on sword brought home to Kelanim that she had to do something.

This was her doing. It was the nagi and the centaur. She had made him weak to make him hers—and now he might well die for it. The mistress threw down her fan and grabbed his hand.

"Come with me," she said with a gasp.

Her looked at her, and for an instant she thought she was looking into the Void itself. He had nothing of any strength behind those eyes. Only sadness and loss looked back at her, so that she felt stripped and tiny in his gaze.

The unfortunate truth was, she still loved him, and she knew that she could mend that hurt. "Please come with me," she repeated, though so softly maybe he couldn't hear it over the tumult in the throne room.

He turned and yanked the staff off the wall. It was a ridiculous thing to be dragging about, but something of his expression told Kelanim that there would be no changing his mind. The sound of the fighting quieted slightly as they ran through the corridors of Perilous and Fair. The mistress was no warrior, but she knew that the few soldiers in the throne room could not hold off the Swoop for long. They had come for the Caisah's head, and they knew the corridors of this place as well as any.

Yet Kelanim knew many places even the Swoop did not. The mistresses traveled through a series of concealed exits and entrances that made up a maze in Perilous and Fair. Many people had attempted to map all of them, and been flummoxed. Kelanim knew them better than most everyone. She had made it one of her priorities to learn as many of the twists and turns as the eunuchs knew. It kept her rivals on their toes when she turned up in unexpected places.

"Here," she said, pushing aside one of the garish tapestries and fumbling for the slightly rough edge of the wall. It had been many, many years since the Vaerli lived in their city, but their engineering still worked very well. The door slid aside, and the Caisah followed her into the corridors.

They stood panting in the semi-darkness. Or at least Kelanim was panting. The Caisah was absolutely quiet, holding his staff and staring off to nowhere.

His mistress leaned her head back against the stone wall and listened. The thickness of the walls muffled any sound that might have reached them, and there was a certain comfort in that. "We'll just wait until the Swoop is beaten back," she whispered. "The Rutilians will chase them off sooner or later . . . we just have to wait . . ."

"We cannot do that," the Caisah replied, his hands clenching and unclenching on the staff. She did not like the tone of his voice.

"Well, we can't stay here either." It was hard not to be a little frustrated. Kelanim was beginning to suspect that she might have gone too far with the taming of her love. He seemed unlike himself, and she had loved that part of him. She thought of her grandfather's stallions, the ones he had raised before he lost the farm gambling. They changed when they were gelded, and she was terrified that she had done the very same thing to the Caisah.

"It is time to go . . ." He jerked free of her hand. In the half-light she was sure that there was the suggestion of light around him. It couldn't be.

"We can't," she protested. "This is our home!"

When he turned on her, his eyes gleamed with eldritch light. Perhaps she had not sufficiently gelded him after all. "This is *not* home!" he barked at her. "This was never my home!"

Kelanim leaned against the wall for support and blinked up at him, wondering if his mind had broken completely. She went to touch him and he batted her hand aside. Then his fingers closed on her wrist—hard.

She winced, but didn't fight back; she knew all too well where that would end. For a moment she was sure that he would dash her head against the rock, or choke the life from her. Kelanim was sure that she deserved it.

But then she tried to breathe. It was like sucking in ice water. Her body went into shock and her mind into a panic. Everything around her flared a burning white, and for a long dreadful moment she wondered what had happened.

Then it all stopped. Now she was bathed in warm air and standing in a night-time forest. Clutching her arms to her chest and breathing heavily, she looked around. How they had come here she had no idea, but when she turned and looked at the Caisah she knew immediately it was his doing. He had a broad grin on his face. "We're nearly there." He held out his hand to her, and she hesitantly took it.

"How . . ." she stopped and cleared her throat. "How did we get here?"

He shrugged. "How do you think I can do all the things I have done?" He leaned forward until his breath was hot on her face. "Think about it hard, Kelanim . . ."

Her love's gaze was so intent on her that she froze in fear. "I . . . I don't know . . ."

At the moment she would have appreciated it if the centaur, or even the nagi, had appeared from under the dark branches. This version of the Caisah was not one she knew or trusted, so she did the thing she had learned as a way to survive his moods; she kept her mouth shut and her eyes open.

After letting out an irritated, half-muttered curse, as if she were too stupid to understand anything, he tugged her.

Together they scrambled down the slight slope to a clearing that seemed familiar to the Caisah. Moonlight was gleaming on a building, and Kelanim knew immediately it had to be Vaerli.

It was certainly a strange one, too. It looked like nothing more than a dais with a series of three steps leading up to it. As they got closer, it looked as though it were made of ice, but ice that had intricate patterns of words carved into it.

Kelanim had lived long enough within the walls of Perilous and Fair to know word magic when she saw it. To see so much in such a desolate place made her shiver even in the warmth. She did not want to go any closer, but the Caisah pulled her toward the strange structure.

When he finally allowed them to stop, he stood there, staring at the stairs as if all the answers were written there; perhaps they were.

"Beautiful, isn't it?" the Caisah whispered to her.

She nodded, but he wasn't really watching her. "Where are we?" she ventured to ask.

"The *Arohai tuan*, the Steps of Sacrifice," came the reply, though that did not enlighten her. The Caisah shot her a look over one shoulder. "This is where I first set foot in Conhaero."

She was getting what she wanted; he was telling her his story. Now that it was coming, she did not know if she wanted to hear it.

"This is where I came from. This is as near to home as I may come." The Caisah spoke slowly, as if by doing so he could somehow make her understand.

Suddenly the mistress wanted to shout at him very badly.

CHAPTER FIFTEEN

THE LESSONS OF THE DEAD

The spectre of Putorae, the Last Seer of the Vaerli, had certainly not lost any of her strength of will by being dead. For three days, Talyn, Ysel, and Finn sat cross-legged by the pool on one of the islands of Elraban and listened to her. At their back, Fida, the Vaerli who had deliberately lost herself, watched with arms crossed. It was like trying to cram too many clothes into too small a saddlebag—at least, that was the conclusion that Talyn came to.

The role of a seer was a complicated one; she already knew that from her brief time with her family before the Harrowing. They stood in the currents of time, both reminding the people of where they had come from, and telling them where they should go. They were not leaders, but advisors, and highly venerated.

Ellyria had been the first, and her twin daughters had been the first pair of born and made. If anyone had ever mentioned that there should be any change to that, Talyn had not heard it. According to Putorae, times and needs had altered.

They spent the first day learning to be still and let time flow over them. The yester-thoughts all had to wash past them, and they would have to grasp what they could from them. Ysel was naturally better at that, since he had only recently been with the Kindred, who found time a far more fluid concept than even the Vaerli did.

The second day, the three of them turned toward the future-thoughts. For this Fida was involved, striking at them with a staff procured from the tale-spinners. Talyn was best at this task, since in the Caisah's employ she had been struck at numerous times. Finn was terrible at it, and by the end of the day ended up battered, bruised and angry.

It was near the tail of that day that Talyn noticed the sliver of Putorae was growing thinner and less visible in the air she occupied. It was amazing she had lasted this long, but Talyn did not point it out to anyone else. She was certain they saw what she did, anyway.

On the final day, the Last Seer finally set about teaching the manipulation of the White Void that would be their only chance of survival when they reached the Belly. She stood, her body only a vague sketch against the blue of the sea and sky, and lectured them on the dangers.

"The White Void will find whatever weakness you have," she cautioned. "It will magnify that, and since we all have flaws there is no use in me trying to tell you to lose them."

The three new seers shared a worried look at that.

"However, with the use of the Gifts, you may pass through." She floated before Talyn first. "Hold onto the First Gift, the earth sense. No place shall be strange to you, even the Void."

Then she slid across to Ysel, looking down at him with a maternal smile. "The Fifth Gift, the control of memory, will keep your minds from flying apart in the White Void. It can do terrible things to your sense of self. So keep a good hold on that Gift as you journey."

Putorae drifted to stand before Finn.

"Finally, the Second Gift, empathy." Her face, now almost a sketch on the breeze, flitted into a form that might have been sadness. "Often overlooked, but in the old days, we could not harm another without feeling it ourselves. In the White Void, that will bind you together and give you strength you do not have on your own."

"Unfortunately, there is no way to practice." Finn spoke, saying what Talyn had been thinking all day. "And the Gifts . . . I cannot feel them . . ."

"That is because they must be given back by the Kindred." Talyn was trying to remain positive, but this venture felt ill-prepared and dangerous. "Until that time, we will be traveling almost blind."

"Wahirangi will take us to the Belly," Finn reminded her. "I would rather have him at our side when we get there. If we can convince the rest of Kindred that the Vaerli will accept their role in the Pact, then we will be fine."

Perhaps as a talespinner he had been trained to look for the happy ending, but Talyn had not. She did not voice her fears.

They spent the rest of the day discussing the many ways the White Void could kill them or drive them mad. They also discussed the Phage, with Talyn sharing what little she knew of them. The mere fact that they could Name Kindred, and that Finn had seen one Named dragon, was enough to depress all three of them by the end.

Putorae, or at least this remaining sliver of her, did not seem put off, but by the time the sun had began to slip below the horizon, she was more a whisper than even a physical presence.

"This is the last." Talyn saw that Ysel and Finn, like she, struggled to hear what the seer was saying. "Only one more memory of me remains in Conhaero, and that is not meant for you, my sons." The sketch of her peerless eyes flickered against the dying sun. "I hope I have given you enough to find your way. I hope I have atoned for not helping my people to see their duty."

This last was said so wistfully that Talyn moved from her spot on the earth beside Finn. She stood close to the remaining portion of the Last Seer, and suddenly wished that she could find some way to communicate her admiration. "You thought of them," was finally all she could offer. "You gave us a chance."

Putorae's eyes flickered over Ysel and Finnbarr; so different and yet so very important. Her pale hand rose as if to touch them, and then she was washed away into nothing.

Her sons sat for a moment staring at the space where she had been, but it was Ysel who finally moved. He jerked himself away, as Fida hastened to his side.

"I think I will get some sleep," he said, in that odd and eerily mature way he had about him. "Tomorrow the tide will be upon us." He held up his arms, and Finn got down on one knee to hug him.

It was strange to consider that they should have been the same age, but there were many strange things in Conhaero.

As Ysel and his protector walked to the woven bridge, Finn let out a long sigh, shaking his head. "Taking a child into battle just feels wrong."

"He is far more than a child," Talyn reminded him, "just as you are far more than a talespinner."

He nodded, though he didn't look entirely convinced. He tapped his toe in the very edge of the pool.

"Amazing how she came right out of here," he commented. "All the time I was training on this spot, and she was here watching over me. I never knew she was so close. Never imagined."

Talyn shook her head. "The son of Putorae and the Caisah. That will take some getting used to."

He shot her a look out of the corner of his eye. "I hope it doesn't make any difference. I know the Caisah isn't your favorite person and . . ."

It all came flooding back to her now—the reason why she had first fallen in love with the talespinner. It was his willingness to be vulnerable, and to share those feelings. She had known too much deception and conspiracy in her life, when she'd met him. Talyn wished she had a scion to pray to, that she might try a prayer that he kept his vulnerability.

Death or madness certainly awaited them. It was not the White Void that made her afraid; it was the Phage. They would never even let them get close to the Belly.

Talyn stopped his worries and protestations by pressing her hand against his mouth. "I have to let go of all that, Finn." When she pulled her fingers away, she did not move away from him. "What has all my anger and hatred got me? I've been led by it into some dreadful places, done dreadful things."

Her throat clenched as she thought on it. "My father tried to warn me, turn me aside from that path, but I wouldn't listen to him. I thought he was the fool, and I sent him away."

Tears, which she should have shed long ago, began to leak from the corners of her eyes, and she dropped her head, ashamed at them. Rather than wipe them away, Finn gathered her into his arms and let them come.

She had yet to tell him all the other things that she had done, even if he knew many of them. She pulled back, and looked him in the eye as best she could. "I chose to forget you too, Finn. I was afraid what I felt for you made me weak, and would stop me on my path. If I hadn't, things would be different."

He pressed his lips together for a moment, and then gave a slight shrug. "To be honest, I have never understood why anyone would think love makes them weak. The old stories tell differently. Perhaps if you'd listened to those instead . . ."

It was a feeble attempt at a joke, but Talyn let out a little laugh. "I remember you used to tell wonderful stories to me after . . ." She stopped on the thought. They both remembered where he had told her most of the stories.

Talyn, the once-Hunter, knew that she was on the edge of another precipice. The Phage would not let her go, and the Conflagration, the arrival of the White Void was upon them. Soon there would be no time for anything else, and she desperately wanted Finn to remind her that she was more than the mistakes she had made.

When he looked at her, she felt like more than the angry fool who had let vengeance and rage guide her.

Talyn leaned over and kissed him, because she knew very well he would not move until she did. The after-thoughts washed back over her, and the remembrance made the kiss all the sweeter. When he ran his hand up her neck and into her hair, she let out a muffled sigh against his lips.

Talyn wanted to touch all of him. She wanted to take back her love and her lover. She wanted to mend herself back into the person she should have been. When they finally pulled apart to breathe, she smiled.

"The end is coming, Finnbarr the Fox." Her whisper was directly into his ear. "And I would rather not get naked in front of your mother."

His laughter was almost a startled bark, but Finn got to his feet and pulled her with him. "I have a room, but I warn you, like all the rooms in the village, it can get a little drafty."

"I am sure we'll find a way to make it warm," she replied, and let herself be led off the tiny island and across the swaying rope bridges to a swinging pod that hung far above the sea. It was attached to the rope system and had a sturdy floor as well as a cocoon of blankets and thick rush mattress.

"More of a nest than a bedroom," Finn said, holding aside the reed door which afforded a modicum of privacy. "It is all the students have, so I am used to it. I'm not really used to sharing it with anyone, though."

"Well," Talyn replied tartly, "we shall just have to hope we don't shake it loose of its moorings."

His laugh was low and honeyed as he let the door swing shut behind them. Starlight and moonlight filtered through the cracks in the woven nest, and it was just enough for them both to be able to see what they were doing.

The sound of the pounding surf below, and the smell of the sea was different than anything Talyn had experienced for a long time. Those were sensations that she associated with Finn very much. The memories of their nights shut in the tiny cabin were overlaid over this experience.

The swaying, however, was something new. As they stripped off each other's clothes in somewhat of a frenzy, they found themselves giggling.

"What a shame it would be if two seers died like this," Finn chuckled, while his hands trailed over her naked skin. "All the plans of my mother and the Vaerli would be upset."

"They would be quite angry," Talyn agreed, before running the flat of her tongue over the line of his neck.

They slid down into the tangle of blankets, where the chill wind off the sea could not reach, and began getting reacquainted with the curves and plains of each other's bodies.

It had been a long time since Talyn had lain with a man, but she found the experience with Finn different. It was not just about getting some relief for her primitive urges, but also about making her lover feel joy and pleasure too. She was glad to be able to see his face in the half-darkness, and gained great pleasure when he groaned her name.

For a while, all time was filled with finding each other once again. Sweat and a few tears came between them, but they held each other and savored even the twinges of loss.

When they were finally done, the tide had turned underneath them, and there was only warmth and smiles. Talyn lay nestled against Finn, and felt the swaying of the nest subside a little.

"I guess they make these things stronger than I thought," she said with a smile.

"I guess so," Finn replied with a warm chuckle, "quite surprising really."

They lay there in silence, neither apparently wanting to sleep or lose the moment. Until Finn let out a soft curse and sat up.

He lit a nearby lantern, and hung it on the hook. As he sat up in bed and pulled her toward him, the light flickered pleasantly on his torso.

"Now you find the light?" she murmured with a slight grin. Then she got a better look at his expression and she did not like it. A jolt of cold intruded on her warmth.

His blue eyes were dark in the shadows cast by the lantern.

"Talyn, why did the Phage send you all this way with a blank piece of paper they said could only be destroyed by dragon flame? What possible reason could there be for that except that they wanted you to find me, and that would mean . . ."

That was when the screams reached them—the screams of the talespinners as their village began to burn.

It was darkness so complete and deep that Byreniko could sense nothing—not even his own body. Pelanor was a distant memory, though what he had seen in the chambers beneath the Salt still burned in his mind. Most of all, his blade sliding into his mother's flesh. That would never go away.

This darkness, then, was almost a blessing. He wanted to stay in this between state, cut off from everything and everyone.

Yet it was not to be. He was not completely alone.

"I always wanted to know my people, now I wish I did not," he whispered to himself.

You must live one last thing, the Kindred whispered into Byre's hollow head in the total darkness. *Live the past to save the future.*

"I don't want to see any more," he said, his voice swallowed by the emptiness around him. "Give me the flames Ellyria endured, the pain and loss of her body. I don't want to know anymore about the Vaerli. They are dead to me."

They made mistakes, sacrificed their own children, and would not take up their responsibilities. They were afraid. The Kindred's voice was soft, and maybe he was trying to imagine it but there seemed to be some sadness in its tone. *You must see that they do not all deserve death for it. They are worth saving, because some of them had faith.*

"Do I have a choice?" Byre felt a great weariness flood over him.

There is always a choice. You chose to go on this journey, to search out the truth. Even when your father was dead, you had a choice to not come to us. This is who you are, and it makes you perfect for what is to come.

"And what is that?"

You will find the answer to that in the last place we send you. It will be deeper, and you must go alone.

Byre hung there in the darkness, and it was impossible to tell for how long. He wondered if it were all a trick; if the Kindred was telling him how special he was along this journey, only to drop him from a great height later on.

Even in this odd in-between state, he felt the sting of curiosity, and the knowledge that the Kindred was right. For all the terrible things the Vaerli had done out of fear and ignorance, he would not condemn them all.

"Then I will go," Byre said finally, and then he fell.

The darkness swirled around him and he wondered where he would land . . . until he realized he already had. He was on his knees on the Salt, sobbing, while screams echoed around him. Salt crystals were cutting his knees, and it was hard to catch his breath when he was sobbing and screaming. A thousand fractured thoughts raced through his brain, and he could not catch hold of any of them. Honor. Fear. His mother's face begging him not to go. The White Void luring away another of his soldiers to death and madness.

Byre tried to stop, to catch his breath, but then he realized this wasn't his body to stop. The hands clutching onto the salt were paler than his own, and the Kindred's explanation of going deeper now made sense.

He was not observing the Caisah. He was the Caisah. This would have been so much more outrageous if he had not just gained a little more insight into the man—but apparently he had not gained enough for the Kindred.

Byre could not move even the man's smallest finger, but he could feel the rumble of his thoughts, like a swirling caldron just at his back. It was a terrifying sensation, this loss of control. He was choking on it.

"Are you all right?" a voice seemed to reach out and wrap itself around the madness, soothing and calm, like the hand that was placed on his shoulder. The relief of it was dizzying.

The Caisah did not recognize the voice, but Byre did. He had been young when he last heard it, but it was the kind of beautiful voice that left a mark. It promised kindness and understanding.

The Caisah turned and looked up at the face. Putorae, the Last Seer of the Vaerli, was looking down at him. She had not been at the terrible final meeting of the council, but it had all been too much of a blur for Byre to think overly much on it. She was the born seer of her generation, and thus the *pae atuae* would only show on her skin when she used her powers. At the moment her golden-brown skin was unmarked, but her eyes were still full of stars.

The Caisah's brain was bursting with life, but it felt . . . better somehow. "You are the seer," the interloper choked out, "so why did you not stop me? You must have seen what would happen . . ."

She placed her hand beneath his elbow and brought him to his feet. The seer was far shorter than he, her tiny frame making him instantly want to protect her. She was the most beautiful thing in all the worlds, because she really did see. The Caisah knew instantly that she saw beyond what the Kindred and the White Void had made of him. She saw the man who had walked into the mist and become lost. That had been a good man.

Putorae was also the saddest creature he had ever laid eyes on. Every line of her body spoke of weariness and mourning. Her hand remained on his shoulder, as if she had forgotten it. "Some things must happen. Even the worst things in the world must be borne to untangle what must be untangled."

The Caisah looked at her curiously, wondering at the feelings bubbling up inside him; he wanted to protect her and make her smile again.

Putorae closed her eyes, her hand now unconsciously rubbing his back, but this time leaning into him as if to hold her up. Byre, riding way back in the tyrant's head, felt his own heart go out to her. When she opened her eyes, their darkness was still full of circling stars.

"What is your name?" she asked softly.

It had never occurred to Byre that the man they were all so terrified of had a name aside from the Caisah—yet, that was only a title. Something was bubbling up from before; memories that were not Byre's.

He caught a glimpse of an army of men, and pride in them nearly choked his throat. Then mist, descending around them as they marched, but they were proud and they went on. The White Void's light enveloped them, and the dangers of it began to take his soldiers, his men, his duty. The struggle to keep them alive wore on the leader's strength, tore at him, but made him something else.

He had a name.

"Vitus," the Caisah whispered. "My name is Vitus."

"And you are a scion," Putorae replied. "The Eagle King." Her hand now touched his face, and suddenly the broken parts of Vitus' brain and soul seemed to make a whole. The seer held him together, even as she looked so sad. "You are the scion with whom I shall bear the future."

In those dark eyes, Byre fell once more to darkness, suddenly sorry to be leaving the head of his enemy.

When he woke, he was on the reassuringly painful ground, his own knees cracked and bleeding. It was Pelanor who was touching him, her hand on his back.

He shrugged her off and rose. Once more he was back under the earth in the rocky cavern that they had first entered, and he could feel the Kindred not far off. Now he was angry; he had felt the kind of man this Vitus was. A good one, until the Kindred had placed too much faith in him.

"Why did you choose him?" Byre raged, pacing up and down their tiny prison. He was screaming at the walls, but he knew that they had ears to hear him.

"Who?" Pelanor asked softly. "Who did they choose? What do you mean?"

Byre could feel that he was ready to snap. He wanted to break something, to see something crack open, like he felt he might. "The Caisah! They needed someone to bring the Vaerli back into line, so they picked him as their messenger . . . but he couldn't hold that much power. He broke. He was not Vaerli, but they used him anyway!"

What would you have had us do? The Kindred with its flaming eyes pulled itself free of the stone wall, stepping toward them. *The Vaerli had stopped listening to us. They had begun to bolster their own power with other races from the Void. We needed one to speak for us. Someone who was outside the Pact.*

Byre stared at the creature of chaos and tried to imagine how mortal creatures looked to them. They could not understand fear and loss the way that even the Vaerli did. To them, their allies of the Pact had been weak and foolish. Neither had they been able to understand the limits of one man's strength.

Everything was rock and chaos. Yet something drove them, and he had to know what.

"What was so urgent about the Vaerli going into the White Void anyway?" Byre walked over and stood only a foot from the Kindred. He raked his eyes over the creature, and examined it as probably no other living being had in a long time. He took in the flaming eyes, the formless gray and brown shape that looked as if it came from the earth itself. It could be anything, but it was nothing. The Kindred were part of Conhaero and they were obsessed with the White Void.

This world is special. The Kindred spoke finally, while its eyes blazed brighter. *A center of chaos and change across all the worlds. Beyond time, it is the font of forces that fight entropy. It burns. See it as we see it.*

The prison walls changed from simply earth to something else entirely: a shifting wall of flame and beauty with infinite patterns. It swirled and pulsed with a rhythm that seemed to penetrate his bones and he suddenly comprehended truly the beauty of change. Without change, all was stagnation and arrogance. Change made mortals rise to challenges and feel the true depth and joy of being alive. Even in adversity they found themselves. The patterns that Conhaero wove could bring down Empires of tyrants and benevolent kings, but all needed to be shaken to the foundation.

Pelanor, who had been standing at Byre's shoulder, fell to her knees, a beatific smile on her face. "It is what I saw on the edge of death. The twelfth maw of the goddess, the beginning and end of all things." Red tears escaped the corners of her eyes and poured down over her cheeks.

She was obviously seeing something different than Byre was—but it was just as affecting.

We may be outside time, but time still changes what we do. The White Void has grown more vast and dangerous over time, stretching wider than we can travel from Conhaero. Yet, change and chaos must reach all worlds or everything would be as it is forever.

"The Vaerli were meant to be those heralds," Byre croaked out as the words of the Pact came back to him. "We were made to ride the White Void for you."

We must always remain with Conhaero. The Pact was indeed made so that you could take change and chaos into all the worlds connected by the Void.

"You didn't see it as we did." He looked up into the flaming implacable eyes. "You are not creatures of flesh and bone. What you thought of as a simple thing terrified the Vaerli—even with all the gifts you gave them."

He quickly recalled the complete lack of understanding the Kindred had displayed when he was being tortured. They looked on the Vaerli as they were, themselves, and could have little comprehension of what their allies in the Pact felt.

They had threatened the Vaerli, and the Vaerli had acted in fear.

Byre took a long breath. "The past is gone, and even the Kindred cannot bring it back. What about the Gifts—will you return them to us?"

The Kindred leaned in closer, so that Byre could feel the uncomfortable heat of the creature's body and smell the sulphur coming from him. "If the Pact is restored and the seers stand before us, then the Gifts will be needed by our warriors. You must be there, at the end. A chance remains to answer that call."

He was going to have to take that as a yes.

The seers. His mind raced. He knew of Nyree, the seer that was Putorae's acolyte, but the born seer had not revealed herself. So, one seer who might or might not be dead, and another that he didn't even know the name of.

"The White Void is coming," he muttered to Pelanor. "How am I supposed to find these seers in time to stop it?"

She was a Phaerkorn, she could have no answers, but she tried her best. "Maybe there is something in Perilous. Some hint to the born seer and her whereabouts . . . some . . ."

The Kindred moved so fast that even in the before-time Byre was not certain he could have tracked it. It was suddenly on Pelanor, leaning over her. The Blood Witch froze, her eyes raised to the force of chaos. If menace could have been conveyed in a better way, Byre could not think of it.

The flaming eyes raked over the Phaerkorn, measuring her and weighing her worth in ways that not even the Vaerli could tell.

When the Kindred's voice finally issued from the impassive stone, the tone was hungry. "You have her stain on you, the hint of a seer awakened."

Pelanor and Byre stared at each other, but it was the Vaerli that spoke. "She has my blood . . . are you saying I am the seer?"

"No." It was bluntly put, and Byre had never more thoroughly put in his place. Considering his history, that was quite impressive.

"But the only other blood I have had is . . ." The Phaerkorn gasped, choking under sudden understanding, and then looked up at Byre, her eyes wide. "Is . . . is that possible?"

"My sister . . . the born seer?" When Byre thought of her, the only image he had was her face set in pain. She had found him the best home she could at short notice. The curse, even then, had been eating its way into them. Soon they would burn, but her dark eyes had filled with tears, even as she began to walk away. He had heard many stories of his sister since then, some from his father—and they had not been good. His sister had become a Hunter for the Caisah, and though he knew the tyrant was not all that his people had thought, in his madness he had made his sister do terrible things.

She is revealed, the Kindred spoke softly. *The end game is upon us, and the arrival of the White Void has bought her power to the surface, like magma will rise.*

"And the Gifts?" Byre asked. "I have walked the ways to the past, seen more than I ever wanted about my own people, and I understand now. Will you return the Gifts to my people?"

One last walk for you, one last test to prove that you are the Vaerli to lead your people. The seers see the path, but you as Chief must hold your people to it. Show them the way, and finally share a road for a time with your sister.

The Kindred was now at his side, breathing flame and promises onto his skin. He could see that this was where his father had hoped the journey would end. He would take up the mantle of leadership that his mother had carried. The trail would lead to reforming the council, showing it bravery and steadfastness.

First, though, he would have to master the White Void, and learn to travel it as his ancestors had always been meant to do.

"Take me with you," Pelanor said simply, putting her hand in his. "I have seen the twelfth mouth of the goddess. I am not afraid of anything. The White Void or your relatives." Her smile was brief and bright. "Besides, I have seen your sister much more recently than you have. I might have to make introductions."

Part of Byre wanted to deny her place, but she had walked the path with him, and her strength and company had saved him.

He cleared his throat, feeling his body tense like he was about to dive into deep and unknown water. "How do I use it, then?"

The Void is so close now. The Kindred stepped back into the darkness and embrace of the earth. *It is within you. Find it.*

Byre thought of his mother dying alone on the Salt, her bones washed clean by the wind. He thought of his father, dying in his arms, cut off from the Vaerli. Then he thought of Ellyria Dragonsoul, her strength and kindness shining through her eyes. She was how a Vaerli ought to be, brave and compassionate.

He wanted to be that person. He wanted to be the things his parents had always striven to help him be.

Byreniko wrapped the fingers of his right hand around Pelanor's, and then reached out with his left. The White Void was close. He could feel it tingling on the tips of his extended hand, chill and terrifying.

Like his ancestors, he felt the terror of it. So many things could happen in the White Void. He accepted that terror, let it in to become part of him.

Then he moved his fingers; the faintest flutter divided reality, and the glare of the between worlds was there. Somehow, he knew the way.

"It's not far." He turned back and whispered to Pelanor. "Don't let go."

"I won't," she returned, with the faintest of smiles.

Byre led the way into the White Void.

CHAPTER SIXTEEN

RETRACING THE STEPS

Kelanim looked around her, feeling the chill of the evening cut right down to her bones. She was not dressed for this sudden foray into the wilds; her thin silk dress and beaded wrap were no match for this cold night. "Why are we here?" she stammered out through lips that were already turning blue.

"Because she is here." It was impossible to read the Caisah's eyes in the shadows of all these trees.

The way he spoke those words filled her with a kind of dread that only ghost stories she had shared with other harem women could. She licked her lips before daring to ask, "She who?"

He held out his hand to her. "Come, I will introduce you . . ."

She had nowhere to run at this point, but the mistress was trembling as she put her hand in his. He led her closer to the Steps, which gleamed like cut ice in the moonlight. Like the walls of Perilous and Fair, this edifice was covered in the word magic that the Vaerli favored. She wanted to know what it said, but was also glad to be ignorant. The sinuous lines of the writing made her uneasy.

"What happened here?" she whispered, more to herself, but the Caisah answered.

"This was the place where it all began." He pointed to the top of the steps, a circular space that Kelanim would not have stepped within even if her life depended on it. "That is where the Vaerli slit the throats of their first born children, so that the White Void would open its center and the other peoples that journeyed in it could come through. If you listen, you can hear the screams of the little ones." He brought them to a stop within only a few feet of the first step, and cocked his head.

Kelanim forgot to breathe, her ears straining to make out what he was hearing. In this dark and mysterious place it was easy for her racing brain to imagine the howls and sobs of children being dragged to the top of those three steps. She shuddered at the terror they must have felt. Even if they had known why their parents were doing these things, they must have been out of their minds with horror.

The mistress had always wanted the Caisah's children so badly that her whole body ached at the thought of it.

He shook his head, as if trying to clear it of what he had heard. "But she is waiting to meet you." He took her trembling hand in his, and she followed. What other choice did she have?

Not too far from the Steps, he knelt down and pulled her with him. It just looked like another piece of ground to the mistress, but the Caisah had a soft smile on his face. "The Steps travel, you see, moving with the Chaos, but they always take her with them. She's very special, you see."

Kelanim looked around, but they were totally alone. No sound even emanated from the forest that surrounded them. She shivered, and chose her words as carefully as she could. "There's no one here, my lord. Let's go back."

His head flicked around. "We can't go back. Perilous and Fair is no longer ours, and we are far from alone."

He started scrabbling at the ground, and Kelanim felt the edge of panic creep closer. The dirt was flying, and inside her head she could hear a voice telling her to get up and run as far and fast as she could. She did not want to see what he was doing.

This was the Caisah who could move mountains at his command, who was a force of nature, and yet here he was, digging like some madman. That voice in the back of her mind told her to get up and walk away now. It didn't matter that they were alone and the forest was dark and frightening—it couldn't be any more frightening than this man at her side.

He was also the man she loved, whom she had sacrificed much for, and whom she had condemned to weakness because of her own desires. Kelanim knew that she had to stay. She leaned back on her heels and watched with dull eyes as the Caisah dug up what she knew it had to be.

Bones. They gleamed as white as the Steps they were tethered to. Vague remnants of clothing still clung to them, what might once have been a beautiful dress. Vaerli bones, by their size, small and delicate.

They must have been there a long time, because there was no stench of death about them.

"This is Putorae," the Caisah said, and sighed as if he were finally content. "Putorae, this is Kelanim." He glanced back at the mistress, and the gleam of madness in his eye pinned her to the spot.

She did not know what to say but, "Hello, Putorae." Apparently she was as deep in this madness as he was.

"Putorae is the mother of my children," the Caisah went on, his fingertips brushing the clean, white bone as if he were stroking beloved flesh.

That jolted Kelanim from her stunned reverie. "M . . . Mother?"

"Yes, mother," he said, his eyes never leaving the patch of dirt. "My only children; twin boys. She was bad, though; she hid them from me. Gone, I do not know where . . ."

Of all the things that her love could have said to her, this was the worst. Kelanim's eyes filled with tears, and she sank back onto the moist earth as sobs clogged her throat. He could have children? All of her effort and time had been spent to the thought that it was the Caisah who could not have children. Everyone thought so, and yet here he was so blindly revealing this fact to her. It would have been better, she thought, if he had simply punched her to a pulp.

Breathing was hard since her raw sobs were choking her. She retched and gagged, but nothing came out; she simply hadn't eaten enough recently to be able to be sick.

When Kelanim finally regained herself, she sat up. The Caisah was watching her with all the interest of a person watching a bug die.

"You . . ." she paused, marshaled her thoughts as best she could, and went on. "You can have children. All those mistresses, all those lovers and never one child, except for her?" She threw an ugly look at the stark white bones.

"Yes." The Caisah said his head tilting at an odd angle. Suddenly he looked nothing like a human at all. "She was special. The Last Seer of the Vaerli. She helped me."

And there it was. He had loved her. Kelanim's hands clenched into tight fists as it dawned on her. He had loved her. Some long dead woman, someone he had killed and buried, he still loved. Not her. Not Kelanim the needy. Not Kelanim the clingy.

She found herself on her feet, backing away from him, even as he continued to lovingly clear the dirt from her bones, all the while muttering soft, sweet things to someone who had been dead for centuries.

"Do not judge him," a voice whispered in her ear, and it was not inside her head this time.

When Kelanim spun around, a woman, gleaming in the moonlight, stood in front of the Steps. Her eyes were dark but full of stars, and every inch of her naked body was covered in the same writing that decorated the edifice.

Kelanim realized that she could see right through her. She darted a glance back at the Caisah, but he had not moved from his ministrations. Her eyes shot back to the woman, who was still there, and she understood. "That . . . that's you in there?"

The dead Vaerli's expression softened. "Yes. He killed me when I wouldn't tell him where I had hidden our sons. He is so broken that it happened quickly. All I remember is earth all around me, and then . . . nothing . . ."

"Are you a . . . ghost?" Kelanim managed to choke out. She had always had her eyes so firmly set on her goal, she had never considered that such things could exist.

"No," the seer said, her long dark hair slowly waving in unfelt breezes. "I am a sliver of memory, a portion of myself that I put away. I saw so many dangers ahead that I placed little pieces across Conhaero. Some for my sons, some for others. Like you."

Her eyes were now locked on Kelanim. "I saw one who would love him as I did. One who would weaken him at the behest of the Phage."

"The who?"

"You know who I speak of." Darkness seemed to gather around the Vaerli's form. "They come in many shapes, some beautiful and enticing."

Kelanim thought of the centaur, and the alluring smell of him that had perhaps driven her to recklessness. Blood rushed to her cheeks. "I . . . I thought it would . . ."

An icy thrill ran through her when the apparition reached down and touched her cheek. "Don't fear, child. They thought to use you to break him, because they must. He, despite all his flaws, is a gift of the Kindred. By reminding him of his past you have opened his eyes. Look!"

Kelanim turned back to the Caisah and felt another portion of her insides crack. Her love was kneeling over the grave, and weeping—truly weeping. Emotion of any kind but rage was something so seldom seen that she had to grit her teeth to hold back an exclamation.

"He sees what he has done," the shade of Putorae whispered into Kelanim's ear. "After all these centuries he remembers what he has done."

The mistress would have run then and there to his side, but the suggestion of an icy grip on her upper arm stopped her. "They are coming now, child. To finish what you have begun. This is not the Caisah that they wanted from you. Help him, and quickly!"

Kelanim was released and she dashed to the side of her love. Wrapping her arms around him, she rocked him back and forth while her eyes darted from shadow to shadow, feeling menace in each of them. The shade of the seer was no longer there, disappeared back to whatever place she occupied, or perhaps unravelled completely.

"They" was what she had said, and Kelanim knew at least two of the forms that would come. They had tried to trick her into destroying the person she loved, and she could feel her own rage at that bubbling like a sickness in her belly.

Her ears were straining as hard as her eyes, and she suddenly discerned a rustle of pine needles and leaves deep within the forest. Some large animal was moving back there, and her imagination conjured what it could be.

"She forgives you," Kelanim said to the Caisah, rubbing his back, and trying her best to pass along some of the warmth of her body to his. "You weren't meant for this. Putorae understands that. She wants you to live."

The seer hadn't actually said that, but why else would see have bothered to warn the mistress of the onrushing danger?

The Caisah looked up at her, his eyes bleak, and his whole body rigid. "I didn't know what would happen. I was just so angry with her, and then it bubbled up. The earth listened to my rage, and it took her. I couldn't . . . I couldn't stop it. I tried."

All those powers the Kindred had given him, and he hadn't known how to control any of them. Kelanim's heart went out to him, imagining herself easily lost in all that magic. Underneath it all he was just a man.

At this moment she needed him to be more than that, because even though she didn't look over her shoulder, she could hear more movement. It was no longer stealthy at all. She had no weapons, and even if she did, Court life had not prepared her for battle. All Kelanim had was the man at her side, the one she had unhinged.

So she grabbed hold of his hands and pulled his attention to her. "You have to fight on, love. Your sons and this world need you." She had no idea if this were true, but she had to find some way to reach him. "I need you, too . . ."

His young face, with those old, weary eyes shifted from upset to something that might have been determination. Together they rose from the dirt and looked around at the forest.

The sounds were now emerging into forms around them. With the glow of the Steps the only light, the creatures of myth and legend stepped nearer to the Caisah. The centaur was at their lead, his dark, shaggy head bent, but his gleaming eyes remained fixed on them both.

They darted once to the uncovered bones. "Another of your victims, abomination. My masters will be glad to know that you have finally begun to remember all that you have done. At the end, it all comes back."

The nagi emerged with a rustle of dry skin on leaves. Its many heads, with many flickering tongues, darted forward and back as if eager to taste flesh.

Kelanim felt her skin trying to crawl off her body. "How did they follow us?" she whispered under her breath, but the centaur heard her.

"We are Kindred. Beneath it all, we remain." His front hoof stamped the ground with an impact that made the mistress jump. "All of Conhaero is open to us. We fold it around us, much as your tyrant here does."

"I struck her down once," the Caisah spoke, ignoring the centaur's jibes. "When we met in the Salt, she came at me, and I turned her aside. I would think she hasn't forgotten that."

"Indeed not," the nagi hissed, "but this time she is not alone. The Phage have grown, and become more powerful with time. The arrival of the White Void brings strength to them that would take it."

More movement sounded around them; the Named were encircling them.

"It seems fitting that this is the place you will die," the centaur continued with a grim smile. "The first place you touched our sacred soil will be the last place, too. You shall lie with the fool Putorae once again—but this time in the earth."

The forest was suddenly full of forms rushing at them; faceless crones with bony arms, women with the faces of foxes, and stout green men with only one eye. Kelanim only had time to catch glimpses of them before the Caisah whipped her behind him.

It was a gesture to make her weep. She had done this, brought them here in her own way, and yet here he was protecting her. As the Named began to circle, she blurted out the truth.

"I did this to you! I did!" She would not resort to tears. She would stand up and own up to her part in this.

For all his strange behavior, the Caisah heard her. He turned and his eyes darted to her face, searching it for answers.

"Your lover gave you up so easily," the centaur stood a little away from them, in the shadows of the trees, and pronounced the death of Kelanim's hopes. "She wanted you to be hers, even if it meant giving up your immortality."

The mistress understood betrayal—she had seen it many times in the harem—and she also understood the twisting of the knife. The Named had meant to do this all along. The only way to draw out the poison was to confront it.

"I love you," was her only reply. "I am not sorry for that, but I am for what I did."

He looked at her steadily, not as the implacable Caisah, but with a touch of vulnerability in his gaze. "Is this how you want me?" he asked softly. "You want me mortal?"

Kelanim nodded, keeping herself erect and ready for whatever punishment might come.

The Caisah looked around at the circle of Named, with long teeth and knives ready for him. "Well then," he said simply. "Then my name is Vitus, but my men in the Void called me the Eagle King."

That was enough; the Named charged at him, snarling and hungry for his blood. Vitus spread his arms wide, and the earth obeyed him.

It rolled up around them. A small cry of alarm escaped Kelanim as the earth took them, and she thought of the body of the Last Seer. Was that to be her fate, too?

However, he was with her, whispering in her ear, something that sent shivers up her spine. "Now is the time, Eagle King."

When Kelanim looked into his eyes, they were clear and seeing her for perhaps the first time.

The howls of the Named seemed like nothing at all when compared to that. It was just as the legends had said: the Caisah commanded the very earth.

This was why the Named, and whoever their masters were, had wanted him removed.

He crushed them, taking them down into the depths of the world. Blood and bone, even of the Named Kindred, could not resist that.

When the earth had finished with them, it rolled back, leaving them in a circle of red and mangled flesh. Kelanim smiled up at him. She had been a fool to want him mortal. He was magnificent like this. He shone.

"It is time to go to the Belly," he said. "The Eagle King will be free, and then you will truly know him."

CHAPTER SEVENTEEN
DEATH AT HOME

Finn and Talyn leapt from the bed. They shoved their clothes on as best they could in the darkness.

He grabbed Talyn's hand, since she had no idea of the layout of the village, and pulled her along with him. His first thought was of what was happening to Ysel. Could Fida protect him properly without the Gifts? Concern for his brother's life made his legs pump harder.

"Wahirangi!" he bellowed, as behind him he heard Talyn draw her sword with her free hand. Talespinners were racing past them, many in states of undress and wide-eyed. Still, they had spoken enough tales about surprise attacks, so they didn't start screaming. They were making for the entrance, while Finn and Talyn were working their way in the opposite direction. It was lucky he knew the village so well or the twists and turns would have stymied him. Hours upon hours traversing the swaying bridges as a child now held him in good stead; he kept his feet and quickly found the nest where his brother had gone to sleep for the night.

Fida was standing on the swaying netting, her sword drawn, and seemed eager for some kind of target. Ysel was calm and ready, too.

"The Phage have found us," he said simply looking up at his brother.

"How?" Talyn demanded. "They had no idea where Finn was . . . even I didn't until . . ." Her face turned pale. "Could . . . could they have some way of tracking me here?"

It appeared from her expression that Fida wanted to strike Talyn down right there and then. Ysel merely looked her up and down, his head tilted to one side. "Perhaps . . ."

That was when the leader of the Swoop appeared, diving down in eagle form and taking her human shape before them. She had her armor on and was wide-eyed.

"Talyn!" She grabbed hold of the Vaerli's arm. "You need to get out of here now!"

Azrul was a brave soul, since at any time she could have used her wings and escaped. Instead, she tugged her friend after her. Finn, and Fida with Ysel kept protectively behind her, followed the two women as they ran through the perilously shaking rope bridges toward the one entrance. It had seemed like a fine idea at first—one entrance in and out—but now the attack was from above and they were out of options.

"Fire!" Fida cried out a warning, as scarlet flames engulfed the structure around them. It wrapped around them so suddenly that there was no chance to turn about and escape it. Finn caught a glimpse of the once-Vaerli turning and throwing Ysel away from her, back to the rocky outcrop they had just passed. Then fire swallowed her. She didn't even scream as flames took her clothes and then her flesh in the blink of an eye.

There was no time to mourn her loss or celebrate her bravery, because Finn, Talyn, and Azrul were falling. The talespinners' bridges were not made to withstand fiery attacks, and theirs had given way to flame. The sound of the Whitefoam eagle's cry filled Finn's ears, but the roar of the ocean below was louder.

The impact of dragon talons around him nearly made the talespinner bite his own tongue off. His neck felt as though it had almost snapped, but he wrapped his hands around Wahirangi's claws that held him so delicately, and looked to his right. Sometimes it was a fine thing to have friends in the air.

Talyn looked as shocked as he felt about this current change in circumstance. She glanced up at the golden head of the dragon gleaming in the moonlight, and her lips curled in the faintest smile.

From this vantage point Finn could make out the attackers and the defenders. It was not the dragon that he and Wahirangi had tussled with on their way to the island, but it was something nearly as terrifying.

A swarm of winged creatures: griffins, baykok with their skeletal frames and red eyes, phoenix, and many more that Finn could only catch glimpses of. It had to be the flaming tails of the birds that had set the village alight. Meanwhile, the predatory birds of the Swoop were harassing and attacking the Named as best they could, but there was little they could do against such powerful beings.

Finn smiled wickedly. "Turn around, Wahirangi, and show these Named what flames really are."

Instead, the dragon just carried them higher, circling away from the devastation without comment. Talyn closed her eyes as if she knew something he did not. Through the rush of wind, even if she yelled, Finn doubted he would be able to make it out.

Perhaps Wahirangi had not heard him. "I said . . ."

"I must protect you," the dragon spoke, even as he did not meet Finn's eye. "And I will not kill my kind. They may be Named, but those are Kindred. They have no choice what they do; the Phage have made them slaves. I will not slay them."

Finn beat on the dragon's talons, even though he knew it would do no good. "You seemed ready to kill that dragon we tussled with before!"

"I was not trying to kill my kin, I was trying to kill the abomination on her back," Wahirangi replied, even as his head turned to follow the actions of the Named below.

Apparently, whatever the Phage had done to the Kindred was different than what Finn had done, but he had to try. "I command you to go back there and defend the village."

Now a massive opal-colored eye turned on him. "You Named me, and now you would command me?"

Opposite him, Talyn was shaking her head desperately from side to side.

Finn knew better than not to take the hint. He looked up at the dragon, and changed his tack. "You would not let innocent people die simply because I went among them. Dragon-fear is powerful, is it not?"

Wahirangi did not answer, but he tucked his two passengers in tight against his warm belly, and folded his wings about him.

The lesser-winged creatures didn't have a chance. The dragon dived among them, turning this way and that. Even his fellow Named fled before him. The flock of birds that were the Swoop also scattered.

Wahirangi drove them all before him, and even sent a blast of dragon-flame slicing harmlessly through the air. Those Named by the Phage obviously did not know that he had such scruples.

When the great beast was done quartering the sky, roaring, flaming, and making a great show, the Named had fled to whatever dark place they had come from. Eventually the Swoop ventured back, but only after the dragon had landed by the devastated entrance to the village.

A small scattering of survivors, blackened by soot and terrified, huddled there. For once the talespinners were not telling the story—they were in it. They did not look happy about it.

Wahirangi put Talyn and Finn back on the earth as gently as if he were their mother. Then he took off, only to return with Ysel. The boy looked more like a boy than he ever had before, Finn thought—wide-eyed, pale and terrified. In the meantime, the nykur appeared out of the darkness and nuzzled Talyn's side. He too was a creature of chaos, but apparently no friend of the Phage; he had blood on his horns and teeth. So there was one creature that did not mind what had happened tonight.

The dragon looked down on them, and though he had no human expressions, the talespinner felt sorrow radiating from him.

"You see," the dragon intoned, "there is no sanctuary for you now, nor for those you care for. You must go to the Belly; there you will find peace or death."

Finn took a long, deep breath. His brother's clothes were singed, but he was not crying. Talyn looked as determined as she had when he first saw her all that time ago—but there was something different; a light in her eyes. He'd never seen that before in her, but he guessed what it might be. She now had a reason to live, and a goal to achieve. That was when Finn realized he would not be alone.

The Swoop—or what was left of them—alighted on the cliff face and transformed back to human form. They were a tough looking collection of women, and the last remnant of scion goodness in the world.

"We will follow where Talyn goes," Azrul said, her hand wrapping around her sword hilt. "One-eyed Baraca is gone; killed by these same Named."

If it had not been for the power of the Phage and the White Void that waited, Finn might have felt confident.

"I'm ready," he said, and hoped his voice did not waver.

"Then I will open the way, and we will go together." Wahirangi's head lowered until it was brushing against Finn's chest. He could feel the heat and comfort of it all the way through him. "You know, son of Putorae, your ability to make yourself small must and can be reversed. You must make yourself so big that the White Void cannot swallow you or your brother. Remember the lessons of your time on Conhaero."

Those were many, and all of them crowded his brain at once. Finn felt as though he had plunged into icy water and could not catch his breath.

"Then let's go," he said, because that was all there was left to say. Talyn silently took a place at his shoulder, with Ysel on the other side. His brother and his lover—two people he would have never thought to have.

The dragon turned and delicately extended his taloned fingers. Like Putorae had shown them, he flicked aside reality as if it were a child's tricks. The white light of the Void nearly burned Finn's eyes, but he heard Wahirangi's comforting voice wrap around him—even if the words themselves were not comforting.

"Stay close, the Belly is not far at all."

A BROTHER'S TRUE FORM

All of the Ahouri flew west out over the sea, with Equo, Varlesh, and Si at their head. They wore the form of the dragonets, and they did not sing any songs as they went. If they had, they would have been songs of war.

Waves lashed at them, as if in an attempt to bring the flock down. Equo narrowed his eyes and flew on all the harder. The strength of his brothers was at his back and his love was ahead of him. He would go anywhere she needed him to be.

He felt dreadful that he had for a moment doubted her. It was imperative that he apologize for that, and there was something else he had to do.

In those awkward days when they had first known each other, when he had been following her around like a young pup, he had told her often that he loved her. Back then, she had brushed him off with good graces. Now he wished he had said something far more recently. They were older and perhaps a little wiser, and had known the end was coming. Why had he not said anything?

The fractured remains of his people did not seem like much to take into the fight, but they had come when he asked. They had returned from their mission to inform the Vaerli, but they had not shared what the response had been. Alone then, and creatures of wing, they flew on.

The Belly was an angry plain of an island in the middle of the slate-gray sea. Billowing, sulfurous clouds clenched above it, obscuring the top of the one hill that rose out of the middle. Occasionally, red flame lit up the inside of the clouds as the mountain proved it was more a volcano. This was the place the Vaerli would not come, and the sole domain of Kindred. Yet, as the singing Ahouri flock flew closer, Equo saw that this was not exactly true any longer.

Other wings had taken up residence, and down on the plain before the volcano were groups of other beings. They had to be more Named, a seething mass of creatures birthed from every myth and legend of all the peoples who had come to Conhaero. Not the best of enemies to have.

Varlesh, in his black dragonet form, flew a little faster and was able to reach Equo's side. One of his red eyes caught his brother's, and there was doubt in it—but not fear.

The Ahouri had one advantage that their small size belied; they had the Songs of the nature. Varlesh began it, singing from the throat of his form, the strains of the melody of flesh. Even the Named had form and shape. They would remake it and it would be most unpleasant.

The flock of Ahouri dived down on those on the plain. Equo kept scanning for signs of Nyree, but there were none. Still, the Song was having an effect. All of the Named looked up in horror as it washed over them.

Some centaurs fell to their knees, bellowing like struck bulls. Snakes hissed and coiled on themselves as if they had been speared. None were able to take much notice of the Ahouri swinging down over them, let alone strike back. It was a most excellent start.

The Song was so beautiful and deadly that the Form Bards grew confident. They let the rhythm carry them higher, so that the notes of it would reach the creatures of the air. It was their shield.

Now everything above them was struck by the wave of music. As the flock of Ahouri flew higher, the other forms scattered before them, trying to escape the sound. Equo was elated. They were like eagles with sparrows fleeing before them.

Now they were in the clouds, and caught glimpses of the rough and rocky surface below them. He led them on, further up, following the line of the volcano toward its rim; that was where he was sure he would find the entrance to the interior of Conhaero. That was also where he was sure the Kindred and the Phage would be—and where they would most likely have Nyree.

As they went though, the Song was becoming harder to hold. The physical effort of it and flying drained his energy, so he knew the other Ahouri would also be suffering. It had been a long time since they had sung this together. The melody was beginning to fall apart, and though he tried to strengthen it, he knew that it could not hold for long. Some of the notes were off, too.

Just a little longer, he thought to himself, since he could not spare his voice to tell them so. The green form of Si drew closer, and Equo's energy reserves came back.

The ahouri swooped around a thick rock formation, almost scraping their wingtips on it, and there was the top of the volcano; the very edge of Conhaero. Two figures stood there, and one Equo recognized immediately. Nyree and her *pae atuae* were glowing, while standing at her side was a woman with a strange ruffle around her neck.

Equo was not so foolish as to attack immediately. He led the flock of Ahouri around the basin, though the smell of sulphur and the reflected heat were painful. The Song was having no effect on either of the women, but the one with the odd neckwear was following their path with her gaze.

The Ahouri flock soared around the edge and came back again. Equo was already readying another song, this one to confuse the mind rather than the flesh, when he saw and finally understood what was around her neck.

The horror of trapped Kindred twisting and turning, as if trying to escape, nearly drove all thought from his mind. To the Form Bards this was the greatest abomination. They had to be freed.

He let out a shriek of outrage and dived toward them, not caring if the others followed. That was when the woman pointed to the thick clouds over their head. The dragon roared out from it, plummeting down toward the Ahouri. She was not alone. Other dragons made their appearance with mind-bending roars and displays of different colored fire. Equo swiveled his head around desperately and realized there were at least five dragons in all.

The flock of Form Bards scattered before them, but several were not fast enough. They were snatched from the air as snakes might catch birds.

The howls of his dying people and their songs urged Equo to action. Si and Varlesh were on each side of him, matching his wing beats and keeping pace with him as he climbed up toward the dragon with the dire rider.

The beast was massive and loomed over the roaring volcano, the red glow of the magma lighting up her belly and her eyes. Her cavernous mouth opened and she roared.

The Ahouri darted past her, as if she were a wagon and they more nimble riders. Equo and his brothers could not use dragon fire, especially with the song being their more powerful weapon. They sang of the frailness of flesh as they flew along her flanks, peppering her rough hide with melody as they went. It would have turned any other creature to a mass of ill-defined flesh, but this creature was made of sterner stuff.

CHAPTER EIGHTEEN 🐉 A BROTHER'S TRUE FORM   239

The granite dragon turned and snapped at them, as her rider called out something to her. Equo banked left as they reached the end of her lashing tail. Varlesh, just fractionally behind him, had to twist to avoid being skewered by it.

If only they knew the Name of this beast, he thought frantically, they could make a Song for it. Creating such a piece while in flight and in peril would not be an easy thing, but it would at least give them a hope.

Varlesh and Si separated from him, turning around and flying back on either side of the dragon, acting like midges on a dog. She snapped and lunged at them, but they flipped and dodged so much that the dragon could not bring her fire to bear properly. They sang as they went; even if it made no difference, it was their way.

Equo took the chance that his brothers and the rest of the Ahouri were giving him. He turned hard, high above the dragon, and drove down not at the dragon, but at her rider. The Ahouri plummeted down upon her, and wrapped teeth and claw about her.

Like the woman below, this dire child seemed to have nascent Kindred trapped in a ring around her shoulders. It made him feel better about menacing someone who was apparently so young. She screamed, and the Kindred bit and struck at his wings and talons.

"Barmethesis, help me!" she howled as Equo snapped at her face. It was all he had wanted. He let go of her and dropped off the back of the dragon with a shriek of triumph.

As he circled the beast, trying to find sounds and tunes that would do what he required, he took a quick note of Nyree. She was struggling with the woman on the edge of the volcano, hair was flying around both women from the heat—and there was something else happening behind her. Figures appearing from nowhere. Maybe they were Kindred, maybe not.

Equo couldn't stop to see. The dragons were all lashing out around him, and the Ahouri were dying. He had to think quickly. Finally the song came to him. With Si and Varlesh following in his wake and picking up the tune, he turned and spun, singing. He'd woven the name Barmethesis into it, and the difference was immediately obvious.

The rocky gray skin rippled as he flew past howling the tune, and the dragon screamed in response. Now she was forgetting about the bothersome Ahouri and concentrating all of her attention on the one that was paining her.

Rider and dragon began to chase the brothers. Her wing beats and her hot breath were on them. Yet the song was not bringing down the dragon; it was hurting her, but she flew on. Barmethesis' flame passed close to them, narrowly missing Si, and Equo realized abruptly what had to be done.

He had no way of telling his brothers, but he deliberately slowed his wing beats, dropping back from them. The idea was a perfect crystal in his head. The moment was a long one.

Then Equo turned, spun and fell toward the creature's mouth. By some stroke of luck he had timed it perfectly, landing near the dragon's jaws but not in them. Her foul breath raked over him, but her teeth did not reach him. He only a moment to get this mad venture right.

Raising himself up, Equo sang directly into the mouth of the dragon. She snapped desperately, but the call of flesh went past that thick, rocky hide and into the softest part of the Named's flesh and brain.

You cannot fly, Barmethesis, the Song whispered seductively. *You are Kindred, of the earth and that is all you are.*

Barmethesis did not scream. Her wings slowed a fraction. She listened—then she began to fall.

Equo felt the whistle of the air around him, but he couldn't push free of her. Her fall was his fall. They were locked together as he had known they would be.

The dragon hit the ground near the rim of the volcano. Equo felt an explosion of pain, and knew his form and all his forms would not walk or fly from this. He caught a glimpse of Si and Varlesh turning and dropping toward him. It was good to see them, to know that they were safe.

He was grateful also that he could see Nyree from here. Though he wished he could sing one more song, he dimly heard the Ahouri flying above, continuing on. The melody and words were so beautiful that it was all worth it. Nyree probably knew he loved her, and that would have to do.

CHAPTER NINETEEN

THE COMING OF THE DRAGON

T he Swoop flew through the gap in the White Void, chilly avian breaths suddenly escaping into a far warmer climate, and erupted in a flurry of feathers and calls above a steaming and angry volcano.

Finn, Wahirangi, Syris, Ysel, and Talyn walked through behind them, but also felt the sudden wave of warmth like a blow. The nykur tossed his head, and lowered it like a bull ready for a fight. It appeared he was likely to get one.

A volcano. The Belly of the World was a volcano. Finn might have guessed that. Looking up, he stumbled on the unstable rocks, and it was Talyn who helped him up. They both watched the Swoop circle back down the flank of the volcano, and already they had plenty of enemies. A mass of Named were racing up the slopes on feet and hooves, while shapes were moving in the clouds above.

Talyn called out, but far too late; Syris was already racing down the slope to join the fray. Anywhere that blood was flowing was where his nature would take him. Chaos would meet chaos. The nykur, who was supposed to be a silent creature, let out a noise like a screaming hawk. It was an eerie battle cry.

"Sister," Wahirangi spoke, and all of them jerked around, alerted to something far closer but a lot less dangerous. The shape of a felled dragon lay half buried in the earth. Ysel crowded closer to his brother, a strangely childish gesture from a boy who claimed so many powers. Finn recognized the dragon immediately—it was the same creature that had attacked them on the way to Elraban.

While that knowledge burned its way into his brain, a small figure was climbing down from atop it. Such a crash should have shaken anyone, but there was a disconcerting sureness about the child's steps. The talespinner felt his jaw clench the closer it got. He hadn't forgotten anything of their last encounter with this thing.

"There's Nyree," Talyn called, pulling his attention away from the oncoming child for just a moment.

A woman, her skin alive with the *pae atuae*, was struggling with another who appeared to have Kindred attached to her neck and shoulders. Finn did not need to be told which one was not on their side.

"And that is Circe," Talyn went on, unsheathing her sword, and unholstering her pistol. "She and I are due a reckoning. I will deal with her. Can you take care of that thing?" Her mouth twisted as she pointed at the black-eyed child.

Two Phage, and she was giving him and his brother the smaller one—pretty generous, Finn thought.

"Go," he said as calmly as this situation would allow. "Get Nyree!"

It spoke of her confidence in them that Talyn was instantly running as directed. He did not want that to be misplaced. As the child drew slowly nearer, he tried to judge how this could possibly go. Ysel remained silent, but his fists were clenched as if he wanted to punch the girl desperately.

Screams above caught their attention. The predatory birds of the Swoop were engaged in battling what looked like two kinds of dragons; some small, some large. Flames were lighting up the clouds, and reptilian screams were filling the air.

"Those are not Phage," Ysel said, matter-of-factly.

Wahirangi's head dipped toward the brothers. "The Swoop are confused. It is as Ysel says; the small ones are not Phage, but Ahouri. I must get everyone fighting their shared enemies, not each other." His opal eyes raked over the black-eyed girl child, but Finn knew what held him back from killing her with fire; the Pact still bound the Kindred from killing Vaerli. The Phage had taken full advantage of that fact.

"Quickly, then," Finn urged, seeing that many of their friends were in danger. The Ahouri might mean that his friends Varlesh, Equo, and Si were up there. "Help them!"

Gathering his legs beneath him, the golden dragon surged into the sky, blue flames jetting from his mouth. Finn didn't see any way that the beast could now avoid killing his own kin. It was the nature of battle that blood was set against blood.

All that he and Ysel were left with was a child. She didn't stand much taller than Finn's brother, but she had even less of the child about her.

Her solid black eyes were even more disconcerting as she drew nearer. Finn noted that from under her dress lone dark lines were drawn upon her skin—they looked awfully like *pae atuae*.

One glance to his left told him that whatever Talyn was doing had now moved out of sight behind the bulk of the dead dragon. As Finn watched the child moving toward them slowly and deliberately, he began to wonder if a dragon might not be the lesser of two great evils.

"Half-Vaerli," she said, cocking her head and smiling slightly at the brothers. "You two are the things left behind by Putorae. The anchors needed." Her laugh was cold. "You are so broken and so unprepared."

It was obvious she was trying to rattle them, but Finn was too busy examining what sort of threat she was. Plenty of stories told of terrifying children, eldritch and dangerous, but that was usually on lonely roads and in misty swamps. This creature, though she was terrifying looking, did not even have a blade. He was not stupid enough to point that out.

Just as he was thinking that, her head turned toward Ysel. "Despite what you look like, you actually have the better training." Her grin spread wider. "So you will know of the Phage, and how the Gifts the Vaerli possessed are still ours, just twisted. The Gift of flesh, for example."

She didn't make a move, but suddenly Ysel let out a howl that sounded as though he had been stabbed. His eyes bulged, and as Finn watched in horror, bruises began to appear all over his body as if he were being crushed by some unseen force. He put out his hand to comfort him, but there was little he could do.

"And time," the girl went on, the twisted *pae atuae* shimmering on her skin. "You should feel the weight of time, as well."

Wahirangi screamed above, and for a moment Finn hoped that help might come from that quarter, but Named creatures were now engaging the Swoop and his dragon.

It is just one little girl, Finn reminded himself, and she was hurting his newly found brother. He would have to stop her himself.

Until she turned her attention to him. Those black eyes bored into him. Suddenly, every bone creaked and groaned in pain. He felt the weight of the world focusing on him through those completely black orbs of hers. Suddenly movement was not an option.

As he fell to his knees, he caught a glimpse of Ysel in the same position.

"So much for Putorae's sons," the girl said, standing over them, a disparaging look on her young face. "Weak like their mother, and unfinished like their father."

The memory of the Last Seer fading before his eyes somehow reached Finn, and gave him enough energy to reach out with his hands. It was a small gesture, but it was enough to make contact.

In that moment before she shook him off, he reached for that Gift that was not from the Vaerli. It was from his father, something that he had always thought of more as a curse than a blessing. It had saved him many times, and this time was to prove no different.

All those times that he had been shunned, laughed out of town, mocked by his classmates for being an orphan rushed back to the talespinner. Every moment where he had been overlooked, and gone hungry because no one cared about him filled his mind.

You are small. Insignificant. Nothing. His gift said, but this time it was not saying it to him, it was saying it to the Phage child. It was burying that message inside her, pushing aside the one that said she was special.

It would have been a terrible thing to do to a child, but this was no child. Finn had to remind himself of that. She had been made to be the seer, a creature of darkness, birthed by twisted beings that did not deserve the name of Vaerli.

While he concentrated, the Phage staggered back, losing her grip on Ysel. The boy was quick-witted; he darted forward, pulled his knife free of its sheath, and struck with all of his might. He did not aim for the black-eyed girl herself, but instead at the circle of Kindred struggling around her shoulders.

He pulled them away from her body and with remarkable precision cut them free. The girl screamed, as if he had cut her instead. Ysel threw the Kindred away behind him. They landed like patches of magma, yet far brighter and more vengeful. As Finn watched from where he was sprawled on the ground, they grew from small patches to fully sized Kindred. They once more were like their kin, without expression or limbs; simply looming rocky beings. Except they rounded on the girl with something that was easily iden-tifiable as vengeance.

Finn scrambled up from where he had fallen and grabbed hold of Ysel. He yanked him away before either of them could see what terrible retribution the Kindred would favor her with. No one needed to see that.

Besides, they were far from safe. They had to find Talyn, because now he could feel it. The White Void was coming. It was coming and they did not have four seers.

CHAPTER TWENTY

HUNTER, SEER, AND VOID

Talyn wrenched Circe off Nyree by the most expedient method: wrapping her hand around the snapping shape of one of the Kindred and yanking hard. Perhaps she might have chosen hair, normally, but the trapped creatures of chaos provided better grip. The Phage spun around with a hiss, but was not as put off as Talyn had hoped, since she delivered a strong sidekick to the made seer that sent her slipping down the inside of the rim of the volcano.

Circe then rounded on Talyn, while Nyree struggled desperately to find her footing on the loose rock down below. Magma bubbled and hissed only a few feet from her. One wrong move and there would never be four seers to keep the White Void and the Kindred happy. They would be lost.

"You are surplus to requirements now," Circe said with a nasty grin, while her trapped Kindred began to howl loudly in despair.

Talyn had never heard them make that noise before; usually their torment was soundless, but she suspected it was not in response to the Phage's comments. They felt something else entirely—as much as she could. The White Void was preparing to open and either be satisfied or rip Conhaero apart. Talyn knew she did not have much time to converse with Circe.

She had a much better reply than words. The once-Hunter whipped her pistol up and out of her holster. In one smooth movement she took aim and fired at the other woman's head—with the trapped Kindred, it made for a rather large target.

The before-time, though, was not working in her favor—it was now working for her enemy. Circe stepped away from the bullet with ease and somehow ended up closer to Talyn. The once-Hunter had a moment to grasp that her fellow seer had managed to get hold of an outcrop and was levering herself back up the slope, but that was the only good thing about the situation.

Nyree wouldn't get there in time to help Talyn. The Gifts of the Vaerli had been withdrawn from her by the Phage, and not yet returned by the Kindred. It was a shame, since she would have liked to have them available to her at this point. It seemed unfair to have come through so many painful years and be denied.

Circe didn't have a weapon, but when her fist connected with Talyn's ribcage, the Vaerli was reminded that the Gift of strength would have also been most useful. Talyn staggered back with the impact, but used it to get enough distance that she might unsheath her sword. It was not her mother's, she missed that one terribly, but this one could still do the job.

While the Phage woman had the Gifts, she also had the advantage. Circe dodged Talyn's strike with her sword. Instead she stepped in past her defense and twisted the weapon from her hands as if taking it from a child. Talyn was now getting a lesson in how terrible it was to be on the receiving end of that particular Gift. It was deeply unpleasant, and she had sudden empathy for her victims through the years.

One of Circe's hands wrapped around Talyn's throat and she began to squeeze. The once-Hunter had a blurry impression of the Phage's face, and the watchful heads of Kindred who could do nothing to save her. It seemed like a shameful way to die, but no matter how much she scrambled at the fingers, they were more powerful than she could imagine.

The world went from the elemental red of the volcano, to gray, and then dark spots began to widen in front of her eyes.

Then Talyn was falling, but not into the embrace of death; to the ground. She gasped for breath as her knees stung with pain, and heard a voice she had never expected to find here of all places.

"I understand you are looking for me?" the Caisah said mildly to the Phage. He sounded different somehow, but it was hard to place why through the ringing in her ears.

By the time Talyn levered herself up to catch sight of the Caisah, with Kelanim standing next to him holding his hand, the Phage woman had forgotten Talyn existed. Circe was staring at them while her Kindred whipped into a frenzy around her face. She bent and calmly picked up Talyn's sword.

"You are the lynchpin, the final abomination that must be cleansed," Circe said through clenched teeth. "Once you are dead, the Kindred's curse will be lifted. It will end and my brothers and sisters will take possession of the White Void. We will be stronger than you were, and all those worlds will learn to obey the Phage."

Talyn knew that look intimately. She had worn it herself quite often. It was the look of the fanatic. It was also the path to arrogance and short-sightedness.

Which Circe was about to learn, because while the Phage enjoyed her moment of victory, she had missed another moment altogether: the one where Nyree managed to clamber high enough to reach Talyn. Her hand brushed against the exposed part of the Vaerli's foot.

"The *pae atuae* is yours," Talyn whispered as Putorae had taught her. "I as the born do give it you, the made." These were the required words, creating the bound between born and made seers, linking them forever in their guardianship.

The silvered writing, like an impossible plant given light, crawled up her leg in an instant. She could feel it like ice running over her skin, covering every inch of it. The sensation was painful, and yet everything Talyn needed now and forever. She was finally what she had always been, the born seer.

"No," she said, with a savage smile at Circe, "I think *you* are the true abomination." With that, Talyn stepped into the before-time as easily as she drew breath. It was bliss to do so. She foresaw the sweep of the Phage and her blade. Circe moved slowly, weighed down by so many Kindred around her, and Talyn was able to move in and past her blade with ease.

The sudden impact of the once-Hunter's sword piercing Circe's gut shuddered up Talyn's arm. It was a plain blade for such good work. The born seer twisted it once, savagely, and heard the trapped Kindred cry out in delight. Finally, they would be free. Then, with her boot, Talyn pushed the Phage from her, off the blade, to her fate. The woman tumbled away, falling past Nyree and into the distant pit of burning, unforgiving magma. It was a fitting end.

Talyn dropped immediately to the ground, threw out her arm, and her made seer caught her hand. With a grunt, Talyn pulled her up, until they both sat panting on the edge of the pit. The cries of battle around them didn't exist for a moment. It was the sound of footsteps approaching that made them both look up.

"And now me," the Caisah said with a sad smile. "You must do the same for me."

The mistress at his back was weeping, and for once Talyn saw clearly. Kelanim did actually love the Caisah—that was why she had been so jealous, not because she craved power. It was an odd thing to notice here, of all places. Empathy, one of the Vaerli Gifts, was making its presence felt. It was painful but worth feeling.

The Caisah took Kelanim's hand in his, but did not change his mind. "I am the lynchpin, the final piece that is holding back the return of the Vaerli Gifts. The Phage had it right. I am an abomination. The broken piece."

Talyn slowly clambered to her feet, feeling as though every bone was aching. She looked at him, her head tilted to one side. "Once the idea of slaying you would have filled me with delight. It wasn't that long ago, really. Now that it comes to it, I don't know if I can . . ."

She looked up suddenly, for coming around the corner of the dragon's fallen carcass were Finn and Ysel, but with them was another man. It was her brother. She knew that instantly, as well as she knew her own face in a mirror. For a second she didn't register who he had with him. He filled her vision completely. A slow, rather wet blink of her eyes, and she noticed that the ranks of the Vaerli for which she had sacrificed her pride, her honor and herself, were finally there behind Byre. He had led them, and he would lead them in the future.

For a long moment she drank them all in, as would a woman who had not tasted water for years. Her eyes darted along the impossible rank of delight. Byre looked very like their father, but with their mother's jet-black hair. The Vaerli were all there—the remains of her people gathered together after so long from her sight. None of them were burning, and there was no pain.

The curse was nearly extinguished. She let her eyes take them all in, filing away each precious, uncertain face. They looked tired, ragtag, though she could see in them the memory of pride. She wanted that in them—but not arrogance. Arrogance had brought them so close to destruction, and Talyn did not want to taste it again.

When she held out her arms in mute offering, Byreniko rushed to her. He smelled of sulphur and sweat. Yet, he was a stranger to her, no longer the little boy with the huge eyes. He had real strength in his arms. It was the kind of strength their trials had brought him. Over his shoulder Talyn saw the intense gaze of the Blood Witch she had sent to help him and keep him safe. She mouthed a thank you to her, and Pelanor smiled, showing her pointed teeth.

"It is good to see you, sister," Byre said, in a voice that spoke of strength and endurance. He must have had both to have reached here, after all the years. His eyes ran over her skin with dawning delight. "The born seer, then." The way his shoulders sagged, she realized he knew what that meant; not for her the easy life, even after all of this.

"You too, brother," she said, as Finn reached her. He did not embrace Talyn, letting her have her reunion, but his eyes gleamed with tears. This wasn't the kind of meeting she had dreamed about, but it was one none the less.

"Talyn," Finn whispered into her ear, and she felt, rather than heard the White Void rumbling toward them. It would not be put away.

Kindred had appeared at the edge of the volcano; silent sentinels to what the Vaerli's choice would be. They made no comment. They only watched.

The seers, four now, all turned to the Caisah, who was watching them with the faintest suggestion of a smile in the corner of his mouth. Now, at the end, it seemed he wanted to offer an explanation.

"They came to me in the Void, you know, when all my men were gone, and madness was only a breath away." He looked out over the heaving magma and the silent Kindred with a kind of resignation that bordered on happiness. "They told me I could not save my men, but that I would be the savior of others, and that I would be remembered." He looked up at the eagle mounted on the staff he carried. "All I wanted was to die honorably."

The earth was beginning to shake under their feet.

He looked Talyn directly in the eye. "I was never meant to be the Caisah. My name is Vitus. I am glad at the end to have it back." He spun about and clasped Kelanim to him, kissing her passionately in a way Talyn had never seen him kiss any other woman. Then, before the mistress could protest, he ripped himself away from her, and simply dived into the volcano.

It was an elegant way to go, and swift too, no doubt. Talyn watched him fall with dry eyes and a strangely hollow place in her chest. She had spent a long time hating him, but now in this moment she felt very little.

His mistress fell to her knees sobbing, but she did not throw herself after. Despite how much she loved the man, Talyn realized she had judged her properly; the woman was a survivor. How deep the wound went was another story entirely, and one that Kelanim would have to decide for herself.

The Caisah was the last link to the curse. She felt it dropping away like something rotten. The Vaerli were free. Talyn swayed on her feet, and it was Finn who held her up. One hand in the small of her back mattered so much in this momentous time.

Nyree was smiling slightly. "Your eyes are full of stars again," she said matter-of-factly to Talyn.

"Then I better earn them." Talyn turned to the Vaerli. They were strangers to her, many lost in her nemohira memories that she had discarded so flippantly along the way. She would have to learn their names all over again, so it would be like starting anew. It would be as if none of the intervening centuries had even happened.

She pushed her hair back from her face, tasting tears and sulphur on her mouth as she spoke to them. "We Vaerli mistook our path. We gave in to fear, which is always much easier to do than be brave. We had so many gifts that we became arrogant."

Finn was watching her, and she took a moment to enjoy feeling worthy of his pride and love. Those were the gifts of bravery, and they were worth earning.

"I know all about arrogance, and fear," Talyn said, dropping her eyes from them for just a moment. "I lived them for far too long, and they blinded me." Her gaze darted to Finn. "Someone showed me how foolish that was, and now I want to live differently. The question is . . . do you feel the same?"

Behind her the magma of the volcano began to spurt into the air. Great red flames were giving way to the blinding white of the Void. The heat was almost unbearable, coming from the center of Conhaero in terrible waves that set Talyn's hair whipping about her.

Just as it seemed the heat would cook them all from the inside, the wind from it suddenly turned cold, and now it was the relentless whine of the Void that came at them. It was as terrifying as her ancestors had said. It spoke of so many worlds, so many pains. Talyn held onto one fact: in there, scions and Vitus had survived. They had none of the Gifts that the Vaerli had, and somehow had managed it.

When she spun around, it was to kiss Finnbarr, the Fox, the talespinner and the seer. He and his brother would indeed be the anchor. "My compass," Talyn whispered into his hair as she drew in the smell of him. "I will come back to you when I can. Make Conhaero what it needs to be, for me and for all its people. I believe you, of all the souls in the chaos, can do that."

At that moment, Wahirangi CloudLord descended. Even the dragon had not come away unscathed; one of his wings was torn, and many of his scales were scorched, yet he preformed an admiring bow to the female seers. For an instant Talyn thought she saw the impression of another dragon in his place, one silver with blue eyes.

Perhaps it was a before-thought, or one from her ancestors. She would take it as a blessing for what they had to do next.

Then, before her courage could desert Talyn called into the crowd. "Syris!"

The nykur came to her, tossing his shaggy green head and not looking one bit daunted by the White Void before them. He too had blood on him, some was even his, but none of his spirit was broken. Already he was rolling his eyes and tossing his head.

She climbed onto his back, and then, turning around, held out her hand to Nyree. They were sisters of a sort now. When she was seated behind her, Talyn looked to their people.

She had never been more afraid than when she next spoke. "We need to answer the call. Sing in the Void as we were meant to." Talyn ran her eyes over all the people she had dreamed for so many years of seeing again. It was hard to judge their faces, marked as they were by sadness, deprivation and loss. "Some must stay here and rebuild, but I hope some of you will come with me. Will you?" she asked them, her heart hammering in her chest.

Slowly, Vaerli picked their way out of the crowd, and she could tell every one of them was a warrior through and through. Like her, after years of being alone, they were looking for community and purpose.

The last thing she saw was Finn standing at the end of reality, Ysel at his side. The talespinner's eyes were full of stars and a bright smile was on his lips. At that moment, Talyn realized that she was suddenly an optimist. Yes, she would walk the White Void as the Pact demanded, but one day she and her warriors would come back to Conhaero and those who waited for them.